"Grafton, who consistently turns out grade-A novels, has outdone herself with her latest . . . chilling, poignant."
—*Forbes*

"TAUT, TERRIFYING, TRANSFIXING . . . The best and strongest book in the series . . . Solana is one of the most evil, calculating characters Grafton has created."
—*USA Today*

"[A] FIRECRACKER OF A TALE . . . The masterful last few chapters are among the most frightening and suspenseful in the series, proving that Grafton has yet to reach her zenith on the way to Z." —*The Courier-Journal*

Kinsey Millhone's elderly neighbor, Gus Vronsky, may have been the original inspiration for the term "Grumpy Gus." A miser and a hoarder, Gus is so crotchety that after he takes a bad fall, his only living relative is anxious to find him some hired help and get back home as soon as she can.

To help, Kinsey runs a check on the applicant, Solana Rojas. Social Security, driver's license, nursing certification: It all checks out. And it sounds like she did a good job for her former employers. So Kinsey gives her the thumbs-up, figuring Gus will be the ideal assignment for this diligent, experienced caregiver.

And the real Solana Rojas was indeed an excellent caregiver. But the woman who has stolen her identity is not, and for her, Gus will be the ideal victim . . .

"Gripping . . . one of the series' high points."
—*Publishers Weekly*

"As usual, Ms. Grafton mixes deadly serious topics, in this case identity theft and elder abuse, with offbeat Kinsey-esque humor." —*The Dallas Morning News*

"Great writing . . . It may be two years before we get what U is for . . . but if it's half as good as *Trespass*, it will be worth the wait." —*USA Today*

"Particularly well crafted." —*Los Angeles Times*

continued . . .

Praise for the Kinsey Millhone novels

"A refreshing heroine." —*The Washington Post Book World*

"Millhone is all too human, and her humanity increases with each novel, each investigation . . . An incredibly even and satisfying series, one that keeps the reader interested in the plot—and in the continuing development of Kinsey Millhone." —*Richmond Times-Dispatch*

"Grafton's prose is lean and her observational skills keen." —*Chicago Tribune*

"In a few strokes, she creates vivid, real people." —Cleveland *Plain Dealer*

"A confident, likable sleuth with a good sense of humor." —*Orlando Sentinel*

"A long-lived and much-loved series." —*Publishers Weekly*

"A stellar series." —*The Baltimore Sun*

"The spunkiest, funniest, and most engaging private investigator in Santa Teresa, California, not to mention the entire detective novel genre." —*Entertainment Weekly*

"Grafton's alphabet thrillers just keep getting better." —*USA Today*

"[Grafton] has mastered the art of blending new and old in novels that are both surprising and familiar." —*The San Diego Union Tribune*

"Grafton deserves an A for maintaining her series's high standard of excellence." —*Library Journal*

"Returning for another visit with the perpetually grumpy, smart-alecky, and utterly dedicated Kinsey is a treat." —Cleveland *Plain Dealer*

"Kinsey Millhone is Grafton's best mystery, one that has been unfolding deliciously since the letter 'A.'" —*San Francisco Chronicle*

"[A] first-class series." —*The New York Times Book Review*

"Book for book, this may be the most satisfying mystery series going." —*The Wall Street Journal*

Titles by Sue Grafton

Kinsey Millhone Mysteries

A is for Alibi
B is for Burglar
C is for Corpse
D is for Deadbeat
E is for Evidence
F is for Fugitive
G is for Gumshoe
H is for Homicide
I is for Innocent
J is for Judgment
K is for Killer
L is for Lawless
M is for Malice
N is for Noose
O is for Outlaw
P is for Peril
Q is for Quarry
R is for Ricochet
S is for Silence
T is for Trespass
U is for Undertow
V is for Vengeance
W is for Wasted
X

and

Kinsey and Me: Stories

IS FOR TRESPASS

SUE GRAFTON

G. P. Putnam's Sons
New York

T

PUTNAM

G. P. Putnam's Sons
Publishers Since 1838
An imprint of Penguin Random House LLC
375 Hudson Street
New York, New York 10014

First Marian Wood/G. P. Putnam's Sons hardcover edition / December 2007
Berkley mass-market edition / December 2008
First G. P. Putnam's Sons premium edition / March 2016
G. P. Putnam's Sons premium edition ISBN: 978-0-399-57521-1

Printed in the United States of America
10 9 8 7 6 5 4 3 2 1

Cover design by Lisa Amoroso

For Elizabeth Gastiger, Kevin Frantz,
and Barbara Toohey,
with admiration and affection

ACKNOWLEDGMENTS

The author wishes to acknowledge the invaluable assistance of the following people: Steven Humphrey; Joe B. Jones, pharmacist (retired); John Mackall, Counselor-at-Law, Seed Mackall LLP; Dan Trudell, President, ARS, Accident Reconstruction Specialists; Robert Failing, M.D., forensic pathologist (retired); Sylvia Stallings and Pam Taylor of Sotheby's International Realty; Sally Giloth; Barbara Toohey; Greg Boller, Deputy District Attorney, Santa Barbara County District Attorney's Office; Randy Reetz, Santa Barbara Chamber of Commerce; Sam Eaton, Attorney, Eaton & Jones, Attorneys at Law; Ann Cox; Ann Marie Kopeikan, Director of Vocational Nursing, Lorraine Malachak, Nursing Programs Support Specialist, and Eileen Campbell, Administration, Santa Barbara City College; Christine Estrada, Santa Barbara County Court Administrator, Superior Court Information Records & Filing; Liz Gastiger; Boris Romanowski, Parole Agent, State of California Department of Corrections; Lynn McLaren, private investigator; Maureen Murphy, Maureen Murphy Fine Arts; Laurie Roberts, photographer; and Dave Zanolini, United Process Servers.

T
IS FOR TRESPASS

PROLOGUE

I don't want to think about the predators in this world. I know they exist, but I prefer to focus on the best in human nature: compassion, generosity, a willingness to come to the aid of those in need. The sentiment may seem absurd, given our daily ration of news stories detailing thievery, assault, rape, murder, and other treacheries. To the cynics among us, I must sound like an idiot, but I do hold to the good, working wherever possible to separate the wicked from that which profits them. I know there will always be someone poised to take advantage of the vulnerable: the very young, the very old, and the innocent of any age. I know this from long experience.

Solana Rojas was one . . .

1

SOLANA

She had a real name, of course—the one she'd been given at birth and had used for much of her life—but now she had a new name. She was Solana Rojas, whose personhood she'd usurped. Gone was her former self, eradicated in the wake of her new identity. This was as easy as breathing for her. She was the youngest of nine children. Her mother, Marie Terese, had borne her first child, a son, when she was seventeen and a second son when she was nineteen. Both were the product of a relationship never sanctified by marriage, and while the two boys had taken their father's name, they'd never known him. He'd been sent to prison on a drug charge and he'd died there, killed by another inmate in a dispute over a pack of cigarettes.

At the age of twenty-one, Marie Terese had married a man named Panos Agillar. She'd borne him six children in a period of eight years before he left her and ran off with someone else. At the age of thirty, she found herself alone and broke, with eight children ranging in age from thirteen years to three months. She'd married again, this time to a hardworking, responsible man in his fifties. He fathered Solana—his first child, her mother's last, and their only offspring.

During the years when Solana was growing up, her siblings had laid claim to all the obvious family roles: the athlete, the soldier, the cut-up, the achiever, the drama queen, the hustler, the saint, and the jack-of-all-trades. What fell to her lot was to play the ne'er-do-well. Like her mother, she'd gotten pregnant out of wedlock and had given birth to a son when she was barely eighteen. From that time forward, her progress through life had been hapless. Nothing had ever gone right for her. She lived paycheck to paycheck with nothing set aside and no way to get ahead. Or so her siblings assumed. Her sisters counseled and advised her, lectured and cajoled, and finally threw up their hands, knowing she was never going to change. Her brothers expressed exasperation, but usually came up with money to bail her out of a jam. None of them understood how wily she was.

She was a chameleon. Playing the loser was her disguise. She was not like them, not like anyone else, but it had taken her years to fully appreciate her differences. At first she thought her oddity was a function of the family dynamic, but early in elementary school, the truth dawned on her. The emotional connections that bound others to one another were absent in her. She operated as a creature apart, without empathy. She pretended to be like the little girls and boys in her grade, with their bickering and tears, their tattling, their giggles, and their efforts to excel. She observed their behavior and imitated them, blending into their world until she seemed much the same. She chimed in on conversations, but only to feign amusement at a joke, or to echo what had already been said. She didn't disagree. She didn't offer an opinion because she had none. She expressed no wishes or wants of her own. She was largely unseen—a mirage or a ghost—watching for little ways to take advantage of them. While her classmates were self-absorbed and oblivious, she was hyperaware. She saw everything and cared for nothing. By the age of ten, she knew it was only a matter of time before she found a use for her talent for camouflage.

By the age of twenty, her disappearing act was so quick and so automatic that she was often unaware she'd absented herself from the room. One second she was there, the next she was gone. She was a perfect companion because she mirrored the person she was with, becoming whatever they were. She was a mime and a mimic. Naturally, people liked and trusted her. She was also the ideal employee—responsible, uncomplaining, tireless, willing to do whatever was asked of her. She came to work early. She stayed late. This made her appear selfless when, in fact, she was utterly indifferent, except when it was a matter of furthering her own aims.

In some ways, the subterfuge had been forced on her. Most of her siblings had managed to put themselves through school, and at this stage in their lives they appeared more successful than she. It made them feel good to help their baby sister, whose prospects were pathetic compared with their own. While she was happy to accept their largesse, she didn't like being subordinate to them. She'd found a way to make herself their equal, having acquired quite a bit of money that she kept in a secret bank account. It was better they didn't know how much her lot in life had improved. Her next older brother, the one with the law degree, was the only sibling she had any use for. He didn't want to work any harder than she did and he didn't mind bending the rules if the payoff was worthwhile.

She'd borrowed an identity, becoming someone else on two previous occasions. She thought fondly of her other personas, as one would of old friends who'd moved to another state. Like a Method actor, she had a new part to play. She was now Solana Rojas and that's where her focus lay. She kept her new identity wrapped around her like a cloak, feeling safe and protected in the person she'd become.

The original Solana—the one whose life she'd borrowed—was a woman she'd worked with for months in the convalescent wing of a home for seniors. The real Solana, whom she now thought of as "the Other," was an LVN. She, too, had studied to become a licensed vocational nurse. The only difference between them was that the Other was certified, while she'd had to drop out of school before she'd finished the course work. That was her father's fault. He'd died and no one had stepped forward to pay for her education. After the funeral, her mother asked her to quit school and get a job, so that was what she'd done. She found work first cleaning houses, and later as a nurse's aide, pretending to herself that she was a real LVN, which she would have been if she'd finished the program at City College. She knew how to do everything the Other did, but she wasn't as well paid because she lacked the proper credentials. Why was that fair?

She'd chosen the real Solana Rojas the same way she'd chosen the others. There was a twelve-year difference in their ages, the Other being sixty-four years old to her fifty-two. Their features weren't really similar, but they were close enough for the average observer. She and the Other were roughly the same height and weight, though she knew weight was of little consequence. Women gained and lost pounds all the time, so if someone noticed the discrepancy, it was easily explained. Hair color was another insignificant trait. Hair could be any hue or shade found in a drugstore box. She'd gone from a brunette to a blonde to a redhead on previous occasions, all of which were in stark contrast to the natural gray hair she'd had since she was thirty.

Over the past year, she'd darkened her hair little by little until the match with the Other was approximate. Once, a new hire at the convalescent home had mistaken the two for sisters, which had thrilled her to no end. The Other was Hispanic, which she herself was not. She could pass if she chose. Her ethnic forebears were Mediterranean; Italians and Greeks with a few Turks thrown in—olive-skinned and dark-haired, with large dark eyes. When she was in the company of Anglos, if she was quiet and went about her business, the assumption was that she didn't speak much English. This meant many conversations were conducted in her presence as though she couldn't understand a word. In truth, it was Spanish she couldn't speak.

Her preparations for lifting the Other's identity had taken an abrupt turn on Tuesday of the week before. On Monday, the Other told the nursing staff she'd given two weeks' notice. Soon her classes were starting and she wanted a break before she devoted herself to school full-time. This was the signal that it was time to put her plan into operation. She needed to lift the Other's wallet because a driver's license was crucial to her scheme. Almost as soon as she thought of it, the opportunity arose. That's what life was like for her, one possibility after another presenting itself for her personal edification and advancement. She hadn't been given many advantages in life and those she had, she'd been forced to create for herself.

She was in the staff lounge when the Other returned

from a doctor's appointment. She'd been ill some time before, and while her disease was in remission, she'd had frequent checkups. She told everyone her cancer was a blessing. She was more appreciative of life. Her illness had motivated her to reorder her priorities. She'd been accepted to graduate school, where she would study for an MBA in health care management.

The Other hung her handbag in her locker and draped her sweater over it. There was only the one hook, as a second hook had a screw missing and dangled uselessly. The Other closed her locker and snapped shut the combination lock without turning the dial. She did this so it would be quicker and easier to pop the lock open at the end of the day.

She'd waited, and when the Other had gone out to the nurse's station, she'd pulled on a pair of disposable latex gloves and given the lock a tug. It hadn't taken any time at all to open the locker, reach into the Other's bag, and remove her wallet. She'd slipped the Other's driver's license from its windowed compartment and put the wallet back, reversing herself as neatly as a strip of film. She peeled off the gloves and tucked them into the pocket of her uniform. The license she placed under the Dr. Scholl's pad in the sole of her right shoe. Not that anyone would suspect. When the Other noticed her license was gone, she'd assume she'd left it somewhere. It was always this way. People blamed themselves for being careless and absentminded. It seldom occurred to them to accuse anyone else. In this case, no one would think to point a finger at her, because she made such a point of being scrupulous in the company of others.

To execute the remaining aspect of the plan, she'd waited until the Other's shift was over and the administrative staff were gone for the day. All the front offices were empty. As was usual on Tuesday nights, the office doors were left unlocked so a cleaning crew could come in. While they were hard at work, it was easy to enter and find the keys to the locked file cabinets. The keys were kept in the secretary's desk and needed only to be plucked up and put to use. No one questioned her presence, and she doubted anyone would remember later that she'd come and gone. The cleaning crew was supplied by an outside agency. Their job was to vacuum, dust, and empty the trash. What did they know about the inner workings of the convalescent wing in a senior citizens' home? As far as they were concerned—given her uniform—she was a bona fide RN, a person of status and respect, entitled to do as she pleased.

She removed the application the Other had filled out when she applied for the job. This two-page form contained all the data she would need to assume her new life: date of birth, place of birth, which was Santa Teresa, Social Security number, education, the number of her nursing license, and her prior employment. She made a photocopy of the document along with the two letters of recommendation attached to the Other's file. She made copies of the Other's job evaluations and her salary reviews, feeling a flash of fury when she saw the humiliating gap between what the two of them were paid. No sense fuming about that now. She returned the paperwork to the folder and replaced the file in the drawer, which she then locked. She put the keys in the secretary's desk drawer again and left the office.

2

DECEMBER 1987

My name is Kinsey Millhone. I'm a private investigator in the small Southern California town of Santa Teresa, ninety-five miles north of Los Angeles. We were nearing the end of 1987, a year in which the Santa Teresa Police Department crime analyst logged 5 homicides, 10 bank robberies, 98 residential burglaries, 309 arrests for motor vehicle theft and 514 for shoplifting, all of this in a population of approximately 85,102, excluding Colgate on the north side of town and Montebello to the south.

It was winter in California, which meant the dark began its descent at five o'clock in the afternoon. By then, house lights were popping on all over town. Gas fireplaces had been switched on and jet blue flames were curling up around the stacks of fake logs. Somewhere in town, you might've caught the faint scent of real wood burning. Santa Teresa doesn't have many deciduous trees, so we aren't subjected to the sorry sight of bare branches against the gray December skies. Lawns, leaves, and shrubberies were still green. Days were gloomy, but there were splashes of color in the landscape—the salmon and magenta bougainvillea that flourished through December and into February. The Pacific Ocean was frigid—a dark, restless gray—and the beaches fronting it were deserted. The daytime temperatures had dropped into the fifties. We all wore heavy sweaters and complained about the cold.

For me, business had been slow despite the number of felonies in play. Something about the season seemed to discourage white-collar criminals. Embezzlers were probably busy Christmas shopping with the money they'd liberated from their respective company tills. Bank and mortgage frauds were down, and the telemarketing scamsters were listless and uninterested. Even divorcing spouses didn't seem to be in a battling mood, sensing perhaps that hostilities could just as easily carry over into spring. I continued to do the usual paper searches at the hall of records, but I wasn't being called upon to do much else. However, since lawsuits are always a popular form of indoor sport, I was kept busy working as a process server, for which I was registered and bonded in Santa Teresa County. The job put a lot of miles on my car, but the work wasn't taxing and netted me sufficient money to pay my bills. The lull wouldn't last long, but there was no way I could have seen what was coming.

At 8:30 that Monday morning, December 7, I picked up my shoulder bag, my blazer, and my car keys, and headed out the door on my way to work. I'd been skipping my habitual three-mile jog, unwilling to stir myself to exercise in the predawn dark. Given the coziness of my bed, I didn't even feel guilty. As I passed through the gate, the comforting squeak of the hinges was undercut by a brief wail. At first I thought *cat, dog, baby, TV.* None of the possibilities quite captured the cry. I paused, listening, but all I heard were ordinary traffic noises. I moved on and I'd just reached my car when I heard the wailing again. I reversed my steps, pushed through the gate, and headed for the backyard. I'd just rounded the corner when my landlord appeared. Henry's eighty-seven years old and owns the house to which my studio apartment is attached. His consternation was clear. "What was *that*?"

"Beats me. I heard it just now as I was going out the gate."

We stood there, our ears attuned to the usual sounds of morning in the neighborhood. For one full minute, there was nothing, and then it started up again. I tilted my head like a pup, pricking my ears as I tried to pinpoint the origin, which I knew was close by.

"Gus?" I asked.

"Possibly. Hang on a sec. I have a key to his place."

While Henry returned to the kitchen in search of the key, I covered the few steps between his property and the house next door, where Gus Vronsky lived. Like Henry, Gus was in his late eighties, but where Henry was sharp, Gus was abrasive. He enjoyed a well-earned reputation as the neighborhood crank, the kind of guy who called the police if he thought your TV was too loud or your grass was too long. He called Animal Control to report barking dogs, stray dogs, and dogs that went doo-doo in his yard. He called the City to make sure permits had been issued for minor construction projects: fences, patios, replacement windows, roof repairs. He suspected most things you did were illegal and he was there to set you straight. I'm not sure he cared about the rules and regulations as much as he liked kicking up a fuss. And if, in the process, he could set you against your neighbor, all the better for him. His enthusiasm for causing trouble was probably what had kept him alive for so long. I'd never had a run-in with him myself, but I'd heard plenty. Henry tolerated the man even though he'd been subjected to annoying phone calls on more than one occasion.

In the seven years I'd lived next door to Gus, I'd watched age bend him almost to the breaking point. He'd been tall once upon a time, but now he was round-shouldered and sunken-chested, his back forming a C as though an unseen chain bound his neck to a ball that he dragged between his legs. All this flashed through my mind in the time it took Henry to return with a set of house keys in hand.

Together we crossed Gus's lawn and climbed the steps to his porch. Henry rapped on the glass pane in the front door. "Gus? Are you okay?"

This time the moaning was distinct. Henry unlocked the door and we went into the house. The last time I'd seen Gus, probably three weeks before, he was standing in his yard, berating two nine-year-old boys for practicing their ollies in the street outside his house. True, the skateboards were noisy, but I thought their patience and dexterity were remarkable. I also thought their energies were better spent mastering kickflips than soaping windows or knocking over trash cans, which is how boys had entertained themselves in my day.

I caught sight of Gus a half second after Henry did. The old man had fallen. He lay on his right side, his face a pasty white. He'd dislocated his shoulder, and the ball of his humerus bulged from the socket. Beneath his sleeveless undershirt, his clavicle protruded like a budding wing. Gus's arms were spindly and his skin was so close to translucent I could see the veins branching up along his shoulder blades. Dark blue bruises suggested ligament or tendon damage that would doubtless take a long time to mend.

I felt a hot rush of pain as though the injury were mine. On three occasions, I've shot someone dead, but that was purely self-defense and had nothing to do with my squeamishness about the stub ends of bones and other visible forms of suffering. Henry knelt beside Gus and tried to help him to his feet, but his cry was so sharp, he abandoned the idea. I noticed that one of Gus's hearing aids had come loose and was lying on the floor just out of his reach.

I spotted an old-fashioned black rotary phone on a table at one end of the couch. I dialed 9-1-1 and sat down, hoping the sudden white ringing in my head would subside. When the dispatcher picked up, I detailed the problem and asked for an ambulance. I gave her the address and as soon as I hung up, I crossed the room to Henry's side. "She's saying seven to ten minutes. Is there anything we can do for him in the meantime?"

"See if you can find a blanket so we can keep him warm." Henry studied my face. "How are you doing? You don't look so good yourself."

"I'm fine. Don't worry about it. I'll be right back."

The layout of Gus's house was a duplicate of Henry's, so it didn't take me long to find the bedroom. The place was a mess—bed unmade, clothes strewn everywhere. An antique chest of drawers and a tallboy were cluttered with junk. The room smelled of mildew and bulging trash bags. I loosened the bedspread from a knot of sheets and returned to the living room.

Henry covered Gus with care, trying not to disturb his injuries. "When did you fall?"

Gus flicked a pain-filled look at Henry. His eyes were blue, the lower lids as droopy as a bloodhound's. "Last night. I fell asleep on the couch. Midnight, I got up to turn off the television and took a tumble. I don't remember what caused me to fall. One second I was up, the next I was down." His voice was raspy and weak. While Henry talked to him, I went into the kitchen and filled a glass with water from the tap. I made a point of blanking out my view of the room, which was worse than the other rooms I'd seen. How could someone live in such filth? I did a quick search through the kitchen drawers, but there wasn't a clean towel or dishrag to be found. Before I returned to the living room, I opened the back door and left it ajar, hoping the fresh air would dispel the sour smell that hung over everything. I handed the water glass to Henry and watched while he pulled a fresh handkerchief from his pocket. He saturated the linen with water and dabbed it on Gus's dry lips.

Three minutes later, I heard the high-wailing siren of the ambulance turning onto our street. I went to the door and watched as the driver double-parked and got out with the two additional paramedics who had ridden in the back. A bright red Fire Rescue vehicle pulled up behind, spilling EMT personnel as well. The flashing red lights were oddly syncopated, a stuttering of red. I held the door open, admitting three young men and two women in blue shirts with patches on their sleeves. The first guy carried their gear, probably ten to fifteen pounds' worth, including an EKG monitor, defibrillator, and pulse oximeter. One of the women toted an ALS jump bag, which I knew contained drugs and an intubation set.

I took a moment to close and lock the back door, and then waited on the front porch while the paramedics went about their business. This was a job where they spent much of their time on their knees. Through the open door I could hear the comforting murmur of questions and Gus's tremulous replies. I didn't want to be present when the time came to move him. One more of his yelps and they'd be tending to me.

Henry joined me a moment later and the two of us retreated to the street. Neighbors were scattered along the sidewalk, attentive in the wake of this undefined emergency. Henry chatted with Moza Lowenstein, who lived two houses down. Since Gus's injuries weren't life-threatening, we could talk among ourselves without any sense of disrespect. It took an additional fifteen minutes before Gus was loaded into the back of the ambulance. By then, he was on an IV line.

Henry consulted with the driver, a hefty dark-haired man in his thirties, who told us they were taking Gus to the emergency room at Santa Teresa Hospital, referred to fondly by most of us as "St. Terry's."

Henry said he'd follow in his car. "Are you coming?"

"I can't. I have to go on to work. Will you call me later?"

"Of course. I'll give you a buzz as soon as I know what's going on."

I waited until the ambulance departed and Henry had backed out of his drive before I got in my car.

On the way into town, I stopped off at an attorney's office and picked up an Order to Show Cause notifying a noncustodial spouse that a modification of child support was being sought. The ex-husband was a Robert Vest, whom I was already fondly thinking of as "Bob." Our Bob was a freelance tax consultant working from his home in Colgate. I checked my watch, and since it was only a few minutes after ten, I headed to his place in hopes of catching him at his desk.

I found his house and passed at a slightly slower speed

than normal, then circled back and parked on the opposite side of the street. Both the driveway and the carport were empty. I put the papers in my bag, crossed, and climbed his front steps to the porch. The morning newspaper lay on the mat, suggesting that Bobby wasn't yet up. Might have had a late night. I knocked and waited. Two minutes passed. I knocked again, more emphatically. Still no response. I edged to my right and took a quick peep in the window. I could see past his dining room table and into the darkened kitchen beyond. The place had that glum air of emptiness. I returned to my car, made a note of the date and time of the attempt, and went on to the office.

3

SOLANA

Six weeks after the Other left her job, she gave notice herself. This was a graduation day of sorts. It was time to say good-bye to her work as a lowly nurse's aide and advance her career as a newly credentialed LVN. Though no one else knew it, there was now a new Solana Rojas in the world, living a parallel life in the same community. Some people saw Santa Teresa as a small town, but Solana knew she could go about her business without much risk of running into her namesake. She'd done it before with surprising ease.

She'd acquired two new credit cards in Solana Rojas's name, substituting her own street address. To her way of thinking, her use of the Other's license and credit wasn't fraudulent. She wouldn't dream of charging merchandise that she didn't intend to pay for. Far from it. She took care of her bills the minute they came in. She might not cover the entire outstanding balance, but she was prompt about writing her newly printed checks and mailing them off. She couldn't afford to be in arrears, because she knew if an account was turned over to a collection agency, her duplicity might come to light. This would never do. There must be no black marks against the Other's name.

The only tiny snag she could see was that the Other's cursive was distinct and her signature impossible to duplicate. Solana had tried, but she couldn't master the slapdash way of it. She worried that some overzealous store clerk would compare her signature to the miniature signature reproduced on the Other's license. To avoid questions arising, she carried a wrist brace in her purse and strapped it around her right wrist before she shopped. This allowed her to claim carpal tunnel syndrome, which netted her sympathy instead of suspicion at her clumsy approximation of the Other's signature.

Even then, there'd been a close call at a department store downtown. As a treat, she was buying brand-new sheets, a new spread, and two down pillows, which she'd taken to the counter in the linen department. The saleswoman had rung up the items, and when she glanced at the name on the credit card, she looked up with surprise. "I can't believe this. I just waited on a Solana Rojas less than ten minutes ago."

Solana smiled and waved aside the coincidence. "That happens all the time. There are three of us in town with the same first and last names. Everybody gets us mixed up."

"I can imagine," the saleswoman said. "It must be irksome."

"It's really no big deal, though it's comical sometimes."

The saleswoman glanced at the credit card, her tone of voice pleasant. "May I see some ID?"

"Absolutely," Solana said. She opened her handbag and made a show of rooting through the contents. She realized in a flash that she didn't dare show the woman the stolen driver's license when the Other had just been there. By now, the Other would have a duplicate license in her possession. If she'd used it for identification purposes, the saleswoman would be looking at the same one twice.

She stopped searching through the bag, her tone perplexed. "For heaven's sake. My wallet's gone. I can't think where I could have left it."

"Did you do any other shopping before you came here?"

"You know what? I did. I remember now I took out my wallet and put it on the counter when I was buying a pair of shoes. I was sure I picked it up again because I took out my credit card, but I must have left it behind."

The saleswoman reached for the phone. "I'll be happy to check with the shoe department. They're probably holding it."

"Oh, it wasn't here. It was in a store down the street. Well, no matter. Why don't you set these aside and I'll pick them up and pay for them as soon as I have my wallet back."

"Not a problem. I'll have your purchases right here."

"Thank you. I'd appreciate it."

She left the store, abandoning the bedding, which she ended up buying at a shopping mall miles from downtown. The encounter frightened her more than she cared to admit. She gave the matter a great deal of thought in the days that followed and finally decided there was too much at stake to take chances. She went down to the hall of records and got a duplicate of the Other's birth certificate. Then she went to the DMV and applied for a driver's license under the name Solana Rojas, using her own Colgate address. She reasoned that there was surely more than one Solana Rojas in the world, just as there was more than one John Smith. She told the clerk her husband had died and she'd just learned to drive. She had to take a written exam and go through the motions of a driving test with an officious fellow sitting next to her, but she'd passed both with ease. She'd signed the forms and had her photo taken, and in return, she was given a temporary license until the permanent one could be processed in Sacramento and sent to her by mail.

That done, she had another perhaps more practical matter to address. She had money, but she didn't want to use it to support herself. She kept a secret stash in case she wanted to disappear—which she knew she would at some point—but she needed a regular income. After all, she had her son, Tiny, to provide for. A job was essential. To that end, she'd been combing the classifieds day after day for weeks without luck. There were more jobs for machinists, house cleaners, and day laborers than there were for health care professionals, and she resented the implications. She'd worked hard to get where she was, and now it appeared that there was no demand for her services.

Two families were advertising for live-in child care. One specified experience with infants and toddlers, and the other made mention of a preschool-age child. In both instances, the ads said Mom was working outside the home. What kind of person opened her door to anyone who was bright enough to read? Women these days had no sense. They behaved as though mothering was beneath them, a trivial job that could be meted out to any stranger walking in off the street. Didn't it occur to them that a pedophile could check the paper in the morning and have himself ensconced with his latest victim by the end of the day? All the attention paid to references and background checks was meaningless. These women were desperate and would snap up anyone who was polite and looked halfway presentable. If Solana were willing to settle for long hours and bad pay, she'd apply for those positions herself. As it was, she'd set her sights on something better.

She had Tiny to consider. The two of them had shared the same humble apartment for close to ten years. He was the object of much discussion among her siblings, who saw him as spoiled, irresponsible, and manipulative. The boy's given name was Tomasso. In the wake of his thirteen-pound-six-ounce arrival, she'd suffered an infection in her female parts, which had cured her of both the desire for other children and the ability to bear them. He was a beautiful infant, but the pediatrician who examined him at birth said he was defective. She couldn't remember the term for it now, but she'd ignored the doctor's somber words. Despite her son's size, his cry was feeble and mewing. He was listless, with poor reflexes and very little muscle control. He had difficulty sucking and swallowing, which created feeding problems. The doctor told her the boy would be better off in an institution, where he could be cared for by those accustomed to children like him. She was having none of it. The child needed her. He was the light and joy of her life, and if he had problems, she'd find a way to deal with them.

Before he was a week old, one of her brothers had tagged him with the nickname "Tiny," and he'd been known by that name since. She thought of him fondly as "Tonto," which seemed fitting. Like the Tonto in old Western movies, he was her tagalong, a loyal and faithful sidekick. He was thirty-five years old now, with a flat nose, deep-set eyes, and a smooth baby face. He wore his dark hair pulled back in a ponytail, exposing ears set low on his head. He wasn't an easy child, but she'd devoted her life to him.

By the time he was in the special-education equivalent of sixth grade, he weighed 180 pounds and had a doctor's standing order excusing him from PE. He was hyperactive and aggressive, given to temper tantrums and destructiveness when thwarted. He'd done poorly through grade school and junior high because he suffered a learning disorder that made reading difficult. More than one school counselor suggested he was mildly retarded, but Solana scoffed. If he had trouble concentrating in class, why blame him? It was the teacher's fault for not doing her job better. It was true he had a speech problem, but she had no trouble understanding him. He'd been held back twice—in the fourth grade and again in the eighth—and finally dropped out in his sophomore year of high school the day he turned eighteen. His interests were limited, and this, coupled with his size, precluded his holding a regular job, or any kind of job at all. He was strong and useful, but he really wasn't cut out for much in the way of work. She was his sole support and that suited them both.

She turned the page and checked the "Help Wanted." She missed the ad at first glance, but something made her scan the entries again. There it was, near the top, a ten-line ad for a part-time private-duty nurse for an elderly female dementia patient who needed skilled care. "Dependable, reliable, own transportation," the ad read. Not a word about honest. There was an address and phone number listed. She'd see what information she could solicit before she actually went out for an interview. She liked having the opportunity to evaluate the situation in advance so she could decide if it was worth her while.

She picked up the phone and dialed the number.

4

At 10:45 I had an appointment to discuss a case that was actually my prime concern. The week before, I'd had a call from an attorney named Lowell Effinger, who was representing the defendant in a personal-injury suit filed as the result of a two-car accident seven months earlier. The previous May, on the Thursday before the Memorial Day weekend, his client, Lisa Ray, driving her white 1973 Dodge Dart, had been making a left-hand turn out of one of the City College parking lots when she was struck by an oncoming van. Lisa Ray's vehicle was badly damaged. Police and paramedics were called. Lisa suffered a bump to the head. The paramedics examined her and suggested a trip to the ER at St. Terry's. Though shaken and upset, she declined medical assistance. Apparently, she couldn't bear the idea of waiting hours, just to be sent home with a set of cautions and a prescription for a mild pain reliever. They told her what to watch for in terms of a possible concussion and advised her to see her own physician if needed.

The driver of the van, Millard Fredrickson, was rattled but essentially unhurt. His wife, Gladys, sustained the bulk of the injuries, and she insisted on being taken to St. Terry's, where the findings of the ER physician indicated a concussion, severe contusions, soft-tissue injuries to her neck and lower back, and torn ligaments in her right leg. Subsequent X-rays showed a cracked pelvis and two cracked ribs. She was treated and referred to an orthopedist for follow-up.

That same day, Lisa had notified her insurance agent, who passed on the information to the adjuster at California Fidelity Insurance, with whom (coincidentally) I'd once shared office space. On Friday, the day after the accident, the adjuster, Mary Bellflower, had contacted Lisa and taken her statement. According to the police report, Lisa was at fault since she was responsible for making the left turn safely. Mary went out to the accident site and took photographs. She also photographed the damage to both vehicles, then told Lisa to go ahead and get estimates for the repair work. She thought the car was beyond help, but she wanted the figures for her records.

Four months later, the Fredricksons filed suit. I'd seen a copy of the complaint, which contained sufficient whereases and wherefores to scare the pants off your average citizen. Plaintiff was said to be "injured in her health, strength, and activity, sustaining serious and permanent physical injury to her body, shock and emotional injuries to her person, which have caused and will continue to cause Plaintiff great emotional distress and mental and physical pain and suffering, subsequently resulting in loss of consortium . . . (and so on and so forth). Plaintiff is seeking damages including but not limited to, past and future medical expenses, lost wages, and any and all incidental expenses and compensatory damages as permitted by law."

Plaintiff's attorney, Hetty Buckwald, seemed to think a million dollars, with that comforting trail of zeros, would be sufficient to soothe and assuage her client's many agonies. I'd seen Hetty a couple of times in court when I was there on other matters, and I generally came away hoping I'd never have occasion to come up against her. She was short and chunky, a woman in her late fifties with an aggressive manner and no sense of humor. I couldn't imagine what had left her with such a chip on her shoulder. She treated opposing attorneys like scum and the poor defendant like someone who ate babies for sport.

Ordinarily, CFI would have assigned one of its attorneys to defend such a suit, but Lisa Ray was convinced she'd do better with a lawyer of her own. She was adamant about not settling and she'd asked Lowell Effinger to represent her, sensing perhaps that CFI might roll over and play dead. Police report to the contrary, Lisa Ray swore she wasn't at fault. She claimed Millard Fredrickson was speeding and that Gladys wasn't wearing her seat belt, which was, in itself, a violation of California traffic law.

The file I'd picked up from Lowell Effinger contained copies of numerous documents: Defendant's Request for Production of Documents, Supplemental Request for Production of Documents, medical records from the hospital emergency room, and reports from the various medical personnel who'd treated Gladys Fredrickson. There were also copies of the depositions taken from Gladys Fredrickson; her husband, Millard; and the defendant, Lisa Ray. I did a quick study of the police report and leafed through the transcripts of Interrogatories. I took my time over the photographs and the sketch of the site, which showed the relative positions of the two vehicles, before and after the collision. At issue, from my perspective, was a witness to the accident, whose comments at the time suggested he supported Lisa Ray's account of the event. I told Effinger I'd look into it and then turned around and set up the midmorning meeting with Mary Bellflower.

Before I walked through the California Fidelity Insurance offices, I donned my mental and emotional blinders. I'd worked here once upon a time and my relationship with the company had not ended well. The arrangement was one whereby I was given office space in exchange for investigating arson and wrongful-death claims. Mary Bellflower was a recent hire in those days, a newly married twenty-four-year-old with a fresh, pretty face and a sharp mind. Now she had four years' experience under her belt and she was a pleasure to deal with. I checked her desktop as I sat down, looking for framed photos of her husband, Peter, and any small tykes she might have given birth to in the interim. None were in evidence and I wondered what kind of luck she'd had with her baby plans. I thought it best not to inquire so I got on with the business at hand.

"So what's the deal here?" I'd asked. "Is Gladys Fredrickson for real?"

"It looks that way. Aside from the obvious—cracked ribs, cracked pelvis, and torn ligaments—you're talking about soft-tissue injuries, which are difficult to prove."

"All this from a fender-bender?"

"I'm afraid so. Low-impact collisions can be more serious than you'd think. The right front fender of the Fredricksons' van struck the left side of Lisa Ray's car with sufficient force that it spun both vehicles in a post-collision rotation. There was a second impact when Lisa's right rear fender came in contact with the van's left rear fender."

"I get the general idea."

"Right. These physicians are all doctors we've dealt with before, and there's no hint of fraudulent diagnoses or padded bills. If the police hadn't cited Lisa, we'd be a lot more inclined to dig in our heels. I'm not saying we won't fight, but she's clearly in the wrong. I sent the claim on up the line so ICPI could take a look. If the plaintiff is claim-happy, her name should show up in their database. On a minor note—and we don't think it pertains to this situation—Millard Fredrickson was handicapped in an automobile accident some years ago. Talk about someone plagued by misfortune."

Mary went on to say she thought Gladys would end up accepting a hundred thousand dollars, not including her medical expenses, a bargain from the company's perspective as they could sidestep the threat of a jury trial with its attendant risks.

I said, "A million bucks reduced to a hundred grand? That's a hefty discount."

"We see it all the time. The attorney tacks on a big price tag so the settlement will look like a good deal to us."

"Why settle at all? Maybe if you stand your ground the woman will back off. How do you know she's not exaggerating?"

"Possible, but not likely. She's sixty-three years old and overweight, which is a contributing factor. With the office visits, physical therapy, chiropractic appointments, and all the medications she's on, she's not able to work. The doctor's suggesting the disability may be permanent, which is going to add yet another headache."

"What kind of work does she do? I didn't see it mentioned."

"It's in there somewhere. She does billing for an assortment of small businesses."

"Doesn't sound lucrative. How much does she make?"

"Twenty-five thousand a year, according to her. Her tax returns are privileged, but her attorney says she can produce invoices and receipts to back up her claim."

"And Lisa Ray says what?"

"She saw the van approach, but she felt she had ample time to make the turn, especially since Millard Fredrickson had activated his right-turn signal and slowed. Lisa started into the turn and the next thing she knew the van was bearing down on her. He estimated his speed at less than ten miles an hour, but that's nothing to sniff at when a thirty-two-hundred-pound vehicle is banging into you. Lisa saw what was coming but couldn't get out of the way. Millard swears it was the other way around. He says he slammed on his brakes, but Lisa had pulled out so abruptly there was no way to avoid plowing into her."

"What about the witness? Have you talked to him?"

"Well, no. That's just it. He's never turned up, and Lisa has precious little in the way of information. 'Old guy with white hair in a brown leather bomber jacket' is as much as she recalls."

"The cop at the scene didn't take his name and address?"

"Nope, nor did anyone else. He'd disappeared by the time the police arrived. We posted notices in the area and we ran ads in the 'Personals' section of the classifieds. So far no response."

"I'll meet with Lisa myself and then get back to you. Maybe she'll remember something I can use to track this guy down."

"Let's hope. A jury trial's a nightmare. We end up in court and I can just about guarantee Gladys will show up in a wheelchair, wearing a collar and a nasty-looking leg brace. All she has to do is drool on herself and that's a million bucks right there."

"I hear you," I said. I went back to the office, where I caught up with paperwork.

There are two items I suppose I should mention at this point:

(1) Instead of my 1974 VW sedan, I'm now driving a 1970 Ford Mustang, manual transmission, which is what I prefer. It's a two-door coupe, with a front spoiler, wide-track tires, and the biggest hood scoop ever placed on a production Mustang. When you own a Boss 429, you learn to talk this way. My beloved pale blue Bug had been shoved nose-first into a deep hole on the last case I worked. I should have bulldozed the dirt in on top and buried it right there, but the insurance company insisted that I have it hauled out so they could tell me it was totaled: no big surprise when the hood was jammed up against the shattered windshield, which was resting on or about the backseat.

I'd spotted the Mustang at a used-car lot and bought it the same day, picturing the perfect vehicle for surveillance work. What was I thinking? Even with the gaudy Grabber Blue exterior, I'd assumed the aging vehicle would fade into the landscape. Silly me. For the first two months, every third guy I met would stop me on the street to have a chat about the hemi-head V-8 engine originally developed for use in NASCAR racing. By the time I realized how conspicuous the car was, I was in love with it myself and I couldn't bear to trade it in.

(2) Later, when you watch my troubles begin to mount, you'll wonder why I didn't turn to Cheney Phillips, my erstwhile boyfriend, who works for the Santa Teresa Police Department—"erstwhile" meaning "former," but I'll get to that in a bit. I did call him eventually, but by then I was already in the soup.

5

I have my office in a little two-room bungalow with a bath and kitchenette, located on a narrow side street in downtown Santa Teresa. It's in walking distance of the courthouse, but more importantly it's cheap. My unit is the middle one of three, set in a squat row like the cottages of the Three Little Pigs. The property is perpetually for sale, which means I could be evicted if a buyer comes along.

After Cheney and I broke up, I won't say I was depressed, but I really didn't feel like exerting myself. I hadn't run for weeks. Perhaps "run" is too kind a word, as running is properly defined as six miles an hour. What I do is a slow jog, which is better than a brisk walk, but not by much.

I'm thirty-seven years old and many women I know were whining about weight gain as a side effect of aging, a phenomenon I was hoping to avoid. I had to concede that my eating habits were not what they should have been. I devour a lot of fast food, specifically McDonald's Quarter Pounders with Cheese, while simultaneously consuming fewer than nine servings of fresh fruits and vegetables daily (actually, fewer than one, unless you want to count the french fries). In the wake of Cheney's departure, I'd been driving up to the take-out window more often than was good for me. The time had now come to shake off the blues and take myself in hand. I vowed, as I did almost every morning, to start jogging again first thing the next day.

Between phone calls and clerical work, I made it to the noon hour. For lunch, I had a carton of nonfat cottage cheese with a dollop of salsa so fierce it brought tears to my eyes. From the time I removed the lid until I tossed the empty container in the trash, the meal took less than two minutes—twice as long as it took me to consume a QP with Cheese.

At 1:00 I got in my Mustang and drove over to the law firm of Kingman and Ives. Lonnie Kingman is my attorney, who'd also rented me office space after I'd been relieved of the position with California Fidelity Insurance that I'd enjoyed for seven years. I won't go into the humiliating details of my being fired. Once I was out on the street, Lonnie offered me the use of an empty conference room, providing a temporary haven in which I could lick my wounds and regroup. Thirty-eight months later, I opened an office on my own.

Lonnie was hiring me to serve an Ex Parte Order of Protection on a Perdido man named Vinnie Mohr, whose wife had accused him of stalking, threats, and physical violence. Lonnie thought his hostility might be defused if I delivered the restraining order instead of a uniformed deputy from the county sheriff's office.

"How dangerous *is* this guy?"

"Not that bad unless he's drinking. Then anything can set him off. Do what you can, but if you don't like the feel of it, we'll try something else. In an odd way he's chivalrous . . . or at any rate, partial to cute girls."

"I'm neither cute nor girlish, but I appreciate the thought."

I checked the paperwork, making sure I had the correct address. In the car again, I consulted my *Thomas Guide to Santa Teresa and San Luis Obispo Counties Streets*, flipping from page to page until I'd pinpointed my destination. I took surface streets to the closest freeway on-ramp and headed south on the 101. There was very little traffic and the drive to Perdido took nineteen minutes instead of the usual twenty-six. There's no nice reason I can think of to be dragged into court, but by law a defendant in a criminal or civil suit must be given proper notice. I delivered summonses, subpoenas, garnishments, and assorted court orders, preferably by hand, though there were other ways to get the job done—by touch and by refusal being two.

The address I was looking for was on Calcutta Street in midtown Perdido. The house was a sullen-looking green stucco with a sheet of plywood nailed across the picture window in front. In addition to breaking the window, someone (no doubt Vinnie) had kicked a big knee-high hole in the hollow-core front door and then ripped it off its hinges. A series of strategically placed two-by-fours had since been nailed across the frame, rendering the door impossible to use. I knocked and then bent down and peered through the hole, which allowed me to see a man approaching from the other side. He wore jeans and had thin knees. When he leaned toward the hole on his side of the door, all I could see of his face was his stubble-covered cleft chin, his mouth, and a row of crooked bottom teeth. "Yeah?"

"Are you Vinnie Mohr?"

He withdrew. There was a brief silence and then a muffled reply. "Depends on who's asking."

"My name's Millhone. I have papers for you."

"What kind of papers?" His tone was dull but not belligerent. Fumes were already wafting through the ragged hole: bourbon, cigarettes, and Juicy Fruit gum.

"It's a restraining order. You're not supposed to abuse, molest, threaten, stalk, or disturb your wife in any way."

"Do what?"

"You have to stay away from her. You can't contact her by phone or by mail. There's a hearing next Friday and you're required to appear."

"Oh."

"Could you show me some ID?"

"Like what?"

"A driver's license would suffice."

"Mine's expired."

"As long as it bears your name, address, and likeness, that's good enough," I said.

"Okay." There was a pause and then he pressed his license against the hole. I recognized the cleft chin, but the rest of his face was a surprise. He was not a bad-looking guy—a bit squinty through the eyes, but I couldn't afford to be judgmental as the photo on my driver's license makes me look like I top the list of the FBI's Ten Most Wanted.

I said, "You want to open the door or should I put the papers through the hole?"

"Hole, I guess. Man, I don't know what she said, but she's a lying bitch. Anyways, she drove me to it, so I'm the one should be filing papers on her."

"You can tell the judge your side of it in court. Maybe he'll agree," I said. I rolled the papers into a cylinder and pushed them through the hole. I could hear paper crackle on the other side as the document was unfurled.

"Hey, come *on* now! Dang. I never did what's wrote here. Where'd she get this? She's the one hit me, not the other way around." Vinnie was assuming the "victim" role, a time-honored move for those who hope to claim the upper hand.

"Sorry I can't help you, Mr. Mohr, but you take care."

"Yeah. You, too. You sound cute."

"I'm adorable. Thanks for your cooperation."

In the car again, I logged the time I'd spent and the mileage on my car.

I drove back into downtown Santa Teresa and parked in a lot near a notary's office. I took a few minutes to fill out the affidavit of service, then went into the office, where I signed the return and had it notarized. I borrowed the notary's fax machine and made two copies, then walked over to the courthouse. I had the documents file-stamped and left the original with the clerk. One copy I retained and the other I'd return to Lonnie for his files.

Once in my office again, I found a call from Henry waiting on my machine. The message was brief and required no reply. "Hi, Kinsey. It's a little after one and I just got home. The doctor popped Gus's shoulder back in, but they decided to admit him anyway, at least for tonight. No broken bones, but he's still in a lot of pain. I'll go over to his house first thing tomorrow morning and do some cleaning so it won't be so disgusting when he gets home. If you want to pitch in, great. Otherwise, no problem. Don't forget cocktails after work today. We can talk about it then."

I checked my calendar, but I knew without looking

that Tuesday morning was clear. I diddled at my desk for the rest of the afternoon. At 5:10, I locked up and went home.

A sleek black 1987 Cadillac was parked in my usual spot in front so I was forced to cruise the area until I found a stretch of empty curb half a block away. I locked the Mustang and walked back. As I passed the Cadillac, I noted the license plate, which read I SELL 4 U. The car had to be Charlotte Snyder's, the woman Henry'd dated off and on for the past two months. Her real estate success was the first thing he'd mentioned when he'd decided to pursue the acquaintance.

I went around to the rear patio and let myself into my studio apartment. There were no messages on my home machine and no mail worth opening. I took a minute to freshen up and then crossed the patio to Henry's place to meet the latest woman in his life. Not that he'd had many. Dating was new behavior for him.

The previous spring, he'd been smitten with the art director on a Caribbean cruise he took. His relationship with Mattie Halstead hadn't worked out, but Henry had bounced back, realizing in the process that female companionship, even at his age, wasn't such a terrible idea. A number of other women on the cruise had taken a shine to him and he'd decided to contact two who were living within geographic range. The first, Isabelle Hammond, was eighty years old. She was a former English teacher, still the subject of legend at Santa Teresa High School when I attended some twenty years after she retired. She loved to dance and she was passionate about reading. She and Henry had gone out on several occasions, but she'd quickly decided the chemistry was off. Isabelle was looking for sparks, and Henry, while flinty, had failed to ignite her flame. This she told him straight out, greatly offending him. He believed men should do the wooing, and, further, that courtship should proceed with courtesy and restraint. Isabelle was cheerfully aggressive and it soon became clear the two of them were ill-suited. In my opinion, the woman was a nincompoop.

Now Charlotte Snyder had entered the picture. She lived twenty-five miles south, just past Perdido, in the seaside community of Olvidado. At age seventy-eight, she was still active in the workplace and apparently showed no inclination to retire. Henry had invited her for drinks at his house and then for dinner at a lovely neighborhood restaurant called Emile's-at-the-Beach. He'd asked me to join them for cocktails so I could check her out. If I didn't think Charlotte was suitable, he wanted to know. I thought the assessment was his to make, but he'd asked for my opinion, so that's what I'd be there to give.

Henry's kitchen door was open, his screen on the latch, so I could hear them laughing and chatting as I approached. I picked up the scent of yeast, cinnamon, and hot sugar, and guessed, correctly as it turned out, that Henry had dealt with his predate nerves by baking a pan of sweet rolls. In his working days he was a baker by trade, and as long as I've known him, his skills have never ceased to amaze. I tapped on the screen and he let me in. He'd dressed up for his date, exchanging his usual shorts and flip-flops for loafers, tan slacks, and a short-sleeved sky blue dress shirt that exactly matched his eyes.

I gave Charlotte high marks on sight. Like Henry, she was trim and she dressed with classic good taste: a tweed skirt, white silk blouse over which she wore a yellow crewneck sweater. Her hair was a soft reddish brown, cut short, expensively dyed, and brushed away from her face. I could tell she'd had her eyes done, but I didn't write it off to vanity. The woman was in sales, and her personal appearance was as much an asset as her experience. She looked like someone who could walk you through an escrow without a hitch. If I'd been in the market for a house, I'd have bought one from her.

She was leaning against the kitchen counter. Henry'd fixed her a vodka and tonic while he was having his usual Jack Daniel's over ice. He'd opened a bottle of Chardonnay for me and he poured me a glass as soon as Charlotte and I had been introduced. He'd set out a bowl of nuts and a tray of cheese and crackers, with clusters of grapes tucked here and there.

I said, "While I'm thinking about it, Henry, I'd be happy to help you clean tomorrow if we can finish before noon."

"Perfect. I've already told Charlotte about Gus."

Charlotte said, "Poor old guy. How's he going to manage when he gets home?"

"That's what the doctor asked. He's not going to release him unless he has help," he said.

"Does he have any family left?" I asked.

"Not that I've heard. Rosie might know. He talks to her every other week or so, mostly to complain about the rest of us."

"I'll ask when I see her," I said.

Charlotte and I went through the usual exchange of small talk, and when the subject shifted to real estate, she became more animated. "I was telling Henry how much these older homes have appreciated in recent years. Before I left the office, just out of curiosity, I checked the MLS for properties in the area and the median price—median, mind you—was six hundred thousand. A single-family residence like this one would probably sell for close to eight, especially since it has a rental attached."

Henry smiled. "She says I'm sitting on a gold mine. I paid ten-five for this place in 1945, convinced it was going to put me in the poor house."

"Henry's offered me a tour. I hope you don't mind if we take a minute for that."

"Go right ahead. I'll be fine."

The two left the kitchen, moving through the dining room to the living room. I could track their progress as he showed her through the place, the conversation becoming largely inaudible when they reached the bedroom he used as a den. He had two other bedrooms, one facing the street, the other looking out onto his garden in the rear. There were two full baths and a half-bath off the entrance. I could tell she was being complimentary, exclaiming in a way that probably had some dollar signs attached.

When they returned to the kitchen, the subject segued from real estate to housing starts and economic trends. She could talk downturns, yields on government bonds, and consumer confidence with the best of them. I was a teeny tiny bit intimidated by her confidence, but that was my problem, not his.

We finished our drinks, and Henry put the empty glasses in the sink while Charlotte excused herself and retreated to the nearest bathroom. He said, "What do you think?"

"I like her. She's smart."

"Good. She seems nice and she's well informed—qualities I appreciate."

"Me, too," I said.

When Charlotte returned, her lipstick had been brightened and she had a fresh dusting of blusher on her cheeks. She gathered her handbag and the two of us preceded Henry out the door, allowing him a moment to lock up.

"Could we take a quick look at the studio? Henry told me he designed the space and I'd love to see what he did."

I made a face. "I should probably tidy up first. I'm a neatnik by nature, but I've been gone all day." In truth, I didn't want her casing the joint, calculating how much the studio would add to the asking price if she persuaded him to sell.

"How long have you been renting?"

"Seven years. I love the location and Henry's the perfect landlord. The beach is half a block that way and my office downtown is only ten minutes from here."

"But if you owned your own home, think of the equity you'd have built up by now."

"I understand the advantages, but my income is up and down and I don't want to be saddled with a mortgage. I'm happy to let Henry worry about taxes and upkeep."

Charlotte gave me a look—too polite to express her skepticism at my shortsightedness.

As I left them, she and Henry had taken up their conversation. She was talking about rental properties, using the equity from his place as leverage for a triplex she'd just listed in Olvidado, where housing wasn't so expensive. She said the units needed work, but if he made the necessary improvements and then flipped the place, he'd net a tidy profit, which he could then reinvest. I tried not to shriek in alarm, but I sincerely hoped she wasn't going to talk him into something absurd.

Maybe I didn't like her quite as much as I thought.

6

Under ordinary circumstances, I'd have walked the half block to Rosie's Tavern to eat supper that night. She's Hungarian and cooks accordingly, leaning heavily on sour cream, dumplings, strudels, creamed soups, cheesy noodles, cabbage-related side dishes, plus your choice of beef or pork cubes cooked for hours and served with tangy horseradish sauce. I was hoping she'd know whether Gus Vronsky had relatives in the area and if so, how to make contact. Given my newfound goal of better balanced meals and more wholesome nutrition, I decided to postpone the conversation until after I'd eaten supper.

My evening meal consisted of a peanut-butter-and-pickle sandwich on whole wheat bread with a handful of corn chips, which I'm almost certain could be considered a grain. I grant you peanut butter is nearly 100 percent fat, but it's still a good source of protein. Further, there was bound to be a culture somewhere that classified a bread-and-butter pickle as a vegetable. For dessert, I treated myself to a handful of grapes. The latter I ate while I lay on my sofa and brooded about Cheney Phillips, whom I'd dated for two months. Longevity has never been my strong suit.

Cheney was adorable, but "cute" isn't sufficient to sustain a relationship. I'm difficult. I know this. I was raised by a maiden aunt who thought to foster my independence by giving me a dollar every Saturday and Sunday morning, and turning me out on my own. I did learn to ride the bus from one end of town to the other and I could cheat my way into two movies for the price of one, but she wasn't big on companionship, and because of that, being "close" makes me sweaty and short of breath.

I'd noticed that the longer Cheney and I dated, the more I was entertaining fantasies of Robert Dietz, a man I hadn't heard from in two years. What that told me was that I preferred to bond with someone who was always out of town. Cheney was a cop. He liked action, a fast pace, and the company of others, where I prefer to be alone. For me, small talk is hard work and groups of any size wear me down.

Cheney was a man who started many projects and finished none. During the time we were together, his floors were perpetually covered with drop cloths and the air smelled of fresh paint though I never saw him lift a brush. The hardware had been removed from all the interior doors, which meant you had to stick your finger through a hole and pull when you passed from room to room. Behind his two-car garage he had a truck up on blocks. It was out of sight and the neighbors had no complaints, but the same crescent wrench had been rained on so often the rust formed a wrench-shaped pattern on the drive.

I like closure. It drives me nuts to see a cabinet door left ajar. I like to plan. I prepare in advance and leave nothing to chance, while Cheney fancies himself a free spirit, taking life on the wing. At the same time, I buy on impulse, and Cheney spends weeks doing market research. He likes thinking aloud whereas I get bored with debates about matters in which I have no vested interest. It wasn't that his way was any better or worse than mine. We were simply different in areas we couldn't negotiate. I finally leveled with him in a conversation so painful that it doesn't bear repeating. I still don't believe he was as wounded as he led me to believe. On some level, he must have been relieved, because he couldn't have enjoyed the friction any more than I did. Now that we'd split, what I loved was the sudden quiet in my head, the sense of autonomy, the freedom from social obligations. Best was the pleasure of turning over in bed without bumping into someone else.

At 7:15 I roused myself from the sofa and tossed out the napkin I was using as a dinner plate. I rounded up my shoulder bag and jacket, locked my door, and walked the half block to Rosie's. Her tavern is a homely mix of restaurant, pub, and neighborhood watering hole. I say "homely" because the rambling space is largely unadorned. The bar looks like every other bar you ever saw in your life—a brass foot rail along the front and liquor bottles against mirrored shelves behind. On the wall above the bar there's a big stuffed marlin with a jockstrap hanging from its spike. This unsavory garment was tossed there by a sports rowdy in a game of chance that Rosie has since discouraged.

Crude booths line two walls, their plywood sections hammered together and stained a dark sticky hue. The remaining tables and chairs are of garage-sale quality, mismatched Formica and chrome with the occasional short leg. Happily, the lighting is bad, so many of the flaws don't show. The air smells of beer, sautéed onions, and certain unidentified Hungarian spices. Absent now is the cigarette smoke, which Rosie'd banished the year before.

As this was still early in the week, the drinking population was sparse. Above the bar, the television set was tuned to *Wheel of Fortune* with the sound on mute. Instead of sitting in my usual booth at the back, I perched on a barstool and waited for Rosie to emerge from the kitchen. Her husband, William, poured me a glass of Chardonnay and set it down in front of me. Like his brother, Henry, he's tall, but much more formal in his attire, favoring highly polished lace-up shoes while Henry prefers flip-flops.

William had removed his suit jacket and he'd made cuffs out of paper toweling, secured with rubber bands, to save the snow white sleeves of his dress shirt.

I said, "Hey, William. We haven't chatted in ages. How're you doing?"

"I've a bit of chest congestion, but I'm hoping to avoid a full-blown upper-respiratory infection," he said. He took a packet from his pants pocket and popped a tablet in his mouth, saying, "Zinc lozenges."

"Good deal."

William was a bellwether of minor illnesses, which he took very seriously lest they carry him off. He wasn't as bad as he'd once been, but he kept a keen eye out for anyone's imminent demise. "I hear Gus is in a bad way," he remarked.

"Bruised and battered, but aside from that, he's fine."

"Don't be too sure," he said. "A fall like that can lead to complications. A fellow might seem fine, but once he's laid up in bed, pneumonia sets in. Blood clot's another risk, not to mention a staph infection, which can take you out just like that."

The snap of William's fingers put an end to any misplaced optimism on my part. Gus was as good as buried as far as William was concerned. William stood at the ready when it came to death. In large part, Rosie had cured him of his hypochondria in that her culinary zeal generated sufficient indigestion to keep his imaginary ills at bay. He still leaned toward depression and found there was nothing quite like a funeral to provide a temporary emotional boost. Who could fault the man? At his age, he'd be hard-hearted indeed not to experience a little lift at the sight of a newly departed friend.

I said, "I'm more worried about what happens when Gus gets home. He'll be out of commission for a couple of weeks."

"If not longer."

"Right. We were hoping Rosie knew of a family member who'd agree to look after him."

"I wouldn't count on relatives. The man is eighty-nine years old."

"The same age as you, and you've got four living siblings, three of them in their nineties."

"But we're from hardier stock. Gus Vronsky smoked most of his life. Still does for all we know. Your best bet is a home health care service like the Visiting Nurses Association."

"You think he has health insurance?"

"I doubt it. He probably didn't imagine he'd live long enough to enjoy it, but he'll be covered by Medicaid or Medicare."

"I suppose so."

Rosie came out of the kitchen through the swinging door, backside first. She had a dinner plate in each hand, one heaped with pan-fried pork steak and stuffed cabbage rolls, and the other with Hungarian beef stew over egg noodles. She delivered the entrees to the day drinkers at the far end of the bar. I was sure they'd been there since noon and she might well be comping their dinner in hopes of sobering them up before they staggered home.

She joined us at the bar and I filled her in briefly on the nature of our concerns about Gus. "Has a great-niece," she said, promptly. "She hasn't seen him in years so she's very fond of him."

"Really. That's great. Does she live here in town?"

"New York."

"That won't do him any good. The doctor won't release him unless he has someone to look after him."

Rosie waved the notion aside. "Put in nursing home. Is what I did with my sister . . ."

William leaned forward. ". . . who died soon afterward."

Rosie ignored him. "Is a nice place. Where Chapel crosses Missile."

"What about his niece? Do you have any idea how I might get in touch with her?"

"He has her name in a book he keeps in his desk."

"Well, that's a start," I said.

When the alarm went off Tuesday morning at 6:00, I dragged my sorry butt out of bed and pulled on my Sauconys. I'd slept in my sweats, which saved me one step in my newly inaugurated morning ritual. While I was brushing my teeth, I stared at myself in the mirror with despair. During the night, my errant hair had formed a cone on top that I had to dampen with water and flatten with my palm.

I locked my front door and tied my house key into the

lace of one running shoe. As I pushed through the gate, I paused and made a big show of stretching my hamstrings in case anybody cared. Then I headed over to Cabana Boulevard, where I trotted along the bike path for a block with the beach to my right. In the weeks since I'd last jogged, the sun was slower to rise, which made the early morning hour seem even darker. The ocean looked sullen and black, and the waves sounded cold as they pounded on the sand. Some miles out, the channel islands were laid against the horizon in a dark ragged line.

Ordinarily, I'd have given little thought to my route, but when I reached the intersection of Cabana and State Street, I glanced to my left and realized there was something reassuring about the bright band of lights strung out on each side. There was no one else out at that hour and the storefronts were dark, but I followed my instincts and left the beach behind, heading toward downtown Santa Teresa, which was ten blocks north.

Lower State plays host to the train station, a bicycle-rental lot, and a Sea & Surf establishment where boards, bikinis, and snorkeling gear are sold. Half a block up, there was a T-shirt shop and a couple of fleabag hotels. The more upscale of the two, the Paramount, had been the lodging of choice in the forties when the Hollywood darlings journeyed to Santa Teresa by train. It was a short walk from the station to the hotel, which boasted a pool fed by natural hot springs. The pool had been shut down after workers discovered that seepage from an abandoned service station was leaking toxic chemicals into the aquifer. The hotel had changed hands and the new owner was rehabilitating the once-grand facility. The interior work had been completed and a new pool was now under construction. The public was invited to peek through holes in the temporary barrier erected to protect the site. I'd stopped to look myself one morning, but all I could see were piles of rubbish and sections of the old mosaic tile.

I continued running for ten blocks and then turned around, tuning in to my surroundings as a way of taking my mind off my heaving lungs. The chilly predawn air felt good. The sky had turned from charcoal to ashen gray. Nearing the end of my run, I could hear the early morning freight train rumble slowly through town with a muted blast from its horn. Dinging merrily, the signal gates came down. I waited while it passed. I counted six boxcars, a tank car, an empty livestock car, a refrigerator car, nine container cars, three hard-top gondolas, a flat car, and finally the caboose. When the train was out of sight I continued at a walk, using the last few blocks to cool down. Mostly, I was happy to have the run out of the way.

I skipped my shower, figuring I might as well stay grungy for the housework to come. I rounded up rubber gloves, sponges, and assorted cleaning products, all of which I tossed in a plastic bucket. I added a roll of paper toweling, rags, laundry soap, and black plastic trash bags. Thus armed, I went out to the patio, where I waited for Henry. There's nothing like the danger and the glamour of a private eye's life.

When Henry appeared, we went over to Gus's place. Henry did a walkabout to assess the situation and then returned to the living room and gathered up the many weeks' worth of newspapers scattered on the floor. For my part, I stood assessing the furnishings. The drapes were skimpy and the four upholstered pieces (one couch and three easy chairs) were encased in dark brown stretchy slipcovers of the one-size-fits-all variety. The tables were made of a chipped laminate veneer meant to look like mahogany. Just being in the room was discouraging.

My first self-assigned task was to search Gus's rolltop desk for his address book, which was tucked in the pencil drawer, along with a house key with a round white tag marked PITTS.

I held it up. "What's this? I didn't know Gus had a key to your place."

"Sure. That's why I have a key to his. Believe it or not, there was a time when he wasn't such a grouch. He used to bring in the mail and water my plants when I went off to Michigan to visit the sibs."

"Will wonders never cease," I said, and returned to the task at hand while Henry carried the stack of papers to the kitchen and stuffed them in the trash. Gus's financial dealings were well organized—paid bills in one pigeonhole, the unpaid in another. In a third, I found his checkbook, two savings account books, and his bank statements bound by rubber bands. I couldn't help but notice the amount of cash he had in his accounts. Well, okay, I studied the numbers carefully, but I didn't take notes. There was close to two thousand dollars in his checking account, fifteen thousand in one savings account, and twenty-two thousand in another. This might not be the whole of it. He struck me as the sort of fellow who stuck hundred-dollar bills between the pages of his books and kept untouched accounts in a number of different banks. The regular deposits he made were probably Social Security or pension checks. "Hey, Henry? What'd Gus do for a living before he retired?"

Henry stuck his head around the corner from the hallway. "He worked for the railroad back East. Might have been the L&N, but I'm not sure in what capacity. What makes you ask?"

"He's got a fair amount of money. I mean, the guy's not rich, but he has the means to live a lot better than this."

"I don't think money and cleanliness are connected. Did you find his address book?"

"Right here. The only person living in New York is a Melanie Oberlin, who has to be his niece."

"Why don't you go ahead and call?"

"You think?"

"Why not? You might as well put it on his phone bill. Meanwhile, I'll start on the kitchen. You can take his bedroom and his bath as soon as you're done."

I placed the call, but as is usually the case these days, I didn't talk to a live human being. The woman on the answering machine identified herself as Melanie, no last name, but she wasn't able to take my call. She sounded pretty cheerful for someone who told me at the same time just how sorry she was. I gave a brief account of her uncle Gus's fall and then left my name, my home and office numbers, and asked her to return the call. I tucked the address book in my pocket, thinking I'd try again later if I didn't hear from her.

I toured Gus's house as Henry had. In the hall, I could smell the fug of mouse droppings and perhaps a mouse corpse of recent vintage trapped in a wall nearby. The second bedroom was filled with an accumulation of unlabeled cardboard boxes and old furniture, some of it quite good. The third bedroom was devoted to items the old man evidently couldn't bring himself to toss. Bundles of twine-bound newspapers had been stacked head-high, with aisles laid out between the rows for easy access in case someone needed to get in and collect all the Sunday funnies from December of 1964. There were empty vodka bottles, cases of canned goods and bottled water sufficient to withstand a siege, bicycle frames, two rusted lawn mowers, a carton of women's shoes, and three stingy-looking TV sets with rabbit-ear antennas and screens the size of airplane windows. He'd filled an old wooden crate with tools. An old daybed was buried under jumbled mounds of clothing. An entire set of green-glass Depression-era dinnerware was stacked on a coffee table.

I counted fifteen ornate picture frames laid up against one wall. I flipped the frames forward and peered at the paintings from above, but I didn't know what to make of them. The subject matter was varied: landscapes, portraits, one painting of a lush but drooping bouquet, another of a tabletop adorned with cut fruit, a silver pitcher, and a dead duck with its head hanging off the edge. The oil on most had darkened so much it was like looking through a tinted window. I know nothing about art, so I had no opinion about his collection, except for the dead duck, which I thought was in questionable taste.

I got busy in the bathroom, thinking to get the worst of it out of the way. I disconnected my emotional gears, much as I do at the scene of a homicide. Revulsion is useless when you have a job to do. For the next two hours, we scrubbed and scoured, dusted and vacuumed. Henry emptied the refrigerator and filled two large trash bags with unidentified rotting foodstuffs. The cupboard shelves held canned goods that bulged along the bottoms, signaling imminent explosion. He ran a load of dishes while I tossed a mound of dirty clothes in the washer and ran that as well. The bedding I left in a heap on the laundry room floor until the washer was free.

By noon we'd covered as much ground as we could. Now that a modicum of order had been restored, I could see how depressing the house was. We could have worked another two full days and the result would have been the same—dinginess, neglect, a pall of old dreams hovering midair. We closed up the house, and Henry rolled two big garbage cans out to the curb in front. He said he'd get cleaned up and then hit the supermarket to restock Gus's shelves. After that he'd call the hospital and find out when he was being released. I went home, took a shower, and got dressed for work in my usual jeans.

I decided I'd make a second try at delivering the Order to Show Cause to my pal Bob Vest. This time when I parked and crossed the street to knock on his door, I noticed two newspapers lying on the porch. This was not a good sign. I waited, on the off chance that I'd caught him on the john with his knickers down around his knees. While I stood there, I spotted a scratching post on one side of the porch. The carpeted surface was untouched as the cat apparently preferred to sharpen its claws by shredding the welcome mat. A sooty-looking cat bed was matted with hair, dander, and flea eggs, but no visible cat.

I went out to the mailbox and checked the contents: junk mail, catalogs, a few bills, and a handful of magazines. I tucked the pile under my arm and crossed the lawn to his neighbor's house. I rang the bell. The door was answered by a woman in her sixties, cigarette in hand. The air around her smelled of fried bacon and maple syrup. She wore a tank top and pedal pushers. Her arms were scrawny and her pants rested loosely on her hips.

I said, "Hi. Do you know when Bob's getting back? He asked me to bring in his mail. I thought he was getting home last night, but I see his newspapers haven't been taken in."

She opened the screen door and peered past me at his

drive. "How'd he manage to rope you in? He asked me to mind his cat, but he never said a word about the mail."

"Maybe he didn't want to bother you with that."

"I don't know why not. He's happy to bother me about everything else. That cat thinks he lives here as often as I look after him. Scruffy old thing. I feel sorry for him."

I wasn't crazy about Bob's neglect of the cat. Shame on him. "Did he mention when he'd be home?"

"He said this afternoon, if you put any stock in that. Sometimes he claims he'll be gone two days when he knows it'll be a week. He thinks I'm more likely to agree to shorter absences."

"Oh, you know Bob," I said, and then held up the mail. "Anyway, I'll just leave this on his doorstep."

"I can take it if you like."

"Thanks. That's nice of you."

She studied me. "None of my business, but you're not the new gal he keeps talking about."

"Absolutely not. I've got problems enough without taking him on."

"Good. I'm glad. You don't look like his type."

"What type is that?"

"The type I see leaving his house most mornings at six A.M."

When I got to the office, I put a call through to Henry, who brought me up to date. As it turned out, the doctor had decided to keep Gus an extra day because his blood pressure was high and his red blood cell count was low. Since Gus was spaced out on pain medication, Henry was the one who dealt with the discharge planner in the hospital social services department, trying to find a way to accommodate Gus's medical needs once he got the boot. Henry offered to explain to me the intricacies of Medicare coverage, but it was really too boring to take in. Beyond Part A and Part B, everything seemed to have three initials: CMN, SNF, PPS, PROs, DRGs. On and on it went in that vein. Since I wouldn't have to navigate those rapids for another thirty years, the information was simply tedious. The guidelines were diabolically cunning, designed to confuse the very patients they were meant to educate.

There was apparently a formula that determined how much money the hospital could make by keeping him for a specified number of days and how much the same hospital could lose by keeping him one day longer. Gus's dislocated shoulder, while painful, swollen, and temporarily debilitating, wasn't considered serious enough to warrant more than a two-night stay. He was nowhere close to using up the days allotted him, but the hospital was taking no chances. On Wednesday, Gus was discharged from St. Terry's to a skilled nursing facility, otherwise known as an SNF.

7

Rolling Hills Senior Retreat was a rambling one-story brick structure on a tenth of an acre without a hill of any sort, rolling or otherwise. Some attempt had been made to tart up the exterior by adding an ornamental birdbath and two iron benches of the sort that leave marks on the seat of your pants. The parking lot was a stern black and smelled as though the asphalt had just been redone. In the narrow front yard, ivy formed a dense carpet of green that had swarmed up the sides of the building, across the windows, and over the edge of the roof. In a year, the place would be covered by a jungle of green, a low amorphous mound like a lost Mayan pyramid.

Inside, the lobby was painted in bright primary colors. Maybe the elderly, like babies, were thought to benefit from the stimulation of strong hues. In the far corner, someone had taken a fake Christmas tree from its box and had gone so far as to stick the aluminum "branches" in the requisite holes. The conformation of branches looked about as realistic as recently transplanted hair plugs. So far, there were no ornaments and no tree lights. With so little late-afternoon sunlight penetrating the windowpanes, the overall effect was cheerless. Linked chairs of chrome, with bright yellow plastic seats, lined the room on two sides. Of necessity, lamps were turned on, but bulbs were the same paltry wattage used in cheap motels.

The receptionist was concealed behind an opaque sliding window, of the sort that greets you in a doctor's office. An upright cardboard rack held brochures that made Rolling Hills Senior Retreat look like a "golden years" resort. In a montage of photographs, handsome, energetic-looking oldsters sat on a garden patio engaged in happy group-chat while playing a game of cards. Another image showed the cafeteria, where two ambulatory couples enjoyed a gourmet repast. In reality, the place had stimulated my hopes for an early and sudden death.

On the way over, I'd stopped at a market, where I'd stood for some time staring at the magazine rack. What kind of reading would amuse a cranky old man? I bought *Model Railroading Magazine*, a *Playboy*, and a book of crossword puzzles. Also, a giant-sized candy bar, in case he had a sweet tooth and hankered for one.

I hadn't been in the lobby long, but since no one had opened the receptionist's window, I tapped on the partition. The window slid back three inches and a woman in her fifties peered out. "Oh, sorry. I didn't realize anyone was out there. Can I help you?"

"I'd like to see a patient, Gus Vronsky. He was admitted earlier today."

She consulted her Rolodex and then made a phone call, keeping her palm close to the mouthpiece so I couldn't read her lips. After she hung up, she said, "Have a seat. Someone will be out shortly."

I sat down in a chair that allowed me a view of a corridor with administrative offices opening off each side. At the end, where a second corridor crossed the first, a nurse's station diverted foot traffic like water flowing around a rock in the middle of a stream. I was guessing hospital rooms were located down the two peripheral halls. Living quarters for the active, healthy residents must be somewhere else. I knew the cafeteria was close because the smell of food was strong. I closed my eyes and sorted the meal into its component parts: meat (perhaps pork), carrots, turnips, and something else—probably yesterday's salmon. I pictured a row of heat lamps beaming down on ten-by-thirteen stainless-steel food pans: one filled to the brim with chicken parts in milk gravy, another filled with glazed sweet potatoes, a third with mashed potatoes stiff and slightly dried around the edges. By comparison, how bad could it be to eat a Quarter Pounder with Cheese? Facing this muck at the end of life, why deny myself now?

In due course, a middle-aged volunteer in a pink cotton smock came and fetched me from the reception area. As she led me down the hallway, she didn't say a word, but she did so in a very pleasant manner.

Gus was in a semiprivate room, sitting upright in the bed closest to the window. The only view was of the underside of ivy vines, dense rows of white roots that looked like the legs of millipedes. His arm was in a sling and the bruises from his fall appeared from the various gaping holes in his gown. His Medicare coverage didn't provide private-duty nursing, a phone, or a television set.

His roommate's bed was surrounded by a curtain on a track, pulled in a half circle that delivered him from sight. In the quiet, I could hear him breathing heavily, a cross between a rasp and a sigh that had me counting his inhalations in case he stopped and it was up to me to perform CPR.

I tiptoed to Gus's bedside and found myself using my public library voice. "Hello, Mr. Vronsky. I'm Kinsey Millhone, your next-door neighbor."

"I know who you are! I didn't fall on my head." Gus spoke in his normal tone, which came across as a shout. I glanced uneasily toward his roommate's bed, wondering if the poor guy would be jarred out of his sleep.

I placed the items I'd bought on the rolling table beside Gus's bed, hoping to appease his ill temper. "I brought you a candy bar and some magazines. How're you doing?"

"What's it look like? I hurt."

"I can just imagine," I murmured.

"Quit that whispering and talk like a normal human being. If you don't raise your voice, I can't hear a word."

"Sorry."

"Sorry doesn't help. Before you ask another stupid question, I'm sitting up like this because if I lie on my back the pain is worse. Right now, the throbbing's excruciating and it makes my whole body feel like hell. Look at this bruise from all the blood they've drawn. Must have been a quart and a half in four big tubes. The lab report says I'm anemic, but I didn't have a problem until they started in."

I kept my expression sympathetic, but I was fresh out of consolation.

Gus snorted with disgust. "One day in this bed and my backside is raw. I'll be covered with sores if I'm here one more day."

"You ought to mention it to your doctor or one of the nurses."

"What doctor? What nurses? No one's been in for the past two hours. Anyway, that doctor's an idiot. He has no idea what he's talking about. What did he say about my release? He better sign it soon or I'm walking out. I may be sick, but I'm not a prisoner—unless getting old is a crime, which is how it's regarded in this country."

"I haven't talked to the floor nurse, but Henry will be here in a bit and he can ask. I did call your niece in New York to let her know what was going on."

"Melanie? She's useless, too busy and self-absorbed to worry about the likes of me."

"I didn't actually talk to her. I left a message on her machine and I'm hoping to hear back."

"She's no help. She hasn't come to visit me for years. I told her I'm taking her out of my will. You know why I haven't done it? Because it costs too much. Why should I pay a lawyer hundreds of dollars to make sure she doesn't get a cent. What's the point? I've got life insurance, too, but I hate dealing with my agent because he's always trying to talk me into something new. If I take her name out as beneficiary, I have to figure out who to put in. I don't have anyone else and I won't leave a thing to charity. Why should I do that? I worked hard for my money. I say let other people do the same."

"Well, there's that," I said, for lack of anything better.

Gus looked at the semicircle of curtain. "What's the matter with him? He better quit that gasping. It's getting on my nerves."

"I think he's asleep."

"Well, it's damned inconsiderate."

"If you want, I can hold a pillow over his face," I said. "Just kidding," I added when he didn't laugh. I took a peek at my watch. I'd been with him the better part of four minutes. "Mr. Vronsky, can I get you some ice before I have to take off?"

"No, just get on with you. To hell with it. You think I complain too much, but you don't know the half of it. You've never been old."

"Great. Okay, well, I'll see you later."

I made my escape, unwilling to spend another minute in his company. I had no doubt his testiness was a result of his misery and pain, but I wasn't required to stand in the line of fire. I retrieved my car from the parking lot, feeling as irritable and out of sorts as he.

As long as I was in a bad mood anyway, I decided to try serving Bob Vest again. He might get away with neglecting his cat, but he better pay attention to his ex-wife and kids. I drove to his house and parked across the street as I had before. I tried my habitual knock on the door to no great effect. Where the hell was the guy? Given that this was my third attempt, I could technically pack it in and file an Affidavit of Inability to Serve Process, but I felt I was getting close and I didn't want to give it up.

I returned to my car and ate the brown-bag lunch I'd packed—an olive pimento cheese sandwich on whole grain bread and a cluster of grapes, which made two servings of fruit in two days. I'd brought a book with me and alternated between reading and listening to the car radio. At intervals, I ran the engine, turned on the heater, and allowed the interior of the Mustang to fill with blessed warmth. This was getting old. If Vest didn't show up by two, I was taking off. I could always decide later whether it was worth another try.

At 1:35, a late-model pickup truck appeared, moving in my direction. The driver turned to look at me as he pulled into the drive and parked. The truck and the license plate matched the vehicle information I'd been given. From the description, this guy was the very Bob I'd been hired to serve. Before I could make a move, he got out, retrieved a duffel from the truck bed, and toted it up the walk. A scruffy gray cat appeared out of nowhere and trotted after him. He unlocked the front door in haste, and the cat was quick to skitter in while he had the chance. Bob glanced in my direction again before he closed the door behind him. This was not good. If he suspected he was being served, he might get cute and scurry out the back door to avoid me. If I could demonstrate a reason for my presence, I might dampen his paranoia and lure him into my trap.

I got out, moved to the front of the car, and lifted the hood. I made a serious display of tinkering with the engine, then put my hands on my hips and shook my head. Gosh, a girl sure is baffled by a big old dirty engine like this. I waited a decent interval and then lowered the hood with a bang. I crossed the street and moved up his walk to the front porch. I knocked on his door.

Nothing.

I knocked again. "Hello? Sorry to bother you, but I wondered if I could use your phone. I think my battery's dead."

I could have sworn he was on the other side of the door, listening to me as I tried listening to him.

No response.

I knocked one more time, and after a minute I went back to my car. I sat and stared at the house. To my surprise, Vest opened the front door and peered out at me. I reached over and busied myself in the glove compartment as though searching for the service manual. Would a seventeen-year-old Mustang even have a service manual? When I looked back again, he had come down the porch steps and was heading in my direction. Oh shit.

Forties, gray at the temples, blue eyes. His face was marked by a series of tight lines—a grimace of perpetual discontent. He didn't seem to be armed, which I found encouraging. Once he was in range, I lowered the window and said, "Hi. How're you?"

"Was that you knocking on my door?"

"Uh-hun. I was hoping to use the phone."

"What's the problem?"

"I can't get the engine to turn over."

"Want me to give it a try?"

"Sure."

I saw his gaze shift to the summons on the front seat beside me, but he must not have registered the reference to Superior Court and all the talk of Plaintive versus the Defendant because he didn't gasp or recoil in dismay. I folded the document and shoved it in my shoulder bag as I emerged from the car.

He took my place in the driver's seat, but instead of turning the key, he put his hands on the steering wheel and shook his head with admiration. "I used to own one of these babies. Jesus, the Boss 429, king of all muscle cars and I sold mine. Sold, hell. I as good as gave it away. I'm still kicking myself. I don't even remember what I needed the money for—probably something dumb. Where'd you find it?"

"In a used-car lot on lower Chapel. I bought it on a whim. The dealer hadn't had it half a day. He told me there weren't many made."

"Four hundred ninety-nine total in 1970," he said. "Ford developed the 429 engine in 1968 after Petty started eating up NASCAR wins with his 426 Hemi Belvedere. Remember Bunkie Knudsen?"

"Not really."

"Yeah, well right around that same time, he left GM and took over as the new boss at Ford. He's the one talked 'em into using the 429 engine in the Mustang and Cougar lines. Sucker's so big the suspension had to be relocated and they had to stick the battery in the trunk.

Turned out to be money losers, but the Boss 302 and the 429 are still the hottest cars ever made. What'd you pay for it?"

"Five grand."

I thought he'd bang his head on the steering wheel, but he shook it instead, one of those slow wags denoting copious regret. "I never should have asked." With that, he turned the key in the ignition and the engine fired right up. "You must have flooded the engine."

"Silly me. I appreciate the help."

"No biggie," he said. "You ever want to sell the car, you know where I am." He got out and stood aside to let me into the car.

I pulled the papers from my bag. "You're not Bob Vest by any chance?"

"I am. Have we met?"

I held out the summons, which he took automatically when I tapped him on the arm. "Nope. Sorry to have to say this, but you're served," I said, as I slid under the steering wheel.

"I'm what?" He looked down at the papers and when he saw what he had, he said, "Well, shit."

"And by the way. You ought to take better care of your cat."

When I got back to the office, I put in a second call to Gus's niece. With the three-hour time difference, I was hoping she'd be home from work. The phone rang so long that I was startled when she finally picked up. I repeated my original report in an abbreviated form. She seemed to draw a blank, like she didn't have any idea what I was talking about. I went through my spiel again in a more elaborate rendition, telling her who I was, what had happened to Gus, his move to the nursing home, and the need for someone, namely her, to come to his aid.

She said, "You're kidding."

"That's not quite the response I was hoping for," I said.

"I'm three thousand miles away. You think it's really that big of an emergency?"

"Well, he's not bleeding out or anything like that, but he does need your help. Someone has to get the situation under control. He's in no position to take care of himself."

Her silence suggested she wasn't receptive to the idea, in whole or in part. What was wrong with this chick?

"What sort of work do you do?" I asked as a prompt.

"I'm an executive VP in an ad agency."

"Do you think you could talk to your boss?"

"And say what?"

"Tell him—"

"It's a her . . ."

"Great. I'm sure she'll understand the kind of crisis we've got on our hands. Gus is eighty-nine years old and you're his only living relative."

Her tone shifted from resistance to mere reluctance. "I do have business contacts in L.A. I don't know how quickly I could set it up, but I suppose I could fly out at the end of the week and maybe see him Saturday or Sunday. How would that be?"

"One day in town won't do him any good unless you mean to leave him where he is."

"In the nursing home? That's not such a bad idea."

"Yes, it is. He's miserable."

"Why? What's wrong with it?"

"Let's put it this way. I don't know you at all, but I'm

reasonably certain you wouldn't be caught dead in a place like that. It's clean and the care is excellent, but your uncle wants to be in his own home."

"Well, that won't work. You said he's not able to care for himself with his shoulder like it is."

"That's my point. You'll have to hire someone to look after him."

"Couldn't you do that? You'd have a better idea how to go about it. I'm out of state."

"Melanie, it's your job, not mine. I barely know the man."

"Maybe you could pitch in for a couple of days. Until I find someone else."

"Me?" I held the phone away from me and stared at the mouthpiece. Surely she didn't think she could drag me into it. I'm the least nursey person I know and I have people who'd back me up on the claim. On the rare occasions when I've been pressed into service, I've bumbled my way through, but I never liked it much. My aunt Gin took a dim view of pain and suffering, which she felt were trumped up purely to get attention. She couldn't tolerate medical complaints and she thought all so-called serious illnesses were bogus, right up to the moment she was diagnosed with the very cancer she died of. I'm not quite as coldhearted but I'm not far behind. I had a sudden vision of hypodermic syringes and I thought I was on the verge of blacking out, when I realized Melanie was still wheedling.

"What about the neighbor who found him and called 9-1-1?"

"That was me."

"Oh. I thought there was an old guy who lived next door."

"You're talking about Henry Pitts. He's my landlord."

"That's right. I remember now. He's retired. My uncle's mentioned him before. Wouldn't he have time to look in on Gus?"

"I don't think you get it. He doesn't need someone 'looking in on him.' I'm talking about professional nursing care."

"Why don't you contact social services? There has to be an agency to handle things like this."

"You're his niece."

"His great-niece. Maybe even great-great," she said.

"Uh-hun."

I let a silence fall into which she did not leap with joy, offering to fly out.

She said, "Hello?"

"I haven't gone anywhere. I'm just waiting to hear what you're going to do."

"Fine. I'll be out, but I don't appreciate your attitude."

She hung up resoundingly to illustrate her point.

8

After dinner Friday night, I went with Henry to a Christmas-tree lot on Milagro to help him choose a tree—a decision he takes very seriously. Christmas was still two weeks away, but Henry's like a little kid when it comes to the holidays. The lot itself was small, but he felt the trees were fresher and the selection better than at the other lots he'd tried. In the six-foot height he preferred, he had several choices: a balsam fir, a Fraser fir, a blue spruce, a Nordman, the Norway, or the noble spruce. He and the man who owned the lot got into a long discussion about the merits of each. The blue spruce, the noble, and the Norway had poor needle retention, and the Nordmans had spindly tips. He finally settled on a dark green balsam fir with a classic shape, soft needles, and the fragrance of a pine forest (or Pine-Sol, depending on your frame of reference). The tree branches were secured with heavy twine, and we hauled it to his station wagon, where we tied it across the top with an elaborate configuration of rope and bungee cords.

We drove home along Cabana Boulevard, the darkened ocean to our left. Offshore the oil rigs twinkled like a regatta with the capacity for spills. It was close to eight by then and the restaurants and motels across from the beach were ablaze with lights. The glimpse we caught of State Street in passing showed a steady march of seasonal decorations as far as the eye could see.

Henry parked in his driveway and we eased the tree out of its restraints. With him toting the trunk end and me struggling along at the midpoint, we wrestled the evergreen around to the street, up his short walk, and in the front door. Henry had rearranged the furniture to clear a place for the tree in one corner of the living room. Once we'd stabilized it in its stand, he tightened the T-bolts and added water to the reservoir below. He'd already pulled six boxes marked X-MAS from his attic and stacked them nearby. Five were filled with carefully wrapped ornaments, and the sixth box contained a formidable tangle of Christmas-tree lights.

"When are you doing the lights and ornaments?"

"Tomorrow afternoon. Charlotte has an open house from two until five and she'll stop by when she's done. You're welcome to join us. I'm making eggnog to get us in the proper spirit."

"I don't want to horn in on your date."

"Don't be silly. William and Rosie are coming, too."

"Have they met her?"

"William has and he gave her a thumbs-up. I'm curious about Rosie's reaction. She's a tough one."

"Why the opinion poll? You either like her or you don't."

"I don't know. Something about the woman bothers me."

"As in what?"

"You don't find her a bit single-minded?"

"I've only talked to her once and I got the impression she was good at what she does."

"It feels more complicated. She's smart and attractive, I'll give you that, but all she talks about is sell, sell, sell. We took a walk after supper the other night and she calculated the value of every house on the block. She was ready to go door-to-door, drumming up sales, but I put my foot down. These are my neighbors. Most are retired and their homes are paid off. So she talks someone into selling, then what? They end up with a pile of cash but no place to live and no way to buy another home because the market's so high."

"What was her response?"

"She was good about it and backed off, but I could see the wheels going round and round."

"She's a go-getter. No doubt about that. In fact, I was worried she'd talk you into selling this place."

Henry gestured his dismissal. "No danger there. I love my house and I'd never give it up. She's still lobbying to get me into rental properties, but that doesn't interest me. I have one tenant already so why do I need more?"

"Okay, so maybe she's ambitious. That doesn't constitute a character flaw. You get hung up in all the fretting and you'll spoil what you have now. If it doesn't work out, then so be it."

"Very philosophical," he said. "I'll remember you said that and quote it back to you one day."

"No doubt."

At 9:30 I went back to my place and let myself in. I flipped off the porch light and hung up my jacket. I was ready to settle down with a glass of wine and a good book when I heard a knock at my door. At that hour, chances were good it was someone trying to sell me something, or passing out poorly printed pamphlets predicting the End of the World. I was surprised anyone would brave the walk to my door since the streetlights don't penetrate Henry's backyard and patio.

I turned on the outside light and peered through the porthole in my front door. The woman standing on my porch wasn't anyone I knew. She was in her midthirties with a pale square face, thinly plucked eyebrows, bright red lipstick, and a thick bunch of auburn hair that she'd caught in a knot on the top of her head. She wore a black business suit, but I didn't see a clipboard or a sample case so maybe I was safe. When she saw me looking out at her she smiled and waved.

I put the chain on and then opened the door a crack. "Yes?"

"Hi. Are you Kinsey?"

"I am."

"My name is Melanie Oberlin. Gus Vronsky's niece. Am I disturbing you?"

"Not at all. Hang on." I closed the door and slid the chain off the track, then let her in. "Wow. That was quick. I talked to you two days ago. I didn't expect to see you so soon. When did you get in?"

"Just now. I have a rental car out front. Turns out my boss thought the trip was a fabulous idea, so I flew into L.A. last night and met with clients all day. I didn't start the drive up until seven, thinking I'd be clever and avoid the rush-hour traffic, but then I got stuck behind a six-car pile-up in Malibu. At any rate, I'm sorry to barge in, but it just dawned on me I don't have a key to Uncle Gus's place. Is there any way to get in?"

"Henry has a set of keys and I'm sure he's still up. It won't take me a minute, if you want to come on in and wait."

"I'd love to. Thanks. Do you mind if I use the loo?"

"Be my guest."

I showed her into the downstairs bathroom, and while she went about her business, I crossed the patio to Henry's back door and tapped on the glass. The kitchen lights were out, but I could see the reflected flicker of the television set in the living room beyond. A moment later, he appeared in the doorway and flipped on the kitchen light before he unlocked the door. "I thought you were in for the night," he said.

"I was, but Gus's niece showed up and she needs a house key."

"Hang on."

He left the door open while he found the set of keys in his kitchen junk drawer. "The way you described your phone conversation, I didn't think she'd come at all, let alone this fast."

"Me, neither. I was pleasantly surprised."

"How long will she stay?"

"I haven't asked her yet, but I can let you know. You may end up dealing with her anyway since I have to go into the office first thing tomorrow morning."

"On Saturday?"

"I'm afraid so. I've got paperwork to catch up on and I like the quiet."

When I returned to the studio, Melanie was still in the bathroom, and the sound of running water suggested she was washing her face. I took two glasses from the cabinet and opened a bottle of Edna Valley Chardonnay. I poured six ounces for each of us and when she came out, I handed her Gus's house key and a glass of wine.

"I hope you like wine. I took the liberty," I said. "Have a seat."

"Thanks. After three hours on the freeway, I could

use a drink. I thought Boston drivers were bad, but people out here are lunatics."

"You're from Boston?"

"More or less. We moved to New York when I was nine, but I went to school in Boston and still visit friends from my BU days." She sat down in one of the director's chairs and did a quick visual survey. "Nice. This would be a palace in the city."

"It's a palace anywhere," I said. "I'm glad you made it out here. Henry was just asking how long you might stay."

"Until the end of next week if all goes well. In the interest of efficiency, I called the local paper and placed a classified ad that starts tomorrow and runs all next week. They'll put it in the 'Help Wanted' section—companion, private-duty nurse, that sort of thing—and they'll also run it in the 'Personals.' I wasn't sure Uncle Gus had an answering machine so I gave his address. I hope that wasn't a mistake."

"I don't see why it would be. You probably won't be swamped with applicants at this time of year. A lot of people postpone job hunting until after the holidays."

"We'll see how we do. In a pinch, I can always try to scare up a temp. I do apologize for my response when you called. I haven't seen Gus in years so you caught me off guard. Once I decided to fly out, I thought I might as well do it right. Speaking of Uncle Gus, how is he? I should have asked about him first thing."

"I didn't get over there to see him today, but Henry did and says he's about as you'd expect."

"In other words, screaming and shouting."

"Pretty much."

"He's been known to throw things, too, when he's really on a tear. Or he did way back when."

"How are you related? I know he's your uncle, but where on the family tree?"

"My mother's side. He was actually her great-uncle, so I guess that makes him a great-great to me. She died ten years ago this past May, and once his brother passed on, I was the only one left. I feel guilty I haven't seen him for so long."

"Well, it can't be easy if you're on the East Coast."

"What about you? You have family out here?"

"Nope. I'm an orphan child as well, which is probably for the best."

We chatted for ten or fifteen minutes and then she glanced at her watch. "Oops. I better get going. I don't want to keep you up. In the morning, you can give me directions to the nursing home."

"I'll be out of here early, but you can always knock on Henry's door. He'll be happy to help. I take it you'll be staying next door?"

"I'd hoped to, unless you think he'd object."

"I'm sure he won't care, but I should warn you the place is grim. We cleaned what we could, but it's iffy in my opinion. Who knows when Gus last had a go at it himself."

"How bad?"

"It's gross. The sheets are clean, but the mattress looks like something he dragged in from the curb. He's a hoarder as well, so two of the three bedrooms aren't usable at all, unless you're looking for a place to toss trash."

"He hoards? That's new. He didn't used to do that."

"He does now. Dishes, clothing, tools, shoes. It looks like he has newspapers from the past fifteen years. There were items in the fridge that were probably capable of spreading disease."

She wrinkled her nose. "You think it's better if I stay somewhere else?"

"I would."

"I'll take your word for it. How hard is it going to be to find a hotel at this hour?"

"It shouldn't be a problem. We don't get many tourists at this time of year. There are six or eight motels just two blocks from here. When I run in the mornings, I always see the vacancy signs lighted."

Maybe it was the wine, but I was noticing how friendly I felt, possibly because I was so grateful she'd arrived. Or maybe ours was one of those relationships where you butt heads up front and get along swimmingly from that point on. Whatever the dynamic, the next thing I knew I was saying, "You can always stay here. For tonight, at any rate."

She seemed as surprised as I. "Really? That'd be great, but I wouldn't want to put you out."

Having offered, of course, I could have bitten off my tongue, but I felt bound by etiquette to assure her of my sincerity, while she swore it'd be no big deal to bumble around in the dark in search of accommodations—clearly something she was hoping to avoid.

In the end, I made up a bed for her on the fold-out sofa in my living room. She already knew where the bathroom was so I took a few minutes to show her how to work the coffeemaker and where the cereal box and bowls were stowed.

At 11:00 she retreated to her bed and I climbed the spiral staircase to the loft. Since she was still on East Coast time, she turned her light out long before I did. In the morning, I got up at 8:00 and by the time I came downstairs, showered, and dressed, she was already up and gone. Like a good guest, she'd stripped the sheets, which she'd folded neatly and placed on the lid of my washing machine, along with the damp towel she'd used for her shower. She'd refolded the sofa bed and put the cushions back in place. According to the note she'd left, she'd gone in search of a coffee shop and expected to be back by 9:00. She offered to buy me dinner if I was free that night, which as it happened, I was.

I left for the office at 8:35 that morning and I didn't see her again for six days. So much for dinner.

9

Late Saturday afternoon, I joined Henry and Charlotte for the tree-trimming festivities. I declined the eggnog, which I knew contained a stunning quantity of calories, not to mention fat and cholesterol. Henry's recipe called for a cup of superfine sugar, a quart of milk, twelve large eggs, and two cups of whipping cream. He'd made a nonalcoholic version, which allowed his guests to add bourbon or brandy to taste. By the time I arrived, the Christmas-tree lights had been threaded through the branches, and Rosie had already been there and gone. She'd accepted a cup of eggnog and then she'd left for the restaurant, as her dictatorial presence was required in the kitchen.

Henry, William, Charlotte, and I unwrapped and admired the ornaments, most of which had been in Henry's family for years. Once the tree was trimmed, William and Henry had their annual argument about how to apply tinsel. William was of the one-strand-at-a-time method, and Henry thought the effect was more natural if the tinsel was tossed and allowed to form picturesque clumps. They settled on a little bit of both.

At 8:00 we walked the half block to Rosie's. William went to work behind the bar, which left the table to Henry, Charlotte, and me.

I hadn't paid attention to how much either had had to drink, which may or may not explain what followed. The menu that night was the usual strange assortment of Hungarian dishes, many of which Rosie had determined in advance would be our free choice for the occasion.

While we waited for the first course, I turned to Henry. "I saw lights on at Gus's so I'm assuming you and Melanie connected this morning after I left for work."

"We did and I found her most forceful and effective. She's accustomed to dealing with the hassles of life in New York so she knows how to get things done. We were at Rolling Hills by nine fifteen. Of course, there was no sign of the attending physician and no way to get Gus released without the doctor's official sanction. Somehow Melanie managed to hunt him down and get his signature on the form. She orchestrated the process with such efficiency, we had Gus out of there and back at his place by eleven ten."

"She found a place to stay?"

"She checked into the Wharfside on Cabana. She also did the grocery shopping and ordered a wheelchair from a rental company. She had it delivered and was out pushing Gus around the neighborhood this afternoon. The attention worked wonders. He was really quite nice."

I was about to make a comment in response, when Charlotte spoke up. "Who built that row of houses on your block? They seem very much alike."

Henry turned and looked at her, faintly disconcerted by the change in subject. "Not so. My house and Gus's are direct images of one another, but the house just past the vacant lot and Moza Lowenstein's place, which is one more door down, have a very different feel. They might have been constructed around the same time, but with the changes people have made in the intervening years, it's hard to tell what the original floor plans were like."

Henry and I exchanged a quick look that Charlotte didn't catch. Sure enough, she'd steered the conversation around to real estate. I hoped her question was idle, but she was apparently pursuing a train of thought.

"I take it none of them were designed by a name architect?"

"Not that I know. Over the years, a series of builders bought up the lots and threw together whatever was easy and cheap. What makes you ask?"

"I was thinking about the restrictions on houses over fifty years old. If a house has no historical significance, a buyer would be free to demolish the structure and build something new. Otherwise, you're more or less limited to the footprint, which reduces the potential."

"Why is that relevant? None of my neighbors have expressed any interest in selling."

She frowned. "I understand there hasn't been much turnover, but given the advanced ages of home owners in the area, some of these houses are bound to come up for sale—Gus's being a case in point."

"And?"

"What will happen when he dies? Melanie won't have the first idea how to market his place."

I flicked another look at Henry, whose face was now carefully composed. In the seven years I've known him, I've seen him lose his temper a handful of times, and his manner was always unfailingly mild. He didn't quite look at her. "What are you proposing?"

"I'm not proposing anything. I'm saying someone

from out of state might misread the situation and underestimate the market value."

"If Gus or Melanie should raise the question, I'll give them your business card and you can rush right in."

Charlotte looked at him. "Excuse me?"

"I didn't realize you were here to cultivate clients. Are you planning to farm the area?" he asked. He was referring to the real estate practice of working an area—sending out flyers, calling on the residents, planting the seeds in hopes of harvesting a sale.

"Of course not. We've already discussed the subject and you made it clear you disapproved. If I offended you in some way, that wasn't my intent."

"I'm sure it wasn't, but it does seem callous to be estimating home prices predicated on the deaths of people I've known for years."

"Oh, for heaven's sake, Henry. You can't be serious. There's nothing personal in this. People die every day. I'm seventy-eight myself and I think estate planning is important."

"Doubtless."

"You needn't take that tone. After all, there are tax implications. And what about the beneficiaries? For most people, a house is the largest asset they have, which is certainly true in my case. If I don't have a clue about property values, how can I determine a fair division among my heirs?"

"I'm sure you'll have it calculated down to the penny."

"I wasn't speaking literally. I'm talking about the average person."

"Gus isn't as average as you seem to think."

"Where in heaven's name is all the hostility coming from?"

"You're the one who brought it up. Kinsey and I were discussing something else entirely."

"Well, I'm sorry to interrupt. It's clear you have your nose out of joint, but I haven't done anything except express an opinion. I don't understand what you're afraid of."

"I don't want my neighbors to think I endorse solicitors."

Charlotte picked up her menu. "I can see this is a point on which we can't agree so why don't we leave it that way?"

Henry picked up his menu as well and opened it. "I'd appreciate that. And while we're about it, perhaps we could talk about something else."

I could feel my face flush. This was like marital bickering except these two weren't that well acquainted. I thought Charlotte would be embarrassed by his tone, but she didn't bat an eye. The moment passed. The rest of the dinner conversation was unremarkable and the evening seemed to end on a pleasant note.

Henry saw her to her car, and while the two said good night, I debated about mentioning the clash, but decided it wasn't my place. I knew what made him so touchy on the subject. At the age of eighty-seven, he had to be thinking about the financial aspects of his own demise.

After Charlotte pulled away, we fell into step, walking the half block home. "I suppose you think I was out of line," he remarked.

"Well, I don't think she's as mercenary as you implied. I know she's focused on her work, but she's not crass."

"I was irritated."

"Come on, Henry. She didn't mean any harm. She believes people should be informed about property values, and why not?"

"I suppose you're right."

"It's not a question of who's right. The point is if you're going to spend time together, you have to take her as she is. And if you don't intend to see her again, then why pick a fight?"

"Do you think I should apologize?"

"That's up to you, but it wouldn't do any harm."

Late Monday afternoon I'd scheduled an appointment with Lisa Ray to discuss her recollections about the accident, for which she was being sued. The address she'd given me was a new condominium development in Colgate, a series of frame town houses standing shoulder to shoulder in clusters of four. There were six exterior styles and four types of building materials: brick, frame, fieldstone, and stucco. I was guessing six floor plans with mix-and-match elements that would make each apartment unique. The units were arranged in varied combinations—some with shutters, some with balconies, some with patios out front. Each foursome sat on a square of well-tended lawn. There were shrubs and flower beds and small hopeful trees that wouldn't mature for another forty years. In lieu of garages, the residents kept their vehicles in long carports that ran between the town houses in horizontal rows. Most of the parking spaces were empty, which suggested people off at work. I saw no evidence of children.

I found Lisa's house number and parked on the street out front. While I waited for her to answer the door, I sampled the air without detecting the scent of any cooking under way. Probably too early. I imagined the neighbors would trickle home between five thirty and six. Dinner would be delivered in vehicles with signs on the top or pulled from the freezer in boxes complete with gaudy food photos, the oven and microwave instructions printed in type so small you'd have to don your reading glasses.

Lisa Ray opened the door. Her hair was dark, cut short to accommodate its natural curl, which consisted of a halo of perfect ringlets. She was fresh-faced, with blue eyes and freckles like tiny beige paint flecks across the bridge of her nose. She wore black flats, panty hose, a red pleated skirt with a short-sleeved red cotton sweater. "Yikes. You're early. Are you Kinsey?"

"That's me."

She opened the door and let me in, saying, "I didn't expect you to be so prompt. I just got home from work and I'd love to get out of these clothes."

"That's fine. Take your time."

"I'll be back in a second. Have a seat."

I moved into the living room and settled on the couch while she took the stairs two at a time. I knew from the file that she was twenty-six years old, a part-time college student who paid her tuition and expenses by working twenty hours a week in the business office at St. Terry's Hospital.

The apartment was small. White walls, beige wall-to-wall carpet that looked new and smelled of harsh chemicals. The furniture was a mix of garage-sale finds and items she'd probably managed to cadge from home. Two mismatched chairs, both upholstered in the same fake leopard print, flanked a red-plaid couch, with a coffee table filling the space between. A small wooden dinette table and four chairs were arranged at the far end of the room with a pass-through to the kitchen off to the right. Checking the magazines on the coffee table, I had my choice of back issues of *Glamour* or *Cosmopolitan*. I picked *Cosmopolitan*, turning to an article about what men like in bed. What men? What bed? I hadn't had a close encounter with a guy since Cheney left my life. I was about to calculate the exact number of weeks, but the idea depressed me before I even started to count.

Five minutes later Lisa reappeared, trotting down the stairs in jeans and a sweatshirt with the University of California Santa Teresa logo on the front. She took a seat in one of the upholstered chairs.

I set the magazine aside. "Is that where you went to school?" I asked, indicating her shirt.

She glanced down. "This is my roommate's. She's a secretary in the math department out there. I'm at City College part-time, working on an AA degree in radiography. St. Terry's has been great about my hours, pretty much letting me work when I want," she said. "Have you talked to the insurance company?"

"Briefly," I said. "As it happens, I used to be associated with California Fidelity, so I know the adjuster, Mary Bellflower. I chatted with her a few days ago and she gave me the basics."

"She's nice. I like her, though we're in total disagreement about this lawsuit."

"I gathered as much. I know you've been over this half a dozen times, but could you tell me what happened?"

"Sure. I don't mind. This was Thursday, right before the Memorial Day weekend. I didn't have classes that day, but I'd gone up to the college to do a review in the computer lab. After I finished, I picked up my car in the parking lot. I pulled up as far as the exit, intending to take a left onto Palisade Drive. There wasn't a ton of traffic, but I had my signal on, waiting for a few cars to pass. I saw the Fredricksons' van approaching from maybe two hundred yards away. He was driving and he'd activated the right-turn signal and reduced his speed, so I figured he was turning into the same lot I was pulling out of. I glanced right and checked to make sure I was clear in that direction before I accelerated. I was partway through the turn when I realized he was going faster than I thought. I tried speeding up, hoping to get out of the way, but he caught me broadside. It's a wonder I'm not dead. The driver's-side door was caved in and the center post was bent. The impact knocked my car sideways about fifteen feet. My head snapped right and then hit the window so hard it cracked the glass. I'm still seeing a chiropractor for that."

"According to the file, you declined medical attention."

"Well, sure. Bizarre as it sounds, I felt fine at the time. Maybe I was in shock. Of course, I was upset, but I didn't have any actual medical complaints. Nothing broken or bleeding. I knew I'd have a big old bruise on my head. The paramedics thought I should be seen in the ER, but basically, they said it was my choice. They ran me through a couple of quick tests, making sure I wasn't suffering memory loss or double vision—whatever else they're concerned about when your brain's at stake. They urged me to see my own physician if anything developed. It wasn't until the next day my neck seized up. I tell you my weekend plans were really screwed. I lay around at my mom's house all day, icing my neck and popping expired pain pills from some dental work she'd had done a couple of years ago."

"What about Gladys?"

"She was hysterical. By the time I managed to wrench open my door, her husband was already out of the van in his wheelchair, screaming at me. She was shrieking and crying like she was on the verge of death. I thought it was a put-on myself. I walked around some, taking a look at both cars so I could get a sense of the damage, but I started shaking so hard I thought I was going to pass out. I went back to my car and sat with my head down between my knees. That's when this old guy showed up and came over to see how I was doing. He was nice. He just kept patting my arm and telling me everything was fine and not to worry, it wasn't my fault, and stuff like that. I know Gladys heard him because all the sudden, she went into this big theatrical slump, moaning and doing this fake boo-hoo stuff. I could see her getting herself all worked up, like my three-year-old niece, who barfs at will if things don't go her way. The old guy went over and helped Gladys to the curb. By then, she was having fits. I don't mean that literally, of course, but I know she was faking."

"Not according to the ER report."

"Oh, please. I'm sure she was banged up, but she's milking the situation for all it's worth. Have you talked to her?"

"Not yet. I'll call and see if she'll agree to it. She isn't required to."

"No sweat on *that* score. She won't pass up the chance to tell her side of it. You should have heard her with the cop."

"Back up a minute. Who called the police?"

"I don't know. I guess somebody must have heard the crash and dialed 9-1-1. The police and paramedics showed up about the same time. A couple of other motorists had pulled over by then and a woman came out of her house across the street. Gladys was moaning like she was in all this pain, so the paramedics started on her first, you know, doing vital signs and stuff like that, trying to calm her down. The cop came over and asked me what happened. That's when I realized the old guy who helped me was gone. Next thing I knew, Gladys was being rolled into the back of the ambulance strapped to a board with her head immobilized. I should've figured out right then how much trouble I was in. I felt terrible about the whole thing because I wouldn't wish pain and suffering on anyone. At the same time, I thought her behavior was bullshit, pure showmanship."

"According to the police report, you were at fault."

"I know that's what it says, but that's ridiculous. The way the law's written, they had the right-of-way so I'm technically the guilty one. When I first saw the van it was creeping along. I swear he wasn't going more than three miles an hour. He must have floored it when he realized he could catch me before I finished the turn."

"You're saying he hit you deliberately?"

"Why not? He had the opportunity of a lifetime staring him in the face."

I shook my head. "I don't understand."

"To collect the insurance money," she said impatiently. "Check it out for yourself. She's essentially self-employed. She works as an independent contractor, so she probably doesn't have long-term medical coverage and no disability insurance. What a great way to support themselves in their retirement years, suing the shit out of me."

"You know that for a fact?"

"What, her having no disability insurance? No, I don't know it for a *fact*, but I'd be willing to bet."

"I can't picture it. How could Millard be sure she'd survive the crash?"

"Yeah, well, he wasn't going *that* fast. Relatively speaking. I mean, he wasn't driving sixty miles an hour. He must have known neither one of us would *die*."

"Risky nonetheless."

"Maybe that depends on the stakes."

"True, but auto insurance fraud is usually highly organized and involves more than one person. The 'mark' might be maneuvered into rear-ending another vehicle, but it's all a setup. The 'victim,' the lawyer, and the doctor are in cahoots on the claim. I can't believe Gladys or Millard are part of anything like that."

"They don't have to be. He might have read about it in a book. It wouldn't take a genius to figure how to set it up. He saw a chance for big bucks and acted on the spur of the moment."

"How are we going to prove that?"

"Find the old guy and he'll tell you."

"What makes you so sure he saw the accident?"

"He must have because I remember catching sight of him as I approached the exit to the parking lot. I didn't pay much attention because I was focused on the street ahead."

"You saw him where?"

"On the far side of Palisade."

"Doing what?"

"I don't know. I guess he was waiting to cross the street, so he must have seen the van about the same time I did."

"What age would you say?"

"What do I know about old guys? He had white hair and his jacket was brown leather, sort of dry-looking and cracked."

"Can you recall anything else? Did the old guy wear glasses?"

"I don't remember."

"What about the shape of his face?"

"Kind of long."

"Clean shaven?"

"I think so. For sure, he didn't have a beard, but he might've had a mustache."

"No moles or scars?"

"Can't help you there. I was upset so I didn't pay much attention."

"What about height and weight?"

"He seemed taller than me and I'm five-six, but he wasn't heavy or rail thin or anything like that. I'm sorry I can't be more specific."

"What about his hands?"

"Nope, but I remember his shoes. They were those old-time black leather lace-up shoes like the kind my granddad wore to work. You know the ones with holes punched around the instep?"

"Wing tips?"

"Yeah, them. They needed polishing and the sole on his right shoe was coming loose."

"Did he have an accent?"

"Not one that I noticed."

"What about his teeth?"

"A mess. Kind of yellow like he smoked. I'd forgotten about that."

"Anything else?"

She shook her head.

"What about your injuries, aside from whiplash?"

"I had headaches at first, but those have gone away. My neck's still sore and I guess that's what's throwing my back out of alignment. I lost two days at work, but nothing beyond that. If I sit for any length of time, I have to get up and walk around for a while. I guess I'm lucky things weren't worse."

"You got that right," I said.

* * *

During that next week, I didn't have occasion to talk to Melanie, but Henry kept me informed about her hassles with Gus, whose prickly disposition had resurfaced. Twice, in the early morning, I saw her arrive from the motel. I knew she stayed late, looking after him. I suppose I could have invited her to my place for a glass of wine or reminded her of her offer to buy dinner. Better yet, I could have put together a nourishing casserole, thus providing a meal for the two of them in the manner of a kindly neighbor. But does that sound like me? I didn't extend myself for the following reasons:

(1) I can't cook.

(2) I'd never been close to Gus, and I didn't want to get caught up in the turbulence surrounding him.

In my experience, the urge to rescue generates aggravation for the poor would-be heroine without any discernible effect on the person in need of help. You can't save others from themselves because those who make a perpetual muddle of their lives don't appreciate your interfering with the drama they've created. They want your poor-sweet-baby sympathy, but they don't want to change. This is a truth I never seem to learn. Problematic in this case was that Gus hadn't generated his troubles. He'd opened a window and in they'd crept.

Henry told me that the first weekend Gus was home, the Rolling Hills nursing director had recommended a private-duty nurse who was willing to work an eight-hour shift on Saturday and again on Sunday. This relieved Melanie of the more odious of medical and personal hygiene responsibilities while simultaneously providing Gus with someone else to abuse when his mood went sour, which it did on an hourly basis.

Henry had also told me Melanie had had no response from the classified ad she'd run. She'd finally contacted an agency and had been interviewing home companions, hoping to find someone to step into the breach.

"Has she had any luck?" I asked.

"I wouldn't call it *luck* exactly. She's hired three so far, and two didn't make it to the end of the day. The third fared better, but not by much. I could hear him blasting her from across the back hedge."

I said, "I guess I should have offered to help, but I decided I'd be better off if I learned to cope with my guilt."

"How're you doing with it?"

"Pretty well."

10

SOLANA

Solana parked the car and rechecked the ad in the "Personals," making sure the address was correct. There was no phone number listed, which was just as well. The last classified ad she'd responded to had been a dead end. The patient was an elderly woman living in her daughter's house, confined to a hospital bed that had been installed in the dining room. The house was lovely, but the makeshift sick bay ruined the overall effect. High ceilings, light pouring in, all the furnishings done in exquisite taste. There was a cook and a housekeeper on the premises, and that put a damper on Solana's enthusiasm.

Solana was interviewed by the daughter, who wanted someone to attend to her mother's needs but felt she shouldn't be required to pay private-duty rates since she would be present in the home as well. Solana would be expected to bathe, feed, and diaper the senile mother, change linens, do her laundry, and administer medication. These were responsibilities she was capable of handling, but she didn't like the daughter's attitude. She seemed to view a nursing professional as a household servant, on a par with a laundress. Solana suspected that the housekeeper would be treated better than she.

The haughty daughter made notes on her clipboard notepad and said she had several other job applicants to interview, which Solana knew was a bald-faced lie. The daughter wanted her to feel competitive, as though she'd be fortunate to be offered the position, which consisted of nine-hour days, one day off a week, and no personal calls. She'd be allowed two fifteen-minute coffee breaks, but she was expected to provide her own meals. And with a cook working right there in the next room!

Solana asked a good many questions, showing how interested she was, making sure the daughter spelled out particulars. In the end she agreed to everything, including the low wages. The daughter's manner went from cold to prim to pleased with herself. It was clear she felt smug for having talked someone into accepting such ridiculous terms. Solana noticed there was no further mention of the other candidates.

She explained she didn't have time just then to do the paperwork, but she'd bring the completed application with her when she came to work the next morning at eight. She jotted down her phone number in case the daughter thought of anything else she wanted to discuss. By the time Solana left, the daughter was falling all over herself, relieved that she'd managed to solve her problem at so little cost. She shook Solana's hand warmly. Solana returned to her car, knowing she'd never see the woman again. The phone number she'd provided rang through to the psychiatric ward in a Perdido hospital, where Tiny had once spent a year.

Now Solana sat across the street and a few doors down from the address she'd been looking for. This was in response to an ad she'd seen over the weekend. She'd dismissed the possibility at first since there wasn't a telephone number listed. As the week went on and no other jobs of interest appeared, she'd decided the house might be worth a quick look. The setting didn't seem promising. The place had a neglected air, especially compared with the other houses on the block. The neighborhood was close to the beach and consisted almost entirely of single-family dwellings. Sandwiched here and there, between the small depressing houses, she could see a new duplex or fourplex in the Spanish-style architecture common to the area. Solana's guess was that many of the residents were retired, which meant fixed incomes and little in the way of discretionary spending.

To all appearances, she was of a similar economic status. Two months before, one of her brothers had given her a banged-up convertible he was eager to junk. The car she'd been driving had thrown a rod, and the mechanic told her the repair bill would be two thousand dollars, which was more than the car was worth. At the time, she had no cash to spare, and when her brother offered her the 1972 Chevrolet, she'd accepted—though not without a certain sense of humiliation. Clearly, he thought the junker was good enough for her. She'd had her eye on a better car and she'd even been tempted to take on the hefty payments, but good sense prevailed. Now she was grateful she'd settled for the secondhand Chevrolet, which resembled so many other cars parked along the street. A newer model would have sent the wrong message. No one was interested in hiring help who appeared to be more prosperous than they.

So far she had no information about the patient beyond the brief clues in the ad. It was good he was eighty-nine years old and tottery enough to fall and hurt himself. His need for outside help suggested there weren't any close relatives willing to pitch in. These days, people were self-centered—impatient about anything that interfered with their own comfort or convenience. From her perspective, this was good. From the patient's, not so much. If he were surrounded by loving kids and grandkids, he'd be no use to her at all.

What worried her was his ability to pay for the in-home care. She couldn't bill through Medicare or Medicaid because she'd never survive official scrutiny, and the chances of his having adequate private insurance didn't look good. So many of the elderly made no provision for long-term disability. They drifted into their twilight years as though by mistake, surprised to discover themselves with limited resources, unable to cover the monstrous medical bills that accrued in the wake of acute, chronic, or catastrophic illness. Did they think the necessary funds would fall from the sky? Who did they imagine would shoulder the burden for their lack of planning? Fortunately, the last patient she'd taken on had ample means, which Solana had put to good use. The job had ended on a sour note, but she'd learned a valuable lesson. The mistake she'd made there was one she wouldn't make again.

She debated the wisdom of inquiring about a job in such a modest neighborhood, but finally decided she could at least knock on the door and introduce herself. Since she'd driven in from Colgate, she might as well explore the possibility. She knew certain wealthy types took pride in maintaining a humble facade. This fellow might be one. Just two days before, she'd read an article in the paper about an elderly woman who'd died and left two million dollars to an animal shelter, of all things. Friends and neighbors had been stunned because the woman had lived like a pauper, and no one suspected she had so much money tucked away. Her prime concern was for her six ancient cats, which the estate attorney had ordered euthanized before the woman was even cold in her grave. This freed up thousands of dollars to pay the subsequent legal bills.

Solana checked her reflection in the rearview mirror. She was wearing her new glasses, a cheap pair she'd found that were a close match to the glasses on the Other's driver's license. With her hair dyed dark, the resemblance between them was passable. Her own face was thinner, but she wasn't worried about that. Anyone comparing her face to the photo would simply think she'd lost weight. The dress she'd chosen for the occasion was a crisply ironed cotton that made a comforting rustling sound when she walked. It wasn't a uniform per se, but it had the same simple lines and it smelled of spray starch. The only jewelry she wore was a watch with big numbers on the face and a sweeping second hand. A watch like that implied a quick and professional attention to vital signs. She took out her compact and powdered her nose. She looked good. Her complexion was clear and she liked her hair in this new darker shade. She tucked her compact away, satisfied that she looked the part—faithful companion to the old. She got out of her car and locked it behind her, then crossed the street.

The woman who answered the door was in her thirties and had a gaudy look about her—bright red lipstick, dark red hair. Her skin was pale, as though she seldom exerted herself and never went outdoors. She was definitely not a California type, especially with those eyebrows plucked to thin arches and darkened with pencil. She wore black boots and a narrow black wool skirt that hit her midcalf. Neither the shape nor the length was flattering, but Solana knew it was the current rage, as were the dark red nails. The woman probably thought she had an eye for high fashion, which wasn't the case. She'd picked up the "look" from the latest magazines. Everything she wore would be dated and out of style before the new year rolled around. Solana smiled to herself. Anyone who had so little self-awareness would be easy to manipulate.

She held the paper up, folded so that the ad was in view. "I believe you placed an ad in the paper."

"I did. Oh, how nice. I was beginning to think no one would ever respond. I'm Melanie Oberlin," she said, and extended her hand. Solana might as well have been a fly-fisherman, casting out her line.

"Solana Rojas," she replied, and shook Melanie's hand, making sure her grip was strong. The articles she'd read all said the same thing. Keep the handshake firm and look your prospective employer in the eye. These were tips Solana committed to memory.

The woman said, "Please come in."

"Thank you."

Solana stepped into the living room, taking in the whole of it without any visible evidence of curiosity or dismay. The house smelled sour. The wall-to-wall carpet was beige, shabby and stained, and the upholstered furniture was covered in a dark brown crepey fabric she knew would be gummy to the touch. The lamp shades were tinted a deep parchment color by the infusion of large quantities of cigarette smoke over a long period of time. She knew if she put her nose against the drapes, she'd inhale decades' worth of secondhand tar and nicotine.

"Shall we sit down?"

Solana took a seat on the sofa.

This was a place where a man had lived alone for many

years, indifferent to his surroundings. A superficial order had been imposed, probably quite recently, but the rooms would have to be gutted to eliminate the many layers of grime. She knew, sight unseen, that the kitchen linoleum would be a dead gray and the aged refrigerator would be small and hunched. The interior light would be out and the shelves would be crusty with years of accumulated food spills.

Melanie looked around, seeing the place through her visitor's eyes. "I've been trying to tidy up since I got into town. The house belongs to my uncle Gus. He's the one who fell and dislocated his shoulder."

Solana loved her apologetic tone because it signified anxiety and a desire to please. "And your aunt is where?"

"She died in 1964. They had one son who was killed in World War Two and a daughter who died in a traffic accident."

"So much sadness," Solana said. "I have an uncle in much the same situation. He's eighty-six and living in isolation after the loss of his wife. I've spent many weekends with him, cleaning, running errands, and preparing food for the coming week. I think it's the company he enjoys more than anything."

"Exactly," Melanie said. "Uncle Gus seems grumpy, but I've noticed how his mood improves with company. Would you like a cup of coffee?"

"Thank you, no. I had two cups this morning and that's my limit."

"I wish I could say the same. I must go through ten cups a day. In the city, we think of it as the addiction of choice. Are you a native of California?"

"Fourth generation," Solana said, amused at the roundabout way the woman had come up with to ask if she was Mexican. She hadn't actually said she was, but she knew Melanie Oberlin would imagine a once wealthy Spanish family. Solana said, "You yourself have an accent, no?"

"Boston."

"I thought so. And this is 'the city' you referred to?"

Melanie shook her head in the negative. "New York."

"How did you hear of your uncle's unfortunate accident? Is there another family member here in town?"

"I'm sorry to say there's not. One of the neighbors called. I flew out expecting to stay a few days, but it's been a week and a half."

"You came all the way from New York? That was very good of you."

"Well, I didn't have much choice," Melanie said. Her smile was self-deprecating, but it was clear she agreed.

"Family loyalty is so very rare these days. Or that's my observation. I hope you'll forgive the generalization."

"No, no. You're right. It's a very sad commentary on the times," she said.

"It's unfortunate there was no one else living close enough to help."

"I come from a very small family and everyone else is gone."

"I'm the youngest of nine. But no matter. You must be anxious to get home."

"'Frantic' is a better word. I've been dealing with a couple of home health care agencies, trying to get someone on board. So far, we haven't been able to make anything work."

"It's not always easy to find someone suitable. Your ad says you're looking for a registered nurse."

"Exactly. With my uncle's medical problems, he needs more than a home companion."

"To be truthful, I'm not an RN. I'm a licensed vocational nurse. I wouldn't want to misrepresent my qualifications. I do work with an agency—Senior Health Care Management—but I'm more like an independent contractor than an employee."

"You're an LVN? Well, that's pretty much the same thing, isn't it?"

Solana shrugged. "There's a difference in training and, of course, an RN earns far more than someone of my humble origins. In my own behalf, I will say that most of my experience has been with the elderly. I come from a culture where age and wisdom are accorded respect."

Solana went on in this vein, inventing as she went along, but she needn't have bothered. Melanie believed every word she said. She wanted to believe so she could make her escape without feeling guilty or irresponsible. "Does your uncle need around-the-clock care?"

"No, no. Not at all. The doctor's concerned about his managing on his own during his recovery. Aside from the shoulder injury, he's been in good health, so we might only need someone for a month or so. I hope that's not a problem."

"Most of my jobs have been temporary," she said. "What are the duties you had in mind?"

"The usual, I guess. Bathing and grooming, light housekeeping, a little laundry, and maybe one meal a day. Something along those lines."

"What about grocery shopping and transportation to his doctor's appointments? Won't he need to be seen by his primary care physician?"

Melanie sat back. "I hadn't thought about that, but it'd be great if you'd be willing."

"Of course. There are usually other errands as well, at least in my experience. What about the hours?"

"That's up to you. Whatever you think would work best."

"And the pay?"

"I was thinking somewhere in the neighborhood of nine dollars an hour. That's the standard rate back East. I don't know about out here."

Solana covered her surprise. She'd meant to ask for seven fifty, which was already a dollar more than she usually earned. She lifted her brows. "Nine," she said, infusing the word with infinite regret.

Melanie leaned forward. "I wish I could offer more, but he'll be paying out of his own pocket and that's as much as he can afford."

"I see. Of course, in California, when you're looking for skilled nursing care, that would be considered low."

"I know and I'm sorry. We could maybe make it, you know, like nine fifty. Would that work for you?"

Solana considered. "Perhaps I could manage, assuming you're talking about a straight eight-hour shift, five days a week. If weekends are necessary, my rate would go up to ten an hour."

"That's fine. If it comes down to it, I can contribute a few dollars to help offset the expense. The important thing is that he has the help he needs."

"Naturally, the patient's needs are paramount."

"When would you be able to start? I mean, assuming you're interested."

Solana paused. "This is Friday and I do have a few things to take care of. Could we say early next week?"

"Would Monday be at all possible?"

Solana shifted with apparent uneasiness. "Ah. I might be able to rearrange my schedule, but much would depend on you."

"Me?"

"You have an application you want me to complete?"

"Oh, I don't think that's necessary. We've covered the basics, and if something else comes up, we can discuss it at the time."

"I appreciate your confidence, but you should have the information for your files. It's better for both of us if we put our cards on the table, so to speak."

"That's very conscientious. Actually, I do have some forms. Hang on a second."

She got up and crossed the room to a side table where her handbag was sitting. She took out a folded set of papers. "You need a pen?"

"That's not necessary. I'll complete the application at home and bring it over first thing tomorrow morning. That will give you the weekend to verify my references. By Wednesday, you should have everything you need."

Melanie furrowed her brow. "Couldn't you go ahead and start work on Monday? I can always make calls from New York when I get home."

"I suppose I could. It's really a matter of your peace of mind."

"I'm not worried about that. I'm sure everything's in order. I feel better just having you here."

"Your decision."

"Good. Why don't I introduce you to Uncle Gus and I can show you around."

"I'd like that."

As they moved into the hall, she could see Melanie's anxiety surface again. "I'm sorry the place is such a mess. Uncle Gus hasn't done much to keep it up. Typical bachelor living. He doesn't seem to notice all the dust and disrepair."

"He could be depressed. Elderly gentlemen in particular seem to lose their zest for life. I see it in their lack of personal hygiene, indifference to their surroundings, and limited social contacts. Sometimes there are personality changes as well."

"I hadn't thought about that. I should warn you he can be difficult. I mean, really, he's a sweetheart, but sometimes he gets impatient."

"Short-tempered, in other words."

"Right."

Solana smiled. "I've seen it before. Believe me, the shouting and tantrums roll right over me. I don't take any of it personally."

"That's a relief."

Solana was introduced to Gus Vronsky, in whom she took an avid interest, though she said very little to him. There was no point working to ingratiate herself. Melanie Oberlin was doing the hiring and she'd soon be gone. Whatever the old man was like, foul-mouthed or disagreeable, Solana would have him to herself. There'd be plenty of time for the two of them to sort themselves out.

That Friday afternoon, she sat at the round Formica table that served as her desk in the dining area of her small apartment. Her kitchen was cramped, with scarcely enough counter space to prepare a meal. She had an apartment-sized refrigerator, a four-burner stove that looked as inadequate as a toy, a sink, and cheap wall-mounted cabinets. She paid bills from this table, which was usually covered with paperwork and therefore useless for eating purposes. She and her son ate sitting in front of the television set, resting their plates on the coffee table.

She had the Vronsky job application in front of her. Close by she had the copy of the application she'd taken from the Other's personnel file. Fifteen feet away, the television thundered, but Solana scarcely noticed. The living room was actually the long part of the L-shaped combination living-dining room with no discernible difference between the two. Tiny, her Tonto, was sprawled in his recliner, his feet elevated, his eyes fixed on the set. He was hard of hearing, and he usually had the volume turned up to levels that made her wince and encouraged her close neighbors to pound on the walls. After he dropped out of school, the only work he could find was as a bagger at a nearby supermarket. That didn't last long. He thought the job was beneath him and he quit six months later. He was then hired by a landscape company to mow lawns and clip hedges. He complained about the heat and swore he was allergic to grass and tree pollens. Often he went to work late or he called in sick. When he did show up, if he wasn't properly supervised, he'd leave when it suited him. He quit or was fired, depending on who was telling the tale. After that he made a few attempts to find work, but the job interviews came to nothing. Because of his difficulties making himself understood, he was often frustrated, lashing out at random. Eventually he stopped making any effort at all.

In some ways, she found it easier to have him at home. He'd never had a driver's license so when he was employed it was up to her to take him into work and pick him up afterward. With the shifts she worked at the convalescent home, this presented a problem.

At the moment, he had a beer balanced on the arm of the chair and an open bag of potato chips resting against his thigh like a faithful hound. He munched while he watched his favorite program, a game show with lots of sound effects and lights. He liked to call out the answers to questions in that strange voice of his. He didn't seem embarrassed that all his answers were wrong. What difference did it make? He enjoyed participating. In the mornings he watched soap operas, and later in the afternoon, he watched cartoon shows or old movies.

Solana studied the Other's employment history with a familiar feeling of envy, mixed with a certain degree of pride since she was now claiming the résumé as her own. The letters of reference talked about how reliable and responsible she was, and Solana felt the attributes exactly described the sort of person she was. The only problem she could see was an eighteen-month gap, during which the Other was out on medical leave. She knew the details because the subject had been much discussed at work. The Other had been diagnosed with breast cancer. She'd subsequently undergone a lumpectomy, followed by chemotherapy and radiation.

Solana had no intention of incorporating that information in the application. She was superstitious about disease and didn't want anyone to think she'd suffered from something so embarrassing. Breast cancer? My god. She didn't need the pity or the fawning concern. In addition, she worried about a prospective employer voicing curiosity. If she included the talk of cancer, someone might inquire about her symptoms, or the nature of the drugs they'd used, or what the doctors had told her about her chances of recurrence. She'd never had cancer in her life. No one in her immediate family had ever had cancer, either. In her mind, having cancer was as shameful as being an alcoholic. Also, she was worried that if she wrote it down, the disease might actually manifest itself.

But how could she explain that interval when the real Solana—the Other—had been off work? She decided she'd substitute a position she herself had held right around that time. She'd worked as a companion for an old lady named Henrietta Sparrow. The woman was now dead so no one could call her to ask for a letter of reference. Henrietta was beyond complaining now (as she had at the time) that she was mistreated. All of that had gone to the grave with her.

Solana consulted a calendar and wrote the start and end dates for the job along with a brief description of the chores she'd been responsible for. She wrote in neat block letters, not wanting a sample of her handwriting to appear anywhere. When the application was completed, Solana joined her son in front of the TV set. She was satisfied with herself and decided to celebrate by ordering three large pepperoni pizzas. If it turned out Gus Vronsky didn't have two nickels to rub together, she could always quit. She looked forward to Melanie Oberlin's departure, and the sooner the better.

11

The following Monday, I stopped by my apartment at lunchtime, hoping to avoid the temptation of fast food. I heated a can of soup, of the do-not-add-water type, that I knew had enough sodium to approximate my swallowing a tablespoon of salt. I was washing up afterward when Melanie knocked on my door. Her black cashmere coat was form-fitting and long enough to bisect her black leather boots. She'd folded a wide black-and-red paisley shawl into a voluminous triangle and secured it across her shoulders. How did she have the confidence to carry it off? If I tried it, I'd look like I'd inadvertently walked through a clothesline and gotten tangled in a sheet.

I opened the door and stepped aside, letting her in. "Hi, how's it going?"

She breezed by me and sat down on the couch, extending her legs in a gesture of collapse. "Don't even ask. The man is driving me insane. I saw you parking your car and thought I'd catch you before you went out again. Is this a bad time? Please tell me it's fine or else I'll have to kill myself."

"It's fine. What's going on?"

"I'm just being dramatic. He's no better or worse than he's always been. Anyway, I can't stay long. I have a gal who started work this morning, which is what I want to talk to you about."

"Sure. What's up?"

"This woman . . . this *angel* . . . named Solana Rojas showed up Friday morning for an interview. We chatted back and forth—Uncle Gus, his injury, and the kind of help he needs. Stuff like that. She said this was right up her alley and she'd be happy to have the job. She even ended up staying through the afternoon without charging a cent. I was afraid to expose her to the real Uncle Gus for fear she'd quit, but I felt honor-bound. I thought she should know what she was getting into and she seems fine with it."

"So what's the problem?"

"I'm on a flight to New York tomorrow and I don't have time to call and verify her references."

"I'm surprised you stayed this long."

"You're not the only one," she said. "I was scheduled to fly back last Friday, but Gus—as you well know—turned into a royal pain. Ditto my boss. I mean, she's great and she was fine about my coming, but she called this morning in a lather. She's got problems at work and she wants me back there. 'Or else,' is how she put it."

"That's too bad."

"I should have known she'd do this. She's generous until the first time it inconveniences her," Melanie said. "I suppose I should be grateful for anything that gets me out of here. Which brings me to my point. Henry tells me you're a PI. Is that true?"

"I thought you knew that."

"I can't believe I never asked. Naughty me," she said.

"I was hoping you could do a quick background check and let me know Solana's okay. Of course, I'd pay you for your time."

"How soon would you need to know?"

"Soon. For the next five days, she's agreed to work an eight-hour shift. After that, assuming all goes well, we'll tinker with the schedule until we figure out what suits. For now, she starts at three and leaves at eleven, which will take Gus through the supper hour, medications, and preparation for bed. As frail as he is, I know he needs more than that, but it's the best I could do. Before she leaves at night, she'll set up his breakfast for the following day. I've arranged for Meals on Wheels to deliver a hot noon meal and something simple for his supper. She offered to cook for him, but I thought it was too much to ask. I didn't want to take advantage."

"It sounds like you've got it covered."

"Let's hope. I'm a wee bit concerned about leaving on such short notice. She seems honest and conscientious, but I never laid eyes on her before Friday, so I probably shouldn't take anything for granted."

"I don't think you have anything to worry about. If she was referred by an agency, she'll be fine. Any home health care service would make sure her references were good. She'd have to be licensed and bonded before they sent her out."

"That's just it. She works with an agency, but she called on her own in response to the ad. Matter of fact, hers was the only call I got, so I should count myself fortunate in that respect."

"What's the agency?"

"I have the business card right here. Senior Health Care Management. It's not listed in the phone book and when I tried the number, it turned out to be a disconnect."

"Did she have an explanation?"

"When I asked, she was completely apologetic. She said the number on the card was an old one. The company has since moved and she hadn't had a chance to have new cards made up. She gave me the new number, but all I get is an answering machine. I left two messages and I'm hoping someone will call me back."

"Did she fill out an application?"

"I have it right here." She opened her handbag and took out the pages, which she'd folded in thirds. "This is a generic form I found in a legal kit. I hire people all the time at work, but the head of personnel has usually vetted them first. I'm a good judge of character when it comes to my field, but I don't have a clue about nursing care. She's an LVN, not an RN, but she's worked with geriatric patients and it doesn't bother her. Naturally, Uncle Gus was crabby and impossible, but she took it all in stride. She's a better man than I am. The way he behaved, I was tempted to pop him one."

I ran an eye down the page, which had been filled out by hand with a ballpoint pen. The information was rendered in tidy block letters, all caps, with no cross-outs. I checked the statement at the bottom of the page where the woman had signed her name, certifying that all the information she'd given was accurate and true. Built into the paragraph was a release, authorizing a prospective employer to verify her qualifications and employment history. *"I understand and agree that any misstatement or omission of material facts will cause forfeiture on my part of all rights of employment."*

"This should cover it. I'll handle some of it by phone,

but many interviews are better done in person, especially when it comes to character issues. Most past employers are reluctant to put anything derogatory in writing for fear of being sued. Face-to-face, they're more likely to offer up the salient details. How far back do you want me to go?"

"Honestly, a spot-check is fine—her degree, the last place she worked, and a couple of references. I hope you don't think I'm being paranoid."

"Hey, I do this for a living. You don't have to justify the job to me."

"Mostly, I want to know she's not a killer on the lam," she said, ruefully. "Even that's not so bad if she can get along with him."

I refolded the application. "I'll run a duplicate at the office in the morning and get this back to you."

"Thanks. I'm heading back down to Los Angeles at nine for a noon flight out. I'll call you on Wednesday."

"It's probably better if I call you when I have something to report."

I pulled a boilerplate contract from my top desk drawer and took a few minutes to fill in the blanks, detailing the nature and substance of our agreement. I jotted my home and office numbers at the top of the page. Once we'd both signed, she took out her wallet and gave me a business card and five hundred bucks in cash. "Will that suffice?"

"It's fine. I'll attach an itemized account when I send you my report," I said. "Does she know about this?"

"No, and let's keep it between the two of us. I don't want her to think I don't trust her, especially after I made such a point of hiring her on the spot. It's fine if you want to tell Henry."

"I'll be ever so discreet."

* * *

I'd mapped out a visit to the City College campus where Lisa Ray's accident had occurred. Time to scout the area and see if I could run the missing witness to ground. It was close to 3:15 by the time I reached the Castle off-ramp and turned right onto Palisade Drive, which angled up the hill. The day was gloomy, the sky overcast in a way that made me think of rain, but California weather can be deceptive. In the East, dense gray clouds would signal precipitation, but here we're subject to a marine layer that doesn't mean much of anything.

Santa Teresa City College sits on a bluff overlooking the Pacific Ocean, one of 107 colleges in the California system of community colleges. The grounds are spread out over considerable acreage, east campus and west campus divided by a street called High Ridge Road, which forms a gentle downhill run to Cabana Boulevard and the beach. Driving by, I could see parking lots and various campus buildings.

There weren't any retail establishments in the immediate vicinity, but a mile to the west, at the intersection of Palisade and Capillo, there was a string of storefront businesses: a café, a shoe-repair shop, a market, a card shop, and a drugstore that serviced the neighborhood. Closer to campus there was a gas station and a large chain supermarket that shared a parking lot with two fast-food restaurants. The old guy might live near the college or he might have had business in the area. From Lisa's account, it wasn't clear whether he was on foot or on his way to or from his car. There was also a possibility he was on the faculty or staff of the college itself. At some point, I'd have to start knocking on doors, fanning out from the site of the accident.

I passed the campus, circled back, and finally pulled in at the curb across from the entrance where Lisa Ray's car had been stopped in preparation for her left-hand turn. There was a time when a private investigator might have done much of the digging in a lawsuit of this type. I'd once known a gumshoe whose specialty was making scale diagrams of accidents, taking measurements of street widths and reference points relevant to a collision. He'd also take photographs of tire tracks, angles of visibility, skid marks, and any other physical evidence left at the scene. Now this data is assembled by the accident-reconstruction experts, whose calculations, formulas, and computer models eliminate most of the speculation. If the lawsuit reached court, the expert's testimony could make or break the case.

I sat in my car and reread the file, starting with the police report. The police officer, Steve Sorensen, was not one I knew. In the various categories that denoted conditions, he'd checked clear weather, midday, dry roadway surface, and no unusual conditions. Under "movement preceding collision," he indicated that the Fredricksons' Ford van (Vehicle 1) was proceeding straight, while Lisa's 1973 Dodge Dart (Vehicle 2) was making a left-hand turn. He'd included a rough sketch with the proviso that it was "not to scale." In his opinion, Vehicle 2 had been at fault, and Lisa had been cited for I 21804, public or private property, yield to approaching vehicles, and 22107, unsafe turn, and/or without signaling. Lowell Effinger had already hired a Valencia accident-reconstruction specialist, who'd assembled the data and was now in the process of preparing his report. He was also doubling as a biomechanical expert and would use the information to determine if Gladys's injuries were consistent with the dynamics of the collision. With regard to the missing witness, old-fashioned legwork seemed to be my best bet, especially since I couldn't come up with any other plan.

The few black-and-white views the traffic officer had shot at the time didn't seem that helpful. Instead, I'd turned to the assortment of photos, both color and black-and-white, that Mary Bellflower had taken of the scene and the two vehicles. She'd arrived within a day of the collision, and her pictures showed fragments of glass and metal visible in the road. I scanned the street in both directions, wondering who the witness was and how I was going to find him.

I went back to the office, checked the file again, and found the number listed for Millard Fredrickson.

His wife, Gladys, answered on the third ring. "What is it?"

In the background, a dog barked incessantly in a range that conjured up images of a small, trembling breed.

"Hi, Mrs. Fredrickson. My name is . . ."

"Just a minute," she said. She put a palm over the mouthpiece. "Millard, would you shut that dog up? I'm trying to talk on the phone here. I said, SHUT THAT DOG UP!" She removed her palm and returned to the conversation. "Who is this?"

"Mrs. Fredrickson, my name is Kinsey Millhone . . ."

"Who?"

"I'm an investigator looking into the accident you and your husband had last May. I'm wondering if I might have a chat with the two of you."

"Is this about the insurance?"

"This is about the lawsuit. I'm interested in taking your statement about what happened, if you'd be so kind."

"Well, I can't talk now. I've got a bunion on my foot that's giving me fits and the dog's gone berserk because my husband went out and bought a bird without so much as a by-your-leave. I told him I don't intend to clean up after anything lives in a cage and I don't give a hang if it's lined with paper or not. Birds are filthy. Full of lice. Everybody knows that."

"Absolutely. I can see your point," I said. "I was hoping I might stop by in the morning, say at nine o'clock?"

"What's tomorrow, Tuesday? Let me check my calendar. I might be scheduled to see the chiropractor for an adjustment. You know I've been going in twice a week, for all the good it's done. With all the pills and folderol, you'd think I'd be fine. Hold on." I could hear her flipping pages back and forth. "I'm busy at nine. It looks like I'll be here at two, but not much after that. I have a physical therapy appointment and I can't afford to be late. They're doing another ultrasound treatment, hoping to give me some relief from all the lower-back pain I got."

"What about your husband? I'll want to talk to him as well."

"I can't answer for him. You'll have to ask him yourself when you get here."

"Fine. I'll be in and out of there as quickly as possible."

"You like birds?"

"Not that much."

"Well, all right then."

I heard a high-pitched, astonished yelp, and Gladys slammed the phone down abruptly, possibly in order to save the dog's life.

12

In the office Tuesday morning, I made a copy of Solana Rojas's application and tucked the original in an envelope I addressed to Melanie. The five-hundred-dollar advance was my usual charge for one day's work, so I thought I'd jump into it and make it worthwhile for both of us.

I sat at my desk and studied the application, which included Solana's Social Security number, her driver's license number, her date and place of birth, and her LVN certification number. Her home address in Colgate showed an apartment number, but the street itself wasn't one I knew. She was sixty-four years old and in good health. Divorced, with no minor children living at home. She'd earned an AA degree from Santa Teresa City College in 1970, which meant she'd gone back for her degree when she was in her midforties. She'd applied for nursing school, but the waiting list was such that it took another two years before she was accepted. Eighteen months later, having completed the requisite three semesters in the nursing program, she had her certification as an LVN.

I studied her job history, noting a number of private-duty assignments. Her most recent employment was a ten-month stint at a convalescent home, where her duties had included the application and changing of bandages, catheterizations, irrigations, enemas, collecting specimens for lab analysis, and the administering of medications. The salary she listed was $8.50 an hour. Now she was asking $9.50. Under the heading "Background," she indicated she'd never been convicted of a felony, that she wasn't currently awaiting trial for any criminal offense, and that she'd never initiated an act of violence in the workplace. Good news, indeed.

The list of her employers, starting with the present and working backward, included addresses, telephone numbers, and the names of supervisors, where appropriate. I could see that the dates of employment formed a seamless progression that covered the years since she'd been licensed. Of the elderly private-duty patients she'd cared for, four had been moved into nursing homes on a permanent basis, three had died, and two had recovered sufficiently to live on their own again. She'd attached photocopies of two letters of recommendation that said just about what you'd expect. *Blah, blah, blah* responsible. *Blah, blah, blah* competent.

I looked up the number of Santa Teresa City College and asked the operator to connect me with Admissions and Records. The woman who took the call was in the throes of a head cold and the act of answering the phone had triggered a coughing fit. I waited while she struggled to get the hacking under control. People shouldn't go to work with head colds. She probably prided herself on never missing a day while everyone around her came down with the same upper-respiratory distress and used up their annual sick leave.

"Excuse me. Whew! I'm sorry about that. This is Mrs. Henderson."

I gave her my name and told her I was doing a pre-employment background check on a Solana Rojas. I spelled the name and gave her the date she'd graduated from the STCC nursing program. "All I need is a quick confirmation that the information's accurate."

"Can you hold?"

I said, "Sure."

While I was listening to Christmas carols, she must have popped a cough drop in her mouth because when she came back on the line, I could hear a clicking sound as the lozenge was shifted across her teeth.

"We're not allowed to divulge information on the telephone. You'll have to make your request in person."

"You can't even give me a simple yes or no?"

She paused to blow her nose, a sloppy transaction with a honking sound attached. "That's correct. We have a policy about student privacy."

"What's private about it? The woman's looking for a job."

"So you claim."

"Why would I lie about something like that?"

"I don't know, dear. You'll have to tell me."

"What if I have her signature on a job application, authorizing verification of her educational background and employment history?"

"One moment," she said, aggrieved. She put a palm across the telephone mouthpiece and murmured to someone nearby. "In that case, fine. Bring the application with you. I'll make a copy and submit it with the form."

"Can you go ahead and pull her file so the information's waiting when I get there?"

"I'm not allowed to do that."

"Fine. Once I get up there, how long will it take?"

"Five business days."

I was annoyed, but I knew better than to argue with her. She was probably hyped up on over-the-counter cold medications and eager to shut me down. I thanked her for the information and then I rang off.

I made a long-distance call to the Board of Vocational Nursing and Psychiatric Technicians in Sacramento. The clerk who took my call was cooperative—my tax dollars at work. Solana Rojas's license was active and she'd never been the subject of sanctions or complaints. The fact that she was licensed meant she'd successfully completed a nursing program somewhere, but I'd still need to make a trip to City College to confirm. I couldn't think why she'd falsify the details of her certification, but Melanie had paid for my time and I didn't want to shortchange her.

I went over to the courthouse and made a run through public records. A check of the criminal index, the civil index, the minor offenses index, and the public index (which included general civil, family, probate, and criminal felony cases) showed no criminal convictions and no lawsuits filed by or against her. The records of the bankruptcy court came up blank as well. By the time I drove up to City College, I was reasonably certain the woman was just as she represented herself.

I slowed to a stop at the information kiosk on campus. "Can you tell me where I can find Admissions and Records?"

"Admissions and Records is in the Administration Building, which is right there," she said, pointing at the structure dead ahead.

"What about parking?"

"It's open in the afternoons. Park anyplace you like."

"Thanks."

I pulled into the first open slot I came to and got out, locking my car behind me. From my vantage point, there was a view of the Pacific through the trees, but the water was gray and the horizon was obscured by mist. The continued overcast made the day feel colder than it was. I slung my bag across one shoulder and crossed my arms for warmth.

The architectural style of most campus buildings was plain, a serviceable mix of cream-colored stucco, wrought iron railings, and red-tile roofs. Eucalyptus trees cast mottled shadows across the grass, and a light breeze ruffled the fronds of the queen palms that towered above the road. There were six or eight temporary classrooms in use while additional facilities were being built.

It was odd to remember that I was enrolled here once upon a time. After three semesters, I realized I wasn't cut out for academic studies even at the modest level of Everything 101. I should have known myself better. High school had been a torment. I was restless, easily distracted, more interested in smoking dope than learning. I don't know what I thought I was going to do with my life, but I sincerely hoped I wouldn't have to go to school to do it. That ruled out medicine, dentistry, and the law, along with countless other professions that I didn't find appealing in the least. I realized that without a college degree, most corporations wouldn't have me as a president. Oh dang. However, if I read the Constitution correctly, my lack of education didn't preclude me from becoming the President of the United States, which only required me to be a natural-born citizen and at least thirty-five years of age. Was that exciting or was it not?

At eighteen and nineteen, I'd drifted through an assortment of entry-level jobs, though with most the "entry" part was about as far as I could get. Shortly after I turned twenty, for reasons I don't remember now, I applied to the Santa Teresa Police Department. By that time, I'd cleaned up my act, as bored with dope as I was with menial work. I mean, how many times can you refold the same stack of sweaters in the sportswear department at Robinson's? The pay scale was pathetic, even for someone like me. I did discover that if you're interested in low wages, a bookstore ranks below retail clothing sales, except the hours are worse. The same holds for waiting tables, which (as it turned out) required more skill and finesse than I had at my disposal. I needed a challenge and I wanted to see just how far my street smarts might take me.

By some miracle, I survived the department's selection process, passing the written exam, the physical-agility exam, the medical and controlled-substance screening, and various other interviews and evaluations. Somebody must have been asleep at the wheel. I spent twenty-six weeks in the Police Officer Standards and Training Academy, which was tougher than anything I'd ever done. After graduation I served as a sworn officer for two years and found, in the end, that I was not that well suited for work in a bureaucracy. My subsequent shift into an apprenticeship with a firm of private investigators proved to be the right combination of freedom, flexibility, and daring.

By the time I'd taken this split-second detour down memory lane, I'd entered the Administration Building. The wide corridor was bright, though the character of the light streaming through the windows was cold. There were Christmas decorations here and there, and the absence of students suggested that they'd already left for the holidays. I didn't remember the place feeling so friendly, but that was doubtless a reflection of my attitude during that period.

I went into the Admissions and Records Office and asked the woman at the desk for Mrs. Henderson.

"Mrs. Henderson's gone home for the day. Is there something I can help you with?"

"Gee, I sure hope so," I said. I felt the thrill of a lie leaping to my lips. "I chatted with her an hour ago and she said she'd pull some information from the student files. I'm here to pick it up." I put Solana's job application on the counter and pointed to her signature.

The woman frowned slightly. "I don't know what to tell you. That doesn't sound like Betty. She never said a word to me."

"She didn't? That's too bad. As sick as she was, it probably slipped her mind. Could you check the records for me since I'm already here?"

"I suppose so, though it might take a minute. I don't know the files as well as she does."

"That's fine. No hurry. I'd appreciate it."

Seven minutes later I had the confirmation I needed. Unfortunately, I wasn't able to coax any further information from the woman. I thought if Solana was a C– student, a prospective employer was entitled to know. As a friend of mine used to say, "On an airplane, you better hope your bomb-sniffing dog didn't graduate at the bottom of his class."

I returned to my car and pulled out my *Thomas Guide* covering Santa Teresa and San Luis Obispo counties. I had the address of the nursing home where Solana had last worked, which turned out to be walking distance from my office.

* * *

Sunrise House was a combination convalescent hospital and assisted-living facility, with room for fifty-two residents, some temporary and some permanent. The building itself was a one-story frame structure, with a number of additions laid nose-to-nose, in vertical and horizontal wings as random as a Scrabble board. The interior was tasteful, the decor done in shades of green and gray that were soothing without being apologetic. The Christmas tree here was also fake, but it was a thickly flocked specimen with tiny lights and silver ornaments in place. Eight large handsomely wrapped presents had been arranged on a white felt tree skirt. I knew the boxes were empty, but their very presence suggested wonderful surprises to come.

A large antique desk occupied the place of honor in the middle of an Oriental carpet. The receptionist was in her sixties, handsome, pleasant, and eager to be of help. She probably thought I had an aging parent in need of accommodations.

When I asked to speak to the head of personnel, she led me through a maze of corridors to the assistant administrator's office. Over her shoulder, she said, "We don't have a personnel department per se, but Mrs. Eckstrom can help you."

"Thanks."

Eloise Eckstrom was roughly my age, late thirties, very tall and thin, with glasses and a full head of bright red hair. She wore a vibrant green twin set, a plaid wool skirt, and flats. I'd caught her with her desk in disarray, drawers emptied and the contents arranged on chair seats and tabletops. An assortment of wire baskets and drawer dividers was packed in a box nearby. On the credenza behind her she had five framed photographs of a wirehaired terrier in various stages of maturity.

We shook hands across her desk, but only after she wiped her fingers clean with a moist towelette. She said, "Sorry the place is such a mess. I've been here a month and I swore I'd get organized before the holidays. Have a seat, if you can find one."

I had a choice between two chairs, both of which were stacked with file folders and back issues of geriatric journals.

"That stuff will probably end up in the trash. You can put it on the floor."

I shifted the weight of magazines from the seat to the floor and sat down. She seemed relieved to have the chance to sit as well.

"What can I help you with?"

I laid Solana Rojas's application on the only bare spot I could find. "I'm hoping to verify some information about a former employee. She's been hired to look after an elderly gentleman, whose niece lives in New York. I guess you'd call this 'due diligence.' "

"Of course."

Eloise crossed the room to a bank of gray metal file cabinets and opened a drawer. She pulled Solana Rojas's personnel file, leafing through the pages as she returned to her desk. "I don't have much. According to this, she came to work for us in March of 1985. Her job evaluations were excellent. In fact, in May of that year, she was Employee of the Month. There were no complaints and she was never written up. That's the best I can do."

"Why did she leave?"

She glanced back down at the file. "She apparently decided to go to graduate school. Must not have suited her if she's already applying for private-duty work."

"Is there anyone here who knew her? I was hoping for someone who'd worked with her on a day-to-day basis.

The guy she'll be caring for is a contrarian, and his niece wants someone with patience and tact."

"I understand," she said, and checked Solana's file again. "It looks like she worked on One West, the post-surgery floor. Maybe we can find you someone who knows or remembers her."

"That would be great."

I followed her down the hall, not entirely optimistic about my chances. In doing a background check, fishing for personal data can be a tricky proposition. If you're talking to a friend of the subject's, you have to get a feel for the nature of the relationship. If the two are close buddies or confidantes, there's probably a treasure trove of intimate information, but your chances of retrieving it are dim. By definition, good friends are loyal and, therefore, quizzing them on the down-and-dirty details about a pal seldom yields much of use. On the other hand, if you're talking to a work mate or casual acquaintance, you have a better shot at the truth. Who, after all, can resist the invitation to trash someone else? An interpersonal rivalry can be exploited for potential bombshells. Bad blood, including overt conflicts, jealousies, petty grievances, or an inequity in pay or social status, can produce unexpected riches. For maximum success in prying, what you need is time and privacy so the person you're talking to will feel free to blab to her heart's content. The post-surgery floor wasn't likely to yield the proper atmosphere.

Here I encountered a tiny stroke of luck.

Lana Sherman, the LVN who'd worked with Solana for the better part of a year, was just leaving the nurse's station for a coffee break and she suggested I tag along.

13

On our way down the hall to the staff lounge, I asked her a few questions, trying to get a feel for the kind of person she was. She told me she was born and raised in Santa Teresa, that she'd been at Sunrise House for three years, and she liked it okay. "Effusive" was not an adjective I'd have been tempted to apply. Her dark hair was thin, with layers of drooping ringlets that looked dispirited. Already I wanted her to fire her "stylist" and try someone new. Her eyes were dark and the whites were bloodshot, as though she were trying her first contact lenses without much success.

The staff lounge was small but attractively furnished. There was a table with chairs drawn up to it, a modern couch, and two upholstered love seats arranged around a coffee table. A microwave oven, a toaster, a toaster oven, and a coffeemaker sat on the counter. The refrigerator was decorated with stern warnings about the sanctity of other employees' food. I took a seat at the table while Lana poured coffee in a mug and added two packs of Cremora and two of Sweet'N Low. "You want coffee?"

"No, thanks. I'm fine."

She picked up a tray and carried it to the vending machine, where she put numerous coins in the slot. She punched a button and I watched her selection tumble into the bin below. She brought her tray to the table and off-loaded her coffee mug, her spoon, and a package of miniature chocolate-covered doughnuts.

I waited until she was seated before I went on. "How long have you known Solana?"

She broke the first doughnut in two and popped half in her mouth. "What's the job?"

The question was a bit abrupt, but in the interest of priming the pump, I filled her in. "My next-door neighbor fell and dislocated his shoulder. He's eighty-nine and needs home care while he recuperates."

"So what's she make?"

The doughnut looked dense and dry, and the dark chocolate frosting had the gloss of wax. For ten cents I'd have knocked her down and eaten one myself. I knew now that the many fruits and vegetables I'd consumed over the past few days had only made me hostile—not good in my line of work.

For an instant I'd completely lost my place in the conversation. "What?"

"What's the pay?"

"I don't know. I was asked to talk to people who've worked with her. I'm interested in a character reference."

"In the neighborhood."

"I won't be talking to her neighbors unless I bomb out every place else."

"I'm talking salary. Ballpark. What's the hourly wage?"

"No one's mentioned it. Are you thinking about changing jobs?"

"I might be."

The second doughnut was gone though I'd hardly noticed, distracted as I was by the opening I saw. "If things don't work out for her, I'd be happy to throw your name in the hat."

"I'd consider it," she said. "Remind me before you leave and I'll give you my résumé. I have a copy in my purse."

"Great. I'll pass it along," I said, and then shifted the conversation. "Were you and Solana friends?"

"I wouldn't say we were friends, but we worked together for close to a year and we got along all right."

"What's she like?"

She shrugged. "So-so."

"So-so?"

"I guess she's nice enough. If you like that kind."

"Ah. And what kind is that?"

"Fussy. If anyone was even two minutes late, she made a big deal of it."

"So she was punctual," I suggested.

"Well, yeah, if that's what you want to call it."

"What about personal traits?"

"Like what?"

"Was she patient, compassionate? Honest? Good-natured? That's the kind of thing I'm looking for. You must have had many opportunities to observe her firsthand."

She stirred her coffee, then licked the spoon clean before she laid it on her tray. She put the next doughnut in her mouth whole and chewed while she considered her reply. "You want my honest opinion?"

"I would love it."

"Don't get me wrong. I have nothing against the woman, but she had no sense of humor and she wasn't that good a conversationalist. I mean, you say something to her and maybe she'd answer and maybe not, depending on what suited her. She was all the time sitting with her nose in a chart or out on the floor checking on the patients. It wasn't even her responsibility. She took it on herself."

I said, "Wow. I had no idea. On paper she looks good."

"That's seldom the whole story."

"And that's exactly why I'm here, to fill in the blanks. Did you see her outside work?"

"Hardly. The rest of us, sometimes on Friday nights? We'd go out together, kind of letting our hair down at the end of the week. Solana went straight home. After a while, we didn't even ask her to join us because we figured she'd say no."

"She didn't drink?"

"Nuh-uhn. Are you kidding? She was too uptight. Plus, she was always watching her weight. And on her breaks, she read books. Anything to make the rest of us look bad. Does that help?"

"Enormously."

"You think she'll be hired?"

"It's not up to me, but I'm certainly going to make a note of what you've said."

I left the place at 1:00 P.M. with Lana Sherman's résumé in hand. Walking back to the office, I passed a sandwich shop and realized I hadn't had lunch. In the press of work, I've been known to skip meals, but seldom when I was this hungry. I noticed that eating properly was antithetical to feeling full. A QP with Cheese and a large serving of fries will leave you close to comatose. The sudden onslaught of carbohydrates and fat makes you long for a nap, which means a gap of ten or fifteen minutes before you start thinking about your next meal. I did an about-face and veered into the sandwich shop. What I ordered is none of your business, but it was really good. I ate at my desk while I reviewed the Fredrickson file.

At 2:00, clipboard in hand, I arrived for my appointment with Gladys Fredrickson. She and her husband lived in a modest house near the beach on a street being overtaken by much grander homes. Given the exaggerated prices of local real estate, it made sense for buyers to snap up any house for sale and do extensive remodeling on the existing residence or raze the entire structure and start from scratch.

The Fredricksons' one-story frame house fit the latter category, not so much a fixer-upper as something you'd bulldoze, pile in a heap, and burn. There was a shabbiness about the place that suggested years of deferred maintenance. Along the side of the house, I could see that a strip of aluminum gutter had come loose. Below the gap a clump of rotting leaves lay fallen in a makeshift compost heap. I suspected the carpet would smell damp and the grout between the shower tiles would be black with mildew.

In addition to the wooden porch stairs, there was a long wooden ramp that extended from the drive to the porch to allow wheelchair access. The ramp itself was mottled with dark green algae and doubtless became as slick as glass whenever it rained. I stood on the porch looking down at the ivy beds interspersed with the yellow blooms of oxalis. Inside, the dog was yapping at a rate that would probably net him a swat on his butt. Across the side yard, through a chicken wire fence, I caught sight of an elderly neighbor lady setting out what were probably the annual Christmas decorations on her lawn. These consisted of seven hollow plastic Santa's helpers that could be lighted from inside. Also, nine plastic reindeer, one of which had a big red nose. She paused to stare at me and my quick wave was rewarded with a smile laced with sweetness and pain. There had once been little ones—children or grandchildren—whose memory she celebrated with this steadfast display of hope.

I'd already knocked twice and I was on the verge of knocking again when Gladys opened the door, leaning heavily on a walker, her neck encircled by a six-inch foam collar. She was tall and thick, the buttons of her plaid blouse gaping open across her ample breasts. The elastic waist on her rayon pants had given way and she'd used two large safety pins to affix the trousers to her shirt, thus preventing them from dropping and pooling around her ankles. She wore a pair of off-brand running shoes, though it was clear she wouldn't be running any time soon. On her left foot, a half-moon of leather had been cut away to provide relief for her bunion. "Yes?"

"I'm Kinsey Millhone, Mrs. Fredrickson. We have an appointment to talk about the accident."

"You're with the insurance company?"

"Not yours. I'm working with California Fidelity Insurance. I was hired by Lisa Ray's attorney."

"Accident was her fault."

"So I've been told. I'm here to verify the information she gave us."

"Oh. Well, I guess you better come on in," she said, already turning her walker so she could hump her way back to the La-Z-Boy where she'd been sitting.

As I closed the front door, I noticed a collapsible wheelchair propped up against the wall. I'd been wrong about the carpet. Theirs had been removed, revealing narrow-plank hardwood floors. Staples that once held the padding in place were still embedded in the wood, and I could see a line of dark holes where the tack strips had been nailed.

The interior of the house was so dense with heat that the air smelled scorched. A small brightly colored bird was fanning its way like a moth from one drapery panel to the next while the dog pranced across the sofa cushions, toppling the stacks of magazines, junk mail, bills, and newspapers piled along the length. The dog had a small face, bright black eyes, and a poufy cravat of hair spilling across its chest. The bird had left two white poker chips of poop on the floor between the end table and the chair. Gladys hollered, "Millard? I told you to get that dog out of here! Dixie's up on the couch and I can't be responsible for what she does next."

"Goddamn it. I'm coming. Quit your hollering," Millard called from somewhere down the narrow transverse hall. Dixie was still barking, dancing on her hind legs with her dainty front feet pawing the air, her eyes fixed on the parakeet, hopeful that she would be rewarded for her trick by getting to eat the bird.

A moment later Millard appeared, propelling his wheelchair into view. Like Gladys, I judged him to be in his early sixties, though he was aging better than she. He was a heavyset man with a ruddy face, a thick black mustache, and a head of curly gray hair. He whistled sharply for the dog and she hopped off the sofa, crossed the room rapidly, and leaped onto his lap. He did a rolling pivot and disappeared down the hall, grumbling as he went.

"How long has your husband used a chair?"

"Eight years. We had to have the carpet taken up so he could manage from room to room."

"I'm hoping he's made time for me today. As long as I'm here, I can talk to him as well."

"No, now he said it didn't suit him. You'll have to come back another time if you want to talk to him." Gladys shoved aside a pile of papers. "Make a space for yourself if you care to sit."

I perched gingerly in the clearing she'd made. I set my shoulder bag on the floor and removed my tape recorder, which I placed on the coffee table in front of me. A tower of manila envelopes tilted against my thigh, most by way of a courier service called Fleet Feat. I waited while she maneuvered herself into position and then eased into the recliner with a grunt. During that brief delay, purely in the interest of securing the avalanche of bills, I did fan out the first five or six envelopes. Two had red rims and a hoary warning that read URGENT!! FINAL NOTICE! One was for a gasoline credit card, the other from a department-store chain.

Once Gladys was settled, I tried on my visiting-nurse voice. "I'll be recording this with your permission. Is that agreeable to you?"

"I suppose."

After I pressed the Record button, I recited my name, her name, the date, and the case number. "Just for the record, you're giving this information voluntarily without threats or coercion. Is that correct?"

"I said I would."

"Thank you. I appreciate that. In answering my questions, please respond only with the facts within your knowledge. I'd ask you to avoid opinions, judgments, or conclusions."

"Well, I've got my opinions like everyone else."

"I understand that, Mrs. Fredrickson, but I have to limit my report to information as accurate as you can make it. If I ask a question and you don't know or don't remember, just say so. Please don't guess or speculate. Are you ready to proceed?"

"I've been ready since I sat down. You're the one dragging it out. I didn't expect all this claptrap and folderol."

"I appreciate your patience."

She nodded in response, but before I could formulate the first question, she launched into an account of her own. "Oh hon, I'm a wreck. No pun intended. I can't hardly get around without my walker. I got numbness and tingling in this foot. Feels like it's fell asleep, like I've been laying on it wrong . . ."

She went on describing the pains in her leg while I sat and took notes, doing a proper job of it. "Anything else?" I asked.

"Well, headaches, of course, and my neck's all froze up. Look at this—I can't hardly turn my head. That's why I got this collar here to help give support."

"Any other pain?"

"Honey, pain's all I've got."

"May I ask what medications you're taking?"

"I got a pill for everything." She reached over to the end table, where a number of prescription bottles had been assembled along with a water glass. She picked up the vials one by one, holding them out so I could write down the names. "These two are pain pills. This one's a muscle relaxant, and this here's for depression . . ."

I was scribbling away but looked up with interest. "Depression?"

"I got chronic depression. I can't remember when I've ever felt so low. Dr. Goldfarb, the orthopedic specialist, he sent me to see this psychiatrist who put me on these new pills. I guess the other ones don't do much once you've taken them awhile."

I made a note of the prescription for Elavil that she'd held out for my inspection. "And what were you on before?"

"Lithium."

"Have you had other problems since the accident?"

"Poor sleep and I can't hardly work a lick. He said I might not ever be able to work again. Not even permanent part-time."

"I understand you do the bookkeeping for a number of small businesses."

"The past forty-two years. Talk about a job that gets old. I've about had it with that stuff."

"You have an office in your home?"

She nodded toward the hall. "Second bedroom back there. Thing is, I can't sit for long on account of my hip gives me fits. You oughtta seen the big old bruise I had, all up and down this side. Purple as a eggplant. I still got a patch of yellow as big as the moon. And hurt? Oh my stars. I had tape on these here ribs and then, like I said, I have this problem with my neck. Whiplash and all and a concussion of the head. I call that 'confusion contusions,'" she said, and barked out a laugh.

I smiled politely. "What kind of car do you drive?"

"Nineteen seventy-six Ford van. Dark green in case you mean to ask that next."

"Thank you," I said, and made a note. "Let's go back to the accident. Would you tell me what happened?"

"Be happy to, though it was a terrible, terrible thing for me as you might imagine." She narrowed her eyes and tapped a finger against her lips, looking into the middle distance as though reciting a poem. By the time she was halfway through the second sentence, it was clear she'd told the story so often that the details wouldn't vary.

"Millard and me were driving along Palisade Drive up by the City College. This was Thursday of Memorial Day weekend. What is that, six or eight months back?"

"About that. What time of day was this?"

"Middle of the afternoon."

"What about weather conditions?"

She frowned slightly, forced to think about her answer instead of offering up her usual rote response. "Fine as near as I remember. We'd had rains off and on all last spring, but a dry spell come along and the papers was saying the weekend would be nice."

"And which direction were you heading?"

"Toward downtown. He couldn't have been driving more than five or six miles an hour. Might have been a bit more, but it was way under the posted limit. I'm positive about that."

"And that's twenty-five miles an hour?"

"Something along those lines."

"Can you remember how far away Ms. Ray's vehicle was when you first noticed it?"

"I remember she was over to my right in that entrance to the parking lot up at the City College. Millard was just about passing when she come flying out in front of me. Boom! He slammed on the brakes, but not near quick enough. I was never so surprised in my life and that's the truth!"

"Was her left turn signal blinking?"

"I don't believe it was. I'm sure not."

"What about your turn signal?"

"No, ma'am. He didn't intend to turn. We were fixing to continue on down the hill to Castle."

"I believe there was some question about your seat belt?"

She shook her head emphatically. "I never ride in a car without a seat belt. It might've come loose on impact, but I was wearing one for sure."

I took a moment to review my notes, wondering if there was any way to throw her off her stride. The well-rehearsed data was getting old. "Where were you going?"

That stumped her. She blinked and said, "Where?"

"I'm wondering where the two of you were going when the accident occurred. I'm filling in the blanks." I held up my clipboard as though that explained everything.

"I forget."

"You don't remember where you were going?"

"I just said that. You told me to say so if I couldn't remember and I can't."

"Fine. That's exactly right." I stared at my clipboard and made a mark. "If it would help refresh your memory, could you have been heading for the freeway? From Castle, you can take the north- or southbound on-ramps."

Gladys shook her head. "Ever since the accident my memory's shot."

"Were you running errands? Grocery shopping? Something for dinner perhaps?"

"Must have been errands. I'd say errands. You know, I might have amnesia. Doctor says it's not uncommon in accidents of this type. I can't hardly concentrate. That's why I can't work. I can't sit and I can't think. Work I do, that's all it is, except for add and subtract and stamping envelopes."

I looked down at my notes. "You mentioned a concussion."

"Oh, I banged my head good."

"On what?"

"Windshield, I guess. Might have been the windshield. I still got me a knot," she said, placing a hand briefly on the side of her head.

I placed my hand on the left side of my head as she had. "On the left side up here or in back?"

"Both. I got bumped ever which way. Here, feel this."

I reached forward. She clasped my hand and pressed it against a hard knot about the size of a fist. "My goodness."

"You better make a note of it," she said, pointing at my clipboard.

"Absolutely," I said, scribbling on the page. "What happened after that?"

"Millard was shook up as you might well imagine. He soon discerned he wasn't hurt, but he could see I was out like a light, knocked completely unconscious. As soon as I regained my senses, he helped me out of the van. Wasn't easy for him since he had to get situated in his chair and lever himself down to the pavement. I couldn't hardly tell where I was at. I was all dizzy and discombobulated and shaking like a leaf."

"You must have been upset."

"Why wouldn't I be when she pulled out in front of us?"

"Of course. Let's just see now." I paused to check my notes. "Aside from you and your husband and Ms. Ray, was there anyone else at the scene?"

"Oh, my yes. Someone called the police and they come pretty quick, along with the fellers in the amulance."

"I'm talking about prior to their arrival. Did anyone stop to help?"

She shook her head. "No. I don't believe so. Not that I recall."

"I understood that a gentleman was giving aid and assistance before the traffic officer showed up."

She stared at me, blinking. "Well, yes, now you mention it. I'd forgot about that. While Millard was checking the van, this feller helped me over to the curb. He set me down and put his arm acrost my shoulders, worried I'd go into shock. That flew right out of my head until just now."

"This was another motorist?"

"I believe this was someone come off the street."

"Can you describe the man?"

She seemed to hesitate. "Why do you want to know?"

"Ms. Ray was hoping to find him so she could send a thank-you note."

"Well." She was silent for a full fifteen seconds. I could see her computing the possibilities in her head. She was wily enough to realize that anyone who showed up that quickly might well have been a witness to the accident.

"Mrs. Fredrickson?"

"What?"

"Nothing about the man sticks in your mind?"

"I wouldn't know anything about that. Millard might recall better than me. By then, this right hip was giving me so much pain I'm surprised I was able to stand. If you had the X-ray here, I could point out the injured ribs. Dr. Goldfarb said I was lucky the crack in my hip wasn't more severe or I've been laid up for good."

"What about his race?"

"He's white. I wouldn't go to any other kind."

"I mean the man who helped."

She shook her head with a fleeting annoyance. "I wasn't paying attention to much except I was glad my leg wasn't broke. You'd have been glad, too, in my place."

"What age would you say?"

"Now I can't be answering questions like that. I'm getting all flustered and upset and Dr. Goldfarb says that's not good. Not a bit good he said."

I continued to look at her, noting her gaze flick away from mine and back. I returned to my list of questions and chose a few that seemed neutral and noninflammatory. In the main, she was cooperative, but I could see her patience was wearing thin. I tucked my pen in the clamp of the clipboard and reached for my shoulder bag as I got to my feet. "Well, I think that's all for now. I appreciate your time. Once I type up my notes, I'll stop by and have you read the statement for accuracy. You can make any necessary corrections, and once you're satisfied it's a faithful rendering, you can give me a signature and I'll be out of your hair."

As I clicked off the tape recorder, she said, "I'm happy to help. All we want is what's fair, given the fault was entirely hers."

"Ms. Ray is interested in that as well."

From the Fredricksons' house, I swung up to Palisade Drive and turned right, taking the same route Gladys had taken the day of the accident. I passed City College, eyes flicking to the entrance to the parking lot. I followed the road as it curved down the hill. Where Palisade intersected Castle, I took a left and followed it as far as Capillo, where I turned right. Street traffic was moving freely and it took me less than five minutes to reach the office. The sky was cloudy and there was talk of isolated thunderstorms, which I thought unlikely. For reasons I've never wholly understood, Santa Teresa has a rainy season but seldom any thunderstorms. Lightning is a phenomenon I've witnessed largely by way of black-and-white photographs, showing white threads lying flat against the night sky like irregular cracks in glass.

Once I was back in the office, I set up a file and then typed my notes. I put Lana Sherman's résumé in the folder with Solana Rojas's application. I could have tossed it, but why not hang on to it since I had it in hand?

Wednesday morning, when Melanie called, I gave her the *Reader's Digest* condensed version of my findings, at the end of which, she said, "So she's fine."

"Looks that way," I said. "Of course, I didn't turn over every rock in the garden."

"Don't worry about it. There's no point in going nuts."

"That's that, then. Looks like it's working out as planned. I'll have Henry keep an eye on the situation and if anything comes up, I can let you know."

"Thanks. I appreciate your help."

I hung up, feeling satisfied with the job I'd done. What I had no way of knowing was that I'd just, unwittingly, put a noose around Gus Vronsky's neck.

14

Christmas and New Year's Day slid past, leaving scarcely a wrinkle in the fabric of ordinary life. Charlotte was off in Phoenix, celebrating the holidays with her kids and grandkids. Henry and I spent Christmas morning together and exchanged gifts. He gave me a pedometer and a Sony headset so I could listen to the radio while I did my morning jog. For him, I'd found an antique egg timer six inches tall, an ingenious glass-and-tin device with pink sand inside. To activate it, you flipped up the three-minute timer until it rested against a lever at the top. Once the sand finished falling from the top portion to the bottom, the upper portion tipped over and rang a tiny bell. I also gave him a copy of *Bernard Clayton's New Complete Book of Breads.* At 2:00, Rosie and William joined us for Christmas dinner, after which I went back to my place and took a long holiday nap.

New Year's Eve I stayed home and read a book, happy that I wasn't out risking life and limb with the many drunks on the road. I confess I abandoned my junk food resolve on New Year's Day and enjoyed an orgy of Quarter Pounders with Cheese (two) and a large order of fries doused in ketchup. I did keep my new pedometer affixed to my person while I ate, and I made sure I walked ten thousand steps that day, which I hoped would count in my favor.

I started the first week of 1988 with a dutiful 6:00 A.M. three-mile jog, radio headset in place, after which I showered and ate breakfast. At the office, I whipped out my trusty Smith-Corona and composed a notice for the "Personals" section of the *Santa Teresa Dispatch*, detailing my interest in the witness to a two-vehicle collision that had occurred on Thursday, May 28, 1987, at approximately 3:15 P.M. I included the few particulars I had, listing the man's age as midfifties, which was only a guess. Height and weight I said were medium and his hair, "thick white." I also made reference to his brown leather bomber jacket and black wing tip shoes. I didn't give my name but I posted a contact number and an appeal for help.

While I was about it, I called the Fredricksons' house, hoping to set up an appointment with Millard to discuss the accident. The phone rang countless times, and I was about to put the handset back in the cradle when he picked up.

"Mr. Fredrickson! I'm glad I caught you. This is Kinsey Millhone. I stopped by your house and talked to your wife a couple of weeks ago and she said I should call so I can set up an appointment with you."

"I can't be bothered with this. You already talked to Gladys."

"I did and she was very helpful," I said. "But there are just a couple of points I'd like to go over with you."

"Like what?"

"I don't have my notes with me, but I can bring them

when I come. Would Wednesday of this week work for you?"

"I'm busy . . ."

"Why don't we say next Monday, a week from today. I can be there at two."

"I'm tied up on Monday."

"Why don't you name the day?"

"Fridays are better."

"Fine. A week from this coming Friday, that's the fifteenth. I'll make a note on my calendar and see you at two. Thanks so much." I marked the date and time on my calendar, relieved I wouldn't have to worry about it for another ten days.

At 9:30, I called the *Santa Teresa Dispatch* with the information and was told the ad would appear on Wednesday and would run for a week. Just after the accident, Mary Bellflower had placed a similar query, with negative results, but I thought it was worth another try. That done, I walked over to the copy shop near the courthouse and ran off a hundred flyers, describing the man and further indicating that it was hoped he had information concerning a two-vehicle accident on such-and-such a date. I stapled a business card to each flyer, thinking I might pick up a client in the bargain. Aside from that, I thought it lent an earnest air to my quest.

I spent most of the afternoon canvassing the hillside homes off Palisade across the road from the entrance to Santa Teresa City College. I parked my car on a side street near a two-story apartment complex and proceeded on foot. I must have knocked on fifty doors. When I was lucky enough to find someone at home, I explained the situation and my need to locate a witness to the accident. I underplayed the notion that he might end up testifying on behalf of the defendant. Even the most conscientious of citizens is sometimes reluctant to commit to a court appearance. Given the vagaries of the judicial system, a witness can spend hours sitting in a drafty corridor only to be excused when opposing parties reach a pretrial settlement.

After two hours I'd learned absolutely nothing. Most of the residents I spoke with were unaware of the accident and none had seen a man who matched the description of the witness I sought. If there was no response to my knock, I left a flyer in the door. I also tacked flyers to any number of telephone poles. I considered tucking a flyer under the windshield wipers of the cars I passed, but the practice is annoying and I always toss such notices myself. I did leave a flyer taped to the wooden bench at the bus stop. It was probably illegal to use city property for such purposes, but I figured if they didn't like it, they could hunt me down and kill me.

At 2:10, having covered the area, I returned to my car, drove across the intersection, and into the college parking lot. I shrugged myself into the jacket I'd tossed on the backseat, locked the Mustang, and walked out to the point where the access road emptied onto the four-lane expanse of Palisade. A length of chain-link fence separated the eastbound from westbound traffic. To my right, the road curved gently down along a slope and out of sight. There was no turn lane designated for vehicles intending to enter the lot from either direction, but I could see that from Lisa Ray's perspective, an oncoming vehicle would have been visible for approximately five hundred yards, a fact I hadn't noted on my earlier visit.

I perched on a low fieldstone wall and watched cars speed by. There was a smattering of foot traffic to and from the campus. Most pedestrians were students or working moms there to pick up kids from a college-run day-care facility on the far corner, near the bus stop. I gathered the day-care operation had no parking spots of its own, so the moms took advantage of the City College lots when picking up their tots. Where possible, I engaged these hapless passersby in conversation, detailing my search for the man with white hair. The moms were polite but distracted, barely responding to my questions before they hurried away, anxious to avoid being dinged with after-hours charges. As the afternoon wore on, there was a steady stream of moms with their little tykes in tow.

Of the first four students I approached, two were new to the college and two had left town that Memorial Day weekend. A fifth wasn't even a student, just a woman out looking for her dog. None had anything useful to contribute, but I learned a lot about the intelligence and superiority of the standard poodle. The campus security officer stopped to chat, probably concerned that I was homeless, casing the joint, or flogging designer drugs.

While he was busy quizzing me, I quizzed him in return. He had a dim recollection of the man with white hair but couldn't remember when he'd seen him last. At least his response, though vague, gave me a modicum of hope. I handed him a flyer and asked him to get in touch if he should spot the guy again.

I continued in this manner until 5:15, two hours beyond the time when the accident had occurred. In May, it would have been light until eight. Now the sun set at five. In the back of my mind I was hoping the man had routine business that brought him to the neighborhood the same time each day. I planned to swing by again on Saturday and do a second neighborhood canvass. Weekends I might have better luck finding folks at home. If there was no response to my newspaper ad, I'd return on

Thursday of the following week. I abandoned the project for the day and headed home, feeling tired and out of sorts. In my experience, loitering is an enervating act.

I turned onto my street and made the usual quick search for the parking spot closest to my studio apartment. I was puzzled to see that a bright red Dumpster had been unloaded at the curb. It was easily twelve feet long and eight feet wide, and might have served as housing for a family of five. I was forced to park around the corner and walk back. In passing, I peered over the five-foot-high rim and into the empty interior. What was that about?

I pulled the mail out of my box, went through the gate, and around the side of my studio apartment, which was once a single-car garage. Seven years before, Henry had relocated his driveway, constructed a new two-car garage, and converted the original garage into a rental, which I'd moved into. Three years later, an unfortunate incident with a bomb had flattened the structure. Henry had taken advantage of the free demolition and he'd rebuilt the studio, adding a half story that contained a sleeping loft and bath. The last Dumpster I'd seen on our block was the one he rented to accommodate the construction debris.

I dropped my bag inside my apartment and left the door ajar while I crossed the patio to Henry's. I rapped on his kitchen door and he appeared moments later from his living room, where he was watching the evening news. We chatted briefly about inconsequential matters and then I said, "What's the deal with the Dumpster? Is that ours?"

"Gus's nurse ordered that."

"Solana? That's a bold move on her part."

"I thought so, too. She stopped by this morning to let

me know it was being delivered. She's getting rid of Gus's junk."

"You're kidding."

"I'm not. She cleared it with Melanie, who gave her the go-ahead."

"And Gus agreed?"

"Looks that way. I called Melanie myself just to make sure it was legitimate. She said Gus went through a rough patch and Solana stayed two nights, thinking he shouldn't be alone. She ended up sleeping on the couch, which was not only too short but smelled of cigarettes. She asked Melanie for permission to move in a cot, but there wasn't space for one. His second and third bedrooms are wall-to-wall junk and that's what she intends to toss."

"I'm surprised he said yes."

"He didn't have much choice. You can't expect the woman to make up a pallet on the floor."

"Who's going to haul the stuff out? Must be half a ton of newspapers in that one room alone."

"She's doing most of it herself, at least as much as she can manage. For the bulkier items, I guess she'll hire someone. She and Gus went through everything and he decided what he was willing to part with. He's hanging on to the good stuff—his paintings and a few antiques—the rest is history."

"Let's hope she pulls up the crappy carpet while she's at it," I remarked.

"Amen to that."

Henry invited me in for a glass of wine, and I would have taken him up on the offer but my phone started ringing.

"I better get that," I said, and took off at a trot.

I caught the call just before my answering machine picked up. It was Melanie Oberlin.

She said, "Oh good. I'm glad I caught you. I was afraid you weren't home. I'm just about to dash out, but I have a question for you."

"Sure."

"I called Uncle Gus earlier today and I don't think he knew who I was. It was the oddest conversation. Kind of goofy, you know? He sounded drunk or confused, or maybe both."

"That's not like him. We all know he's crabby, but he always knows exactly where he is and what's going on."

"Not this time."

"Maybe it's his meds. They've probably got him on pain pills."

"At this late date? That doesn't sound right. I know he was on Percocet, but they pulled him off that as soon as they could. Have you talked to him lately?"

"Not since you left, but Henry's been to see him two or three times. If there was a problem, I'm sure he'd have mentioned it. You want me to look in on him?"

"If you don't mind," she said. "After he hung up, I called back and spoke to Solana, hoping to get her assessment of the situation. She thinks he may be showing early signs of dementia."

"Well, that's worrisome," I said. "I'll go over in the next couple of days and have a chat with him."

"Thanks. And could you ask Henry if he's noticed anything?"

"Sure. I'll get back to you as soon as I have something to report."

Tuesday morning, I set aside an hour to serve a three-day pay-or-quit notice on a tenant in a Colgate apartment building. Ordinarily, Richard Compton, the owner of the building, would have delivered the eviction notice himself in hopes of goosing the renter into catching up. Compton had owned the property for less than six months and he'd been busy booting out the deadbeats. People who decline to pay their rent can sometimes be a surly lot and two had offered to punch his lights out. He decided it'd be smart to send someone in his place, namely me. I personally thought it was cowardly on his part, but he'd offered me twenty-five bucks to hand someone a piece of paper, and it seemed like adequate recompense for two seconds' worth of work. Traffic was light and I made the fifteen-minute drive with my radio tuned to one of those talk shows where listeners call in to ask advice about marital and social woes. I'd become a big fan of the hostess and found it entertaining to test my reactions against hers.

I spotted the street number I was looking for and pulled in at the curb. I folded the eviction notice and tucked it in my jacket pocket. As a general rule, in serving papers of any kind, I don't like to show up waving official-looking documents. Better to get the lay of the land before making my purpose clear. I hefted my bag from the passenger seat as I emerged and locked the car behind me.

I took a minute to scan the premises, which looked like a movie version of a prison. I was staring at four three-story buildings, arranged to form a square with the corners open and walkways between. Twenty-four apartments were lumped together in each unadorned block of stucco. Junipers had been planted along the foundations, perhaps in an attempt to soften the facade. Unfortunately, most of the evergreens had suffered a blight that left the branches as sparse as last year's Christmas trees and the remaining needles the color of rust.

Across the front of the nearest building, I could see a short row of slab porches, one step high, furnished with the occasional aluminum lawn chair. An apologetic inverted V of roof had been tacked above each front door, but none were large enough to offer protection from the elements. In the rainy season, you could stand there, house key in hand as you fumbled to get in, and by the time the door finally swung open, you'd be drenched. Summer sunlight would beat down unrelentingly, converting the front rooms into small toaster ovens. Anyone climbing to the third tier would suffer heart palpitations and shortness of breath.

There was no yard to speak of, but I suspected if I went into the interior courtyard, I'd see covered barbecue grills on the second- and third-floor loggias, clotheslines and children's playthings in the grassy patches at ground level. The garbage cans were standing in a ragtag line at one end of the structure that housed empty carports in lieu of closed garages. The complex had a curious unoccupied air, like housing abandoned in the wake of calamity.

Compton had nothing but complaints about his tenants, who were sorry sunza-bitches (his words, not mine). According to him, at the time he'd purchased the property, the units were already overcrowded and ill used. He'd made a few repairs, slapped a coat of paint on the exterior, and raised all the rents. This had driven out the least desirable of the occupants. Those who remained were quick to bellyache and slow to pay.

The tenants in question were the Guffeys, husband and wife, Grant and Jackie respectively. The previous month, Compton had written them a nasty letter about their failure to pay, which the Guffeys had ignored. They were already two months in arrears and perhaps intent on garnering another rent-free month before responding to his threats. I crossed the dead grass, went around the corner of the building, and up a flight of outside stairs. Apartment 18 was on the second floor, the center one of three.

I knocked. After a moment the door was opened to the length of the burglar chain and a woman peered out. "Yes?"

"Are you Jackie?"

A pause. "She's not here."

I could see her left eye, blue, and medium-blond hair caught up on rollers the size of frozen orange juice cans. I could also see her left ear, which had sufficient small gold hoops stuck through the cartilage to mimic a spiral-bound notebook. Compton had mentioned the piercings in his description of her, so I was reasonably certain this was Jackie, lying through her teeth. "Do you know when she'll be back?"

"What makes you ask?"

Now I was the one who hesitated, trying to decide on my approach. "Her landlord asked me to stop by."

"What for?"

"I'm not authorized to discuss the matter with anyone else. Are you related to her?"

A pause. "I'm her sister. I'm from Minneapolis."

The best thing about lying are the flourishes, I thought. I myself am a world-class practitioner. "And your name is?"

"Patty."

"Mind if I write that down?"

"It's a free country. You can do anything you want."

I reached into my shoulder bag and found a pen and a small lined notebook. I wrote "Patty" on the first page. "Last name?"

"I don't have to tell."

"Are you aware that Jackie and her husband haven't paid rent for the past two months?"

"Who cares? I'm visiting. It's got nothing to do with me."

"Well, maybe you could pass along a message from the guy who owns the place."

I handed her the eviction notice, which she took before she realized what it was. I said, "That's a three-day pay or quit. They can pay in full or vacate the premises. Tell 'em to pick one."

"You can't do that."

"It's not me. It's him and he warned them. You can remind your 'sister' of that when she gets home."

"How come he doesn't have to live up to his side of the deal?"

"As in what?"

"Why should they be prompt when the son of a bitch takes his time about making repairs, assuming he gets to them at all. She's got windows won't open, drains backed up. She can't even use the kitchen sink. She has to do all the dishes in the bathroom basin. Take a look around. The place is a dump and you know what the rent is? Six hundred bucks a month. It cost a hundred and twenty dollars to get the wiring fixed or they'd've burned the building down. That's why they haven't paid, because he won't reimburse 'em for the money they spent."

"I can sympathize, but I can't give you legal advice even if I had any to offer. Mr. Compton's acting within his rights and you'll have to do that, too."

"Rights, my ass. What rights? I stay here and put up with his crap or I have to move out. What kind of deal is that?"

"The deal you signed before you moved in," I said.

"You want your side heard, you can join a tenants association."

"Bitch." She slammed the door in my face, at least so far as she could manage with the burglar chain in place.

I got back in my car and headed for the notary's office, so I could dot all my i's and cross my t's.

15

When I got back to the office after lunch, the message light was blinking on my answering machine. I pushed the Play button.

A woman said, "Hello? Oh. I hope this is the right number. This is Dewel Greathouse. I'm calling in regard to a flyer I found in my door yesterday? The thing is, I'm almost sure I've seen that gentleman. Could you give me a call when you get this? Thanks. Oh. I can be reached at . . ." She rattled off the number.

I snatched up a pen and a pad of paper, and jotted down what I remembered, then replayed the message to verify the information. I punched in the number, which rang half a dozen times.

The woman who finally answered was clearly out of breath. "Hello?"

"Mrs. Greathouse? Is that Dewel, or did I misunderstand the name?"

"That's right. Dewel with a *D.* Hang on a second. I just ran up a flight of steps. Sorry."

"Not a problem. Take your time."

Finally, she said, "Whew! I was on my way back from the laundry room when I heard the phone. Who's this?"

"Kinsey Millhone. I'm returning your call. You left a message on my machine in response to one of the flyers I distributed in your neighborhood."

"I sure did. I remember now, but I don't believe you gave your name."

"Sorry about that, but I appreciate your calling."

"I hope you don't mind my asking, but why are you looking for this gentleman? I wouldn't want to get anyone in trouble. The flyer said something about an accident. Did he hit someone?"

I went back through my explanation, making it clear that the man didn't cause or contribute to the accident. I said, "He was more the Good Samaritan. I'm working for an attorney who's hoping he can give us a report of what went on."

"Oh, I see. Well, that's all right then. I don't know that I can be much help, but when I read the description, I knew exactly who you meant."

"Does he live in the area?"

"I don't think so. I've seen him sitting at the bus stop at Vista del Mar and Palisade. You know the one I mean?"

"At City College?"

"That's it, only on the opposite side."

"Okay. Right."

"I've noticed him because that's my street and I pass him as I'm driving home. I have to slow to make the turn and I'm looking in that direction."

"How often do you see him?"

"Couple of afternoons a week for the past year I'd say."

"And this is since last May?"

"Oh yes."

"Can you tell me which days of the week?"

"Not offhand. I moved to my apartment in June of '86 after I took a new part-time job."

"What sort of work do you do?"

"I'm in the service department at Dutton Motors. What's nice is I'm only ten minutes from work, which is why I took this apartment to begin with."

"What time of day, would you say?"

"Midafternoon. I get home at two fifty pretty much without fail. I'm just half a mile away so it doesn't take me long once I'm on the road."

"You know anything about him?"

"Not really. It's mostly what you said. He's got thick white hair and he wears a brown leather jacket. I only see him in passing so I really couldn't guess age or eye color or anything like that."

"You think he works in the neighborhood?"

"That'd be my guess. Maybe as a handyman or something of that nature."

"Could he be employed at City College?"

"I suppose it's possible," she said, sounding skeptical. "He looks too old to be a student. I know a lot of older people are going back to school, but I've never seen him with a backpack or briefcase. All the college kids I see carry something of the sort. Books at the very least. If you want to talk to him, you might catch him at the bus stop."

"I'll try that. In the meantime, if you see him again, could you let me know?"

"Certainly," she said, and with a click she was gone.

I circled her name and number on the desk pad and put it in the file. I was excited to have even a sketchy confirmation of the man's existence. Like a sighting of the Loch Ness Monster or the Abominable Snowman, the report gave me hope.

I worked late that day, paying bills and generally getting my life in order. By the time I got home it was 6:45 and fully dark. The temperature had dropped into the forties from a daytime high of sixty-two degrees, and my turtleneck and blazer offered no protection from the wind picking up. The damp fog emanating from the beach amplified the chill. I knew once I was safely indoors, I wouldn't want to venture out again. I saw lights on at Gus's house and decided it was as good a time as any to pay a visit. I was hoping the supper hour was through so I wouldn't be interrupting his meal.

As I passed, I saw the Dumpster was half full. Solana was evidently making progress in her junk-elimination project. I knocked on Gus's door, my arms crossed tightly as I huddled with the cold. I shifted from foot to foot in a vain attempt to warm myself. I was curious to meet Solana Rojas, whose work history I'd researched three weeks previously.

Through the glass pane in Gus's front door, I watched her approach. She flipped on the porch light and peered out, calling through the glass. "Yes?"

"Are you Solana?"

"Yes." She wore glasses with black frames. Her dark hair was the uniform brown of a home-dye job. If she'd had it done in a salon, some "artiste" would have added a few phony-looking highlights. I knew from the application she was sixty-four, but she looked younger than I'd imagined.

I smiled and raised my voice, hooking a thumb in the direction of Henry's place. "I'm Kinsey Millhone. I live next door. I thought I'd stop by to see how Gus is doing."

She opened the door and a slat of warm air escaped. "The name again is what?"

"Millhone. I'm Kinsey."

"Nice meeting you, Ms. Millhone. Please, come in. Mr. Vronsky will be happy for the company. He's been a little down in the dumps." She stepped back, allowing me to enter.

She was trim but carried a bulkiness in the belly that spoke of child-bearing once upon a time. Young moms often lose the baby weight quickly, but it returns in middle age to form a permanent mocking pouch. Moving past her, I automatically gauged her height, which was five foot two or so to my five foot six. She wore a serviceable-looking pastel green tunic with matching pants—not quite a uniform, but wrinkle-free separates bought for comfort and washability. Stains from a patient's blood or other body fluids would be easy to remove.

I was struck by the sight of the living room. Gone were the chipped veneer tables with their tacky little knickknacks. The stretchy dark brown slipcovers had been removed from the couch and three chairs. The original upholstery material turned out to be a pleasant mix of florals in tones of cream, pink, coral, and green, probably selected by the late Mrs. Vronsky. The limp drapes had come down, leaving the windows looking bare and clean. No dust, no clutter. The mouse-back carpeting was still in place, but a bouquet of dark pink roses now sat on the coffee table, and it took me a moment to realize they were fake. Even the smells in the house had changed from decades-old nicotine to a cleaning product that was probably called "Spring Rain" or "Wild Flowers."

"Wow. This is great. The place has never looked this good."

She seemed pleased. "There's still work to do, but at

least this part of the house is improved. Mr. Vronsky's reading in his room, if you'll come with me."

I followed Solana down the hallway. Her crepe-soled shoes made no sound, and the effect was odd, almost as if she were a hovercraft floating before me. When we reached Gus's bedroom, she peered in at him and then glanced back at me and put a finger to her lips. "He's fallen asleep," she whispered.

I looked past her and saw Gus propped up in bed, supported by a pile of pillows. A book was open across his chest. His mouth was agape and his eyelids were as transparent as a baby bird's. The room was tidy and his sheets looked new. A blanket was neatly folded at the foot of his bed. His hearing aids had been removed and placed close at hand on his bed table. In a low tone, I said, "I hate to bother him. Why don't I come back in the morning?"

"It's entirely up to you. I can wake him if you like."

"Don't do that. There's no hurry," I said. "I leave for work at eight thirty. If he's up, I can visit with him then."

"He's up at six o'clock. Early to bed and early to rise."

"How's he doing?"

She pointed. "We should talk in the kitchen."

"Oh, sure."

She retraced her steps and turned left into the kitchen. I trailed behind, trying to tread as quietly as she did. The kitchen, like the living room and bedroom, had undergone a transformation. The same appliances were in place, yellowed with age, but now a brand-new microwave sat on the counter, which was otherwise bare. Everything was clean, and it looked like the kitchen curtains had been laundered, ironed, and rehung.

In a belated answer to my query, she said, "He has good days and bad. At his age, they don't bounce back so quick. He's made progress, but it's two steps forward, three steps back."

"I gathered as much. I know his niece is concerned about his mental state."

The animation dropped like a veil falling away from her face. "You talked to her?"

"She called me yesterday. She said when they talked on the phone he seemed confused. She asked if I'd noticed any change in him. I haven't seen him for weeks so I really couldn't say, but I told her I'd stop in."

"His memory isn't what it was. I explained that to her. If she has questions about his care she should address them to me." Her tone was slightly testy and the color had risen in her cheeks.

"She isn't worried about his care. She was wondering if I'd picked up on anything myself. She said you suspected dementia . . ."

"I never said any such thing."

"You didn't? Maybe I'm mistaken, but I thought she said you'd mentioned early signs of dementia."

"She misunderstood. I said dementia was one of several possibilities. It could be hypothyroidism or a vitamin B deficiency, both reversible with proper treatment. I wouldn't presume to make a diagnosis. It's not my place."

"She didn't say you'd made any kind of claim. She was just alerting me to the situation."

"'Situation.'" She was looking at me intently, and I could see she'd somehow taken offense.

"Sorry. I guess I'm not expressing myself well. She said he sounded confused on the phone and thought it might have been his medication or something like that. She said she called you right afterward and the two of you discussed it."

"And now she's sent you to double-check."

"On him, not on you."

She broke off eye contact, her manner prickly and stiff. "It's unfortunate she felt the need to have a conversation with you behind my back. Apparently, she wasn't satisfied with my account."

"Honestly, she didn't call to talk about you. She asked if I'd noticed any change in him."

Now her eyes bored into me, hot and dark. "So now you're the doctor? Perhaps you'd like to see my notes. I keep a record of everything, which is what I was taught. Medications, blood pressure, his bowel movements. I'd be happy to send her a copy if she doubts my qualifications or my dedication to her uncle's care."

I didn't actually squint at her, but I felt myself focus on the skewed exchange. Was she nuts? I couldn't seem to extract myself from the misinterpretation. I was afraid if I uttered two more sentences, she'd quit the job in a huff and Melanie would be up a tree. It was like being in the presence of a snake, first hissing its presence and then coiled in readiness. I didn't dare turn my back or take my eyes off her. I stood very still. I let go of my fight-or-flight defense and decided to play dead. If you run from a bear, it gives chase. That's the nature of the beast. Likewise a snake. If I moved, she might strike.

I held her gaze. In that flicker of a moment, I could see her catch herself. Some kind of barrier had come down and I'd seen an aspect of her I wasn't meant to see, a flash of fury that she'd covered up again. It was like watching someone in the throes of a seizure—for three seconds she was gone and then back again. I didn't want her to realize the extent to which she'd revealed herself. I moved on, as though nothing had occurred. I said, "Oh. Before I forget, I wanted to ask if the furnace is working okay."

Her focus cleared. "What?"

"Gus had a problem with the furnace last year. As cold as it's been, I wanted to make sure you were warm enough. You haven't had a problem?"

"It's fine."

"Well, if it starts acting up, feel free to give a yell. Henry has the name of the heating company that worked on it."

"Thank you. Of course."

"I better scoot. I haven't had dinner yet and it's getting late."

I moved toward the door and I could feel her following at my heels. I glanced back and smiled. "I'll pop over in the morning on my way to work."

I didn't wait for a reply. I gave a casual wave and let myself out the front door. As I trotted down the porch steps, I sensed her standing at the door behind me, watching through the glass. I resisted the urge to check. I took a left on the walk and the minute I was out of her sights, I allowed myself one of those shudders that shakes you from head to toe. I unlocked my apartment and spent a few minutes turning on all the lights to dispel the shadows in the room.

In the morning before I took off for work, I made a second trip next door, determined to talk to Gus. I thought it was odd that I'd found him asleep so early in the evening, but maybe that's what old men did. I'd played and replayed Solana's reaction to my question about Gus's mental state. I hadn't imagined the flash of paranoia, but I didn't know where it came from or what it meant. In the meantime, I'd told Melanie I'd check on him and I wasn't going to let the woman scare me away. I knew she didn't start work until midafternoon, and I was just as happy at the notion of avoiding her.

I climbed the porch steps and knocked on the door. There was no immediate response so I cupped my hands against the glass and peered inside. There were no lamps turned on in the living room, but it looked like the kitchen light was on. I rapped on the glass and waited, but there was no sign of anyone. I'd borrowed the key Gus had given Henry, but I didn't think I should take the liberty of letting myself in.

I went around to the back door with its glass upper section. A note had been taped to the inside:

Meals on Wheels Volunteer. Door is unlocked. Please let yourself in. Mr. Vronsky is hard of hearing and may not respond to your knock.

I tried the knob and sure enough, the door was unlocked. I opened it wide enough to stick my head in. "Mr. Vronsky?"

I glanced at the kitchen counters and the stove top. There was no sign he'd eaten breakfast. I could see a box of dry cereal set out beside a bowl and a spoon. No dishes in the sink. "Mr. Vronsky? Are you here?"

I heard a muffled thumping in the hallway.

"Hell and damnation! Would you quit all that hollering? I'm doing the best I can."

Within seconds, the querulous Gus Vronsky appeared in the doorway, holding on to a walker for support as he shuffled into the room. He was still in his robe, bent nearly double by his osteoporosis, which left him staring at the floor.

"I hope I didn't wake you. I wasn't sure you heard me."

He tilted his head and peered up at me sideways. His

hearing aids were in place, but the left one was askew. "With all the racket you made? I went to the front door, but there was nobody on the porch. I thought it was a prank. Kids making trouble. We used to do that when I was young. Knock on the door and run. I was on my way back to bed when I heard the ruckus in here. What in tarnation do you want?"

"I'm Kinsey. Henry's tenant . . ."

"I know who you are! I'm not an imbecile. I can tell you right now I don't know who's president so don't think you can trip me up on that one. Harry Truman was the last decent man in office and he dropped those bombs. Put an end to World War Two, I can tell you that straight off."

"I wanted to make sure you were okay. Do you need anything?"

"*Need* anything? I need my hearing back. I need my health. I need relief from this pain. I fell and put my shoulder out of commission . . ."

"I know. I was with Henry when he found you that day. I stopped by last night and you were sound asleep."

"That's the only privacy I have left. Now there's this woman comes in, pestering the life out of me. You may know her. Solana *something*. Says she's a nurse, but not much of one in my opinion. Not that *that* counts for much these days. I don't know where she's gone off to. She was here earlier."

"I thought she came on at three o'clock."

"What time is it now?"

"Eight thirty-five."

"A.M. or P.M.?"

"Morning. If it were eight thirty-five P.M., it would be dark out."

"Then I don't know who it was. I heard someone

fumbling around and assumed it was her. Door's unlocked, it could have been anyone. I'm lucky I wasn't murdered in my bed." His gaze shifted. "Who's that?"

He was looking past me at the kitchen door and I jumped when I saw someone standing on the porch. She was a heavyset woman in a mink coat, holding up a brown grocery bag. She motioned at the knob. I crossed and opened the back door for her.

"Thank you, dear. I have my hands full this morning and didn't want to have to set this on the porch. How are you?"

"Fine." I told her who I was and she did the same, introducing herself as Mrs. Dell, the Meals on Wheels volunteer.

"How are you doing, Mr. Vronsky?" She set her package on the kitchen table, talking to Gus as she unloaded the bag. "It's awfully cold outside. Nice that you have neighbors concerned about you. Have you been doing well?"

Gus didn't bother to reply and she didn't seem to expect an answer. He made an irritated gesture, waving her away, and moved his walker toward a chair.

Mrs. Dell tucked boxes in the refrigerator. She moved to the microwave oven and put three cartons inside, then punched in some numbers. "This is chicken casserole, a single serving. You can have this with the vegetables packed in the two smaller containers. All you do is push the Start button. I've already set the time. But you be careful when you take it out. I don't want you burning yourself like you did before." She was speaking louder than normal, but I wasn't convinced he'd heard her.

He stared at the floor. "I don't want beets." He said it as though she'd accused him of something and he was setting the record straight.

"No beets. I told Mrs. Carrigan you didn't care for them so she sent you green beans instead. Is that all right? You said green beans were your favorite."

"I like green beans, but not hard. Crisp is no good. I don't like it when they taste raw."

"These should be fine. And there's a half a sweet potato. I put your brown-bag supper in the fridge. Mrs. Rojas said she'd remind you when it's time to eat."

"I can remember to eat! How idiotic do you think I am? What's in the bag?"

"A tuna salad sandwich, coleslaw, an apple, and some cookies. Oatmeal-raisin. Did you remember to take your pills?"

He looked at her blankly. "What say?"

"Did you take your pills this morning?"

"I believe so, yes."

"Well, good. Then I'll be on my way. Enjoy your meal. Nice meeting you, dear." She folded the brown paper bag and tucked it under one arm before she let herself out.

"Meddlesome," he remarked, but I didn't think he meant it. He just liked to complain. For once, I was reassured by the crabbiness of his response.

16

My visit with Gus lasted fifteen minutes more, at which point his energies seemed to flag and mine did as well. That much high-decibel small talk with a cranky old man was about my max. I said, “I have to go now, but I don’t want to leave you in here. Would you like to go into the living room?”

“Might as well, but you bring that bag lunch in and set it on the couch. I get hungry, I can’t be running back and forth.”

“I thought you were having the chicken casserole.”

“I can’t reach that contraption. How am I supposed to manage when it’s up on the counter in the back? I’d have to have arms another three feet long.”

“You want me to move the microwave closer?”

“I never said that. I like to eat my lunch at lunchtime and my dinner when it’s dark.”

I helped him get up out of his kitchen chair and steadied him on his feet. He reached for his walker and shifted his weight from my supporting hands to the aluminum frame. I kept pace beside him as he crept into the living room. I couldn't help but marvel at the inconsistencies of the aging process. The difference between Gus and Henry and his siblings was marked, even though they were all roughly the same age. The journey from the kitchen to the living room had left Gus exhausted. Henry wasn't running marathons, but he was a strong and active man. Gus had lost muscle mass. Holding his arm lightly, I felt bony structure with scarcely any meat. Even his skin seemed fragile.

When he was settled on the couch, I returned to the kitchen and retrieved his lunch from the refrigerator. "You want this on the table?"

He looked at me peevishly. "I don't care what you do. Put it anywhere you like."

I placed the bag on the couch in easy reach. I was hoping he wouldn't topple sideways and crush the damn thing.

He asked me to find his favorite television show, episodes of *I Love Lucy* on an off-channel that probably ran them twenty-four hours a day. The set itself was old and the channel in question had a certain snowy cast to it that I found bothersome. When I mentioned it to Gus, he said that's what his eyesight was like before cataract surgery six years earlier. I fixed him a cup of tea and then made a quick check of the bathroom, where his container of pills was sitting on the rim of the sink. The plastic storage case was the size of a pencil box and had a series of compartments, each marked with a capital letter for each day of the week. Wednesday was empty so it looked like he'd been right about taking his pills. Home again, I left the key to Gus's house under Henry's doormat and headed off to work.

* * *

I spent a productive morning at the office, sorting through my files. I had four banker's boxes, which I loaded with case folders from 1987, thus making room for the coming year. The boxes I stashed in the storage closet at the rear of my office, between the kitchenette and the bathroom. I made a quick trip to an office-supply company and bought new hanging files, new folders, a dozen of my favorite Pilot fine point rolling ball pens, lined yellow pads, and Post-its. I spotted a 1988 calendar and tucked that in my basket as well.

While I drove back to the office, I did some thinking about the missing witness. Hanging out around the bus stop in hopes of spotting him seemed like a waste of time, even if I did it for an hour every day of the week. Better to go to the source. At my desk again, I called the Metropolitan Transit Authority and asked for the shift supervisor. I'd decided to chat with the driver assigned to the route that covered the City College area. I gave the supervisor an abbreviated version of the Lisa Ray two-car accident and told him I was interested in speaking to the driver who handled that route.

He told me there were two lines, the number 16 and the number 17, but my best bet was a guy named Jeff Weber. His circuit started at 7:00 A.M. at the Transit Center at Chapel and Capillo streets, and ran a continuous loop through town, up along Palisade, and back to the center every forty-five minutes. He generally finished his shift at 3:15.

I spent the next couple of hours being a good secretary to myself, typing, filing, and tidying my desk. At 2:45 I locked the office and headed for the Metropolitan Transit Authority barn, which is located adjacent to the Greyhound bus station. I left my car in the pay lot and took a seat in the depot with a paperback novel.

The ticket agent pointed out Jeff Weber as he exited the locker room, a jacket over one arm. He was in his fifties, his name tag still affixed to the pocket of his uniform. He was tall, with a blond crew cut shot through with gray, and small blue eyes under bleached-blond eyebrows. His large nose was sunburned and his shirt sleeves were two inches too short, leaving his bony wrists exposed. If he were a golfer, he'd need clubs especially tailored to his height and the length of his arms.

I caught up with him in the parking lot and introduced myself, handing him my card. He scarcely glanced at the information, but he was politely attentive while I launched into the description of the man I was looking for.

When I finished, he said, "Oh, yes. I know exactly who you mean."

"You do?"

"You're talking about Melvin Downs. What's he done?"

"Nothing at all." Once again, I laid out the details of the accident.

Weber said, "I remember, though I didn't see the accident itself. By the time I pulled up at that stop a police car and ambulance had arrived at the scene and traffic had slowed to a crawl. The officer was doing what he could to move cars along. The delay was only ten minutes, but touchy business nonetheless. That hour, none of my passengers complain, but I can sense when they're annoyed. Many are just off work and anxious to get home, especially at the start of a long holiday weekend."

"What about Mr. Downs? Did you pick him up that day?"

"Probably. I usually see him two days a week—Tuesdays and Thursdays."

"Well, he must have been there because both victims remember seeing him."

"I don't doubt it. I'm just saying I can't remember for sure if he got on the bus or not."

"You know anything about him?"

"Just what I've observed. He's a nice man. He's pleasant enough, but he isn't chatty like some. He sits near the back of the bus so we don't have much occasion for conversation. Bus is crowded, I've seen him give up his seat to the handicapped or elderly. I catch a lot in the rear-view mirror and I've been impressed with how courteous he is. That's not something you see much. Nowadays people aren't taught the same manners we learned when I was growing up."

"You think he works in the neighborhood up there?"

"I'd assume so, though I couldn't tell you where."

"I talked to someone who thought he might do odd jobs or yard work, that sort of thing."

"Possibly. There's a fair number of older women in the area, widows and retired professional ladies, who could probably use a handyman."

"Where do you drop him?"

"I bring him all the way back here. He's one of the last passengers I carry at the end of my route."

"Any idea where he lives?"

"As it happens, I do. There's a residence hotel on Dave Levine Street near Floresta or Via Madrina. Big yellow frame place with a wraparound porch. Weather's nice, I sometimes see him sitting out there." He paused to glance at his watch. "I'm sorry I can't be more help, but my wife's on her way." He held up my business card. "Why don't I hang on to this? Next time I see Melvin, I'll be glad to pass your message along."

"Thanks. Feel free to tell him what I want to talk to him about."

"Well, good. That's good then. I'll be sure to do that. Best of luck to you."

Once in my car again, I circled the block, making a long loop up Chapel and down on Dave Levine, which was one-way. I did a slow crawl, watching for sight of the yellow residence hotel. The neighborhood, like mine, was a curious combination of single-family dwellings and small commercial enterprises. Many corner properties, especially those closer to the heart of town, had been converted to mom-and-pop-style businesses: a minimart, a vintage-clothing store, two antique shops, and a secondhand bookstore. By the time I spotted the hotel, there were cars stacked up behind me, the closest driver making rude hand gestures I could see in my rearview mirror. I turned right at the first corner and drove another block before I found a parking space.

I hoofed back a block and a half, passing a used-car lot offering assorted nondescript vans and pickup trucks with prices and admonitions writ large across the windshields in tempera paint. MUST SEE! $2499.00 DON'T MISS!! SUPER PRICE. $1799.00. AS IS. PRICED TO SELL!! $1999.99. The latter was an old milk truck tricked out as a camper. The rear doors stood open and I could see a wee kitchenette, built-in storage units, and a pair of bench seats that folded down to make a bed. The salesman, arms crossed, was discussing its various advantages with a white-haired man in sunglasses and a porkpie hat. I nearly stopped to inspect the vehicle myself.

I'm a huge fan of tiny spaces and for less than two thousand dollars—well, one penny less—I could easily imagine myself curled up in a camper with a novel and a battery-operated reading light. Of course, I'd park in front of my apartment instead of camping out in Nature, which in my opinion couldn't be more treacherous. A woman alone in the woods is nothing more than bear and spider bait.

The hotel was a Victorian structure that had been modified over time in a helter-skelter fashion. It looked like a rear porch had been added and then closed in. A covered walkway connected the house to a separate building that might be an additional rental. The flower beds were immaculate, the shrubs clipped, and the exterior paint looked fresh. The bay windows on opposite corners of the building appeared to be original, the second-story bay stacked neatly above the first, with crown molding jutting out along the roofline. The elaborate two-foot overhang was supported by ornate wood corbels pierced with circles and half-moons. Birds had built their nests in the eaves, and the shaggy clusters of twigs were as jarring as the sight of an elegant woman's unshaven armpits.

The half-glass front door stood open and a hand-inked sign above the doorbell read, "Bell broken—can't hear knocking—office in rear of hall." I assumed this was an invitation to let myself in.

At the rear of the corridor three doors stood open. Through one I could see a kitchen that looked large and outdated, the linoleum faded to an almost colorless hue. The appliances were like those I'd seen once in a theme park attraction depicting American family life in every decade since 1880. On the far wall I could see a back stairway angle up and out of sight, and I imagined a back door nearby, though I couldn't see it from where I stood.

The second door opened into what must have been a

rear parlor, used now as a dining room by the simple insertion of a chunky oak table and ten mismatched chairs. The air smelled of paste wax, ancient cigar smoke, and last night's cooked pork. A hand-crocheted runner covered the surface of a cumbersome oak sideboard.

A third open door revealed the original dining room, judging by its graceful proportions. Two doors had been blocked off by gray metal file cabinets, and an oversized rolltop desk was jammed up against the windows. The office was otherwise empty. I knocked on the door frame and a woman emerged from a smaller room that might have been a closet converted to a powder room. She was stout. Her gray hair was frizzy and thin, pulled up in a haphazard arrangement, with more hanging down than she'd managed to secure. She wore small wire-rimmed glasses, and her teeth overlapped like sections of sidewalk buckled by tree roots.

I said, "I'm looking for Melvin Downs. Can you tell me what room he's in?"

"I don't give out information about my tenants. I have their safety and privacy to consider."

"Can you let him know he has a visitor?"

She blinked, her expression unchanged. "I could, but there's no point. He's out." She closed her mouth, apparently not wanting to plague me with more information than I'd requested.

"You have any idea when he'll be back?"

"Your guess is as good as mine, dear. Mr. Downs doesn't keep me apprised of his comings and goings. I'm his landlady, not his wife."

"Do you mind if I wait?"

"I wouldn't if I were you. Wednesdays he doesn't get back until late."

"Like what, six?"

"I'd say closer to ten, judging from past behavior. You his daughter?"

"I'm not. Does he have a daughter?"

"He's mentioned one. In point of fact, I don't allow single women to visit the tenants after nine at night. It sends the wrong message to the other residents."

"I guess I'll try another day."

"You do that."

When I got home I went directly to Henry's house and knocked on his door. We hadn't had a chance to visit in days. I caught him in his kitchen pulling a big bowl from one of the lower cabinets. I tapped on the glass, and when he saw me he set the bowl on the counter and opened the door.

"Am I interrupting anything?"

"No, no. Come on in. I'm making bread-and-butter pickles. You're welcome to lend a hand."

In the sink I could see a large colander piled high with cucumbers. A smaller colander held white onions. Small glass jars of turmeric, mustard seeds, celery seeds, and cayenne pepper were lined up on the counter.

"Are those cucumbers yours?"

"I'm afraid so. This is the third batch of bread-and-butter pickles I've made this month and I'm still up to my ears."

"I thought you only bought one plant."

"Well, two. The one seemed so small, I thought I ought to add a second just to keep it company. Now I've got vines taking up half the yard."

"I thought that was kudzu."

"Very funny," he said.

"I can't believe you're still harvesting in January."

"Neither can I. Grab a knife and I'll find you a cutting board."

Henry poured me half a glass of wine and made himself a Black Jack and ice. Occasionally sipping our drinks, we stood side by side at the kitchen counter, slicing cucumbers and onions for the next ten minutes. When we finished, Henry tossed the vegetables with kosher salt in two big ceramic bowls. He pulled a bag of crushed ice out of the freezer and packed ice over the cucumber-onion combination and covered both bowls with weighted lids.

"My aunt used to make pickles that way," I remarked. "They sit for three hours, right? Then you boil the other ingredients in a pot and add the cucumbers and onions."

"You got it. I'll give you six pints. I'm giving Rosie some, too. At the restaurant, she serves them on rye bread with soft cheese. It's enough to bring tears to your eyes."

He filled a big soup kettle with water and put it on the stove to sterilize the pint jars sitting in a box nearby.

"So how was Charlotte's Christmas?"

"She said good. All four kids gathered at her daughter's house in Phoenix. Christmas Eve, there was a power failure so the whole clan drove to Scottsdale and checked into the Phoenician. She said it was the perfect way to spend Christmas Day. By nightfall the power was on again so they went back to her daughter's house and did it all again. Hang on a second and I'll show you what she got me."

"She gave you a Christmas present? I thought you weren't exchanging gifts."

"She said it wasn't Christmas. It's early birthday."

Henry dried his hands and left the kitchen briefly, returning with a shoe box. He opened the lid and pulled out a running shoe.

"Running shoes?"

"For walking. She's been walking for years and wants to get me into it. William may be joining us as well."

"Well, that's a good plan," I said. "I'm glad to hear she's still around. I haven't seen much of her lately."

"Nor have I. She's got a client in from Baltimore and he's driving her nuts. All she does is drive him around looking at properties that somehow don't suit. He wants to build a fourplex or something of the sort, and everything he's looked at is too expensive or in the wrong area. She's trying to educate him about California real estate and he keeps telling her to think 'outside the box.' I don't know where she gets the patience. What about you? How's life treating you these days?"

"Fine. I'm getting my ducks in a row for the coming year," I said. "I did have a curious run-in with Solana. She's a prickly little thing." I went on to describe the encounter and her touchiness when she realized I'd been talking to Gus's niece long-distance. "The call wasn't even about her. Melanie thought Gus was confused and she wondered if I'd noticed anything. I said I'd check on him, but I wasn't meddling in Solana's business. I don't know beans about geriatric nursing."

"Maybe she's one of those people who sees conspiracies everywhere."

"I don't know . . . it feels like there's something more going on."

"From what I've seen of her, I'm not a fan."

"Nor am I. There's something creepy about her."

17

SOLANA

Solana opened her eyes and flicked a look at the clock. It was 2:02 A.M. She listened to the hiss of the baby monitor she'd put in the old man's room beside his bed. His breathing was as rhythmic as the sound of the surf. She folded the covers back and padded barefoot down the hall. The house was dark but her night vision was excellent, and there was sufficient illumination from the streetlights to make the walls glow with gray. She was drugging him regularly, crushing the over-the-counter sleeping medications and adding them to his evening meal. Meals on Wheels delivered a selection of hot foods for the noon meal and a brown-bag supper for later in the day, but he preferred his hot meal at 5:00, which was when he'd always eaten supper. There wasn't much she could do with an apple, a cookie, and a sandwich, but a casserole was excellent for her purposes. In addition, he liked a dish of ice cream before bed. His sense of taste had faded, and if the sleeping pills were bitter, he never said a word.

He was easier to get along with now that she had him on the right routine. At times he seemed confused, but no more so than many of the elderly she'd had in her care. Soon he'd be completely dependent. She liked her patients compliant. Usually the angry and obstructive ones were the first to settle down, as though they'd waited all their lives for her soothing regimen. She was mother and ministering angel, giving them the attention they'd been robbed of in their youth.

It was her belief that the contentious oldsters had been contentious as kids, thus garnering anger, frustration, and rejection from the parents who were meant to give them love and approval. Raised on a steady diet of parental aggression, these lost souls disconnected from most social interactions. Despised and despising, they had a hunger masked by rage and loneliness masquerading as petulance. Gus Vronsky was neither more nor less cantankerous than Mrs. Sparrow, the acid-tongued old harridan she'd tended to for two years. When she'd finally ushered Mrs. Sparrow into the netherworld, she'd gone out as quietly as a kitten, mewing only once as the drugs took effect. The obituary said she'd died peacefully in her sleep, which was more or less the truth. Solana was tenderhearted. She prided herself on that. She delivered them from suffering and set them free.

Now while Gus lay immobilized, she searched his dresser drawers, using a penlight she shielded with her palm. It had taken her weeks of incremental increases in his doses before she'd been able to justify staying overnight. His doctor checked on him just often enough that she didn't want to arouse suspicion. He was the one who suggested that Gus needed the supervision. She told the doctor he sometimes woke up in the middle of the night, disoriented, and would then try to get himself out of bed. She said she'd caught him on two occasions wandering through the house with no idea where he was.

Extending her hours had necessitated cleaning out one of the bedrooms so she'd have a place to stay. As long as she was about it, she'd gone through both spare bedrooms, setting aside items of potential value and discarding the rest. With the Dumpster at the curb, she was able to eliminate most of the junk he'd been saving lo those many years. He'd set up such a howl about it early on that she'd taken to working when he was asleep. He seldom went into those rooms anyway, so he didn't seem to notice how much had disappeared.

She'd searched his bedroom before, but she'd obviously missed something. How could he have so little of value? He'd told her, complainingly, that he'd worked for the railroad all his life. She'd seen his monthly pension checks, which were more than sufficient to cover his monthly expenses. Where had the rest of the money gone? She knew his house was paid off, disgusting as it was, but now he had her salary to pay and she didn't come cheap. Soon she'd start billing Melanie for overtime, though she'd let the doctor suggest the added hours.

The first week she worked she'd found the passbooks for two savings accounts in one of the cubbyholes in his desk. One contained a pathetic fifteen thousand dollars and the other, twenty-two thousand. Obviously he wanted her to believe that was the extent of it. He was taunting her, knowing she had no way to get her hands on the funds. In her previous job, something similar had occurred. She'd persuaded Mrs. Feldcamp to sign countless checks made out to cash, but four more big savings accounts had surfaced after the old woman was gone. Those four held close to five hundred thousand dollars, which made her weep with frustration. She'd taken one last run at the money, backdating withdrawal slips that she forged with the old woman's signature. She thought the effort was credible, but the bank had taken issue. There was even talk of prosecution, and if she hadn't shed that particular persona, all her hard work might have come to nothing. Fortunately she'd been quick enough to vanish before the bank discovered the extent of her chicanery.

At Gus's, the week before, after a diligent search through the chest of drawers in one of the spare bedrooms, she'd found some jewelry that must have belonged to his wife. Most of it was cheap, but Mrs. Vronsky's engagement ring was mounted with a good-sized diamond and her watch was a Cartier. Solana had moved those to a hiding place in her room until she could get to a jeweler's and have them appraised. She didn't want to try a pawnshop because she knew she would net only a small percentage of their value. Items in pawnshops were easily traced and that would never do. Really, she was losing hope of unearthing assets beyond those in hand.

She crept to the closet, lifting the knob as she opened the door. She'd learned the hard way that the hinges screeched like someone stepping on a dog's tail. That had happened the second night she'd spent in the house. Gus had sat up in bed, demanding to know what she was doing in his room. She'd said the first thing that had come into her head. "I heard you yelling and I thought something was wrong. You must have had a bad dream. Why don't I warm you some milk?"

She'd laced the milk with cherry cough syrup, telling him it was a special drink mix for kids, full of vitamins and minerals. He'd swallowed it right down, and she'd made a point of oiling the hinges before she tried again. Now she went back through his jacket pockets, testing his raincoat, his only sports coat, and the robe he'd left hanging on the closet door. Nothing, nothing, nothing, she thought irritably. If the old man was worthless, there was no way she could put up with him. He could go on for years, and what was the point of helping if it netted her nothing? She was a trained professional, not a volunteer.

She gave up the search for the night and returned to bed, frustrated and out of sorts. She lay there, sleepless, roaming the house in her mind, trying to determine how he'd outwitted her. Nobody could live as long as he had without having a substantial sum of money somewhere. She'd obsessed about the subject from day one of her employment when she'd been certain of success. She'd quizzed him about his insurance policies, pretending that she was pondering the issue of whole life versus term. Almost gleefully he'd told her he'd let his policies lapse. She'd been sorely disappointed, though she'd discovered through Mr. Ebersole how difficult it was to insinuate oneself as a beneficiary. She'd done better with Mrs. Prent, though she wasn't at all sure the lesson she'd learned there would apply to this situation. Surely Gus had a will, which might provide another possibility. She hadn't found a copy, but she'd come across a safe-deposit key, which suggested he kept his valuables at the bank.

All the worrying was exhausting. At 4:00 A.M. she rose, put on her clothes, and made her bed neatly. She let herself out the front door and walked the half block to her car. It was dark and cold, and she couldn't shake the sour mood he'd put her in. She drove to Colgate. In long stretches, the highway was deserted, as wide and empty as a river. She pulled into the carport at her apartment complex, her gaze moving across the line of windows to see who was awake. She loved the sense of power she experienced, knowing she was up and about while so many others were dead to the world.

She let herself in and checked to make sure Tiny was home. He seldom went out, but when he did, she might not see him for days. She opened his door with the same stealth she employed in searching Gus's closets. The room was dark, dense with his body smells. He kept his heavy curtains closed because the morning light bothered him, nudging him awake hours before he was ready to get out of bed. He stayed up late at night watching television and he couldn't face life before noon, he said. The soft wash of daylight from the hallway revealed his bulky outline in the bed, one beefy arm on top of the quilt. She closed the door.

She poured a tot of vodka in a jelly glass and sat down at the dining room table, which was piled high with junk mail and unopened bills, among them her new driver's license, which she was thrilled to have in her possession. On top of the closest stack was a blank envelope with her name scrawled across the front. She recognized her landlord's nearly illegible scrawl. He was actually the manager, a position he enjoyed because he paid no rent. The note inside was short and to the point, informing her of a two-hundred-dollar-a-month increase, effective immediately. Two months previously she'd been told the building had been sold. Now the new owner was systematically jacking up the rents, which automatically raised the value of the property. At the same time, he was making a few improvements, if that's what you wanted to call them. He'd taken credit for having the mailboxes repaired when it was actually a post office regulation. The mailman wouldn't deliver to any address where there wasn't a clearly marked box. The dead bushes had been pulled away from the front of the building and left at the curb, where the trash collectors had ignored them for weeks. He'd also installed coin-operated washers and dryers in the communal laundry room, which had been abandoned for years and had served as a storage space for bicycles, many of which were stolen. She knew most of the tenants would ignore the washing machines.

Across the back alleyway from her apartment there was another complex he'd bought—twenty-four units in four buildings, each with its own unlocked laundry room, where a washer and dryer were available without charge. There were only twenty apartments in her building, and many of her fellow tenants took advantage of the free facilities. Small boxes of detergent were available from a vending machine, but it was easy enough to jimmy the mechanism and take what you needed. She wondered what the new owner was up to, probably snapping up properties right and left. Greedy people were like that, squeezing the last penny out of those like herself, who struggled to survive.

Solana had no intention of paying two hundred more a month for a furnished apartment that was barely habitable as it was. For a while Tiny had kept a cat, a big old white male that he'd named after himself. He was too lazy to get up and let the cat in and out, so the animal had taken to pissing on the carpet and using the heat registers to relieve itself in more serious ways. She was used to the smell by now, but she knew if she left the place, the manager would raise hell. She hadn't paid a pet deposit because when the two of them moved in, they didn't have a pet. Now she couldn't see why she should be held responsible when the cat had died of old age. She wasn't even going to think about the medicine cabinet Tiny had ripped out of the bathroom wall or the scorch mark on the laminate counter where he'd set a hot skillet some months before. She decided to hold off on paying the rent while she considered her alternatives.

She went back to Gus's house at 3:00 that afternoon and found him awake and cross as a bear. He knew she'd been sleeping in the house three or four nights a week and he expected to have her at his beck and call. He said he'd been banging and thumping on the wall for hours. The very idea put her in a fury.

"Mr. Vronsky, I told you I was leaving at eleven o'clock last night just as I always do. I made a point of coming into your room to tell you I was on my way home and you agreed."

"Someone was here."

"It wasn't me. If you doubt me, go in my room and look at the bed. You'll see it hasn't been slept in."

She went on in this vein, insistent on her version of events. She could see how befuddled he was, convinced of one thing when she was standing there telling him the opposite.

He blinked rapidly and his face took on the stubborn cast she knew so well. She put a hand on his arm. "It's not your fault. You're overly emotional, that's all. It happens with people your age. You might be having a series of small strokes. The effect would be much the same."

"You were here. You came into my room. I saw you looking for something in the closet."

She shook her head, smiling at him sadly. "You were dreaming. You did that last week. Don't you remember?"

He searched her face.

She kept her expression kind and her tone sympathetic. "I told you then you were imagining things, but you refused to believe me, didn't you? Now you're doing it again."

"No."

"Yes. And I'm not the only one who's noticed. Your niece called me right after she spoke to you on the phone earlier this week. She said you were confused. She was so worried about you, she asked a neighbor to come over and check up on you. Do you remember Ms. Millhone?"

"Of course. She's a private detective and she intends to investigate you."

"Don't be ridiculous. Your niece asked her to pay a visit because she thought you were showing signs of senile dementia. That's why she came, to see for herself. It wouldn't take a private detective to determine how disturbed you've become. I told her it might be any number of things. A thyroid condition, for instance, which I also explained to your niece. From now on, you'd be wise to keep your mouth shut. They'll think you're paranoid and making things up—another sign of dementia. Don't humiliate yourself in the eyes of others. All you'll get is their pity and their scorn."

She watched his face crumble. She knew she could break him down. As cranky and ill-tempered as he was, he was no match for her. He began to tremble, his mouth working. He was blinking again, this time trying to hold back tears. She patted his arm and murmured a few endearments. In her experience, it was kindness that caused the old ones so much pain. Opposition they could take. They probably welcomed it. But compassion (or the semblance of love in this case) cut straight to the soul. He began to weep, the soft, hopeless sound of someone sinking under the weight of despair.

"Would you like a little something to settle your nerves?"

He put a trembling hand over his eyes and nodded.

"Good. You'll feel better. The doctor doesn't want you to be upset. I'll bring you some ginger ale as well."

Once he'd taken his medicine, he sank into a sleep so

deep she was able to pinch him hard on the leg and get no response.

She made up her mind to give notice at the first complaint. She was tired of catering to him.

At 7:00 that night, he'd toddled from the bedroom to the kitchen, where she was sitting. He was using his walker, which made a dreadful thumping sound that got on her nerves.

He said, "I didn't have my dinner."

"That's because it's morning."

He hesitated, suddenly unsure of himself. He flicked a look at the window. "It's dark out."

"It's four A.M. and, naturally, the sun isn't up. If you like, I can fix your breakfast. Would you like eggs?"

"The clock says seven."

"It's broken. I'll have to have it repaired."

"If it's morning, you shouldn't be here. When I said I saw you last night, you told me I'd imagined it. You don't come to work until midafternoon."

"Ordinarily, yes, but I stayed last night because you were upset and confused and I was worried. Sit down at the table and I'll make you something nice for your breakfast."

She helped him into a kitchen chair. She could tell he was struggling to figure out what was true and what was not. While she scrambled eggs for him, he sat, silent and sullen. She put his eggs in front of him.

He stared at the plate but made no move to eat.

"Now what's wrong?"

"I don't like hard eggs. I told you that. I like them soft."

"I'm so sorry. My mistake," she said. She took his plate and dumped the eggs in the trash, then scrambled two more, leaving them so soft they were little more than rivers of slime.

"Now eat." This time he obeyed.

Solana was tired of the game. With nothing to gain, it might be time to move on. She liked her patients with a little fight left in them. Otherwise, what did her victories mean? He was a loathsome man anyway, smelling faintly medicinal and reeking of wet. Right then and there she decided to quit. If he thought he was so smart, he could fend for himself. She wouldn't bother to notify his niece she was leaving. Why waste the time or the energy on a long-distance call? She told him it was time for his regular pain medication.

"I took that."

"No, you didn't. I keep notes for the doctor. You can see for yourself. There's nothing written here."

He took his pills, and within minutes his head was drooping and she helped him to his bed again. Peace and quiet at last. She went to her room and packed her belongings, tucking his wife's jewelry in her overnight case. She'd been paid accumulated overtime the day before by mail, a stingy check from his niece, who hadn't even included a thank-you note. She wondered if she might borrow the car she'd seen sitting in the garage. He probably wouldn't notice it was gone since he so seldom went out. As it was, the car was of use to no one, and Solana's secondhand convertible was a mess.

She'd just finished zipping up her bags when she heard a knock at the door. Why would somebody stop by at this hour? She hoped it wasn't Mr. Pitts from next door inquiring about the old man's welfare. She checked her reflection in the mirror on the dresser. She smoothed her hair back and adjusted the clip she was using to hold it in place. She went into the living room. She flipped on the porch light and peered out. She couldn't place the woman, though she looked familiar. She appeared to be in her seventies and was well put together: low heels, hose, and a dark suit with a froth of ruffles at the neck. She looked like a social worker. Her smile was pleasant as she glanced at the paper she carried, refreshing her memory. She opened the door a crack.

"Are you Mrs. Rojas?"

Solana hesitated. "Yes."

"Am I pronouncing that right?"

"Yes."

"May I come in?"

"Are you selling something?"

"Not at all. My name's Charlotte Snyder. I'm a real estate agent and I was wondering if I could speak to Mr. Vronsky about his house. I know he took a tumble and if he's not feeling up to it, I can come back another time."

Solana made a point of looking at her watch, hoping the woman would get the hint.

"I apologize for the hour. I know it's late, but I've been with a client all day and this was the first chance I've had to stop by."

"What's this about the house?"

Charlotte looked past her into the living room. "I'd prefer to explain it to him."

Solana smiled. "Why don't you come in and I'll see if he's up? The doctor wants him to get as much rest as possible."

"I wouldn't want to disturb him."

"Not to worry."

She let the woman in and left her sitting on the couch while she made a trip to the bedroom. She turned on the overhead light and looked at him. He was down in the depths of sleep. She waited a suitable interval and then flicked off the light switch and returned to the living room. "He's not feeling well enough to come out of his room. He says if you'll explain your business to me, I can pass the information along when he's feeling better. Perhaps you'd be so kind as to tell me your name again."

"Snyder. Charlotte Snyder."

"I recognize you now. You're a friend of Mr. Pitts next door, yes?"

"Well, yes, but I'm not here because of him."

Solana sat and stared at her. She didn't like people who were cagey about stating their business. This woman was uneasy about something, but Solana couldn't figure out what it was. "Mrs. Snyder, of course you should do as you think best, but Mr. Vronsky trusts me with everything. I'm his nurse."

"It's a big responsibility." She appeared to wrestle with the idea, whatever it was, blinking at the floor before deciding to go on. "I'm not here to promote anything one way or the other. This is purely a courtesy . . ."

Solana gestured impatiently. Enough with the preamble.

"I'm not sure Mr. Vronsky understands how much this place is worth. I happen to have a client who's in the market for a property of this sort."

"What sort is that?" Solana's first impulse was to disparage the house, which was small, outdated, and in bad repair. Then again, why give the agent reason to offer less, if that's what she was getting at?

"Are you aware that he owns a double lot? I checked with the county assessor's office, and it turns out when Mr. Vronsky bought this lot, he bought the one next door as well."

"Of course," Solana said, though it had never occurred to her that the vacant lot next door belonged to the old man.

"Both are zoned for multiple-family dwelling."

Solana knew very little about real estate, never having owned a piece of property in her life. "Yes?"

"My client's here from Baltimore. I've shown everything currently listed, but then yesterday, it occurred to me . . ."

"How much?"

"Excuse me, what?"

"You can give me the figures. If Mr. Vronsky has questions, I can let you know." Wrong move. Solana could see the woman's uneasiness return.

"You know, on second thought, it might be better if I come back another time. I should deal with him in person."

"What about tomorrow morning at eleven?"

"Fine. That's good. I'd appreciate it."

"Meanwhile, there's no point wasting his time or yours. If it's too little money, selling is out of the question, in which case it won't be necessary to bother him again. He loves this house."

"I'm sure he does, but being realistic, the land is worth more than the house at this point, which means we're talking about a tear-down."

Solana shook her head. "No, no. He won't want to do that. He lived here with his wife and it would break his heart. It would take a lot to get him to agree."

"I understand. Perhaps this is not a good idea, our discussing . . ."

"Fortunately, I have influence and I might talk him into it if the price is right."

"I haven't done the comps. I'd have to give it some thought, but everything depends on his response. I wanted to feel him out before I went further."

"You must have an opinion or you wouldn't be here."

"I've already said more than I should. It would be highly irregular to mention a dollar amount."

"That's up to you," Solana said, but in a tone that implied the door was closing.

Mrs. Snyder paused again to marshal her thoughts. "Well . . ."

"Please. I can help."

"With the two lots together, I think it would be reasonable to say nine."

" 'Nine'? You're saying nine thousand or ninety? Because if it's nine, you might as well stop right there. I wouldn't want to insult him."

"I meant nine hundred thousand. Of course, I'm not committing my client to a dollar amount, but we've been looking in that range. I represent his interests first and foremost, but if Mr. Vronsky wanted to list the property with me, I'd be delighted to walk him through the process."

Solana put a hand to her cheek.

The woman hesitated. "Are you all right?"

"I'm fine. You have a business card?"

"Of course."

Later, Solana had to close her eyes with relief, realizing how close she'd come to blowing everything. As soon as the woman was gone, she went into the bedroom and unpacked her bags.

18

Driving home from work on Friday, I spotted Henry and Charlotte walking the bike path along Cabana Boulevard. They were bundled up, Henry in a navy peacoat, Charlotte in a ski jacket with a knit hat pulled down over her ears. The two were engrossed in conversation and didn't see me pass, but I waved nonetheless. It was still light out, but the air was the dull gray of dusk. The streetlights had come on. The restaurants along Cabana were open for happy hour and the motels were activating their vacancy signs. The palm trees stood at parade rest, fronds rustling in the sea wind coming in off the beach.

I turned onto my street and snagged the first parking spot I saw, sandwiched between Charlotte's black Cadillac and an old minivan. I locked up and walked to my apartment, checking the Dumpster as I went by. Dumpsters are a joy because they cry out to be filled, thus encouraging us to rid our garages and attics of accumulated junk. Solana had tossed the bicycle frames, the lawn mowers, long-defunct canned goods, and the carton of women's shoes, the weight of the trash forming a compact mass. The mound was almost as high as the sides of the container and would probably have to be hauled away before long. I pulled my mail out of the box and went through the gate. When I rounded the corner of the studio, I saw Henry's brother William standing on his porch in a natty three-piece suit with a muffler wrapped around his neck. The January chill had brought bright spots of color to his cheeks.

I crossed the patio. "This is a surprise. Are you looking for Henry?"

"Matter of fact I am. This upper-respiratory infection has triggered an asthma attack. He said I could borrow his humidifier to head off anything worse. I told him I'd stop by to pick it up, but his door's locked and he's not responding to my knock."

"He's off on a walk with Charlotte. I saw them on Cabana a little while ago so I'd imagine they'll be home soon. I can let you in if you want. Our doors are keyed the same, which makes it easier if I'm out and he has to get into the studio."

"I'd appreciate your help," he said. He stood aside while I stepped forward and unlocked the back door. Henry had left the humidifier on the kitchen table, and William scribbled him a note before he took the apparatus.

"You going home to bed?"

"Not until after work if I'm able to hold out that long. Friday nights are busy. Young people revving up for the weekend. If necessary, I can wear a surgical mask to prevent my passing this on."

"I see you're all dressed up," I said.

"I just came from a visitation at Wynington-Blake."

Wynington-Blake was a mortuary I knew well (Burials, Cremation, and Shipping—Serving All Faiths), having dropped by on previous occasions. I said, "Sorry to hear that. Anyone I know?"

"I don't believe so. This is a visitation I read about when I checked the obituaries in the paper this morning. Fellow named Sweets. No mention of close relations so I thought I'd put in an appearance in case he needed company. How's Gus doing? Henry hasn't mentioned him of late."

"I'd say fair."

"I knew it would come down to this. Old people, once they fall . . ." He let the sentence trail off, contemplating the sorry end of yet another life. "I should call on him while I can. Gus could go at any time."

"Well, I don't think he's on his deathbed, but I'm sure he'd appreciate a visit. Maybe in the morning when he's up and about. He could use some cheering up."

"What better time than now? Raise his spirits, so to speak."

"He could use that."

William brightened. "I could tell him about Bill Kips's death. Gus and Bill lawn-bowled together for many years. He'll be sorry he missed the funeral, but I picked up an extra program at the service and I could talk him through the memorial. Very moving poem at the end. 'Thanatopsis' by William Cullen Bryant. You know the work, I'm sure."

"I don't believe I do."

"Our dad made us memorize poetry when the sibs and I were young. He believed committing verse to memory served a man well in life. I could recite it if you like."

"Why don't you step in out of the cold before you do."

"Thank you. I'm happy to oblige."

I held the door open, and William moved far enough

into my living room so I could close it behind him. The chill air seemed to have followed him in, but he set to work with a will. He held on to his lapel with his right hand, his left tucked behind him as he began to recite. "Just the last of it," he said, by way of introduction. He cleared his throat. " 'So live, that when thy summons comes to join / The innumerable caravan which moves / To that mysterious realm, where each shall take / His chamber in the silent halls of death, / Thou go not, like the quarry-slave at night, / Scourged to his dungeon, but, sustained and soothed / By an unfaltering trust, approach thy grave / Like one who wraps the drapery of his couch / About him, and lies down to pleasant dreams.' "

I waited, expecting a perky postscript.

He looked at me. "Inspirational, isn't it?"

"I don't know, William. It's really not that uplifting. Why not something with a touch more optimism?"

He blinked, stumped for a substitute.

"Why don't you give it some thought," I said. "Meanwhile, I'll tell Henry you stopped by."

"Good enough."

Saturday morning, I made another run over to the residence hotel on Dave Levine Street. I parked out in front and let myself in. I walked down the hall to the office, where the landlady was tallying receipts on an old-fashioned adding machine with a hand crank.

"Sorry to interrupt," I said. "Is Melvin Downs in?"

She turned in her chair. "You again. I believe he went out, but I can check if you like."

"I'd appreciate that. I'm Kinsey Millhone, by the way. I didn't catch your name."

"Juanita Von," she said. "I'm the owner, manager,

and cook, all rolled into one. I don't do the cleaning. I have two young women who do that." She got up from the desk. "This might take a while. His room's on the third floor."

"You can't call?"

"I don't permit telephones in the rooms. It's too costly having jacks installed, so I let them use mine when the occasion arises. As long as they don't take advantage, of course. You might wait in the parlor. It's the formal room to the left as you go down this hall."

I turned and went back to the parlor, where I prowled the perimeter. While the surfaces weren't cluttered, Juanita Von did seem to favor ceramic figures, knock-kneed children with sagging socks and fingers in their mouths. The bookshelves were free of books, which probably saved her cleaning women the effort of dusting. Limp sheer curtains at the window filtered sufficient light to make the air in the room seem gray. The matching sofas were unforgiving, and the wooden chair wobbled on its legs. The only sound was the ticking of the grandfather clock in one corner of the room. What kind of people lived in such a place? I pictured myself coming home to this at the end of each day. Talk about depressing.

I spotted six neatly stacked magazines on the coffee table. I picked up the first, a copy of last week's *TV Guide.* Under it was the November 1982 issue of *Car & Driver* and under that was an issue of *BusinessWeek* from the previous March. A few minutes later Juanita Von reappeared. "Out," she said, sounding entirely too satisfied for my taste.

"Not to get repetitive here, but do you have any idea when he'll be back?"

"I do not. As a proprietor, I'm strictly hands-off. If it's not my business, I don't inquire. That's my policy."

Thinking to endear myself, I said, "This is a wonderful old house. How long have you owned it?"

"Twenty-six years this March. This is the old Von estate. You might have heard of it before. Property once stretched from State Street to Bay and covered twelve square blocks."

"Really. It's quite a place."

"Yes, it is. I inherited this house from my grandparents. My great-grandfather built it at the turn of the century and gave it to my grandparents the day they were married. It's been added onto over the years as you can tell. Corridors go every which way."

"Did your parents live here as well?"

"Briefly. My mother's people were from Virginia, and she insisted that they move to Roanoke, which is where I was born. She didn't much care for California and she certainly had no interest in local history. My grandparents knew she'd talk my father into selling the property once they were gone so they skipped a generation and left it to me. I was sorry to have to break it up into rental units, but it was the only way I could afford the upkeep."

"How many rooms do you have?"

"Twelve. Some are larger than others, but most of them have good light, and they all have the same high ceilings. If I ever come into money, I intend to redo the public rooms, but that's not likely to happen any time soon. I sometimes discount the rent a bit if a tenant wants to paint or fix up. As long as I approve the changes."

She began to tidy the magazines, her attention turned to the task so she wouldn't have to make eye contact. "If you don't mind my asking, what's your business with Mr. Downs? I've never known him to have a visitor."

"We believe he witnessed an accident in May of last

year. This was a two-vehicle collision up near City College and he offered assistance. Unfortunately, one's now suing the other for a large sum of money, and we hope he has information that might help settle the dispute."

"Way too many people suing in my opinion," she said. "I've served on juries in two different lawsuits and both were a waste of time, not to mention the taxpayers' dollars. Now, if we're done chatting, I'll get on with my work."

"Why don't I leave Mr. Downs a note and he can contact me. I don't want to turn into a pest."

"Fine with me."

I took out a pen and a spiral-bound notebook, dashing off a note, asking if he'd get in touch at his earliest convenience. I ripped the leaf from my notebook and folded it in half before I handed it to her with one of my business cards. "There's a machine on both these numbers. If he can't reach me directly, tell him I'll return the call as soon as I can."

She read the card and sent me a sharp look, though she made no comment.

I said, "I don't suppose I could trouble you for a quick tour."

"I don't rent to females. Women are usually trouble. I don't like gossip and petty bickering, not to mention feminine-hygiene products interfering with the plumbing. I'll see Mr. Downs gets your note."

"Fair enough," I said.

I stopped by the supermarket on my way home. For once, the sun was out, and while the temperature was still riding in the low fifties, the sky was a bright clear blue. Charlotte's Cadillac was parked across the street. I let myself in and unloaded my shopping bags. I'd noticed a batch of fresh bread dough proofing in a cradle that Henry kept in the glass-enclosed breezeway between my place and his. He hadn't made bread for ages and the notion put me in a good mood. Having been a professional baker by trade, he'd make eight to ten loaves at a time, and he was generous about sharing. I hadn't talked to Charlotte in a week, so once my kitchen was tidied up, I trotted across the patio and knocked on Henry's door. I could see Henry at work, and judging from the size of the kettle on the stove, he was making chili or spaghetti sauce to go with his bread. William was seated at the table, with a cup of coffee in front of him, an odd expression on his face. Charlotte stood with her arms crossed, and Henry was whacking an onion with a vengeance. He reached over and opened the door for me, but it wasn't until I'd closed it behind me that I tuned in to the tension in the room. At first I thought there was a problem with Gus because the three of them were so silent. I figured William had gone next door to visit him and brought back a bad report, which was only partially true. I found myself looking from one stony face to the next.

I said, "Is everything okay?"

Henry said, "Not really."

"What's going on?"

William cleared his throat, but before he could speak, Henry said, "I'll handle this."

"Handle what?" I asked, still clueless.

Henry used the knife blade to sweep the onion aside. He laid out eight cloves of garlic and used the flat of the same blade to crush the cloves, which he then chopped. "William went over to Gus's for a visit this morning and saw Charlotte's business card on the coffee table."

"Oh?"

"I shouldn't have mentioned it," William said.

Henry sent a hot look in Charlotte's direction and I realized then that there was a dispute under way. "These people are my neighbors. I've known some of them for the better part of fifty years. You went over there to hustle real estate. Gus was under the impression that I sent you over there to talk about the sale of his home when I did no such thing. He has no interest in putting his property on the market."

"You don't know that. He was totally unaware of how much equity he'd built up or the use he could make of it. Of course he knew he'd bought the lot next door, but that was fifty years ago, and he didn't understand how that half-acre ownership enhanced the overall value. People are entitled to information. Just because you're not interested doesn't mean he's not."

"Your efforts reflected poorly on me and I don't appreciate it. From what his nurse says he was close to collapse."

"That's not true. He wasn't the least bit upset. We had a nice chat and he said he'd think about it. I was there less than twenty minutes. There was no pressure whatever. I don't operate that way."

"Solana told William you were there twice. Once to talk to her and then a second time to discuss the matter with him. Maybe you don't call that pressure, but I do."

"He was sleeping the first time and she said she'd pass the information along. I went back at her request because she wasn't sure she'd explained it properly."

"I asked you not to do it at all. You did an end-run around me."

"I don't need your permission to go about my business."

"I'm not talking about permission. I'm talking about simple decency. You don't go into a man's home and cause trouble."

"What trouble are you talking about? Solana's the one who has everyone all riled up. I drove all the way up from Perdido this morning and here you are being pissy with me. Who needs it?"

Henry was silent for a moment, opening a can of tomato sauce. "I had no idea you'd take such liberties."

"I'm sorry you're upset, but I really don't think you have the right to dictate my behavior."

"That's entirely correct. You can do anything you want, but keep my name out of it. Gus has health problems, as you well know. He doesn't need you waltzing in there acting like he's on his deathbed."

"I did no such thing!"

"You heard what William said. Gus was beside himself. He thought his house was being sold out from under him and he was being sent to a nursing home."

Charlotte said, "Stop that. Enough. I have a client who's interested . . ."

"You have a client in the wings?" Henry stopped and stared at her in astonishment.

"Of course I have clients. You know that as well as I do. I haven't committed a crime. Gus is free to do anything he wants."

William said, "At the rate he's going, you'll end up dealing with his estate. That should settle it."

Henry banged his knife down. "Goddamn it! The man is not dead!"

Charlotte snatched her coat from the back of the kitchen chair and shrugged herself into it. "I'm sorry, but this discussion is at an end."

"Conveniently for you," Henry said.

I expected to see her stomping out the door, but the two weren't ready to disengage. As with any clash of wills, each was convinced of his position and righteously annoyed with the other's point of view.

"Nice seeing you," she said to me, buttoning her coat. "I'm sorry you had to be a party to this unpleasantness." She took out a pair of leather gloves and put them on, working the leather over her fingers one by one.

Henry said, "I'll call you. We can talk about this later when we've both calmed down."

"If you think so little of me there's nothing left to say. You've as good as accused me of being insensitive, untrustworthy, and unscrupulous . . ."

"I'm telling you the effect you had on a frail old man. I'm not going to stand by and let you bulldoze right over him."

"I did not bulldoze over him. Why would you take Solana's word over mine?"

"Because she has nothing at stake. Her job is to look after him. Your job is to talk him into selling his house and land so you can take your six percent."

"That's offensive."

"You're damn right it is. I can't believe you'd employ such tactics when I specifically asked you not to."

"That's the third time you've said that. You've made your point."

"Apparently, I haven't. You've yet to apologize. You defend your so-called rights without any regard to mine."

"What are you talking about? I mentioned the value of homes in this area and you assumed I intended to muscle my way in, abusing your neighbors in order to make a few bucks."

"The man was in tears. He had to be sedated. What do you call that, if not abuse?"

"Abuse, my ass. William talked to him. Did you see anything of the sort?" she asked, turning to him.

William shook his head in the negative, studiously avoiding eye contact so one or the other wouldn't suddenly lash out at him. I kept my mouth shut as well. The subject had now shifted from Charlotte's visit to Solana's account of it. At the rate they were going at it, there was no way to cut in and broker a truce. I wasn't good at that stuff anyway, and I was finding it tough to get a handle on the truth.

Charlotte plowed right on. "Did you talk to him yourself? No. Did he call you to complain? I bet not. How do you know she's not making it up?"

"She didn't make it up."

"You really don't want to hear the truth, do you?"

"You're the one who doesn't want to listen."

Charlotte picked up her handbag and let herself out the back door without another word. She didn't slam the door, but there was something in the way she shut it that spoke of finality.

In the wake of her departure, none of us could think of a thing to say.

William broke the silence. "I hope I didn't cause a problem."

I nearly laughed because it was so obvious he had.

Henry said, "I hate to think what might have happened if you hadn't brought it up. I'll talk to Gus myself and see if I can persuade him that he and his house aren't in jeopardy."

William stood and reached for his own overcoat. "I should go. Rosie will be setting up for lunch." He started to say something more but must have thought better of it.

Once he was gone the silence lingered. Henry's chopping had slowed. He was preoccupied, probably replaying the argument in his head. He'd remember the points he scored and forget hers.

"You want to talk about it?" I asked.

"I think not."

"You want company?"

"Not at the moment. I don't mean to be rude about it, but I'm upset."

"If you change your mind, you know where I am."

I went back to my place and got out my cleaning supplies. Scrubbing bathrooms has always been my remedy for stress. Drink and drugs before noon on Saturday was too sordid to contemplate.

In the unlikely event that I hadn't been exposed to enough conflict for one day, I decided to pay a visit to the Guffeys out in Colgate. Richard Compton had left a message the day before on my office machine, indicating that the Guffeys still hadn't paid their rent. He'd gone into court Friday morning and filed a Complaint of Unlawful Detainer, which he wanted me to serve. "You can add it to your invoice. I've got the paperwork right here."

I might have argued the point, but he'd given me a lot of work of late, and Saturday is a good day for catching people at home. "I'll swing by your house on the way out there," I said.

19

I fired up my trusty Mustang and made the detour to Compton's house on the Upper East Side. Then I headed north on the 101. Deadbeats tend to be centrally located. Certain neighborhoods and certain enclaves, being run-down and cheap, apparently attract like-minded individuals. Perhaps some people, even those in the crudest circumstances, were still living beyond their means and therefore got sued, served, and summoned to court by those to whom they were indebted. I could imagine a population of the fiscally irresponsible exchanging tricks of the trade: promises, partial payments, talk of checks in the mail, bank errors, and lost envelopes. These were the people who imagined they were somehow exempt from accountability. Most matters that passed through my hands spoke of those who felt entitled to swindle and deceive. They cheated their employers, stiffed their landlords, and blew off their bills. Why not? Going after them took time and money and netted their creditors little. People without assets are bulletproof. You can threaten all you like, but there's nothing to collect.

I circled the four-building complex, checking the space in the carport assigned to Apartment 18. Empty. Either they'd sold their vehicle (assuming they had one to begin with) or they were out on a happy Saturday jaunt. I continued around the block and pulled up across the street from their apartment. I took a paperback mystery novel from my shoulder bag and found my place. I read in the peace and quiet of my car, glancing up at intervals to see if the Guffeys had come home.

At 3:20, sure enough, I heard a car rattling and coughing like an old crop duster on approach. I looked up in time to see a banged-up Chevrolet sedan turn down the alleyway and into the Guffeys' carport. The vehicle resembled many I've seen advertised by vintage-car nuts who buy and sell "classic" cars composed entirely of rust and dings. Dismantled, the parts were worth more than the whole. Jackie Guffey and a man I pegged as her husband came around the corner of the building with their arms loaded with bulging plastic bags from a nearby discount store. Their failure to pay their rent must have given them lots of extra cash to spend. I waited until they'd disappeared into the apartment and then I got out of my car.

I crossed the street, climbed the stairs, and knocked on their door. Alas, no one deigned to respond. "Jackie? Are you in there?"

After a moment, I heard a muffled "No."

I squinted at the door. "Is that Patty?"

Silence.

I said, "Is Grant home?"

Silence.

"Anyone?"

I took out a roll of duct tape and affixed the notice of unlawful detainer to the front door. I knocked on the door again and said, "Mail's here."

On my way home, I slid by the row of boxes outside the main post office and sent a second copy of the notice to the Guffeys by first-class mail.

Monday morning, I woke early, feeling anxious and out of sorts. Henry's quarrel with Charlotte had unsettled me. I lay on my back, covers pulled up to my chin, and stared up at the clear Plexiglas skylight above my bed. Still dark as pitch outside, but I could see a sprinkling of stars so I knew the sky was clear.

I have a low tolerance for conflict. As an only child, I got along with myself very well, thanks. I was happy being in my room alone, where I could color in my coloring book, using the crayons from my 64-shade box with the sharpener built right in. Many coloring books were dumb, but my aunt made a point of purchasing the better specimens. I could also play with my teddy bear, whose mouth would lever open if you pressed a button under its chin. I'd feed the bear hard candy and then turn him over and undo the zipper in his back. I'd remove the candy from the little metal box that passed for a tummy and eat it myself. The bear never complained. This is still my notion of a perfect relationship.

School was a source of great suffering to me, but once I learned to read, I disappeared into books, where I was a happy visitor to all the worlds that sprang full-blown from the printed page. My parents died when I was five, and Aunt Gin, who took over the parenting, was as unsociable as I. She had a few friends, but I can't say she was intimate with anyone. As a result, I grew up ill prepared for disagreements, differences of opinion, clashes of will, or the need for compromise. I can handle contention in my professional life, but if a personal relationship turns testy, I head for the door. It's simply easier that way. This explains why I've been married and divorced twice and why I don't anticipate making the same mistake again. The spat between Henry and Charlotte was making my stomach hurt.

At 5:36, having abandoned the notion of going back to sleep, I rolled out of bed and into my running clothes. The sun wouldn't rise for an hour. The sky was that odd shade of silver that precedes the dawn. The bike path glowed under my feet as though lit from below. At State, I veered left, following my new jogging route. I was wearing my headset, listening to the local "lite" rock station. The streetlamps were still on, throwing out circles of white, like a series of large polka dots through which I ran. Seasonal decorations were long gone and the last of the browning Christmas trees had been dragged to the curb and left for pickup. On the return I paused to check the progress on the pool rehabilitation at the Paramount Hotel. Gunite was being sprayed over the rebar, which I took as an encouraging sign. I jogged on. Running is a form of meditation, so naturally my thoughts turned to eating, a wholly spiritual experience in my book. I contemplated the notion of an Egg McMuffin, but only because McDonald's doesn't serve QPs with Cheese at so early an hour.

I walked the last few blocks home, taking the time to review events. I hadn't yet had the opportunity to talk to Henry about his falling out with Charlotte, which ran in an endless loop in my head. On reflection, what snagged my attention was the little side trip their argument had taken. Charlotte was convinced Solana Rojas had played a part in the rift between them. That bothered me. Without Solana's help, there was no way Gus could manage living on his own. He was dependent on her. We were all of us dependent on her because she'd stepped into the breach, shouldering the burden of his care. That put her in a position of power, which was cause for concern. How easy it would be for her to take advantage of him.

I'd turned up no hint of trouble in the course of the background check, but even if Solana's record was spotless, people can and do change. She was in her early sixties and maybe she hadn't set anything aside for her retirement years. Gus might not be worth a lot, but he might have more than she did. Financial inequity is a powerful goad. Dishonest folks like nothing better than to shift assets out of the pockets of those who have them and into their own.

I turned the corner from Bay onto Albanil, pausing as I passed Gus's place. Lights were on in the living room, but there was no sign of Solana and no sign of him. I glanced at the Dumpster as I passed. The grungy wall-to-wall carpeting had been ripped up and lay over the discards like a blanket of brown snow. I surveyed the remaining rubbish, as I did most days. It looked like Solana had tipped the contents of a wastebasket into the Dumpster. The avalanche of falling paper had separated, sliding into various crevices and crannies like snow settling on a mountaintop. I could see junk mail, newspapers, flyers, and magazines.

I tilted my head. There was an envelope with a red line around the rim caught in a fold of the wall-to-wall carpeting. I reached down and retrieved it, taking a closer look. The envelope was addressed to Augustus Vronsky and bore the return address of Pacific Gas and Electric. The flap was still sealed. This was one of Gus's utility bills. The red rim suggested a certain stern reprimand, and I was guessing his payment was overdue. What was this doing in the trash?

I'd seen the pigeonholes in Gus's rolltop desk. His

paid and unpaid bills had been neatly segregated, along with receipts, bank statements, and other financial documents. I remembered being impressed that he kept his affairs in such good working order. Despite his deplorable housekeeping skills, it was clear he was conscientious about day-to-day business matters.

I turned the envelope over in my hand. Had he not been paying his bills? That was worrisome. Idly, I picked at the edge of the flap, debating the wisdom of taking a peek. I know the federal regulations related to postal theft. It's against the law to steal someone else's mail—no ifs, ands, or buts. What's also true is that a document placed in a trash container sitting at the curb no longer retains its character as the personal property of the one who tossed it. In this case, it looked like the unopened bill had ended up in the trash by mistake. Which meant it was still hands-off. What was I supposed to do?

If this was a dunning notice and I left it where I'd found it, his utilities might be cut. On the other hand, if I kept the envelope, I might end up in the federal pen. What bothered me was the virtual certainty that Gus wasn't the one who emptied the trash these days. Solana did that. I hadn't seen Gus outside for the past two months. He was barely ambulatory and I knew he wasn't taking care of routine chores.

I climbed his porch stairs and put the bill in the mailbox affixed to his front door frame and then went back to my place. I'd have given anything to find out if Gus was looking after his finances properly. I passed through the gate and rounded the studio to the rear. I let myself in and went up the spiral stairs to the loft, where I stripped off my running sweats and hopped in the shower. Once I was dressed, I ate my cereal, after which I crossed the patio and knocked on Henry's back door.

He was sitting at the kitchen table with a cup of coffee, the paper spread out in front of him. He got up to open the door. I held on to the frame, leaning forward to have a quick look around. "No fights in progress?"

"Nope. The coast is clear. You want coffee?"

"I do."

He let me in and I sat down at the kitchen table while he got out a mug and filled it, then set the milk and sugar in front of me, saying, "That's regular milk, not the usual half-and-half. To what do I owe the pleasure? I hope you're not going to lecture me on my bad behavior."

"I'm thinking about taking Gus some homemade soup."

"You need a recipe?"

"Not quite. I was actually hoping to score soup that was already made. You have any in your freezer?"

"Why don't we have a look? If I'd thought of it, I'd have taken him a batch myself." He opened his freezer and began to pull out a series of Tupperware containers, each neatly labeled with the contents and the date. He studied one. "Mulligatawny soup. I'd forgotten I had that. Doesn't sound like something you'd make. You're more the chicken-noodle type."

"Exactly," I said, watching as he retrieved a quart container from the very back of the shelf. The label was so frost-covered, he had to scrape at it with his thumbnail. "July of '85? I think the vichyssoise is past its sell-by date." He placed the jar in the sink to thaw and returned to his search. "I saw you jogging this morning."

"What were you doing out so early?"

"You'll be proud of me. I walked. Two miles by my count. I enjoyed myself."

"Charlotte's a good influence."

"Was."

"Oh. I don't suppose you want to talk about it."

"Nope." He pulled out another container and read the top. "How about chicken with rice? It's only two months old."

"Perfect. I'll thaw it first and take it over hot. It's more convincing that way."

He closed the freezer and set the rock-hard soup container on the table near me. "What's brought about such a neighborly gesture?"

"I've been worrying about Gus and this is my excuse for a visit."

"Why do you need an excuse?"

"Maybe not an excuse so much as a purpose. Not to get into the issue one way or the other, but Charlotte seemed to think Solana had a hand in putting the two of you at odds. I was wondering why she'd do that. I mean, if she's up to something, how would either of us know?"

"I wouldn't set too much store by what Charlotte says, although to be fair about it, I don't think what she did was necessarily wrong, just opportunistic."

"Is there any chance you'll patch things up?"

"I doubt it. She's not going to apologize to me and I certainly won't apologize to her."

"You sound just like me."

"Surely not that stubborn," he remarked. "At any rate, on the subject of Solana, I thought you did a background check and she was clean."

"Maybe so, maybe not. Melanie asked me to take a quick look and that's what I did. I know she doesn't have a criminal record because I researched that first."

"So you're going over there to snoop."

"More or less. If it comes to nothing, it's fine and dandy with me. I'd rather make a fool of myself than have Gus at risk."

* * *

When I got back to my place, I put the container of frozen soup in the kitchen sink and ran warm water around it to thaw. I found a bowl and set it on the counter, then took out a saucepan. I was already thinking of myself as a domestic little bun. While I waited for the soup to heat, I started a load of laundry. As soon as the soup was ready, I put it back in the Tupperware container and trotted it over to Gus's next door.

I knocked and Solana appeared from the hallway a moment later. A quick glance showed that the red-rimmed envelope was still in the box and I left it where it was. Ordinarily I'd have plucked it out and handed it over with a quick explanation, but given her paranoia, if I made reference to it, she'd think I was spying on her, which of course I was.

When she opened the door, I held up the container. "I made a big pot of soup and thought Gus might enjoy some."

Solana's demeanor was less than welcoming. She took the container, murmured a thank-you, and was on the verge of closing the door when I spoke up in haste, "How's he doing?"

I got the dark flat stare, but she seemed to reconsider the urge to snub me. She dropped her gaze. "He's napping right now. He had a rough night. His shoulder's bothering him."

"I'm sorry to hear that. Henry talked to him yesterday and he was under the impression Gus was doing better."

"Visitors tire him. You might mention it to Mr. Pitts. He stayed longer than he should have. By the time I got here at three, Mr. Vronsky'd taken to his bed. He dozed much of the day, which is why he slept so poorly last night. He's like a baby with his days and nights mixed up."

"I wonder if his doctor would have something to suggest."

"He has an appointment Friday. I intend to mention it," she said. "Was there something else?"

"Well, yes. I'm on my way to the market and wondered if you needed anything?"

"I wouldn't want to trouble you."

"It's no trouble at all. I'm going anyway and I'd be happy to help. I can even sit with Gus if you'd prefer to go yourself."

Solana ignored that offer. "If you'll wait here, I have a thing or two you could pick up."

"Sure." I'd invented the supermarket errand on the spot, desperate to prolong the contact. She was like the keeper at the gate. You couldn't get to Gus unless you went through her.

I watched her move into the kitchen, where she set the soup container on the counter and then vanished, probably finding pen and paper. I stepped into the living room and glanced at Gus's desk. The cubbyhole that had held his bills was empty, but the passbooks for his two savings accounts were still where I'd seen them before. It looked like his checkbook was wedged in there as well. I was panting to scrutinize his finances, at the very least making sure his bills were being paid. I shot a glance at the kitchen door. No sign of Solana. If I'd acted right then, I might have had my way. As it was, my hesitation cost me the opportunity. Solana appeared two beats later, her purse under her arm. The list she gave me was short, a few items scribbled on a piece of scratch paper. I watched her open her wallet and remove a twenty-dollar bill that she held out to me.

"Place looks better with that old ratty carpet gone," I said, as though I'd spent the time she'd been gone admiring her latest handiwork instead of plotting to steal Gus's bankbooks. I was kicking myself. In seconds I could have crossed the room and had the records in hand.

"I do what I can. Ms. Oberlin tells me you and Mr. Pitts did a cleaning before she arrived."

"It didn't amount to much. A lick and a promise, as my aunt used to say. Is this it?" I paused and glanced at the list. Carrots, onions, mushroom broth, turnips, a rutabaga, and new potatoes. Nutritious, wholesome.

"I promised Mr. Vronsky some fresh vegetable soup. His appetite's been off and it's the only thing he'll eat. Meat of any kind makes him nauseous."

I could feel my cheeks tint. "I guess I should have asked first. The soup's chicken with rice."

"Maybe when he's feeling better."

She moved closer, essentially walking me toward the door. She might as well have put a hand on my arm and marched me out.

I took my time at the grocery store, pretending I was shopping for myself as well as Gus. I didn't know what a rutabaga looked like, so after a frustrating search, I had to consult with the clerk in produce. He handed me a big gnarly vegetable like a bloated potato with a waxy skin and a few green leaves growing out one end. "Are you serious?"

He smiled. "You've heard of neeps and tatties? That's a neep; also called a swede. The Germans survived on those in the winter of 1916 to 1917."

"Who'da thunk?"

I returned to my car and headed for home. As I rounded the corner from Bay onto Albanil, I saw the waste-management company had picked up the Dumpster and was hauling it away. I parked in the empty stretch of curb and went up Gus's porch steps with Solana's groceries. To thwart me, she accepted the plastic sack and change from the twenty, then thanked me without inviting me inside. How exasperating! Now I'd have to come up with a fresh excuse to get in.

20

Wednesday, when I came home for lunch, I found Mrs. Dell standing on my porch in her full-length mink coat, holding the brown paper bag containing her Meals on Wheels delivery. "Hi, Mrs. Dell. How are you?"

"Not well. I'm worried."

"About what?"

"Mr. Vronsky's back door is locked and there's a note taped to the glass saying he won't be needing our services. Did he say anything to you?"

"I haven't talked to him, but it does seem odd. The man has to eat."

"If the food wasn't to his liking, I wish he'd mentioned it. We're happy to make adjustments if he has a problem."

"You didn't talk to him?"

"I tried. I knocked on the door as loudly as I could. I know he has trouble hearing and I didn't want to leave if he was already hobbling down the hall. Instead, that nurse of his appeared. I could tell she didn't want to talk, but she finally opened the door. She told me he's refusing to eat and she doesn't want the food to go to waste. Her attitude was very close to rude."

"She canceled Meals on Wheels?"

"She said Mr. Vronsky was losing weight. She took him to the doctor to have his shoulder checked and sure enough, he's down six pounds. The doctor was alarmed. She acted like it was my fault."

"Let me see what I can do."

"Please. This has never happened to me. I feel terrible thinking it was something I did."

As soon as she'd left, I put a call through to Melanie in New York. As usual, I didn't speak to a live human being. I left a message and she returned the call at 3:00 California time when she got home from work. I was in the office by then, but I set aside the report I was typing and told her about my conversation with Mrs. Dell. I thought she'd be startled about Meals on Wheels. Instead, she was irritated.

"And that's why you called? I know all this stuff. Uncle Gus has been griping about the food for weeks. At first Solana didn't pay much attention because she thought he was just being ornery. You know how much he loves to complain."

Having observed the trait myself, I couldn't argue the point. "What's he going to do about meals?"

"She says she can handle them. She offered to cook for him when she first came to work, but I thought it was too much to ask when she was already taking on his medical care. Now, I don't know. I'm leaning in that direction, at least until his appetite returns. Really, I can't see a downside, can you?"

"Melanie, don't you see what's going on here? She's building a wall around the guy, cutting off access."

"Oh, I don't think so," she said, her tone skeptical.

"Well, I do. All he does is sleep and that can't be good for him. Henry and I go over there, but he's quote-unquote 'indisposed' or 'he doesn't feel like company.' There's always some excuse. When Henry did manage a visit, she claimed Gus was so debilitated afterward, he had to take to his bed."

"Sounds about right. When I'm sick, all I want to do is sleep. The last thing I need is someone sitting there making chitchat. Talk about exhausting."

"Have you spoken to him recently?"

"It's been a couple of weeks."

"Which I'm sure suits her fine. She's made it clear she doesn't want *me* over there. I have to rack my brain to get a foot in the door."

"She's protective of him. What's so bad about that?"

"Nothing if he were doing better. The man is going downhill."

"I don't know what to say. Solana and I talk every couple of days and I'm not getting this from her."

"Of course not. She's the one doing it. Something's wrong. I can feel it in my bones."

"I hope you're not saying I should make another trip. I was out there six weeks ago."

"I know it's a hassle, but he needs the help. And I'll tell you something else. If Solana knows you're coming, she'll cover her tracks."

"Come on, Kinsey. She's asked me three or four times if I'd come out to see him, but I can't get away. Why make an offer like that if she were doing something wrong?"

"Because she's devious."

Melanie was quiet and I imagined the little wheels going round and round. I thought maybe I was getting through to her, but then she said, "Are you sure you're okay? Because this is all sounding very weird if you want to know the truth."

"I'm fine. Gus is the one I'm worried about."

"I don't doubt your concern, but all this cloak-and-dagger stuff is a bit melodramatic, don't you think?"

"No."

She made one of those long, low exasperated sounds in her throat, like this was all too much. "Okay, fine. Let's assume you're correct. Give me one concrete example."

Now I was the one silent for a beat. As usual, when confronted with a demand of that sort, my mind went blank. "I can't think of one offhand. If you want my best guess, I'd say she's drugging him."

"Oh, for heaven's sake. If you think she's so dangerous, then fire her."

"I don't have the authority. That's up to you."

"Well, I can't do anything until I talk to her. Let's be fair about it. There are two sides to every story. If I fired her strictly on the basis of what you've said, she'd file a complaint with the labor relations board about unfair treatment or dismissal without cause. You know what I'm saying?"

"Shit, Melanie. If you talk to Solana about this, she'll go ballistic. That was her response the last time around when she thought I was checking up on her."

"How else am I supposed to find out what's going on?"

"She's not going to admit to anything. She's too smart."

"But so far it's just your word against hers. I don't mean to be hard-nosed, but I'm not flying three thousand miles based on a 'feeling' in your bones."

"Don't take my word for it. You think I'm so nuts, why don't you call Henry and ask him?"

"I didn't say you were nuts. I know you better than that. I'll think about it. We're swamped right now at work and taking the time off would be a pain in the butt. I'll talk to my boss and get back to you."

Typical of Melanie, that was the last conversation we had for a month.

At 6:00 I walked up to Rosie's and found Henry sitting at his usual table in the bar. I'd decided my sterling behavior entitled me to a meal out. The place was jumping. This was Wednesday night, which is known as "hump day" to working stiffs, the week being more than half done. Henry got up graciously and held my chair while I slid in next to him. He bought me a glass of wine, which I sipped while he finished his Black Jack over ice. We ordered, or, rather, we listened, while Rosie debated what we'd have. She decided Henry would enjoy her *oz-porkolt*, a venison goulash. I told her about my nutritional goals, begging and pleading to be spared the sour cream and its many variations. She took this in stride, saying, "Is very good. No worry. For you, I prepare *guisada de guilota*."

"Wonderful. What's that?"

"Is quail braised in tomatillo-chili sauce."

Henry shifted in his seat with a look of injury. "Why can't I have that?"

"Okay. You both. I bring right away."

When the food arrived she made sure each of us had a glass of really bad red wine, which she poured with a flourish. I toasted her and sipped, saying, "Oh yum," while my tongue shriveled in my mouth.

Once she'd departed, I took a taste of sauce before I committed myself fully to the quail. "We have a problem," I said, picking at the bird with my fork. "I need to borrow the key to Gus's place."

He looked at me for a moment. I don't know what he saw in my face, but he reached in his pocket and took out a ring of keys. He worked his way through the circle and when he came to the key to Gus's back door, he forced it off the ring and put it in my outstretched palm. "I don't suppose you'd care to explain."

"Better for you if I keep my mouth shut."

"You won't do anything illegal."

I put my fingers in my ears and did that la-la-la business. "I'm not hearing that. Could you ask something else?"

"You never told me what went on when you took him the soup."

I took my fingers out of my ears. "That went fine, except she told me that his appetite was off and any kind of meat made him sick. There I stood having just given her the container full of chicken soup. I felt like an idiot."

"But you talked to him?"

"Of course not. Nobody does. When was the last time you talked to him?"

"Day before yesterday."

"Oh, that's right. And guess what? She says Gus took to his bed because you stayed too long and he was exhausted, which is bullshit. Plus, she canceled Meals on Wheels. I called Melanie to tell her and that conversation went straight into the toilet. She implied I was making things up. Either which way, she feels Solana should have the chance to defend herself. She did suggest it would be helpful if I had a shred of proof to support my suspicions. Thus . . ." I held up the key.

"Be careful."

"No sweat," I said. Now all I needed was the opportunity.

* * *

I believe, as many people do, that things happen for a reason. I'm not convinced there's a Grand Plan in place, but I do know that impulse and chance play a role in the Universe, as does coincidence. There are no accidents.

For instance:

You're on a highway and your tire goes flat, so you pull over to the side of the road in hopes of flagging down help. Many cars go by, and when someone finally comes to your aid, he turns out to be the kid you sat behind in fifth grade. Or maybe you leave for work ten minutes late and because of that you're caught in traffic, while ahead of you, the bridge you cross daily collapses, taking six cars with it. You might just as easily have left four minutes early and down you'd have gone. Life is made up of these occurrences for good or for ill. Some call it synchronicity. I call it dumb luck.

Thursday, I left the office early for no particular reason. I'd grappled with a lot of paperwork that day and maybe I was bored. As I rounded the corner from Cabana onto Bay, I passed Solana Rojas in her rattletrap convertible. Gus was hunched in the front seat, bundled into an overcoat. As far as I knew, he hadn't been out of the house in weeks. Solana was speaking to him intently and neither looked up as I went by. In the rearview mirror I saw her stop at the corner and make a right-hand turn. I figured she was taking him to another doctor's appointment, which later turned out not to be the case.

I whipped into a parking place and locked my car, then trotted up the steps to Gus's front door. I made a show of knocking on the pane of glass in the door. I waved merrily at an imaginary someone inside and then pointed toward the side and nodded, showing I understood. I went around the side of the house to the rear and climbed the back porch steps. I peered through the windowpane in the door. The kitchen was empty and the lights were out—no big surprise. I used the key Henry'd given me to let myself in. The action was not strictly legal, but I put it in the same category as returning Gus's mail. I told myself I was doing a good deed.

The problem was this:

In the absence of an invitation, I had no legitimate reason to enter Gus Vronsky's house when he was home, let alone when he was out. It was pure chance that I'd seen him pass in Solana's car, heading off to god knows where. If I were caught, what possible explanation could I give for being in his house? There'd been no smoke boiling out his windows and no cries for help. No power failure, no earthquake, no gas leak, no break in the water main. In short, I had no excuse beyond my fear for his safety and well-being. I could just imagine how far that would fly in a court of law.

In the course of this home invasion, I was hoping for one of two things: either reassurance that Gus was in good hands or evidence I could act on if my suspicions were justified. I went down the hall and into Gus's bedroom. The bed was neatly made—"a place for everything and everything in place" being Solana Rojas's credo. I opened and closed a few drawers but saw nothing out of the ordinary. I'm not sure what I expected, but that's why you look, because you don't know what's there. I went into his bathroom. His oblong pill organizer was sitting on the sink. The compartments for S, M, and T were empty, as was W. T, F, and S were still filled with assorted pills. I opened the medicine cabinet and scanned his prescription medications. I rooted through my shoulder bag until I found my notebook and pen. I wrote down the information from every bottle I saw: date, physician's name, the drug, the dosage, and instructions.

There were six prescriptions altogether. I'm not well versed in pharmaceutical matters, so I made careful notes and replaced the containers on the shelf.

I left the bathroom and continued down the hall. I opened the door to the second bedroom, where Solana kept clothing and personal items for use on the nights she stayed over. This room was the former warehouse for numerous unlabeled cardboard boxes, all of which had been removed. The few pieces of antique furniture had been dusted, polished, and rearranged. I could see she'd made herself right at home. A handsome carved mahogany bed frame had been reassembled and the linens were as taut as an army cot. There was a burled walnut rocking chair inlaid with cherry, an armoire, and a plump-shouldered fruitwood chest of drawers with ornate bronze drawer pulls. I opened three drawers in succession and saw that all were filled with Solana's clothes. I was tempted to search her room further, but my good angel suggested I was already risking jail and had better cease and desist.

Between the second and third bedrooms there was a full bath, but a quick peek through the open door revealed nothing significant. I did open the medicine cabinet and found it empty except for a number of cosmetics, which I'd never seen Solana wear.

I crossed the hall and opened the door to the third bedroom. Someone had put heavy black-out drapes across the windows so the room was dark and the air dense with heat. In the single bed against the wall there was a massive shape. At first I didn't understand what I was looking at. Oversized pillows? Laundry bags bulging with discarded clothes? I was so accustomed to Gus's hoarding that I assumed this was one more example of his inability to throw things out. I heard a grunt. There was a shifting motion, and the man lying in the bed turned from his left side to his right so he was then facing the door. Though his upper body remained in shadow, a band of daylight bisected the bed, illuminating two glittering slits. Either he slept with his eyes open or he was looking right at me. He didn't react and there was no indication he'd registered my presence. Immobilized, I stood there and held my breath.

In the depths of sleep our animal instincts take over, alerting us to any dangers that arise. Even a subtle shift in temperature, a change in the air as it eddies through the room, the faintest of noises, or an alteration in the light can trigger our defenses. In changing positions, the man had moved up from the deepest recess of sleep. He was reaching for consciousness, ascending slowly like an underwater diver with a circle of open sky above his head. I would have mewed in fear, but I didn't dare make a sound. I backed out of the room, acutely aware of the whisper of my denim jeans as I moved, the press of my boot sole against the wood floor. I closed the door with infinite care, one hand firmly on the knob, the other resting against the edge of the door to prevent even the softest click as the door met the frame and the strike nosed into the plate.

I turned and retraced my steps at the tiptoeing equivalent of a dead run. I held my shoulder bag close to me, aware that the slightest bump of a kitchen chair might bring the fellow bolt upright, wondering who was in the house with him. I crossed the kitchen, let myself out the back door, and crossed the porch with the same caution. I descended the back-porch steps, my ears cued to any sound behind me. The closer I got to safety, the more in jeopardy I felt.

I crossed Gus's grass. Between his property and Henry's there was a short length of fencing and a longer stretch of hedge. When I reached the line of shrubs, I raised my arms to shoulder height and forced my way through a narrow gap between two bushes, then more or less fell onto Henry's patio. I probably left a telltale path of broken twigs behind me, but I didn't stop to check. It wasn't until I was in my apartment with the door locked that I dared take a breath. Who the hell *was* that guy?

I turned the thumb lock on the door, left the lights off, and went around the kitchen counter to the blind cul-de-sac, where my sink, stove, and cupboards form a windowless U. I sank to the floor and sat there with my knees drawn up, waiting for someone to pound on the door and demand an explanation. Now that I was safe, my heart began to pound, banging in my chest like someone trying to break down a door with a battering ram.

In my mind's eye, I ran through the entire sequence of events: the show I'd made of tapping on the window in the front door, pretending to communicate with someone inside. I'd tromped merrily down the front steps and tromped merrily up the back. Once inside, I'd opened and closed doors. I'd slid drawers back and forth on their tracks, checked two medicine cabinets, which by all rights should have squeaked on their hinges. I'd paid no attention to the noise I made because I'd thought I was alone. And all the time, that *gorilla* was sleeping in the next room. Was I out of my freakin' mind?

After thirty seconds in hiding, I started to feel stupid. I hadn't been apprehended like some hot prowl burglar in the process of breaking and entering. No one had spotted me going in or out. No one had called the cops to report an intruder. Somehow I'd escaped detection—as far as I knew. Nonetheless, the incident was meant as an object lesson for yours truly. I should have taken it to heart, but I was struck dumb by the realization that I'd passed up the chance to lift the passbooks to Gus's bank accounts.

21

On the way to work the next morning, I took Santa Teresa Street as far as Aurelia, turned left, and made a detour into a drugstore parking lot. Jones Apothecary was an old-fashioned pharmacy, where the shelves were stocked with vitamins; first-aid remedies; nutritional supplements; ostomy supplies; nostrums; skin, hair, and nail products; and other items meant to alleviate minor human miseries. You could have your prescriptions filled, but you couldn't buy lawn furniture. You could rent crutches and buy arch supports, but you couldn't have film developed. They did offer a free blood-pressure check, and while I waited for service I sat down and affixed the cuff to my arm. After much huffing, squeezing, and releasing, the readout was 118/68 so I knew I wasn't dead.

As soon as the consultation window was free, I stepped up to the counter and caught the eye of the pharmacist, Joe Brooks, who'd been helpful in the past. He was a man in his seventies with snowy white hair that eddied into a swirl in the middle of his forehead. He said, "Yes, ma'am. How're you? I haven't seen you in a while."

"I've been around—staying out of trouble as much as possible," I said. "Right now, I need some information and I thought you might help. I have a friend who's taking a number of medications and I'm worried about him. I think he's sleeping too much and when he's awake, he's confused. I'm wondering about side effects of the drugs he's on. I made a list of what he's taking, but the prescriptions weren't filled here."

"That wouldn't make a difference. Most pharmacists handle patient consultations the same way we do. We make sure the patient understands what the medication does, the dosage, and how and when it should be taken. We also explain any possible food or drug interactions and advise them to call the doctor if they have reactions out of the ordinary."

"That's what I assumed, but I wanted to double-check. If I show you the list, can you tell me what these are for?"

"Shouldn't be a problem. Who's the doctor?"

"Medford. Do you know him?"

"I do and he's a good egg."

I took out my notebook and folded it open to the relevant page. He removed a pair of reading glasses from his jacket pocket and eased the stems over his ears. I watched him trace the lines of print with his eyes, commenting as he worked his way down the line. "These are all standard medications. The indapamide is a diuretic prescribed to lower blood pressure. Metoprolol's a beta-blocker—again, prescribed to treat hypertension. Klorvess is a cherry-flavored potassium replacement that requires a prescription because potassium supplementation can affect heart rhythm and damage the GI tract.

Butazolidin is an anti-inflammatory, probably for treatment of osteoarthritis. Did he ever mention that?"

"I know he complains about his aches and pains. Osteoporosis, for sure. He's just about bent double from bone loss." I was looking over his shoulder, reading the list. "What's that one?"

"Clofibrate is used to reduce cholesterol, and this last one, Tagamet, is for acid reflux. The only thing I see worth scrutiny are his potassium levels. Low blood potassium could cause him to be confused, weak, or sleepy. How old is he?"

"Eighty-nine."

He nodded, tilting his head as he considered the implications. "Age plays a part. No doubt about that. Geriatric individuals don't excrete drugs as promptly as healthy younger people. Liver and kidney functions are also substantially reduced. Coronary output starts declining after age thirty, and by ninety it's down to thirty to forty percent of maximum. What you're describing might be an unrelated medical condition nobody's picked up on. He'd probably benefit from an evaluation by a geriatric specialist if he hasn't seen one."

"He's under doctor's care. He dislocated his shoulder in a fall a month ago and just went in for a recheck. I expected a quicker recovery rate, but he doesn't seem much improved."

"That may well be. Striated muscle also declines with age, so it's quite possible his shoulder repair has been impeded by torn musculature, the osteoporosis, undiagnosed diabetes, or an impaired immune system. Have you talked to his doctor?"

"No, and I doubt it would be productive, given current privacy laws. His office wouldn't acknowledge his being a patient, let alone put his doctor on the phone to chat with some stranger about his care. I'm not even a family member; he's just a neighbor of mine. I'm assuming his caregiver's conveyed all the information to his doctor, but I have no way of knowing."

Joe Brooks thought about that, weighing the possibilities. "If he was given pain pills for the shoulder, he might be abusing his meds. I don't see reference to anything of the sort, but he might have a supply on hand. Alcohol consumption's another consideration."

"I hadn't thought of that. I suppose either one is possible. I've never seen him take a drink, but what do I know?"

"Tell you what: I'd be happy to call his doctor and pass along your concerns. I know this guy socially and I think he'd listen to me."

"Let's hold off on that. His caregiver lives on the premises and she's already hypersensitive. I don't want to step on her toes unless it's absolutely necessary."

"Understood," he said.

I left the office at noon that day, thinking to make myself a quick lunch at home. When I rounded the studio and reached the back patio, I saw Solana knocking frantically on Henry's kitchen door. She'd thrown a coat over her shoulders like a shawl and she was clearly upset.

I paused on my doorstep. "Is something wrong?"

"Do you know when Mr. Pitts is getting home? I've knocked and knocked, but he must be out."

"I don't know where he is. Can I help you?"

I could see the conflict in her face. I was probably the last person on earth she'd be appealing to, but her problem must have been pressing because she clutched the edges of her coat with one hand and crossed the patio. "I need a hand with Mr. Vronsky. I put him in the shower and I can't get him out. Yesterday he fell and hurt himself again so he's afraid of slipping on the tile."

"Can we manage him between us?"

"I hope so. Please."

We walked double-time to Gus's front door, which she'd left ajar. I followed her into the house, dropping my bag on the couch in the living room as we passed. She was talking over her shoulder, saying, "I didn't know what else to do. I was getting him cleaned up before supper. He's had trouble with his balance, but I thought I could handle him. He's in here."

She led me through Gus's bedroom and into the bathroom, which smelled of soap and steam. The bathroom floor had a slippery cast to it and I could see how difficult it would be to maneuver. Gus was huddled on a plastic stool in one corner of the shower. The water had been turned off and it looked like Solana had done what she could to dry him off before she left. He was shivering despite the robe she'd thrown around him to keep him warm. His hair was wet and water was still dripping down his cheek. I'd never seen him without clothes and I was shocked at how thin he was. His shoulder sockets looked enormous while his arms were all bone. His left hip was badly bruised and he was weeping, making a whimpering sound that spoke of his helplessness.

Solana bent over him. "You're fine. You're okay now. I found someone to help. Don't you worry."

She dried him off and then she took his right arm while I took his left, offering support as we hoisted him to his feet. He was shaky and clearly off-kilter, only able to take baby steps. She moved to a position in front of him and held him by the hands, walking backward to stabilize him as he tottered after her. I kept one hand under his elbow as he shuffled into the bedroom. As frail as he was, it was a trick to keep him upright and on the move.

When we reached the bed, Solana stood him close by, leaning him against the mattress for support. He clung to me with both hands while she slipped first his one arm and then the other into his flannel pajama top. Below, the skin sagged from his thighs and his pelvic bones looked sharp. We sat him on the edge of the bed and she slipped his feet through his pajama bottoms. Together we lifted him briefly so she could pull the bottoms up over his flanks. Again, she eased him onto the edge of the bed. When she lifted his feet and rotated his legs to slide them under the covers, he cried out in pain. She had a stack of old quilts nearby and she laid three over him to offset his chill. His trembling seemed uncontrollable and I could hear his teeth chattering.

"Why don't I make him a cup of tea?"

She nodded, doing what she could to make him comfortable.

I moved down the hallway to the kitchen. The teakettle was on the stove. I ran the tap until the water was hot, filled the kettle, then set it on the burner. Hastily I went through the well-stocked cupboards, looking for tea bags. New bottle of vodka? No. Cereal, pasta, and rice? Nix. I discovered the box of Lipton's on my third pass. I found a cup and saucer and set them on the counter. I went to the door and peered around the corner. I could hear Solana in the bedroom, murmuring to Gus. I didn't dare stop to think about the risk I was taking.

I slipped across the hall to the living room and moved to the desk. The pigeonholes were much as they'd been before. No bills or receipts in evidence, but I could see his bank statements, his checkbook, and the two savings account passbooks, held together by a single rubber band. I slipped off the band and took a quick look at the balances in his passbooks. The account that had originally held fifteen thousand dollars appeared to be untouched. The second passbook showed a number of withdrawals, so I shoved that in my bag. I opened his checkbook and removed the register, then put the checkbook cover and the one savings passbook back in the cubbyhole.

I moved to the couch and pushed the items to the bottom of my shoulder bag. Four long strides later I was back in the kitchen, pouring boiling water over a Lipton's tea bag. My heart was banging so hard that when I carried the china cup and saucer down the hall to Gus's bedroom, the two rattled together like castanets. Before I went into the bedroom I had to pour the tea I'd slopped from the saucer back into the cup.

I found Solana sitting on the edge of the bed, patting Gus's hand. I set the cup and saucer on the bed table. The two of us arranged pillows behind his back and secured him in an upright position. "We'll let this cool and then you can have a nice sip of tea," she said to him.

His eyes sought mine and I could see what I swore was a mute appeal.

I glanced at the clock. "Didn't you say he had a doctor's appointment later today?"

"With his internist, yes. Mr. Vronsky's been so shaky on his feet that I'm concerned."

"Is he strong enough to go?"

"He'll be fine. Once he's warm again, I can get him dressed."

"What time is his appointment?"

"In an hour. The doctor's office is only ten minutes from here."

"One thirty?"

"Two."

"I hope everything's okay. I can wait and help you get him in the car, if you like."

"No, no. I can manage now. I'm grateful for your help."

"I'm glad I was there. For now, unless you need me for something else, I'll be on my way," I said. I was torn between wanting to hover and needing to escape. I could feel a trickle of flop sweat in the small of my back. I didn't wait for a word of thanks, which I knew would be in short supply in any event.

I moved through the living room, grabbed my shoulder bag, and went out to my car. With a glance at my watch, I fired up the engine and pulled away from the curb. If I played my cards right, I could make copies of Gus's financial data and get the checkbook and savings account book back in the desk while Solana was taking him to his appointment.

When I reached my office I unlocked the door, slung my bag on the desk, and turned on the copy machine. During the laborious warm-up process, I shifted from foot to foot, groaning at the delay. As soon as the readout announced the machine was ready, I began making copies of the pages in the check register, plus the deposits and withdrawals recorded in the passbook. I'd study the figures later. Meanwhile, if I timed it right, I could head back to my place and hover in the wings. Once I saw Solana drive off with Gus for his doctor's appointment, I could slip in the back door and return the items, leaving her none the wiser. A capital plan. While it depended on proper timing, I was in the perfect position to pull it off—assuming the goon wasn't there.

My copy machine seemed agonizingly slow. The carriage line of white-hot light ticked back and forth across the plate. I'd lift the lid, open the book to the next two pages, lower the lid, and press the button. The copy paper slid out of the machine, still hot to the touch. When I was finished I turned off the machine and reached for my bag. That's when my gaze strayed to my desk calendar. The notation for Friday, January 15, read "Millard Fredrickson, 2:00 P.M." I went around the desk and looked at the entry right-side up. "Shit!"

It took me half a minute to find the Fredricksons' telephone number. In hopes of rescheduling, I snatched up the handset and punched in the numbers. The line was busy. I checked the clock. It was 1:15. Solana'd told me the doctor's office was ten minutes away, which meant she'd leave at 1:30 or so to give herself time to park and ferry Gus into the building. He'd proceed at a creeping pace, especially in light of his recent fall, which must have left him in pain. She'd probably drop him at the entrance, park, and go back, guiding him through the automated glass doors and up the elevator. If I went to the Fredricksons' early, I could conduct a quick interview and beat it back to my place before she returned. Anything I missed, I could ask Millard later in a follow-up call.

The Fredricksons didn't live that far from me, and he'd probably be delighted to have me in and out of his place in the paltry fifteen minutes I had to spare. I picked up my clipboard with the notes I'd taken during my chat with his wife. My anxiety level was way up, but I had to focus on the task at hand.

The drive from my office to the Fredricksons' naturally entailed being caught by any number of red lights. At the intersections controlled by stop signs, I'd do a quick visual survey, making sure there were no cop cars in evidence, and then I'd roll on through without bothering to stop. I turned onto the Fredricksons' street, parked across from the house, and made my way to the front door. I nearly lost my footing on the algae-slick wooden wheelchair ramp, but I caught myself before I went down on my butt. I was pretty sure I'd wrenched my back in a way I'd have to pay for later.

I rang the bell and waited, expecting Gladys to come to the door as she had on my earlier visit. Instead, Mr. Fredrickson opened the door in his wheelchair with a paper napkin tucked in his shirt collar.

"Hello, Mr. Fredrickson. I thought I'd pop in a few minutes early, but if I interrupted your lunch, I can always come back in an hour or so. Is that better for you?" I was thinking *please, please, please*, but I didn't actually clasp my hands in prayer.

He glanced down at the napkin and removed it with a tug. "No, no. I just finished. We might as well get started as long as you're here." He rolled himself back, made a two-point turn, and pushed himself as far as the coffee table. "Grab a chair. Gladys is off at rehab so I've got a couple hours to spare."

The notion of spending two hours with the man made the panic rise anew. "It won't take me that long. A few quick questions and I'll get out of your hair. Is this seat okay?"

I was busy stacking magazines and mail that I moved to one side so I could sit on the couch where I'd sat before. I heard a muffled barking from a back room, but there was no sign of the bird so maybe the dog had had a nice lunch as well. I took out my tape recorder, which I hoped still had juice. "I'll be recording this interview the same way I did with your wife. I hope you're agreeable." I was already punching buttons, getting properly set.

"Yes. Fine. Anything you want."

I recited my name, his, date, time, subject matter, and other particulars talking so fast it sounded like the tape recorder was operating at twice its normal speed.

He folded his hands in his lap. "I might as well start at the beginning. I know how you people are . . ."

I flipped through the pages on my yellow legal pad. "I have most of the information here so all I need is to fill in a few blanks. I'll be out of here shortly."

"Don't hurry on my account. We have nothing to hide. Her and me had a long talk about this and we intend to cooperate. Seems only fair."

I dropped my gaze to the reel turning in the machine and felt my body grow still. "We appreciate that," I said.

The phrase "we have nothing to hide" echoed through my frame. What came immediately to mind was the old saying "The louder he proclaims his honesty, the faster we count the silver." His aside was the equivalent of someone beginning a sentence with the phrase "to be perfectly honest." You can just about bet whatever comes next will be straddling the line between falsehood and an outright lie.

"Any time you're ready," I said, without looking at him.

He related his rendition of the accident in tedious detail. His tone was rehearsed and his account so clearly mimicked what I'd heard from her that I knew they'd conferred at length. Weather conditions, seat belt, Lisa Ray's abruptly pulling into his lane, the slamming on of brakes, which he accomplished with his hand control. Gladys couldn't possibly remember everything she'd told me, but I knew if I spoke to her again, her story would be amended until it was a duplicate of her husband's. I scribbled as he spoke, making sure I was covering the same ground. There's nothing worse than running into an inaudible response when a tape is transcribed.

At the back of my mind I was fretting about Gus. I had no idea how I'd get the financial data back where it belonged, but I couldn't worry about that now. I nodded as Mr. Fredrickson went on and on. I made sympathetic noises and kept my expression a near parody of interest and concern. He warmed to the subject as he proceeded with his narrative. Thirty-two minutes later, when he started repeating himself, I said, "Well, thanks. I think this about covers it. Is there anything else you'd like to add for the record?"

"I believe that's it," he said. "Just a mention of where we were going when that Lisa Ray woman ran into us. I believe you asked my wife and it'd slipped her mind."

"That's right," I said. He fidgeted slightly and his voice had changed so I knew a whopper was about to escape his lips. I leaned forward attentively, pen poised over the page.

"The market."

"Ah, the market. Well, that makes sense. Which one?"

"That one on the corner at the bottom of the hill."

I nodded, taking notes. "And the trip was to buy what?"

"Lottery ticket for Saturday's draw. I'm sorry to say we didn't win."

"Too bad."

I turned off the tape recorder and anchored my pen in the top of my clipboard. "This has been a big help. I'll stop by with the transcript as soon as I have it done."

I drove back to my place without much hope. It was 2:45 and Solana and Gus would probably be back from the doctor's office. If Solana went into the living room and spotted the empty cubbyhole, she'd know what I'd done. I pulled up in front of my place, parked the car, and scanned the cars on both sides of the street. No sign of Solana's. I could feel my heart rate accelerate. Was it possible I still had time? All I needed was to nip inside, shove everything back in the desk, and make a hasty getaway.

I put my car keys in my bag and crossed Gus's grass, following the walkway to the back door. The checkbook register and the savings passbook were in the bowels of my bag. I had my hand on the documents as I climbed the back steps. I could see the note for the Meals on Wheels volunteer still taped to the glass. I peered in the window. The kitchen was dark.

Ten or fifteen seconds was all I required, assuming the goon wasn't waiting for me in the living room. I took out the key, inserted it in the lock, and turned it. No deal. I held the knob and wiggled the key, by way of coaxing. I looked down in puzzlement, thinking Henry'd given me the wrong key. Not so.

The locks had been changed.

I moaned to myself as I headed down the stairs double-time, worried I'd be caught when I hadn't actually accomplished anything. I cut through the hedge between Gus's backyard and Henry's, and let myself into the studio. I locked my door and sat down at my desk, panic rising in my throat like bile. If Solana realized the check register and passbook were missing, she'd know I'd taken them. Who else? I was the only one who'd been in the house except for the fellow in the bed. Henry'd been there a couple of days before so he'd come under suspicion as well. The dread in my gut felt like a bomb about to go off, but there was nothing to be done. I sat quietly for a moment until I'd caught my breath. What difference did it make now? What was done was done and as long as I was screwed, I might as well see what my thievery had netted me.

I spent the next ten minutes looking at the figures in Gus's bank accounts. It didn't take an accountant to see what was going on. The account that had originally held twenty-two thousand dollars had been reduced by half, all of this in the space of a month. I flipped back through the earlier pages of the passbook. It looked like Gus, in his pre-Solana days, was making deposits of two to three thousand dollars at regular intervals. His check register showed that since January 4, money had been transferred from the one savings account into his checking account with a number of checks then written to Cash. None of the canceled checks were available for inspection, but I'd have bet money his signatures were forged. At the back of the passbook, I came across the pink slip to his car that must have migrated from its proper file. To date, she hadn't transferred ownership from his name to hers. I reviewed the numbers with a shake of my head. It was time to quit cocking around.

I pulled out the phone book and turned to the listings for county offices. I found the number for the Domestic/Elder Abuse Telephone Hotline, which I couldn't help but notice spelled the word "DEATH." It had finally dawned on me that I didn't have to prove Solana was doing anything abusive or illegal. It was up to her to prove she wasn't.

22

The woman who answered the phone at the Tri-Counties Agency for the Prevention of Elder Abuse listened to my brief explanation of the reason for my call. I was transferred to a social worker named Nancy Sullivan and I ended up having a fifteen-minute conversation with her while she took the report. She sounded young and her phone manner suggested she was asking questions from a form she had in front of her. I gave her the relevant information: Gus's name, age, address, Solana Rojas's name and description.

"Does he have any known medical problems?"

"Lots. This whole situation started with a fall that dislocated his shoulder. Aside from the injury, it's my understanding that he suffers from hypertension, osteoporosis, probably osteoarthritis, and maybe some digestive problems."

"What about signs of dementia?"

"I'm not sure how to answer that. Solana Rojas reports signs of dementia, but I haven't seen any myself. His niece in New York talked to him on the phone one day and thought he sounded confused. The first time I went over, he was sleeping, but when I stopped by the next morning he seemed fine. Crabby, but not disoriented or anything like that."

I went on, giving her as much detail as I could. I didn't see a way to mention the financial issues without admitting I'd snitched his bankbooks. I did describe his shakiness earlier that day and Solana's report of a fall, which I hadn't personally witnessed. "I saw the bruises and I was horrified at how thin he is. He looks like a walking skeleton."

"Do you feel he's in any immediate danger?"

"Yes and no. If I thought it was a life-or-death matter, I'd have called the police. On the other hand, I'm convinced he needs help or I wouldn't be on the phone."

"Are you aware of any incidents of yelling or hitting?"

"Well, no."

"Emotional abuse?"

"Not in my presence. I live next door to the guy and I used to see him all the time. He's clearly old, but he managed to get around fine. He used to be the neighborhood crank so it's not like any of us were close to him. Can I ask you a question?"

"Of course."

"What happens now?"

"We'll send out an investigator in the next one to five days. It's too late to get anything on the books until first thing Monday morning, and then someone will be asked to look into it. Depending on the findings, we'll assign a caseworker and take whatever action seems necessary. You may be called on to answer additional questions."

"That's fine. I just don't want his caregiver to know I was the one who blew the whistle on her."

"Don't worry. Your identity and any information you give us is strictly confidential."

"I appreciate that. She might make a guess, but I'd just as soon not have it confirmed."

"We're well aware of the need for privacy."

In the meantime, come Saturday morning, I had other business to take care of, chiefly locating Melvin Downs. I'd made two trips to the residence hotel without results and it was time to get serious. I took the Missile off-ramp and swung over to Dave Levine Street. I parked around the corner on the side street, passing the same used-car lot I'd seen before. The converted milk truck/camper offered at $1,999.99 had apparently been sold and I was sorry I hadn't stopped to take a closer look. I'm not a proponent of recreational vehicles, in part, because long-distance driving isn't a means of travel I find amusing. That said, the milk truck was adorable and I knew I should have bought the damn thing. Henry would have let me park it in the side yard and if I'd ever found myself in financial straits, I could have given up my studio and lived in style.

When I reached the hotel I took the porch steps two at a time and went in the front door. The foyer and downstairs hall were empty so I took myself to Juanita Von's office first floor rear. I found her shifting the past year's files and financial records from the cabinet's drawers to a banker's box.

"I just did that," I said. "How are you?"

"Tired. It's a pain, but it has to be done and I do enjoy the feeling of satisfaction afterwards. You may be in luck this time. I saw Mr. Downs come in a while ago, though he could have gone out without my noticing if he used the front stairs. He's a hard one to catch."

"You know what? I really think I've earned the right

to talk to him even if it is upstairs. This is my third trip over here and if I miss him this time, you'll have to explain yourself to the attorney who's handling this case."

She considered my request, taking her time about it so it wouldn't appear she was moved by the threat. "I suppose just this once. Hold on a second and I'll walk you up."

"I can manage it," I said. Secretly, I was longing for the opportunity to snoop. She was having none of it, perhaps imagining I ran a drop-in hooker service for down-at-heel old men.

Before she left the office she paused to wash her hands and locked up her desk against the possibility of thieves. I followed her out of the office and toward the front door, responding politely as she pointed out features along the way. She began to climb the stairs, pulling herself along by the handrail. I stayed two steps behind her, listening to her labored breathing as we reached the second floor.

"This sitting area on the landing is where the tenants gather of an evening. I provide the color television set and I ask them to be considerate about what they watch. Can't have one individual making all the choices for the group."

The landing was large enough to accommodate two couches, a wide-armed upholstered chair, and three smaller wooden chairs, all with padded seats. I pictured a bunch of old guys with their feet on the coffee table, commenting on sports and cop shows. We turned to the right into a short corridor at the end of which she showed me a big glass-enclosed sunporch and a laundry room. We went down two steps to a hallway that extended along the length of the house. All the room doors were closed, but each had a small brass slot with a card in it, printed with the name of the occupant. I watched the brass numbers climb from 1 to 8, which meant that Melvin Downs's room was probably at the rear of the building, near the top of the back stairs.

We rounded the corner and started up the next flight. It felt like it took six minutes getting from the first floor to the third, but eventually we reached the top. I sincerely hoped she didn't intend to hang around to supervise my conversation with Downs. She accompanied me to his room and had me step to one side while she knocked on his door. She stood politely, with her hands crossed in front of her, giving him time to assemble himself and answer the door.

"Must have gone out again," she remarked, as though I wasn't bright enough to figure that out myself. She tilted her head. "Hold on a minute. That might be him now."

Belatedly, I caught the sound of someone coming up the back stairs. A white-haired man appeared, carrying two empty cardboard wine boxes, one tucked inside the other. He had a long face and pointed elfin ears. Age had eroded channels in his face, and there were deep creases worn into each side of his mouth.

Juanita Von brightened. "There you are. I told Miss Millhone it might be you coming up the stairs. You have a visitor."

He was wearing the rumored black wing tip shoes and the brown leather bomber jacket I'd heard about before. I felt myself smiling and realized until now, I hadn't been convinced that he existed at all. I held my hand out. "How are you, Mr. Downs? I'm Kinsey Millhone. I'm delighted to catch up with you."

His handshake was firm and his manner friendly, underlaid with an element of puzzlement. "I'm not sure I know what this is about."

Mrs. Von stirred, saying, "I'll get back to my work and leave the two of you to talk. With respect to the house rules, I don't allow young ladies to visit in the tenants' rooms with the doors shut. If you'll be more than ten minutes, you can have your conversation in the parlor, which is more appropriate than standing in the hall."

I said, "Thanks."

"No trouble," she said. "Long as I'm up here, I'll look in on Mr. Bowie. He's been under the weather."

"Fine," I said. "I know my way out."

She moved down the stairs and I turned my attention to Downs. "Would you prefer to talk in the parlor?"

"The bus driver on my route told me someone had come around asking questions about me."

"That's all he said? Well, I'm sorry if I took you by surprise. I told him he could fill you in."

"I saw a flyer that said something about a car crash, but I've never been in one."

I took a few minutes to go through my oft-repeated tale about the accident, the lawsuit, and the questions we had about what he'd seen at the time.

He stared at me. "How did you manage to locate me? I don't know anyone in town."

"That was a stroke of luck. I distributed flyers in the neighborhood where the collision occurred. That must have been one of the ones you saw. I included a brief description, and a woman called me saying she'd seen you at the bus stop across from City College. I called MTA, got the route number, and then chatted with the bus driver. He was the one who gave me your name and address."

"You go to this much trouble for something that happened seven months ago? That can't be true. Why now, after all this time?"

"The lawsuit wasn't filed until recently," I said. "Is this upsetting you? Because that wasn't my intention. I just want to ask a few questions about the accident so we can figure out what went on and who was at fault. That's all this is about."

He seemed to pull himself together and shift gears. "I don't have anything to say. It's been months."

"Maybe I can help refresh your memory."

"I'm sorry, but I have something I need to take care of. Maybe another day."

"This won't take long. Just a few quick questions and I'll be out of your hair. Please."

After a pause, he said, "All right, but I don't remember much. It didn't seem important, even at the time."

"I understand," I said. "If you'll recollect, this was the Thursday before Memorial Day weekend."

"Sounds about right."

"You were on your way home from work?"

He hesitated. "What difference does that make?"

"I'm just trying to get a feel for the sequence of events."

"After work, then. That's right. I was waiting for my bus and when I looked up I saw a young woman in a white car pull forward, preparing to turn left out of the City College parking lot."

He came to a stop, as though calculating his responses so he could offer the least information possible without being obvious.

"And the other car?"

"The van was coming from the direction of Capillo Hill."

"Heading east," I said. I was trying to encourage a response without too much prompting. I didn't want him simply feeding back the information I fed him.

"The driver was signaling a right-hand turn and I saw him slow."

He stopped. I shut my mouth and stood there, creating one of those conversational vacuums that usually goads the other guy to speak. I watched him avidly, willing him to proceed.

"Before the girl in the first car completed the turn, the driver in the van accelerated and rammed right into her."

I felt my heart give a thump. "He accelerated?"

"Yes."

"Deliberately?"

"That's what I said."

"Why would he do that? Didn't it seem weird?"

"I didn't have time to think about it. I ran out to see if I could help. It didn't look like the girl was seriously hurt, but the passenger, an older woman, had big problems. I could see it in her face. I did what I could, though it didn't amount to much."

"The younger woman, Ms. Ray, had wanted to thank you for your kindness, but she says the next thing she knew, you'd disappeared."

"I'd done as much as I could. Someone must've dialed 9-1-1. I could hear the sirens so I knew help was on the way. I went back to the bus stop and when the bus came, I got on. That's as much as I know."

"I can't tell you how helpful you've been. This is just what we need. The defendant's attorney will want to take your deposition . . ."

He looked at me as though I'd struck him in the face. "You never said anything about a deposition."

"I thought I mentioned it. It's no big deal. Mr. Effinger will go through this again for the record . . . the same sort of questions . . . but you don't have to worry about that now. You'll get plenty of notice and I'm sure he can set it up so you won't have to miss work."

"I didn't say I'd testify about anything."

"You might not have to. The suit might be dropped or settled and you'll be off the hook."

"I answered your questions. Isn't that enough?"

"Look, I know it's a pain. Nobody likes to get caught up in these things. I can have him call you."

"I don't have a phone. Mrs. Von isn't good about messages."

"Why don't I give you his number and you can contact him? That way, you can do it at your convenience." I took out my notebook and scribbled Lowell Effinger's name and office number.

I said, "I'm sorry for the misunderstanding. I should have made myself clear. As I indicated, there's an outside possibility the matter will be resolved. Even if you testify, Mr. Effinger will make it as painless as possible. I can promise you that."

When I tore off the leaf and passed it to him I caught sight of his right hand. A crude tattoo was visible in the webbing between the thumb and index finger. The area was rimmed with what looked like lipstick red that had faded over time. Two round black dots sat on either side of his knuckle. My first thought was *prison*, which might explain his attitude. If he'd had legal problems in the past, it could account for his balkiness.

He put his hand in his pocket.

I glanced away, feigning interest in the decor. "Interesting place. How long have you lived here?"

He shook his head. "I don't have time to chat."

"No problem. I appreciate your time."

* * *

As soon as I reached my desk I put a call through to Lowell Effinger's office, which was closed for the weekend. His machine picked up and I left a message for Geneva Burt, giving her Melvin Downs's name and address. I said, "Don't let it wait. This guy seems antsy. If you don't hear from him first thing Monday, call his landlady, Mrs. Von. She's a tough old bird and she'll crack the whip."

I gave her the number that rang into Juanita Von's office.

23

Having made the call to the county agency that dealt with elder abuse, I expected to feel relieved. The matter was out of my hands and the investigation of Solana Rojas was someone else's responsibility. In reality, I was uneasy about running into her. I'd worked hard to ingratiate myself in an effort to gain access to Gus, but if I cut off all contact and the investigator showed up asking pointed questions, the obvious conclusion would be that I'd made the call, which of course I had. I didn't know how to maintain even the semblance of innocence. In my heart, I knew Gus's safety took precedence over the risk of Solana's wrath, but I fretted nonetheless. Consummate liar that I am, I was now fearful she'd accuse me of telling the truth.

This is how the system works. A citizen sees an instance of wrongdoing and calls it to the attention of the proper authorities. Instead of being lauded, an aura of guilt attaches. I'd done what I thought was right and now I felt like skulking around, avoiding the sight of her. I could tell myself all day long I was being silly, but I was afraid for Gus, worried he'd pay the price for the call I'd made. Solana wasn't a normal human being. She had a ruthless streak and the minute she figured out what I'd done, she was going to crawl up in my hair and take a shit. It didn't help that we lived in such proximity. I unburdened myself to Henry sitting in his kitchen at the cocktail hour—he with Black Jack over ice, me with my Chardonnay.

"Don't you have business that might take you out of town?" he asked.

"Don't I wish. Actually, if I were gone, suspicion would fall on you."

He waved that worry aside. "I can handle Solana. So can you, if it comes down to it. You did the right thing."

"That's what I keep telling myself, but I do have one teeny tiny transgression to confess."

He said, "Oh, lord."

"It's not *that* bad. The day I was helping Solana with Gus, I took advantage of the moment to lift his check register and one of the passbooks for a savings account."

" 'Lift,' as in stole?"

"Well, yes, if you want to be blunt. That's what prompted me to make the call to the county. It was the first proof I'd seen that she was draining his accounts. The problem is, now that she's changed the locks I don't have a way to put them back."

"Oh boy."

" 'Oh boy' is right. What am I supposed to do? If I hang on to the documents, I can't keep them at my place. What if she figures it out, calls the cops, and gets a search warrant?"

"Why can't you put 'em in your safe-deposit box?"

"But I'd still risk getting caught with them. At the same time, I can't destroy them because if Solana's charged with a crime, that would be evidence. Actually if *I'm* charged with a crime, it's evidence against me."

Henry was shaking his head in disagreement. "Don't think so for three reasons. The documents are inadmissible because they're 'fruit of the poison tree.' Isn't that what it's called when evidence is illegally obtained?"

"Pretty much."

"Besides which, the bank has the same records, so if push comes to shove, the DA's office can subpoena the records from them."

"What's number three? I can hardly wait."

"Seal 'em in an envelope and mail them to me."

"I don't want to put you in jeopardy. I'll figure it out. Really, it's enough to make me want to reform," I said. "Oh, yeah, and there's something else. The first time I went in . . ."

"You've been in *twice*?"

"Hey, the second time she invited me. That's when Gus was stranded in the shower. The first time, I used his house key and made a note of all the medications he was on. I wondered if maybe a drug combination was causing his confusion and making him sleep. The pharmacist I talked to suggested possible pain pill or alcohol abuse, which is neither here nor there. This is the point. When I was cruising through the house, thinking Gus and Solana were gone, I opened the door to the third bedroom and there was this three-hundred-pound *goon* asleep in the bed. Who the hell was he?"

"Might have been the orderly she hired. She mentioned him when I was over there. He comes in once a day to help get Gus on and off the toilet and things like that."

"But why was he sleeping on the job?"

"He might have stayed so she could have a day off."

"Don't think so. She was out with Gus running an errand of some kind. Come to think of it, why wasn't the orderly there to help when she had to get Gus out of the shower?"

"Maybe he'd already come and gone. She said he's paid by the hour so he probably isn't there for long."

"If you see him over there again, let me know. Melanie never said a word about Solana hiring help."

I went back to my place at 7:00 with a buzz on. A happy consequence of my anxiety was my appetite was gone. In the absence of food, I was turning into a drunk. I glanced at my desk and saw the message light blinking on my answering machine. I crossed the room and pressed the Play button.

"Hey, Kinsey. Richard Compton here. Could you give me a call?"

What was this about? I'd done a couple of jobs for the man in the previous week, so maybe he had more. I was willing to do just about anything to keep myself out of my own neighborhood. I dialed the number he left and when he picked up, I identified myself.

"Thanks for returning my call. Look, I'm sorry to bother you on a Saturday night, but I need a favor."

"Sure."

"I have to fly up to San Francisco tomorrow at six A.M. I thought I'd better catch you now instead of calling from the airport."

"Good plan. So what's the favor?"

"I got a message from the fellow in the apartment above the Guffeys' place. He thinks they're getting ready to decamp."

"So the unlawful detainer did the trick?"

"Looks that way."

"That's a blessing."

"A big one. Problem is, I'm gone until Friday and I won't have a chance to do the final inspection and pick up the keys."

"You'll be changing the locks anyway, so why sweat the keys?"

"True, but I made them pay a twenty-dollar key deposit, plus a hundred-dollar cleaning deposit. If someone doesn't go out there, they'll swear up and down the place was immaculate and they left the keys in plain sight. Then they'll turn around and want both deposits back in full. Obviously, you don't have to do it right this minute. Any time before noon on Monday would be fine."

"I can go tomorrow if you like."

"No sense inconveniencing yourself. I'll give 'em a call and tell them you'll be there Monday. You want to give me a time?"

"Eleven fifteen? That way I can take care of it before I break for lunch."

"Good. I'll let them know. I'll be staying at the Hyatt on Union Square if you should need to reach me."

He gave me the phone number of his hotel and I jotted it down. "Look, Richard, I'm happy to help you out, but I'm not in the property management business. You should really hire a professional to handle things like this."

"I could, kiddo, but you're much cheaper. A management company would take ten percent of the gross."

I might have responded, but he'd hung up.

When I left my apartment Monday morning, I found myself scanning the street and the front of Gus's house, hoping to avoid an encounter with Solana. I didn't trust myself to have a civil conversation with her. I started my car and pulled away from the curb in haste, unable to resist the urge to crane my neck for some sign of her. I thought I caught movement at the window, but it was probably a fresh surge of paranoia kicking in.

I reached the office and let myself in. I gathered the mail from Saturday that had been shoved through the slot and now lay in a wide lake on the rug in my reception area. My answering machine was winking merrily. I separated the junk mail and tossed it in the wastebasket while I punched the Play button. The message was from Geneva Burt, in Lowell Effinger's office. She sounded harried, but her Mondays were probably like that. I dialed the law firm while I was in the process of opening the bills, the phone pressed between my right ear and my shoulder in a hands-free hunched position. When Geneva picked up on her end I identified myself and said, "What's up?"

"Oh hi, Kinsey. Thanks for returning my call. I'm having a devil of a time connecting with Mr. Downs."

"He's supposed to call *you*. That's why I gave him your number in the first place. He doesn't have a phone so he gets his messages through his landlady. It seemed simpler all around to have him make the contact since he's so difficult to reach."

"I understand and I passed along your comment about how antsy he is. Mr. Effinger's anxious to take his deposition so he asked me to go ahead and call and get something on the books. I've tried three times this morning and I can't get anyone to pick up. I hate to do this to you, but he's leaning on me so I gotta turn around and lean on you."

"Let me see what I can do. I don't think he works

Mondays so I may be able to catch him at home. You have a date and time set? If so, I'll make sure he puts it on his calendar."

"Not yet. We'll accommodate his schedule once we know what's good for him."

"Great. I'll get back to you as soon as I've talked to him. If he's at all resistant, I'll put him in my car and drive him over there myself."

"Thanks."

I got in my car and looped back up Santa Teresa Street and covered the eight blocks, making the two left turns that put me on Dave Levine. The residence hotel came into view, and for once there was a decent parking place out front. I left my car at the curb and took the porch steps two at a time. I pushed open the door and walked down the hall to Mrs. Von's office in the rear. On the counter there was an old-fashioned punch bell and I gave it a ringy-ding.

A young woman came out of the dining room with a feather duster in one hand. She was in her twenties, her hair skinned back and held in place with blue plastic combs. She wore a T-shirt and jeans, and she had a dust rag caught in a belt loop, like a sous-chef. "May I help you?"

"I'm looking for Mrs. Von."

"She's out running errands."

The phone on the desk behind her began to ring. And ring. And ring. She glanced at it, ignoring the obvious solution, which was to answer it. "Is there something I can help you with?"

The ringing stopped.

"Possibly," I said. "Do you know if Mr. Downs is in?"

"He's gone."

"The man's always gone. Any idea when he'll be back?"

"He moved out. I'm supposed to clean the place, but I haven't gotten to it yet. Mrs. Von's putting a notice in the paper that the room's for rent. That's partly what she's doing while she's out."

"You can't be serious. I talked to him on Saturday and he never said a word. When did he give notice?"

"He didn't. He just packed up and left. Whatever you said to him, you must have scared him away," she said with a laugh.

I stood rooted in place. What in the world would I tell Lowell Effinger? Melvin Downs's statement was crucial to his case and now the guy had cut and run.

"Can I take a look at his room?"

"Mrs. Von wouldn't like that."

"Ten minutes. Please. That's all I ask. She doesn't have to know."

She thought about that and seemed to shrug. "Door's unlocked so you can walk around if you want. Not that there's anything to see. I peeked in first thing to see if he'd left a mess behind. It's clean as a whistle as far as I can tell."

"Thanks."

"Don't mention it. And I mean that. I'm busy cleaning the kitchen. I don't know nuthin' about nuthin' if she catches you."

I took the back stairs this time, worried I'd run into the returning Mrs. Von if I used the main staircase. From below I could hear the ringing of the phone start up again. Maybe the cleaning woman was on orders not to answer it. Maybe Cleaning Personnel Union #409 forbade her taking on duties that weren't specified by contract.

When I got to the third floor, just to be on the safe side, I tapped at Melvin Downs's door and waited a beat. When no one responded to my knock, I checked the hall in both directions and then opened the door.

I stepped into his room with the same heightened sense of danger I felt every time I found myself someplace I wasn't supposed to be, which was much of the time these days. I closed my eyes and inhaled. The room smelled of aftershave. I opened them again and did a visual survey. The dimensions were unexpectedly generous, probably sixteen by twenty feet. The closet was large enough to accommodate a wide chest of drawers with two wooden rods for hanging clothes and a shoe rack attached to the back of the door. Above the hanging rods there were empty wood shelves that reached all the way to the ceiling.

The adjacent bathroom was twelve by twelve with an old cast-iron claw-foot tub and a sink with a wide lip, a small glass shelf above. The toilet had a wooden seat and a wall-mounted tank that was operated by a pull-chain. The floors were covered in a parquet pattern of fake-wood linoleum.

In the main room there was a second chest of drawers, a double bed with a white painted iron bedstead, and two mismatched bed tables. The one table lamp was utilitarian—two seventy-five-watt bulbs, a hanging metal chain, and a plain, yellowing shade that looked scorched in places. When I pulled the chain only one bulb came on. The bed had been stripped and the mattress was folded back on itself, revealing the bedsprings. Melvin had made a tidy pile of the linens that would need to be washed: sheets, pillowcases, mattress cover, bedspread, and towels.

Under a bay of windows on the far wall there was a

wooden table painted white and two unfinished wooden chairs. I crossed to a length of kitchen counter with a short run of cabinets above. I checked the shelves. A set of dishes, six drinking glasses, two cereal boxes, and an assortment of crackers. Knowing Mrs. Von as I did by then, a hot plate or any other cooking equipment would be strictly forbidden.

I began to search in earnest, though I didn't see much in the way of hiding places. I pulled each drawer open, looked in and behind, checked the underside, and then closed it and moved on. Nothing in the wastebasket. Nothing under the chest of drawers. I took one of the kitchen chairs and carried it to the closet so I could climb up and get a clear view of the far reaches of the shelves. I pulled the string that controlled the one naked bulb. The light was dull. At first I thought I'd struck out again, but I could see something in one corner against the wall. I stood on my toes, head down, my arm fully extended as I groped blindly across the dusty shelf. My hand closed over the item and I hauled it into view. It was one of those toys with two parallel wooden sticks, which when squeezed makes a small wooden clown do a somersault. I watched the clown do a couple of flips and then climbed down off the chair. I returned the chair to the kitchenette and stuck the toy in my bag before I moved into the bathroom.

The bathroom hadn't been scrubbed, but neither did it contain anything in the way of information. I did see the cardboard insert from a wine box, folded flat and tucked behind the sink. Melvin Downs had been carrying two wine boxes, one tucked inside the other, when we were introduced. Which meant he was already in the process of packing up his things. Interesting. Something had triggered a hasty departure and I hoped it wasn't me.

I left the room and closed the door behind me. As I headed toward the stairs, I heard the faint strains of a radio from the room across the hall. I hesitated and then knocked on the door. What did I have to lose?

The man who answered was missing his upper front teeth and had a prickling two-day growth of beard.

"Sorry to bother you, but I'm wondering what happened to Melvin Downs."

"Don't know. Don't care. I didn't like him and he didn't like me. Good riddance."

"Is there anyone else I might talk to?"

"Him and the fellow in five watched TV together. Second floor."

"Is he here?"

He closed the door.

I said, "Thanks."

I went out to my car and got in, then sat with my hands on the steering wheel while I considered my options. I glanced at my watch. It was close to eleven o'clock. For the moment, there was nothing I could do. I had the Guffeys to contend with, so I turned the key in the ignition and headed for Colgate. If I didn't get a move on, I'd be late.

24

SOLANA

Sunday morning, Solana stood in the kitchen, breaking up a handful of tablets with a mortar and pestle. The pulverized medication was a new over-the-counter sleep aid she'd purchased the day before. She liked to experiment. The old man was currently sedated and she took the opportunity to place a call to the Other, to whom she hadn't spoken since before Christmas. Given the press of the holidays and her care of the old man, Solana hadn't given the Other much thought. She felt safe where she was. She couldn't see how her past could catch up with her, but it never hurt to keep a finger on the Other's pulse, as it were.

After the usual banal conversation, the Other said, "I had the oddest thing happen. I was in the neighborhood of Sunrise House and stopped by to see the gang and say hi. There's a new woman in the administrator's office and she asked me if I was enjoying my new job. When I said I was in school full-time, she gave me this *look*. I can't even tell you how strange it was. I asked what was wrong and she said a private investigator had come in, doing a background check for a private-duty nursing job. I told her she'd made a mistake, that I wasn't doing private duty."

Solana closed her eyes, trying to determine what this meant. "She must have made a mistake, thinking you were someone else."

"That was my reaction, but while I was standing there, she pulled the folder and pointed out the note she'd entered at the time. She even showed me the woman's business card."

Solana focused on the information with a curious sense of detachment. "Woman?"

"It wasn't a name I'd seen before and I can't remember it now, but I don't like the idea of someone asking personal questions about me."

"I have to go. There's someone at the door. I'll call you later."

Solana hung up. She could feel the heat climb her frame like a hot flash. What alarmed Solana was the fact that the young woman from next door was prying into matters that were none of her concern. The revelation was deeply disturbing, but she couldn't stop and worry about that now. She had other business to take care of. She'd set up an appointment at an art gallery, where she was hoping to off-load the paintings she'd found when she first came to work. She knew nothing about art, but the frames were handsome, and she believed they would bring in a tidy sum. She'd gone through the yellow pages and selected five or six galleries in the fancy-pants part of town. As soon as Tiny helped her load the paintings in the trunk of her car, she'd take off, leaving him to babysit Mr. Vronsky while she was out.

* * *

She left the freeway and took the Old Coast Road, which ran through the part of Montebello known as the Lower Village. There was nothing remotely village-like about the area. It was all high-end retail businesses: custom clothing, interior design shops, architects' offices, real estate offices with color photographs of ten- to fifteen-million-dollar homes in the window. She spotted the gallery in the middle of a line of stores. Parking was at a premium and she circled the block twice before she found a space. She opened the trunk of the convertible and took out two of the six paintings she'd brought. On both, the frames were ornate and she was sure the gold leaf was real.

The gallery itself was plain, long and narrow, no carpet, no furniture except for an expensive antique table with a chair on each side. The lighting was good, calling attention to the thirty or so paintings hung along the walls. Some looked no better than the two she'd carried in.

The woman at the desk looked up with a pleasant smile. "You must be Ms. Tasinato. I'm Carys Mumford. How are you today?"

Solana said, "Fine. I have an appointment with the owner to talk about some paintings I want to sell."

"I'm the owner. Won't you have a seat?"

Solana was slightly embarrassed by the error she'd made, but how was she to know someone so young and attractive would own a ritzy place like this? She'd expected a man, someone older and snooty and easy to manipulate. Awkwardly, she set the paintings down, wondering how to proceed.

Ms. Mumford got up and came around the table, saying, "Mind if I have a look?"

"Please."

She picked up the larger of the two paintings and carried it across the room. She leaned it against the wall, then returned for the second painting, which she placed beside it. Solana watched the woman's expression change. She couldn't decipher the woman's reaction and she felt a moment of uneasiness. The paintings looked okay to her, but maybe the gallery owner thought they were inferior.

"How did you acquire these?"

"They're not mine. I work for the gentleman who hopes to sell them because he needs the cash. His wife bought them years ago, but after she died, he didn't have much use for them. They've been stored in a spare room, just taking up space."

Carys Mumford said, "Do you know these two artists?"

"I don't. I never cared for landscapes myself—mountains and poppies or whatever those orange flowers are. Maybe you're thinking these aren't as good as the paintings you have, but the frames are worth a lot," she said, trying not to sound desperate or apologetic.

Carys Mumford looked at her with surprise. "All you're selling are the frames? I assumed you were talking about the paintings."

"I'd be willing to throw those in. Is something wrong?"

"Not at all. This is a John Gamble, one of the plein-air painters from the early part of the century. His work is highly sought after. I haven't seen a painting of this size in years. The other is by William Wendt, another well-known plein-air painter. If you're not in any hurry, I have two or three clients I'm certain would be interested. It's just a matter of reaching them."

"How long would that take?"

"A week to ten days. These are people who travel most of the year and it's sometimes a trick catching up with them. At the same time, they trust my judgment. If I say these are authentic, they'll take my word for it."

"I'm not sure I should leave them. I'm not authorized to do that," she said.

"That's up to you, though an interested buyer would want to see the painting and perhaps take it home for a few days before making a decision."

Solana could just imagine it. This woman would pass the paintings on to someone else and that's the last she'd ever see of them. "This Gamble fellow . . . what would you say that one's worth?" She could feel her palms dampen. She didn't like negotiating in a situation like this where she wasn't on solid ground.

"Well, I sold a similar painting two months ago for a hundred and twenty-five thousand. Another client, a couple, bought a Gamble from me five or six years ago for thirty-five thousand. Now it's worth a hundred and fifty."

"A hundred and fifty thousand dollars," Solana said. Surely her ears weren't deceiving her.

The Mumford woman went on, "If you don't mind my asking, is there a reason you can't leave these with me?"

"It's not me. It's the gentleman I work for. I might talk him into leaving them for a week, but not longer. I'd need a receipt. I'd need two receipts."

"I'd be happy to oblige. Of course, I'd need to see the two bills of sale from the original purchase or some proof the gentleman actually owns the paintings. It's a formality, but in transactions of this magnitude, the provenance is critical."

Solana shook her head, inventing a back story as

quickly as she could. "Not possible. His wife bought them years ago. There was a fire after that and all his financial records were destroyed. Anyway, what difference does it make after all these years? What matters is the current value. This is an authentic Gamble. A big one. You said so yourself."

"What about an appraisal for insurance purposes? Surely he has a rider on his policy to protect himself in case of loss."

"That I don't know about, but I can ask."

She could see the woman turning the problem over in her mind. This business of provenance was just an excuse to bring the price down. Maybe she thought the painting was stolen, which couldn't be further from the truth. The woman wanted the paintings. Solana could see it in her face, like someone on a diet looking at a rack of doughnuts through a plate-glass window. Finally, the gallery owner said, "Let me think about it and maybe we can find a way. Give me a number where you can be reached and I'll get back to you in the morning."

When Solana left the gallery she had the two receipts in hand. The lesser of the two paintings, the William Wendt, was valued at seventy-five thousand. The other four paintings in the trunk she'd hold on to until she was satisfied she'd been treated well. It was worth waiting a week, if she could have that much cash in hand.

Home again, she found herself brooding on the issue of Kinsey Millhone, who seemed determined to snoop. Solana vividly recalled the first time she'd knocked on Mr. Vronsky's door. She'd despised the girl on sight, staring at her through the pane as though she were a tarantula in one of the glass cases at the Museum of

Natural History. Solana had taken Tiny there often as a child. He was fascinated by the variety of disgusting insects and spiders, hairy things that lurked in corners and under leaves. Some had horns and pincers and hard black carapaces. These loathsome creatures could disguise themselves so cunningly that it was sometimes hard to spot them in the foliage where they hid. Tarantulas were the worst. The display case would appear empty and Solana would wonder if the spider had escaped. She'd lean toward the glass, searching uneasily, and suddenly discover the thing was close enough to touch. This girl was like that.

Solana had opened the door to her, picking up her scent as clearly as an animal's, something feminine and floral that didn't suit her at all. She was slim, in her thirties, with a wiry athletic build. That first encounter, she wore a black turtleneck T-shirt, a winter jacket, jeans, and tennis shoes, with a slouchy-looking leather bag slung over one shoulder. Her dark hair was straight and carelessly cut as if she'd done it herself. Since then, she'd presented herself on numerous occasions, always with the same lame compliments and clumsy questions about the old man. Twice Solana had caught sight of her jogging along State Street early in the morning. She gathered the young woman did this weekday mornings before the sun was up. Solana wondered if she went out before dawn to spy on her. She'd seen her peering into the Dumpster when she passed it on the street. What Solana did, what Solana put there, was none of her business.

Solana forced herself to remain calm and polite in dealing with the Millhone woman, though she kept her fixed in an unrelenting stare. The young woman's brows were lightly feathered, green eyes set in a fringe of dark lashes. The hazel of her eyes was eerie—green with gold flecks and a lighter ring around the iris that made her eyes blaze like a wolf's. Watching her, Solana felt a sensation wash over her that was nearly sexual. They were kindred spirits, dark to dark. Usually Solana could look straight into other minds, but not this one. While Kinsey's manner was friendly, her comments hinted at a curiosity Solana didn't care for. She was someone who took in far more than she let on.

The day she'd offered to go to the market, she'd given herself away. Solana had gone to the kitchen to make up her grocery list. She'd hung a mirror in the kitchen beside the back door and she studied herself now. She was fine. She looked good, exactly as she claimed. Caring, concerned, a woman who had her patient's best interests at heart. When she returned to the living room, purse under one arm, her wallet in hand, she saw that instead of waiting on the porch as she'd been asked, she'd stepped into the house. The gesture was small, but it smacked of willfulness. This was someone who did what she wanted and not as she was told. Solana could tell she'd had a quick look around. What had she seen that day? Solana had longed to scan the room to see if anything was amiss, but she'd kept her gaze pinned on the young woman's face. She was dangerous.

Solana didn't like her persistence, though now that she thought about it, she hadn't seen Kinsey for two or three days. This past Friday she'd gone next door, looking for help getting the old man out of the shower. Mr. Pitts was out and Kinsey had come over instead. Solana hadn't cared which of them it was. Her purpose was to drop the remark about the old man's fall. Not because he'd fallen—how could he when she scarcely let him get out of bed—but as a way of accounting for the fresh bruises on his legs. She hadn't seen Kinsey since and that seemed odd. She and Mr. Pitts were always expressing such concern about the old man so why not now? The two were clearly in cahoots, but what were they up to?

Tiny had told her that Thursday while he was napping, he heard someone moving around in Gus's house. Solana didn't see how it could have been Kinsey, because as far as she knew, the woman didn't have a key. All the same, Solana'd called a locksmith and had the locks changed. She thought back to the Other's tale about the woman investigator asking questions at the senior facility where the two of them had worked. Clearly she'd been sticking her nose where it didn't belong.

Solana went back to the old man's room. He was awake and he'd struggled into a sitting position on the side of his bed. His bare feet dangled and one hand was outstretched, clutching the bed table for support.

She clapped her hands loudly. "Good! You're up. Would you like some help?" She'd startled him so badly she could almost feel the jolt of fear that had shot up his spine.

"Bathroom."

"Why don't you wait here and I'll bring the bedpan. You're entirely too wobbly to be prancing around the house."

She held the bedpan for him, but he couldn't pass any urine. No big surprise. That was just an excuse for his getting out of bed. She couldn't imagine what he thought to accomplish. She'd moved his walker to the empty bedroom so in order to get anywhere, he'd have to creep from room to room, holding on to the furniture for support. Even if he reached the back door, or the front door for that matter, he'd have to negotiate the porch steps and then the sidewalk beyond. She thought she might allow him to escape and get as far as the street before she brought him back. Then she could tell the neighbors he'd taken to wandering off. She'd say, *Poor old thing. In his flimsy pajamas, he could catch his death of cold.* She'd say he'd been hallucinating as well, crazy talk about people being after him.

Mr. Vronsky's efforts had left him shaking, which she could have warned him about if he'd asked. She helped him into the living room so he could watch his favorite television show. She sat beside him on the sofa and apologized for losing her temper. Even though he'd provoked her, she swore it wouldn't happen again. She was fond of him, she said. He needed her and she needed him.

"Without me, you'd have to go into a nursing home. How would you like that?"

"I want to stay here."

"Of course you do and I'll do everything I can to help you. But no complaints. You must never talk to anyone about me."

"I won't."

"That young woman who comes over. You know who I mean?"

The old man nodded, not meeting her gaze.

"If you complain to her—if you communicate in any way—Tiny will hurt her badly and the fault will be yours. Do you understand?"

"I won't say anything," he whispered.

"That's a good boy," she said. "Now that you have me, you'll never be lonely again."

He seemed grateful and humble in the wake of her kindness. When his show was over, as a reward for his good behavior, she fondled him in a way that would help him relax. Afterward, he was docile and she sensed the bond that was building between them. Their physical relationship was new, but she'd bided her time, easing him into it day by day. He'd been raised a gentleman and he'd never admit what she did to him.

She'd been smart to get rid of the volunteer from Meals on Wheels. She didn't like leaving the back door unlocked, and she loathed Mrs. Dell, with her fancy salon hairdo and pricey mink coat. She was totally absorbed in her do-gooder image of herself. If Solana was present when she arrived with the meals, she might offer a pleasantry, but there was no conversation between them, and the woman seldom thought to ask about the old man. Solana had put a halt to the service nonetheless. There was always the chance that she might notice something and report it to someone else.

Monday morning, Solana gave the old man a double dose of his "medicine." He'd sleep for two solid hours, which would give her plenty of time to drive to Colgate and back. She needed to get home to see what Tiny was up to. She couldn't quite count on him to stay put. She thought she'd bring him back to the house again so she'd have help getting Gus in and out of the shower when he woke. As long as she kept a close eye on the old man, it was probably a smart move to let him have visitors now and again. Before she left, she unplugged the phone in his room and stood by the bed, watching him. As soon as his breathing was deep and regular, she put on her coat and picked up her purse and car keys.

As she was turning the thumb lock, she heard the muffled slam of a car door and she stopped in her tracks. An engine started up. She stepped over to the window and stood to one side with her back to the wall. From that angle, she had a truncated view of the street, but she wouldn't be visible to anyone outside. When the blue

Mustang passed, she saw Kinsey lean forward, craning as though to get one more look at the house. What was so interesting?

For the second time, Solana turned and surveyed the room. Her gaze brushed past the desk and came back. There was something different. She crossed the room and stood there, studying the cubbyholes, trying to figure out what had changed. She pulled out the packet of bankbooks and suffered a painful stab of surprise. Someone had taken off the rubber band and removed the passbook for one of the savings accounts. In addition, the checkbook seemed thinner, and when she opened it she realized the register was gone. Oh dear god. Her gaze returned to the window. Two people had been in the house during the past week—Mr. Pitts and the infuriating Kinsey Millhone. One of them had done this, but how had they managed it and when?

As she unlocked the door to her apartment, she knew the place was empty. The television set was dark. The kitchen counters were littered with the dregs of his meals over the past few days. She moved down the short hall to Tiny's room and flipped on the overhead light. She was a neat person by nature and she was always appalled by his slovenly ways. She'd badgered him incessantly as a boy, forcing him to tidy his room before she allowed him to do anything else. By the time he reached his teens, he outweighed her by 150 pounds and all the nagging in the world had no effect. He'd sit and look at her with those big cow eyes, but what she said and what she did had no power to move him. She could beat on him all day long, but it only made him laugh. Next to him, she was small and ineffectual. She'd given up her attempts to change or control him. The best she could hope for now was to confine his messes to the home front. Unfortunately, now that she was spending most of her time with the old man, Tiny felt free to live any way he pleased. She checked the bathroom they shared and was annoyed at the sight of his bloody handprints. Sometimes he liked to punch and cut, and he wasn't always good at cleaning up after himself.

She went into her room and spent a few minutes picking up the panty hose, underwear, and discarded clothing strewn on the floor. Some of the flashier garments she hadn't had occasion to wear in years. Having tidied up, she gathered the articles she wanted to take with her to the old man's house. She was beginning to like it there and she was determined to stay. She'd put the machinery in motion, as she had twice before in her search for permanence. She wanted to set down roots. She wanted to feel free, without having to look over her shoulder to see if the law was catching up with her. She was tired of living like a gypsy, always on the move. She had a fleeting fantasy of life without anyone getting in her way. Mr. Vronsky was tiresome, but he had his uses—for now, at any rate. Her current problem was rounding up Tiny, her Tonto, who usually didn't go far by day. If he disappeared after supper, there was no point in wondering where he'd gone or what he was up to.

She locked the apartment and returned to her car, prepared to circle the neighborhood in search of him. There was a service station with an auto-repair garage where he liked to hang out. Something about the smell of hot metal and grease appealed to him. Also the car wash next door. He liked watching the dirty vehicles go in the one end and come out the other end, clean and dripping with water. He could stand for an hour, looking at the swinging lengths of canvas that swished against the sides and over the tops of the cars. He loved the twisted worms of soap that shot out on the tires and the hot wax spray that made the finish shiny. For a while, she hoped he'd get a job there, wiping the beads of moisture from cars at the end of the run. That was something he could do. Tiny thought about life in concrete terms: what was happening right now, what was set in front of him, what he wanted to eat, what warranted a scolding, what netted him a swat. His view of the world was flat and uncomplicated. He was a man with no curiosity and no personal insight. He had no ambition and no urge to do anything except fritter away his time watching television at home, and then doing whatever he did when he went out. Better not to pursue that issue, she thought.

Solana drove the streets slowly and kept a sharp eye out for the bulk of him. He'd be wearing his denim jacket. He'd have his black watch cap pulled down around his ears. No sign of him at the service station. No sign of him at the car wash. She finally spotted him coming out of the corner minimart. She'd passed the mom-and-pop market before, but he must have been inside, buying cigarettes and candy bars with the money she'd left for him. She slowed to a stop and honked. He lumbered over to the car and got in on the passenger's side, slamming the door. He was smoking a cigarette and chewing gum. What a bumpkin he was.

"Put that out. You know I don't allow you to smoke in my car."

She watched him roll the window down and toss out his lighted cigarette. He stuck his hands in his jacket pockets, clearly tickled about something.

Irritated, she went on. "What are you so happy about?"

"Nofing."

"'Nofing's not a word. Say 'noth-thing.' What's in your pocket?"

He shook his head as though he didn't know what she meant.

"Did you steal something?"

He said no, but his tone was grumpy. He was too simple to lie and she knew by the expression on his face that she'd caught him again. She pulled over to the curb. "Empty your pockets right now."

He made a show of disobeying, but she smacked him in the head and he complied, taking out two small bags of M&M's and a packet of beef jerky.

"What's the matter with you? Last time you did this, I told you never again. Didn't I say that to you? What's going to happen if you get caught?"

She rolled the window down and tossed out the treats. He set up a wail, making the mooing sound that so annoyed her. He was the only person she knew who actually said the word *wah* when he cried. "No more stealing. You hear me? And none of that other stuff. Because you know I can send you back to that ward. Do you remember where you were? Do you remember what they did to you?"

"Yeah."

"Well, they can do that again if I say the word."

She studied him. What was the point in reprimanding the boy? He did what he did in the hours when he was gone. Many days she'd caught sight of his hands, knuckles darkly bruised and swollen like mitts. She shook her head in despair. She knew if she pushed him too far, he'd turn on her as he had in the past.

When she reached the block they lived on she turned down the alleyway, searching for a parking spot. Most of the slots in the carport were empty. The apartment complex behind theirs had a constant turnover of tenants, which meant that parking spaces were available on a shifting basis as renters came and went. She caught sight of a blue Mustang parked in the fire lane at the end of the alley, tucked up along the side of the building.

She couldn't believe her eyes. No one parked there. A sign had been posted saying it was a fire lane and had to be kept clear. Solana rolled on by, turning to stare at the vehicle. She knew whose it was. She'd seen it less than an hour before. What was Kinsey doing here? She could feel the ripples of panic rising in her chest. She made a small sound, somewhere between a gasp and a moan.

Tiny said, "What's the matter," leaving out most of the consonants and flattening the vowels.

She turned from the alleyway onto the street. "We're not stopping here right now. I'll take you to the Waffle House and buy you breakfast. You should quit smoking. It's bad for you."

25

At 11:10 Monday morning, I climbed the stairs to the second floor of the three-story apartment building where the Guffeys lived. I could hear a steady splatting of water and assumed the gardener or a maintenance man was hosing down the walks. I hadn't had the pleasure of meeting Grant Guffey, but his wife was hostile and I wasn't looking forward to another pissing contest. Why had I agreed to do this? During the walk-through, even if I saw great gaping holes in the walls, they'd deny responsibility, swearing up and down that the holes had been there from day one. I didn't have a copy of the inspection sheet they'd signed when they took the place. I knew Compton was meticulous about this phase of the rental process, which was what allowed him to be so tough on his tenants when they moved out. If there was visible damage and the Guffeys protested, we'd be reduced to a ridiculous "Did too! Did not!" argument.

I'd left my car in the alleyway below, parked close to the building at an angle where it wouldn't be visible from their back window. Not that they'd know my car, but a touch of caution is never a bad thing. The spot was posted as a fire lane, but I hoped I wouldn't be there long. If I heard sirens or smelled smoke, I'd run like a little bunny and retrieve my poor vehicle before it was crushed by a fire truck. This was the last time I was doing Compton's dirty work. It wasn't like I was doing it for free, but I had other business to take care of. The specter of Melvin Downs flickered across my mind, bringing with it a slow, heavy dread.

When I reached the top of the stairs I could see a widening pool of water pouring from under the door to Apartment 18. The flood was spilling over the edge of the second-floor walkway, hitting the concrete patio below, creating the illusion of rain I'd heard mere moments before. Oh joy. I waded to the front door, creating ripples as I went. The drapes had been pulled across the windows so I couldn't see in, but when I knocked, the door swung inward on a creaking hinge. In movies, this is the moment when the audience wants to scream a warning: Don't go in there, you twit! A door swinging open usually signifies a body on the floor, and the fearless detective will be blamed for the shooting after foolishly picking up the weapon to inspect it for gunpowder residue. I was too smart for that.

Gingerly, I peered in. The water was now flirting with the tops of my tennis shoes, thus soaking my socks. The place was not only empty, but thoroughly trashed. Water was gushing out of the bathroom from numerous ruptured plumbing fixtures: sink, shower, shattered toilet, and tub. The wall-to-wall carpet had been shredded with a sharp instrument, and the strands leaned away from the rush of water like long waving grass in a fast-moving stream. The kitchen cabinets had been ripped off the wall and left in a splintered pile in the middle of the floor.

If the place had come furnished, all the furniture had been stolen or sold, because aside from a few coat hangers, there was nothing else to be seen. At the rate the water was flowing, I thought it was a safe bet to anticipate a virtual rain forest in the apartment below. My tennis shoes made a squishing sound as I backed out the door.

A man said, "Hey."

I looked up. A fellow was bending over the third-floor railing. I shaded my eyes to see him against the glare.

"Got a problem down there?" he asked.

"Can I use your phone? I need to call the police."

"I figured as much so I called 'em myself. If that's your car out back, you better move it or you'll get ticketed."

"Thanks. Do you have any idea where I can find the water shut-off valve?"

"Clueless."

After moving my car, I spent the next hour with the county sheriff's deputy who'd arrived ten minutes after the call went out. While I waited, I'd gone down to Apartment 10 and knocked but couldn't rouse anyone. The tenants were probably off at work and wouldn't learn of the watery disaster until five o'clock that day.

The deputy managed to get the water turned off, which brought out a second round of tenants, outraged and distressed by the interruption to their service. One woman emerged, wrapped in a terry-cloth bathrobe, her hair in a helmet of bubbling shampoo.

I borrowed the upstairs neighbor's phone and called the Hyatt in San Francisco, swearing I'd leave him money for the long-distance charges. Miraculously, Richard Compton was in his hotel room. When I told him what was going on, he said, "Shit!"

He gnawed on the problem for a moment and then said, “Okay. I’ll take care of it. Sorry to put you through this.”

“You want me to call a restoration company about the water damage? They can at least get big fans and dehumidifiers out here. If you don’t get right on it, the floors will warp and you’ll have mold growing in the walls.”

“I’ll get the manager from another building started on that. He can call the company we use. Meantime, I’ll get in touch with my insurance agent and have him send someone out.”

“I guess the Guffeys won’t be getting their deposit back.”

He laughed, but not much.

After we’d hung up, I took a moment to assess the situation.

Between Melvin Downs’s disappearance and the Guffeys’ vandalism, I didn’t see how things could get worse. Which just goes to show how little I know about life.

The rest of Monday was uneventful. Tuesday morning, I took my metaphorical hat in hand and met with Lowell Effinger to deliver the news about Melvin Downs. I’d seen Effinger on two previous occasions and our dealings thereafter had been conducted on the phone. Sitting across the desk from him, I noticed how tired he looked, smoky gray pouches under his eyes. He was a man in his early sixties with a tangle of curly hair that had turned from salt and pepper to white since I’d seen him last. He had a strong chin and jaw, but his face looked as crumpled as a paper bag. I wondered if he had personal problems, but I didn’t know him well enough to ask. He spoke in a deep voice that rumbled up from his chest. "You know where he worked?"

"Not specifically. Probably near City College because that's where he caught the bus. When the driver told me where he lived, I was so busy trying to connect with him there, I didn't worry about where he worked."

"If he moved out of his room, he probably quit his job, don't you think?"

"Well, it's worth pursuing in any event. I'll go back over to the hotel and talk to Mrs. Von. I've seen her so often she might as well adopt me by now. She claims a policy of minding her own business, but I'll bet she knows more than she's told me so far. I can also talk to some of the other residents while I'm there."

"Do what you can. If nothing turns up in the next few days, we'll revisit the issue."

"I wish I'd been quicker. When I talked to him Saturday, he gave no indication he was planning to leave. Of course, he'd just gone out and scored a couple of cardboard boxes, but it didn't occur to me he'd be using them to *pack*."

Thirty minutes later I found myself at the residence hotel for the umpty-ninth time. This round, I caught Mrs. Von coming out of the kitchen with a cup of tea in hand. She wore a sweater over her housedress, and I could see a peek of the tissue she'd tucked up her sleeve. "You again," she said, but with no particular animosity.

"I'm afraid so. Do you have a minute?"

"If it's in reference to Mr. Downs, I have all the time you want. He left without giving notice so that does it for me. This is my afternoon off so if you'd care to come into my apartment, we can talk."

"Happy to," I said.

"Would you like a cup of tea?"

"No, thanks."

She opened a door at the rear of the office. "This was originally the servants' quarters," she remarked as she went in.

I trailed behind her, taking in the rooms at a glance.

"In my grandparents' day, servants were expected to be invisible unless they were hard at work. This was their parlor and the anteroom where they took all their meals. The cook prepared food for them, but nothing like the meals that were served in the formal dining room. The servants' bedrooms were in the attic, above the third floor."

She was using the two rooms as a bedroom and sitting room, both done in pinks and mauves, with a surfeit of family photographs in silver-plated frames. Four Siamese cats lounged on the furniture, barely stirring from their morning naps. Two regarded me with interest, and one eventually got up, stretched, and crossed the room to take a little sniff of my hand.

"Don't mind them. They're my girls," she said. "Jo, Meg, Beth, and Amy. I'm Marmee," she said. She took a seat on the sofa, setting her teacup to one side. "I assume your interest in Mr. Downs has to do with the lawsuit."

"Exactly. You have any guesses about where he went? He must have family somewhere."

"He has a daughter in town. I don't know her married name, but I'm not sure it matters. The two are estranged and they have been for years. I don't know the details, except that she refuses to let him see his grandsons."

"Sounds meanspirited," I said.

"I wouldn't know. He only mentioned her the once. Naturally my ears pricked up."

"Did you ever notice the tattoo on his right hand?"

"I did, though he seemed so self-conscious about it I tried not to look. What did you make of it?"

"I suspect he'd been in prison."

"I wondered about that myself. I will say in the time he lived here, his behavior was exemplary. As far as I was concerned, as long as he kept his room neat and paid his rent on time, I saw no reason to pry. Most people have secrets."

"So if you knew he'd been convicted of a crime, it wouldn't have precluded your taking him as a tenant."

"That's what I said."

"You know what kind of work he did?"

She thought about that briefly and then shook her head. "Nothing that required a degree. He said more than once how much he regretted not finishing high school. Wednesday nights, when he came in late, I thought he was attending night school. 'Adult education,' I believe they call it these days."

"When he first showed up looking for a room, did he fill out an application?"

"He did, but after three years, I destroy them. I have enough paper cluttering my life. Truth is, I'm mighty careful about my tenants. If I'd thought he was a man of low character, I'd have turned him down, whether he'd been in prison or no. As I recall, he listed no personal references, which struck me as odd. On the other hand, he was clean and well spoken, clearly intelligent. He was also gentle by nature, and I never heard him swear."

"I guess if he had something to hide, he'd be too smart to put it on an application."

"That'd be my guess as well."

"I understand he was chummy with a guy on the second floor. You mind if I talk to him?"

"Talk to anyone you like. If Mr. Downs had been honorable about giving notice, I'd have kept my observations to myself." She paused to look at her watch. "Now unless you need something more, I'd best get on with my day."

"What's the name of the gentleman in room number five?"

"Mr. Waibel. Vernon."

"Is he in?"

"Oh, yes. He lives on his disability checks and seldom goes out."

26

Vernon Waibel was a bit more friendly than Melvin's third-floor neighbor, who'd shut the door in my face. Like Downs, Waibel was in his fifties. He had dark brows and dark eyes. His gray hair was thinning and shaved close, as though to anticipate the baldness to come. Like someone facing chemotherapy, he preferred taking charge of the hair loss himself. His skin was tawny, his neck creased from exposure to the sun. He wore a multicolored cotton sweater in earth tones, chinos, and moccasins without socks. Even the tops of his feet were brown. I wondered how he managed to tan if he seldom went out. I saw no evidence of disability, but that wasn't my concern.

I went through the usual, hi-how-are-you stuff. "I hope I'm not disturbing you."

"Depends on what you want."

"I understand Mr. Downs moved out. You have any idea where he went?"

"You a cop?"

"Private detective. He was supposed to be deposed as

a witness to an automobile accident and I need to track him down. He's not guilty of wrongdoing. We just need his help."

"I got a little time to talk if you want to come in."

I thought about Juanita Von's rule about no women visitors in a tenant's room with the door shut. She and I were such good friends by now I thought I'd risk her disapproval. "Sure."

He stepped back and I passed in front of him. His room was not as large as Downs's, but it was cleaner and it had a lived-in feel to it. The furnishings had been augmented with personal items: two plants, a sofa with throw pillows, and a quilt folded over the iron bedstead. He gestured toward the only upholstered chair in the room. "Take a seat."

I sat down and he settled on a plain wooden chair nearby. "You the one put that flyer out about him?"

"You saw that?"

"Yes, ma'am. I did and so did he. Made him nervous, I'll tell you that."

"Is that why he left?"

"He was here and now he's not. Draw your own conclusions."

"I'd hate to think I was the one who scared him away."

"I can't speak to that, but if you're here to ask questions, you might as well get to 'em."

"How well did you know him?"

"Not well. We watched television together, but he never said much. Nothing personal, at any rate. We're both fans of that channel that runs the old movie classics. *Lassie*, *Old Yeller*, *The Yearling*—things like that. Stories that broke your heart. That's about all we had in common, but it was enough."

"Did you know he was leaving?"

"He didn't consult me, if that's what you mean. Neither one of us was looking for a friend, just someone who wouldn't hog the TV when we were hell-bent on hogging it ourselves. *Shane* was another movie he liked. Times we'd be sitting there bawling like babies. Pitiful, but there you have it. Feels good to have a reason to let it all hang out."

"How long have you known him?"

"The five years since he moved in."

"You must have learned something about the man."

"Surface stuff. He was good with his hands. TV went on the blink, he'd tinker until he got it up and running again. He had a knack for anything mechanical."

"For instance?"

He thought briefly. "The grandfather clock in the parlor quit running and Mrs. Von couldn't find anyone to come take a look. She had a couple of numbers for clock-repair guys, but one was dead and the other had retired. Melvin said he wouldn't mind having a go at it. Next thing you know he had it working again. I'm not sure he did us any favors. Middle of the night, I can hear it all the way up here. Times I can't sleep, I count every chime. Four times an hour—it's enough to drive me insane."

"What'd he do for a living?"

"Beats me. He didn't volunteer information of that type. I live on disability so maybe he thought I'd feel bad, him working and me not. He was paid in cash, I know that much, so it might have been something under the table."

"Someone suggested yard work or maybe household repairs."

"I'd say more skilled, though I couldn't tell you what. Small appliances, electronics, something like that."

"What about family?"

"He'd been married once upon a time because he mentioned his wife."

"You know where he was from?"

"Nope. He did say he had some money saved and he had his eye on a truck."

"I didn't think he drove. Why else would he take the bus back and forth across town?"

"He had a license, but no vehicle. That's why he was in the market for one."

"Sounds like he meant to hit the road."

"Might have."

"What about the tattoo on his hand? What was that about?"

"He was an amateur ventriloquist."

"I don't get the connection."

"He could throw his voice, like that Señor Wences guy on the old *Ed Sullivan Show.* He'd flatten his thumb along his index finger and make it move like a mouth. The red in the web between his index finger and his thumb were the lips and the two dots on the knuckle were the eyes. He made like she was a little pal of his named Tía—'Auntie' in Spanish—the two of them talking back and forth. I only saw him do it once, but it was funny. I found myself talking to her like she was real. I guess everybody's got a talent of some kind, even if it's an act you lifted from someone else."

"Had he been in prison?"

"I asked him about that once. He admitted he served time, but he wouldn't say what for." He hesitated, easing a sly peek at his watch. "I don't mean to cut you short, miss, but I got a program about to come on and if I don't get down there, the other fellows on the floor will be all over the set."

"I think that about covers it. If you think of anything

else, could you give me a call?" I found a business card in my bag and gave it to him.

"Sure thing."

We shook hands. I slung my bag across one shoulder and moved to the door. He stepped ahead of me and opened it like a gent.

He said, "I'll just follow you down the hall since I'm headed that way."

We'd nearly reached the landing when he said, "If you want my opinion?"

I turned and looked at him.

"I'd bet you dollars to doughnuts, he didn't leave town."

"Why?"

"He had grandsons."

"I heard he wasn't allowed to see them."

"Doesn't mean he didn't find a way."

As it turned out, the investigator for the Tri-Counties Agency for the Prevention of Elder Abuse was the very same Nancy Sullivan I'd spoken to on the phone, which I learned when she appeared in my office on Friday afternoon. She must have been in her twenties, but she looked a scant fifteen. Her hair was shoulder-length and straight. She had a plain, earnest air about her, leaning forward slightly in her chair, feet together, while she explained what she'd learned in the course of her investigation. The jacket and midcalf skirt she wore looked like they'd been ordered from a travel clothing catalog, a wrinkle-free fabric you could wear for hours on a plane and later wash in a hotel sink. She wore sensible low-heeled shoes and opaque stockings through which I could see evidence of spider veins. At her age? That was troubling. I tried to picture her in a conversation with Solana Rojas, who was so much older, smarter, and wiser in the ways of the world. Solana was cunning. Nancy Sullivan seemed sincere, which is to say clueless. No contest.

After an exchange of pleasantries, she told me she was filling in for one of the investigators usually assigned to evaluate cases of suspected abuse. As she spoke, she tucked a strand of hair behind her ear and cleared her throat. She went on to say she'd talked to her supervisor who'd asked her to do the preliminary interviews. Any follow-up queries deemed necessary would be referred back to one of the regular investigators.

So far it sounded reasonable, and I was politely nodding away like a bobble-head doggie on an auto dashboard. Then, as though by extrasensory perception, I started hearing sentences she hadn't actually said. I felt a small thrill of fear. I knew for a pluperfect fact she was going to drop a bomb.

She took a manila folder from her briefcase and opened it on her lap, sorting through her papers. "Now my findings," she said. "First of all, I want to tell you how much we value the call you made . . ."

I found myself squinting. "This is bad news, isn't it?"

Startled, she laughed. "Oh, no. Far from it. I'm sorry if I gave you that impression. I talked to Mr. Vronsky at length. Our procedure is to make an unannounced visit so the caretaker won't have an opportunity to set the scene, so to speak. Mr. Vronsky wasn't ambulatory, but he was alert and forthcoming. He did seem emotionally fragile and in moments, he was disoriented, none of which was surprising in a man of his age. I asked him a number of questions about his relationship with Mrs. Rojas, and he had no complaints. In fact, quite the contrary. I asked him about his bruises . . ."

"Solana was present through all of this?"

"Oh, no. I asked her to give us time alone. She had work to do so she went about her business while we chatted. Later I talked to her separately as well."

"But she was in the house?"

"Yes, but not in the same room."

"That's happy news. I trust you kept my name out of it."

"That wasn't necessary. She said you told her you were the one who called."

I stared at her. "You're kidding me, right?"

She hesitated. "You didn't tell her it was you?"

"No, dear, I didn't. I'd have to be out of my mind to do such a thing. First words out of her mouth and she's bullshitting you. That was a fishing expedition. She made an educated guess and looked to you for confirmation. Bingo."

"I didn't confirm anything and I certainly didn't tell her who called. She mentioned your name in the context of the dispute because she wanted to set the record straight."

"I'm not following."

"She said the two of you had an argument. She says you distrusted her from the moment she was hired so you were constantly on her case, coming over uninvited to check up on her."

"That's crap for starters. I'm the one who did the background investigation that cleared her for the job. What else did she tell you? I'd be fascinated to hear."

"I probably shouldn't be repeating this, but she mentioned that the day you saw Mr. Vronsky's bruises, you accused her of hurting him and threatened to call the authorities to file a complaint."

"She invented that story to discredit me."

"Perhaps there was a misunderstanding between the two of you. I'm not here to judge. It's not our job to mediate in situations like this."

"Situations such as *what*?"

"People sometimes call when a question comes up about patient care. Usually it's a disagreement between family members. In an effort to prevail . . ."

"Look, there was no disagreement. We never had a conversation on the subject at all."

"You didn't go to Mr. Vronsky's house a week ago to help her get him out of the shower?"

"Yes, but I didn't accuse her of anything."

"But wasn't it after that incident you called the agency?"

"You know when it was. You're the person I spoke to. You said the call was confidential and then you gave her my name."

"No, I didn't. Mrs. Rojas brought it up. She said you told her you were the one who turned her in. I never responded one way or the other. I would never breach confidentiality."

I slouched down on my spine, my swivel chair squeaking in response. I'd been screwed and I knew it, but I couldn't keep pounding on the same point. "Skip it. This is dumb. Just get on with it," I said. "You spoke to Gus and then what?"

"After I spoke with Mr. Vronsky, I had a conversation with Mrs. Rojas and she gave me some of the specifics of his medical status. She talked about his bruises in particular. His anemia was diagnosed when he was in the hospital, and while his blood count's improved, he's still prone to bruising. She showed me the lab reports, which were consistent with her claim."

"So you don't believe he's being physically abused."

"If you'll bear with me, I'm getting to that. I also talked to Mr. Vronsky's primary-care physician and the orthopedist who treated him for his shoulder injury. They say his physical condition's stable, but he's frail and unable to manage on his own. Mrs. Rojas said when she was hired, he was living in such filth she had to get a Dumpster . . ."

"What's that have to do with it?"

"There are also questions about his mental competence. He hasn't paid his bills in months and his doctors both feel he lacks the capacity to give informed consent for his medical treatment. He's also unable to see to his daily needs."

"Which is why she's able to take advantage of him. Don't you get that?"

Her expression became prim, nearly stern. "Please let me finish." She shifted some papers uneasily. Her earnestness returned as though she were moving on to a far brighter note. "What I hadn't realized, and you may not have been aware of this yourself, is that Mr. Vronsky's situation has already come to the attention of the court."

"The court? I don't understand."

"A petition for appointment of a temporary conservator was filed a week ago, and after an emergency hearing a private professional conservator was assigned to manage his affairs."

"A 'conservator'?" I felt like a half-witted parrot, repeating her words, but I was too astonished to do much else. I sat upright and leaned toward her, gripping the edge of the desk. "A *conservator*? Are you nuts?"

I could tell she was flustered because half of the papers slid from her manila folder and spilled out across the floor. In haste, she bent down and swept them into a pile, trying to talk while she gathered everything together.

"It's like a legal guardian, someone to oversee his health care and his finances . . ."

"I know what the word *means.* I'm asking you who? And if you tell me it's Solana Rojas, I'll blow my brains out."

"No, no. Not at all. I have the woman's name right here." She looked down at her notes, her hands shaking as she turned pages right side up and arranged them in rough order. She licked an index finger and sorted through the file until she found what she was looking for. She picked up the paper and turned it toward me as she read the name. "Cristina Tasinato."

"Who?"

"Cristina Tasinato? She's a private professional . . ."

"You said that! When did this happen?"

"Late last week. I've seen the paperwork myself and it was properly executed. Ms. Tasinato worked through an attorney and she put up a bond, which she's required to do by law."

"Gus doesn't need some *stranger* stepping in to take charge of his life. He has a niece in New York. Didn't anyone talk to her? She must have some rights in this."

"Of course. Under probate law, a relative has priority when it comes to an appointment as conservator. Mrs. Rojas mentioned the niece. Evidently, she spoke to her on three separate occasions, describing his condition and begging her to help. Ms. Oberlin couldn't spare the time. Mrs. Rojas felt a conservator was imperative to Mr. Vronsky's well-being . . ."

"That's a complete crock of shit. I talked to Melanie myself and it wasn't like that at all. Sure, Solana called her, but she gave no indication he was in trouble. If she'd known, Melanie would have flown out in a heartbeat."

The prim mouth again. "Mrs. Rojas says otherwise."

"Isn't there supposed to be a hearing?"

"Ordinarily, yes, but in an emergency, the judge can go ahead and grant the request, pending investigation by the court."

"Oh, right. And suppose the court does the same nifty job you did? Where does that leave Gus?"

"There's no need to get personal. All of us have his best interests at heart."

"The man can speak for himself. Why was this done without his knowledge or consent?"

"According to the petition, he has a hearing deficit in addition to periods of confusion. So even if there had been a regular court hearing, he wouldn't have been competent to attend. Mrs. Rojas said you and his other neighbors don't fully comprehend the kind of trouble he's in."

"Well, we sure as fuck know now. How'd this Tasinato woman get wind of it?"

"She might have been contacted by the convalescent facility or one of his physicians."

"So however this went down, she now has total control over him? Finances, real property, medical treatment? All of it?"

Ms. Sullivan declined to respond, which I found infuriating.

"What kind of idiot are you! Solana Rojas played you for a fool. She played us all for fools. And look at the result. You've handed him over to a pack of wolves."

The color was rising in Nancy Sullivan's face and she looked down at her lap. "I don't think we should continue the conversation. You might prefer to talk to my supervisor. I discussed this with her this morning. We thought you'd be relieved . . ."

"Relieved?"

"I'm sorry if I upset you. I may have presented it wrong. If so, I apologize. You called, we've looked into it, and we're convinced he's in capable hands."

"I beg to differ with you."

"I'm not surprised. You've been antagonistic since I sat down."

"Stop. Just stop. This is pissing me off. If you don't get the hell out, I'll start screaming at you."

"You've already screamed," she said tightly. "And believe me, this will go in my report." While she shoved papers in her briefcase and gathered her belongings, I could see the tears splashing down her cheeks.

I put my head in my hands. "Shit. Now I'm the villain of the piece."

27

The minute she was out the door, I grabbed my jacket and shoulder bag and trotted over to the courthouse, where I entered a side door and climbed the wide red-tile steps to the corridor above. Arches in the stairwell were open to the chill winter air and my footsteps echoed against the mosaic tile walls. I went into the county clerk's office and filled out a form, requesting the file on Augustus Vronsky. I'd been in the same place seven weeks previously, doing the background check on Solana Rojas. Clearly, I'd screwed that up, but I wasn't sure how. I sat in one of the two wooden chairs while I waited, and six minutes later I had the record in hand.

I moved to the far side of the room and sat down at a table, occupied largely by a computer. I opened the file and leafed through, though there wasn't much to see. I was looking at a standard four-page form. A pale *X* had been typed into various boxes running down the page. I flipped to the end of the document, where I noted the name of the attorney representing Cristina Tasinato, a man named Dennis Altinova, with an address on Floresta. His phone and fax numbers were listed, as was an address for Cristina Tasinato. Flipping back to the first page, I started again, scanning the headings and subheadings, seeing what I already knew. Augustus Vronsky, designated the conservatee, was a resident of Santa Teresa County. Petitioner was not a creditor or debtor or agent of either. Petitioner was Solana Rojas, asking the court to appoint Cristina Tasinato as conservator for the person and estate of the conservatee. I suspected Solana was at the heart of the matter, but it was still a jolt to see her name neatly typed in the box.

Under "Character and estimated value of the property of the estate," all the particulars were declared "Unknown," including real property, personal property, and pensions. A box was also ticked stating that the conservatee was unable to provide for his or her personal needs for physical health, food, clothing, or shelter. Supporting facts were apparently spelled out in an attachment that was part of the Confidential Supplemental Information and Petition "on file herein." There was no sign of the document, but that's what the term "confidential" implies. In the paragraph below that, a box was ticked indicating that Gus Vronsky, proposed conservatee, was "substantially unable to manage his or her financial resources or resist fraud or undue influence." Again, supporting facts were specified in the Confidential Supplemental Information, which had been filed with the petition but was unavailable as part of the public record. The signatures of the attorney, Dennis Altinova, and the conservator, Cristina Tasinato, were penned at the end. The document had been filed with the Santa Teresa Superior Court on January 19, 1988.

Also part of the file was an invoice for "Caregiver management" costs, broken down according to fees, month, and running total. For the latter half of December 1987 and the first two weeks in January 1988, the amount requested was $8,726.73. That sum was substantiated by an invoice from Senior Health Care Management, Inc. There was also an invoice submitted by the attorney for professional services as of January 15, 1988, listing dates, hourly rates, and the amount charged off to the conservatorship. The balance due him was $6,227.47. These expenses had been submitted for court approval, and just in case the routing of funds wasn't clear, the note at the end read, "Please make checks payable to Dennis Altinova: senior attorney time, $200.00/hour; associate attorney time, $150.00/hour; paralegal time, $50.00/hour." Between them, the newly appointed conservator and her attorney had racked up charges totaling $14,954.20. I was surprised the attorney hadn't attached a stamped, self-addressed envelope to speed the payment along.

I marked the pages I wanted reproduced—which is to say, all of them—and returned the file to the clerk. While I waited for copies, I borrowed a phone book and looked up Dennis Altinova in the white pages. Under his office address and phone number, his home address and home phone were listed, which surprised me. I don't expect doctors and lawyers to make personal information available to anybody smart enough to check. Apparently, Altinova wasn't that worried about being stalked and killed by a disgruntled client. The neighborhood he lived in was pricey, but in Santa Teresa even houses in the shabby parts of town cost staggering amounts. There were no other Altinovas in evidence. I checked the listings for Rojas: many, but no Solana. I looked for the name Tasinato: none.

When the clerk called my name, I paid for the copies and tucked them in my bag.

* * *

Dennis Altinova's office on Floresta was half a block from the courthouse. The police station was on the same street, which came to a dead end at the point where the Santa Teresa High School property picked up. In the other direction, Floresta crossed State Street, ran past the downtown, and eventually butted up against the freeway. Lawyers had staked out the area, settling in to cottages and assorted small buildings whose original tenants had moved on. Altinova was renting a small suite of offices on the top floor of a three-story building with an off-brand savings and loan at street level. If I remembered correctly, the space had once been devoted to an upholsterer's shop.

I studied the directory in the lobby, which really amounted to little more than a walk-in pantry where you could wait for an elevator that moved with all the speed and grace of a dumbwaiter. The rents here weren't cheap. The location was prime, though the building itself was woefully out of date. The owner probably couldn't bear to sacrifice the time, energy, and money required to move tenants out and do a proper remodeling job.

The elevator arrived, a four-by-four cubicle that jerked and shuddered throughout my creeping ascent. This gave me time to examine safety inspection dates and speculate about how many people it would take to exceed the weight limit, which was 2,500 pounds. I figured ten guys at 250 pounds apiece, assuming you could squeeze ten guys into a contraption that size. Twenty women at 125 pounds each was out of the question.

I exited on three. The floor in the corridor was a speckled black-and-white terrazzo marble, rubble in other words, bound with white cement, white sand, and pigment, and reformed as tile. The walls were paneled in oak that was darkened by time. Oversized windows at either end of the hall let in daylight that was augmented by rafts of fluorescent tubing. The entrance doors to the offices were pebbled glass with the names of the occupants stenciled in black. I thought the effect was charming, suggestive as it was of lawyers' and detectives' offices in old black-and-white movies.

Altinova's office was midway down the hall. The door opened into a modest reception area that had been modernized by the addition of a desk made of stainless steel and poured glass. The desktop was bare except for a four-line telephone console. The lighting in the room was indirect. The chairs—four of them—looked as though they'd make your butt go numb minutes after you sat down. There were no side tables, no magazines, no art, and no plants. Certain "interior designers" do shit like this and call it minimalism. What a joke. The place looked like the tenant had yet to move in.

A receptionist came through a door in the back wall marked "private." She was a tall, cool blonde, too pretty to imagine she wasn't banging the boss.

"May I help you?"

"I wonder if I might have a quick word with Mr. Altinova." I thought the word "quick" struck a nice note.

"You have an appointment?"

"Actually, I don't. I was over at the courthouse and decided I'd chance it. Is he in?"

"Can you tell me what this is regarding?"

"I'd prefer to discuss it with him."

"Were you referred?"

"No."

She didn't like my responses so she punished me by breaking off eye contact. Her face was a perfect oval, as smooth, pale, and unblemished as an egg. "And your name is?"

"Millhone."

"Pardon?"

"Millhone. M-I-L-L/H-O-N-E. Accent on the first syllable. Some people pronounce it 'Malone,' but I don't."

"I'll see if he's free."

I was reasonably certain he didn't know who I was, and if he did know, I was hoping he'd be curious what I was up to. I was curious myself. I knew he wouldn't give me a snippet of information. Primarily, I wanted to lay eyes on the man who'd drafted the legal papers that eradicated Gus Vronsky's autonomy. Also, I thought it might be interesting to shake the tree to see if anything ripe or rank hit the ground.

Two minutes later the man himself appeared, holding on to the frame while he stuck his head around the door. Good move on his part. If he'd invited me into his office, he might have given the impression he was interested in what I had to say. His coming out to the reception desk implied that:

(a) he could disappear at will,

(b) that my business wasn't worth sitting down for, and

(c) therefore I'd better get to the point.

I said, "Mr. Altinova?"

"What can I do for you?" His tone was as flat and hard as the look in his eyes. He was tall and dark-haired with sturdy black-framed glasses resting on a sturdy outcrop of nose. Good teeth, fleshy mouth, and a cleft chin so pronounced it looked as if someone had taken a hatchet to his face. I placed him in his late sixties, but he looked fit and he carried himself with the vigor (or perhaps testiness) of someone younger. The receptionist peered over his shoulder from the hallway, watching our interchange like a kid hoping to see a sibling get bawled out and sent to her room.

"I'm looking for a woman named Cristina Tasinato."

His expression showed nothing, but he did peer around the door with mock curiosity, scanning the reception area as though Ms. Tasinato might be playing hide-and-seek in the nearly empty room. "Can't help."

"Name doesn't ring a bell?"

"What sort of work do you do, Ms. Millhone?"

"I'm a private investigator. I have some questions for Ms. Tasinato. I was hoping you could put me in touch."

"You know better than that."

"But she's a client of yours, yes?"

"Ask someone else. We have nothing to discuss."

"Her name appears with yours on a document I saw at the courthouse just now. She was appointed conservator for a man named Gus Vronsky. I'm sure you've heard of him."

"Nice meeting you, Ms. Millhone. You can let yourself out."

Witty rejoinders in short supply, I said, "I appreciate your time."

He closed the door abruptly, leaving me on my own. I waited a beat, but his lovely receptionist didn't reappear. I couldn't believe she was passing up the opportunity to lord it over me. On the pristine glass desktop, line one on the telephone console lit up—Altinova, no doubt, putting a call in to Cristina Tasinato. The desktop was otherwise bare so I couldn't even see a way to snoop. I let myself out as instructed and took the stairs down, not willing to risk the elevator, which was little more than a rickety box hanging by a string.

* * *

I retrieved my car from the public parking garage, circled the block, and headed up Capillo Hill, in my eternal search for Melvin Downs. Having suffered the indignity of Altinova's rebuff, I needed the soothing effects of routine work. Where Capillo crossed Palisade, I took a left and continued on Palisade until I saw the campus of Santa Teresa City College coming up on my right. The bench at the bus stop was empty. I cruised down the long hill that curved away from the campus. At the bottom there was a small nest of businesses: minimart, liquor depot, and a cluster of motels. If Melvin Downs did maintenance or custodial work, it was hard to believe he was employed only two days a week. Those were full-time jobs, 7:00 A.M. to 3:00 P.M., or hours along those lines. Besides which, the hill itself was long and steep, which meant he'd have had to trudge up that half mile at the end of his workday. Why do that when there was a bus stop half a block in the other direction, closer to the beach?

Back up the hill I went. This time I drove past the college and down as far as the two strip malls at the intersection of Capillo and Palisade. Here my choices were many and varied. On my left there was a large drugstore and, behind it, an independent market that handled local organic produce and other natural foodstuffs. Perhaps Melvin unloaded crates or bagged groceries, or maybe he'd been hired to keep the aisles swept and mopped. I parked in the drugstore lot and went in. I did a walk-through, scanning each aisle as I passed. There was no sign of him. This was Tuesday and if he still worked in the neighborhood, he'd be finishing up in an hour or two. I went out the front exit.

Still on foot, I crossed the street. Walking the length of the mall to my right, I passed two mom-and-pop restaurants, one serving Mexican fare and one leaning more toward the breakfast and lunch trade. I glanced through the window at a shoe repair shop, cased the Laundromat, a jewelry store, and the pet-grooming establishment next door. The last small business was a discount shoe store, trumpeting a GOING-OUT-OF-BUSINESS SALE! EVERYTHING REDUCED 30 TO 40 PERCENT. The store was bereft of customers so even the liquidation sale was a dud. I retraced my steps.

At the corner, I waited for the light to change and crossed Capillo to the shops and specialty businesses lined up in a row on the far side of the intersection. I wandered through a craft mart, a drugstore, and a gift-and-card shop, all without success. I returned to my car and sat there wondering if I was completely off base. I'd been encouraged by Vernon Waibel's assertion that Melvin was still in town, but I had no real reason to believe it. It made me happy thinking I could run him to ground through sheer tenacity, a trait I've been blessed with since birth. More to the point, if he'd fled into the world at large, I had no idea how to find him. Better to believe he was still in range.

I started my car and backed out of the slot. I took a right turn onto Capillo and then a left at the light. This put me back on Palisade, moving past a residential neighborhood of small wood-and-stucco homes built in the 1940s. On my right, a road snaked up the hill to houses of a loftier nature with spectacular ocean views. I slowed at a set of crosswalks. A crossing guard watched with care as a string of children made their way from the near corner to the one on the other side. They walked in twos, holding hands, while a teacher and a teacher's assistant hurried them along.

When the guard nodded that traffic could proceed, I followed the slope of the hill down to the beachside park below. I did a slow circle of the parking lot, taking in the smattering of people I could see. I came out of the lot and turned right again, climbing the hill to the more populated section of Palisade I'd cruised before. How much gas was I willing to burn in the hope he was here?

I drove back to City College and parked in range of the bus stop on the same side of the street. For a while I sat, directing my attention to the campus across the way, the child care center on the near corner, and the block of apartments built into the side of the hill. After thirty unproductive minutes, I started the car again and took a left on Palisade. I'd make one last pass before I gave it up for the day. I reached the end of the imaginary territory I'd assigned to my quarry. At the beach park, I made the turn-around and drove back up the hill to the main intersection. I was stopped for a red light when I spotted him a hundred yards away.

Recognition is a complex phenomenon, a nearly instantaneous correlation of memory and perception, where the variables are almost impossible to replicate. What do we note in one another on sight? Age, race, gender, emotion, mood, the angle and rotation of the head; size, body type, posture. Later, it's difficult to pinpoint the visual data that triggers the "click." I was once at a departure gate in Chicago's O'Hare Airport when I caught sight of a man in profile striding through the terminal in a jostling crowd of pedestrians. It was a split-second image, like a stop-action photograph, before the passengers shifted, blocking him from view. The man I'd seen was an officer I'd trained with as a rookie on the force. I barked out his name and he whipped around, as amazed as I was to spot a known face in unfamiliar surroundings.

I'd talked to Melvin once, but seeing his walk and the set of his shoulders created a response. I yelped in surprise, my gaze flicking to the stoplight. Still red. When I looked back, he was gone. I blinked, my gaze moving rapidly from one side of the street to the other. He couldn't have gotten far. The second the light changed and I saw a break in the oncoming traffic, I made a left-hand turn and slid into the alleyway that ran behind the stores. No sign of him. I knew I was right. I'd seen the white hair and the cracked brown bomber jacket in my peripheral vision.

I circled back to the main intersection and began a grid search, mentally dividing the block into smaller sections that I could survey in slow motion. Back and forth I went. I didn't think he'd seen me because he'd been facing the opposite direction, a man on a mission, shutting out all else. At least I'd narrowed the hunt. I continued at a crawl, the drivers behind me merrily beeping their horns in encouragement. I was talking to myself by then, saying, *Shit, shit, shit. Come on, Downs, show your face again just once.*

After twenty minutes I gave up. I couldn't believe he'd vanished. I could have parked my car and done another foot search, but the idea didn't seem productive. I'd return on Thursday and do a proper door-to-door canvass of the area. In the meantime, I figured I might as well go home.

Once in my neighborhood, I parked half a block down, locked my car, and headed for Henry's back door. I could see him through the glass, settling in his rocker with his Black Jack over ice on the table next to him. I knocked. He got up and opened the door with a smile. "Kinsey. Come on in, sweetie. How are you?"

I said, "Fine," and then burst into tears. He shouldn't have called me "sweetie" because that's all it took.

I'll skip over the blubbering I did and the halting hiccuping account of the day's disasters, starting with Melvin Downs, the blunders Nancy Sullivan had made, what I'd learned at the courthouse about the money charged against Gus's bank accounts, and my visit to the lawyer's office, with the whole sorry mess coming back to Melvin at the end. I didn't claim it was the worst day of my adult life. I've been divorced twice and some of that drama was in a league of its own.

But on a professional level, this was low.

I unburdened myself, telling him what I said, what he said, what she said, how I felt, what I wish I'd said, what I thought then and later and in between. Every time I reached the end of my recital, I'd remember some new detail and swing back to incorporate it. "What gets me is everything Solana said was exactly what *I'd* said when I called the county, except she turned it around. I couldn't deny the disgusting state his house was in so most of what she told Nancy Sullivan was true. His anemia, bruises—all of it. How could I argue? While I was using the facts as evidence of abuse, Solana was using the same information to justify the court's taking charge of his affairs. It just seems so *wrong* . . ."

I paused to blow my nose, adding the tissue to the pile of soggy ones I'd tossed in the trash. "I mean, who are these people? A lawyer and a professional conservator? I can't get over it. While I was at the courthouse, I went into the library and pulled *Deering's California Probate Code*. It's all laid out, powers and duties—blah, blah, blah. As nearly as I can tell, there's no licensing process and no agency that oversees or regulates their actions. I'm sure there are conscientious conservators somewhere, but these two have fallen on Gus like vampires."

Two tissues later, my lips feeling fat from all the tears

I'd shed, I said, "I have to give Solana credit—she was clever to invent the business of a quarrel between us. Her claim that I'd threatened her made my call to the agency look like spite on my part."

Henry shrugged. "She's a sociopath. She plays by a different set of rules. Well, one rule. She does what serves her."

"I'll have to change my strategy. To what, I don't know."

"There is one bright note."

"Oh, great. I could use one," I said.

"As long as there's money in his accounts, Gus is worth more to them alive than dead."

"At the rate they're going, it won't take long."

"Be smart. Don't let her suck you into doing anything illegal—aside from the stuff you've already done."

28

Leaving for work Wednesday morning, I spotted Solana and Gus on the sidewalk in front of the house. I hadn't seen him outside for weeks and I had to admit, he was looking good with a jaunty knit cap pulled down over his ears. He was in his wheelchair, bundled into heavy-duty sweats that draped at the shoulder and hung from his knees. She'd tucked a blanket over his lap. They must have just come back from an outing. She'd turned the wheelchair around so she could maneuver it up the front steps.

I crossed the grass. "Can I help you with that?"

"I'll take care of it," she said. Once she'd hauled him up the last step, I put a hand on his chair and leaned closer.

"Hey, Gus. How are you?"

Solana shifted into the space between us, trying to cut off my access. I held up a palm to bar her, which darkened her mood.

"What are you doing?" she asked.

"Giving Gus the chance to talk to me if you don't object."

"He doesn't want to talk to you and neither do I. Please get off this property."

I noticed his hearing aids were gone and it occurred to me it was a neat way of putting him out of commission. How could he interact if he couldn't hear a thing. I put my lips near his ear. "Can I do anything for you?"

The look he sent me was sorrowful. His mouth trembled and he moaned like a woman in the early stages of labor, before she understands how bad it really gets. He peered at Solana, who stood with her hands folded. In her sturdy brown shoes and bulky brown coat, she looked like a prison matron. "Go ahead, Mr. Vronsky. Say anything you like."

He put a finger behind his ear and shook his head, feigning deafness though I knew he'd heard me.

I raised my voice. "Would you like to come next door to Henry's for a cup of tea? He'd love to see you."

Solana said, "He's had his tea."

Gus said, "I can't walk anymore. I'm all wobbly."

Solana caught my eye. "You're not welcome here. You're upsetting him."

I ignored her, dropping down on my haunches to make eye contact with him. Even seated, his spine was so curved he had to turn his head sideways to return my gaze. I smiled at him in what I hoped was an encouraging manner, hard to pull off with Solana hovering over me. "We haven't seen you in ages. Henry's probably got some nice homemade sweet rolls. I can take you over in your chair and have you back in a jiffy. Does that sound like something you'd enjoy?"

"I'm not feeling well."

"I know that, Gus. Is there anything I can do to help?"

He shook his head, his gnarled hands stroking each other in his lap.

"You know we're concerned about you. All of us."

"I thank you for that and for everything."

"As long as you're okay."

He shook his head. "I'm not okay. I'm old."

I spent a quiet morning at the office, tidying my desk and paying some bills. I took care of simple jobs: tossing, filing, taking out the trash. I was still brooding about Gus, but I knew there was no point in going over the same ground again. I had to focus on something else. Like Melvin Downs. Something about the man bothered me, above and beyond the issue of tracking him down, which I was certain I could do.

Once my desktop was orderly, I spent an hour transcribing my interview with Gladys Fredrickson, tracking back and forth through the tape recording. Amazing how background noise interferes with audibility: the rattle of paper, the dog barking, her wheezing breath as she spoke. It would take more than one session to get the interview typed up, but it gave me something to do.

When I wearied of that, I opened the pencil drawer and took out a pack of index cards. In the same drawer, I spotted the toy I'd salvaged from the back of the closet in Melvin Downs's room. I squeezed the two sticks together, watching while a double-jointed wooden clown did a series of maneuvers on the high bar: back giant, clear hip to handstand, three-quarter giant. I had no way of knowing if the toy belonged to him or to the tenant who'd occupied the room before he arrived. I set the toy aside and picked up the stack of index cards.

Card by card, one line each, I jotted down what I knew of him, which didn't amount to much. He most likely worked in the area adjacent to City College, where he caught the bus. He was fond of movie classics that seemed, in the main, to be sentimental yarns about young boys, baby animals, and loss. He was estranged from his daughter, who refused to let him see his grandsons for reasons unknown. He'd been in prison, which might have had a bearing on his daughter's disenfranchising him. He had an imaginary friend named Tía that he created using a lipstick-red mouth tattooed in the U formed between the thumb and index finger of his right hand. Two black dots inked on the knuckle became the hand-puppet's eyes.

What else?

Melvin was mechanically inclined, with a fix-it mentality that allowed him to repair miscellaneous items, including a malfunctioning TV set. Whatever his day job, he was paid in cash. He finished work and sat waiting for a bus on Tuesdays and Thursdays by midafternoon. He was polite to strangers but had no close friends. He'd saved enough money to buy a truck. He'd been in town the past five years, ostensibly to be near the very grandsons he was forbidden to see. His room at the hotel was grim, unless of course he'd taken countless doilies, needlepointed pillows, and other decorative items with him when he left. When he'd seen the flyer I'd distributed, his response was to panic, pack his possessions, and disappear.

When I ran out of facts I shuffled the cards and arranged them randomly to see if enlightenment would ensue. I spread them out on the desk and leaned my head on my hand, thinking, *Which of these facts doesn't belong?*

I could think of one possibility. I pulled two cards forward and stared at them. How did the mechanical clown and Melvin's imaginary friend, Tía, fit into the larger scheme of things? Nothing else I'd learned about him suggested a playful nature. Indeed, there was something furtive in his reluctance to display the lipstick tattoo. So maybe the toys weren't intended for his amusement. Maybe Tía and the toy clown were meant to amuse someone else. Like who? Kids, any number of whom I'd seen at the nearby elementary school and the child care center near the bus stop he frequented.

Was he a pedophile?

I knew child molesters often kept games and videos on hand, befriending children over a period of time until a bond was formed. Physical contact was gradually introduced. In the wake of affection and trust came the fondling and fumbling, until touching and secrets were the intoxicating spice of their "special" relationship. If he was a sex offender, it would explain his fright that he'd been spotted within one thousand yards of a school, a playground, or a day care center. It would also explain his daughter's refusal to let him see his grandsons.

I picked up the phone and called the county probation department. I asked to speak to a parole officer named Priscilla Holloway. I expected to have to leave a message, but she picked up on her end and I identified myself. Her voice was surprisingly light, given what I remembered of her physical stature. She was a big-boned redhead, the sort who'd played rough sports in high school and still had softball and soccer trophies displayed in her bedroom at home. I'd met her the previous July when I was babysitting a young renegade named Reba Lafferty, who'd been paroled from the California Institute for Women.

"I've got a question for you," I said, when we'd dispensed with the chitchat. "How familiar are you with the registered sex offenders in town?"

"I know most of them by name. We all do. Lot of

them are required to come in for drug testing. They also call in changes of address or changes in employment. Who in particular?"

"I'm looking for a fellow named Melvin Downs."

There was a pause and I could almost hear her shaking her head. "Nope. Don't think so. The name doesn't sound familiar. Where'd he do his time?"

"I have no idea, but I'm guessing he was in prison on a child molest. He has a crude tattoo that looks like prison vintage—a lipstick-red mouth in the web between the thumb and index finger on his right hand. I'm told he's an amateur ventriloquist and I'm wondering if he trots out his talent in seducing young kids."

"I can check with the other POs and see if they know him. What's the context?"

"You know an attorney named Lowell Effinger?"

"Sure, I know Lowell."

"He wants to depose Downs as a witness in a personal-injury suit. Downs is a hard man to find, but I finally ran him to ground. He seemed cooperative at first, but then he turned around and bolted so fast it made me wonder if he was in the system somewhere."

"I don't think here, but he might be a fugitive from another state. These guys want out from under, all they have to do is hit the road without telling us. We've got ten to fifteen unaccounted for at any given time. And that's just locally. Statewide, the numbers are mind-boggling."

"Jeez, all those sex offenders on the loose?"

"Sorry to say. Give me your number again and I'll get back to you if I learn anything."

I thanked her and returned the handset to the cradle. My suspicions hadn't been confirmed, but she hadn't shot me down. Altogether, I was feeling a flicker of encouragement.

* * *

As a consequence, early Thursday afternoon, I drove up Capillo Hill again and sat in the parking lot of the organic foods market, looking out at the intersection where I'd seen Downs two days before. Since his work schedule seemed consistently Tuesdays and Thursdays, I hoped I had a decent chance of spotting him. I was bored to tears with the hunt, but I'd brought a paperback novel and a thermos of hot coffee. There was a ladies' room available at the gas station two doors down. What more did a girl require? I read for a while, periodically glancing through the windshield to scan the area.

I paid a visit to the service station, and as I came out of the ladies' room I could see activity across the street. A van pulled in at the curb in front of the Laundromat. Idly, I watched as two men got out and went in. I was already sitting behind the wheel of my car again when they emerged minutes later, toting cardboard boxes, which they stowed in the rear of the van. There was lettering on the side panel, but I couldn't read what it said. I reached into the backseat and snatched up the binoculars I keep close at hand. I adjusted the focus until the lettering became sharp.

Starting Over Christian Charities, Inc.
Your trash is our cash.
We accept gently used clothing, furniture,
small appliances and office equipment.
Tues & Thurs, 9:00 A.M. to 2:00 P.M.

Apparently the two men were picking up donations. From a Laundromat? How weird was that? It was the phrase "small appliances" that caught my attention. Also, the days and times of operation. This was the perfect position for someone like Downs with a penchant for tinkering and a talent as a fix-it man. I pictured him with nonfunctioning vacuum cleaners, hair dryers, and electric fans, salvaging items that would otherwise go into the trash. A Christian charity might also be sympathetic to his prison history.

I tossed my book aside, got out of my car, and locked it behind me. I made a beeline for the crosswalks in the middle of the block. When I reached the storefront, I bypassed the big plate-glass windows and cut between two buildings to the alley in the rear. I'd driven the alley twice, making a study of pedestrians while navigating the lane and a half, barely wide enough for two cars to pass. Once I'd had to stop at that spot when a woman in front of me with a carload of kids slowed to make the turn into her garage.

Now that I knew what I was looking for, the payoff was quick. Above the back door of the Laundromat, there was the same sign I'd seen on the side of the van. This was a drop-off location for Starting Over, an organization that must have rented the two back rooms to accept and sort donations. The rear parking had slots enough for three cars with additional space for a lidded bin that was kept available for hours when the center was closed. The rolling bin had been placed across the opening between the Laundromat and the jewelry store next door. I could see the back end of the vehicle that was parked in the gap. It was one I knew well: an old milk truck outfitted as a camper, originally offered for sale "as is" at $1,999.99. The dealer who sold it had operated the lot right around the corner from the residence hotel where Downs had lived. I might have actually witnessed the transaction the day I saw the salesman in conversation with a white-haired man in sunglasses and a porkpie hat. I hadn't met Melvin at that point so I wouldn't have understood the significance. By the time I'd caught up with him, he was prepared to flee. I took out my notebook and jotted down the license number of the milk truck.

The rear door of the shop stood ajar. I approached with care and peered around the corner. Melvin had his back to me, folding children's clothing into tidy piles that he placed in a cardboard box. Now that I knew where he was, I'd report his location to Lowell Effinger. He'd schedule a date for the deposition and issue a subpoena requiring Downs to appear. I made a note of the address and the contact number printed on the bin and then returned to my car and drove back to my office, where I put in a call to the attorney's office and told his secretary where Downs could be served.

"You'll handle the service?"

I said, "That's not a good idea. He knows me on sight, which means I'd be coming in the front door and he'd be flying out the back."

"But this is your baby. You should have the satisfaction," she said. "I'll let you know when everything's set up, which shouldn't take long. By the way, Gladys told Herr Buckwald there was talk of a missing witness and now she's all over us for his name and address." I was amused by her fake German accent, which exactly captured Hetty Buckwald's nature.

"Good luck," I said. "Call me when you're done."

"I'm on it, kid."

Driving home that afternoon, I became aware of the tension in my neck. I was wary of Solana and hoping to avoid running into her again. She had to be aware I had her in my sights and I didn't think she'd appreciate the interference. As it turned out, our paths didn't cross until Saturday night. So I was worrying before it was absolutely necessary.

I'd been to see a movie and it was close to eleven when I got home. I parked half a block down the street in the only space I could find at that hour. I got out and locked the car. The street was dark and empty. A skittish wind blew, sending a tumble of leaves across my feet like an undulating wave of mice escaping from a cat. The moon was intermittently visible, obscured and then exposed by the erratic movement of the trees. I thought I was the only one out, but as I approached Henry's gate, I caught sight of Solana standing in the shadows. I secured my shoulder bag and shoved my hands in the pockets of my parka.

She stepped forward when I was abreast of her, blocking my path.

I said, "Get away from me."

"You put me in hot water with the county. A bad move on your part."

"Who's Cristina Tasinato?"

"You know who she is. Mr. Vronsky's conservator of record. She says you paid a visit to her attorney. Did you think I wouldn't find out?"

"I don't give a rat's ass."

"Bad language is unbecoming. I gave you more credit than that."

"Or maybe you didn't give me credit enough."

Solana stared at me. "You were in my house. You picked up Mr. Vronksy's pill bottles to see what medications he's on. You set the bottles down *not* quite in the same place so I could tell they'd been moved. I pay attention to such things. You must have thought you were immune from discovery, but you're not. You took his bankbooks as well."

"I don't know what you're talking about," I said, but I wondered if she could hear my heart careen off my chest wall like a handball.

"You've made a serious mistake. People who try getting the best of me are always wrong. They learn the meaning of the word 'regret,' but by then it's too late."

"Are you *threatening* me?"

"Of course not. I'm offering advice. Leave Mr. Vronsky alone."

"Who's the big goon you have living in the house?"

"There's no one living in the house except the two of us. You're a suspicious young woman. Some would call you paranoid."

"Is he the orderly you hired?"

"There's an orderly who comes in, if it's any business of yours. You're upset. I can understand your hostility. You're strong willed, used to doing as you please and having everything your way. We're very much alike, both of us willing to play to the death."

She put a hand on my arm and I shook it away. "Cut the melodrama. You can eat shit and die for all I care."

"Now it's you threatening me."

"You better believe it," I said.

The gate squeaked as I opened it and the sound of the latch catching punctuated the end of the exchange. She was still standing on the walk as I rounded the corner of the studio and let myself into my darkened apartment. I locked the door and shucked my jacket, tossing it on the kitchen counter as I passed. The lights were still off as I moved into the downstairs bathroom and stepped into the shower to check the street outside. By the time I peered out the window, she was gone.

29

As I was letting myself into the office Monday morning I heard my phone ring. A bulky package was leaning against the door, left by a courier service. I tucked it under my arm and unlocked the door in haste, stepping over a pile of mail that had been shoved through the slot. I paused to snatch up the lot of it and scampered into the inner office, tossing the mail on my desk while I made a grab for the phone. I caught it on ring five and found Mary Bellflower on the line, sounding remarkably cheerful. "Did you get the documents Lowell Effinger messengered over to you? He sent me the same batch."

"Must be the package that was left at my door. I just now walked in and haven't had a chance to open it. What is it?"

"The transcript of the deposition he took from the accident expert earlier this week. Call me as soon as you've read it."

"Sure thing. You sound happy."

"I'm curious at any rate. This is good stuff," she said.

I shrugged off my jacket and tossed my shoulder bag

on the floor beside my desk. Before I opened the packet, I walked down the short hall to my kitchenette and set up a pot of coffee. I'd forgotten to bring in a carton of milk so I was forced to use two flat packets of fake stuff once the coffee had finished dripping into the carafe. I returned to my desk and opened the manila mailer. Then I leaned back in my swivel chair and put my feet on the edge of the desk with the transcript opened on my lap, coffee cup to my right.

Tilford Brannigan was a biomechanical expert who doubled, in this case, as the accident reconstructionist, wearing two hats at once. The document was neatly typed. The pages were stapled together at the top left corner. Each eight-by-eleven page had been reduced in size and formatted to fit four to the sheet.

The first page listed correspondence, marked "Plaintiff's Exhibits #6-A Through 6-H," and went on down the numbered lines. Included was Brannigan's curriculum vitae, Gladys Frederickson's medical summaries, Request for Production of Documents, Plaintiff Response to the Defendant Request for Production of Documents, Supplemental Request for Production of Documents. Dr. Goldfarb's medical files had been subpoenaed, as had the files of a Dr. Spaulding. There were numerous depositions, summary/medical records marked Plaintiff's Exhibit #16, along with the police report. Various photographs of the damaged cars and the accident site had been entered as exhibits. I quickly flipped to the last page, just to get a feel for what I was in for. Brannigan's testimony started on page 6 and continued to page 133. The proceedings had begun at 4:30 P.M. and concluded at 7:15.

A deposition is, by nature, a less formal proceeding than an appearance in court since it occurs in a lawyer's office instead of a courtroom. Testimony is given under oath. Both plaintiff's and defendant's attorneys and a court reporter are in attendance, but there's no judge.

Hetty Buckwald was there representing the Fredricksons, and Lowell Effinger was on hand in Lisa Ray's behalf, though neither the plaintiffs nor the defendant were present. Years before, I'd looked up Ms. Buckwald's bona fides, convinced her law degree was from Harvard or Yale. Instead, she'd graduated from one of those Los Angeles law schools that self-promotes by way of big splashy ads pasted on freeway billboards.

I cruised through the repetitious early pages, where Ms. Buckwald worked to suggest that Brannigan was inexperienced and ill qualified, neither of which was true. Lowell Effinger objected at intervals, mostly intoning, "Misstates the prior testimony" or "Asked and answered" in a voice that, even on paper, sounded bored and annoyed. Effinger had tagged certain pages to make sure I didn't miss the import. The gist of it was that, despite Ms. Buckwald's persistently snide and wearing questions that cast aspersions on him wherever possible, Tilford Brannigan was steadfast in his insistence that Gladys Fredrickson's injuries were inconsistent with the dynamics of the collision. There followed fourteen pages of testimony in which Ms. Buckwald picked away at him, trying to get him to yield on whatever minor point she was pursuing. Brannigan held up well, patient and unperturbed. His responses were mild, sometimes amusing, which must have infuriated Ms. Buckwald, who relied on friction and animosity to rattle a witness. If he conceded the smallest detail, she leaped on the admission as though it were a major triumph, completely undermining testimony he'd given before. I wasn't sure whom she was trying to impress.

As soon as I'd read the file, I called Mary Bellflower, who said, "So what did you think?"

"I'm not sure. We know Gladys was injured. We have three inches of medical reports: X-ray results and treatment protocols. She might fake whiplash or a lower-back pain, but a cracked pelvis and two cracked ribs? Please."

"Brannigan didn't say she wasn't injured. He's saying the injuries weren't sustained in the accident. By the time Millard ran into Lisa Ray pulling out of the parking lot, she was already hurt. Brannigan didn't say so flat out, but that's his guess."

"What, like Millard beat the crap out of her or something like that?"

"That's what we need to find out."

"But her injuries *were* fresh, right? I mean, this wasn't anything that'd happened weeks before."

"Right. It could have happened prior to their getting in the van. Maybe he was taking her to the emergency room and he saw his chance."

"Not to be dense about it, but why would he do that?"

"He had liability insurance, but no collision coverage. They'd dropped their home-owner's policy because they couldn't afford the premiums. No catastrophic medical, no long-term disability. They were totally exposed."

"So he deliberately rammed into Lisa Ray's car? That's risky, isn't it? What if Lisa had been killed? For that matter, what if his wife had been killed?"

"He wouldn't have been any worse off. Might have been better for him actually. He could have sued for wrongful death or negligent homicide, half a dozen things. The point was to blame someone else and collect the dough instead of having to pay it out. He'd been badly injured himself and a jury awarded him $680,000. They've probably pissed it all away."

"Jesus, that's cold. What kind of guy is he?"

"Try desperate. Hetty Buckwald went after Brannigan tooth and nail and couldn't get him to back down. Lowell said it was all he could do not to bust out laughing. He thinks this is big. Huge. We just have to figure out what it means."

"I'll go up there again. Maybe the neighbors know something we don't."

"Let's hope."

I returned to the Fredricksons' neighborhood and started with the two neighbors directly across the street. Their knowledge, if any, probably wouldn't come to much, but at least I could rule them out. At the first house, the middle-aged woman who answered the door was pleasant but professed to know nothing about the Fredricksons. When I explained the situation, she said she'd moved in six months before and preferred to keep her distance from her neighbors. "That way, if I have a problem with any one of them, I can complain without worrying about someone's feelings being hurt," she said. "I tend to my affairs and expect them to tend to theirs."

"Well, I can see your point. I've had good luck with my neighbors until recently."

"When neighbors turn on you, there's nothing worse. Your home is supposed to be a refuge, not a fortified encampment in a war zone."

Amen, I thought. I gave her my card and asked her to call me if she heard anything. "Don't count on it," she said, as she closed the door.

I went down her walkway and up the walk leading to the house next door. This time the occupant was a man in his late twenties, thin face, glasses, underslung jaw with a tiny goatee meant to give definition to his weak chin. He wore loose jeans and a T-shirt with horizontal stripes of the sort a mother would select.

"Kinsey Millhone," I said, holding out my hand.

"Julian Frisch. You selling something? Avon, Fuller Brush?"

"I don't think they sell door-to-door these days." Again, I explained who I was and my fact-finding mission with regard to the Fredricksons. "Are you acquainted with them?"

"Sure. She does my books. You want to come in?"

"I'd like that."

His living room looked like a display for computer sales and service. Some of the equipment I could identify on sight—keyboards and the monitors that looked like clunky television screens. There were eight computers set up, with tangled cables that snaked across the floor connecting them. In addition, there were sealed cartons I assumed contained brand-new computers. The few cranky-looking models sitting in one corner might have come in for repair. I'd heard the terms "floppy disk" and "boot up" but I didn't have a clue what they meant.

"I take it you sell or repair computers."

"Little bit of both. What do you have?"

"A portable Smith-Corona."

He half-smiled, as if I were making a joke, and then he wagged a finger at me. "Better catch up with reality. You're missing the boat. Time's going to come when computers will do everything."

"I have trouble believing that. It just seems so *unlikely.*"

"You're not a believer like the rest of us. The day will come when ten-year-olds will master these machines and you'll be at their mercy."

"That's a depressing thought."

"Don't say I didn't warn you. At any rate, that's probably not why you knocked on my door."

"True enough," I said. I redirected my attention and went through my introduction, which I'd just about perfected by then, wrapping up with a reference to the two-car collision on May 28 of the year before. "How long has Gladys Fredrickson handled your books?"

"The past two or three years. I only know her professionally, not personally. She's a mess right now, but she does good work."

"Did or does?"

"Oh, she still handles my accounts. She complains about her aches and pains, but she never misses a beat."

"She told the insurance company she couldn't work because she can't sit for long periods and she can't concentrate. She said the same thing to me when I took her statement."

His expression was pained. "That's a pile of crap. I see the courier service over there two and three times a week."

"Are you sure about that?"

"I work right here. I got a clear view across the street. I don't mean to rat her out, but she's as busy as ever."

Maybe I was falling in love. My heart gave the same pitter-patter and my chest felt warm. I put a hand across my forehead to see if I was suffering a fever of sudden onset. "Hang on a minute. This is too good to believe. Would you mind repeating that on tape?"

"I could do that," he said. "I was thinking about firing her, anyway. Her whining is getting on my nerves."

I sat down on the lone metal folding chair and put my tape recorder on an unopened carton. I took out my clipboard so I could make a written record of the information as well. He didn't have tons to contribute, but what he offered was pure gold. Gladys Fredrickson's claims of disability were fraudulent. She hadn't collected a cent yet, unless she was receiving state disability checks, which was entirely possible. Once he'd gone through his account for the tape recorder, I packed up my gear and shook his hand, thanking him profusely.

He said, "Not a problem. And if you change your mind about becoming computer literate, you know where I am. I could get you up and running in no time."

"How much?"

"Ten grand."

"You lost me there. I don't want to pay ten grand for something that makes me feel inadequate." I left thinking, *Ten-year-old kids? Get serious.*

The neighbor across the street to the right of the Fredricksons' was no help at all. The woman never did quite grasp my purpose, thinking I was selling insurance, which she politely declined. I repeated myself twice and then thanked her and moved over to the house on the other side.

The woman who answered the door was the same woman I'd seen when I arrived at the Fredricksons' house the first time. Given my experience with elderly persons, namely Gus, Henry, and the sibs, I placed this woman in her early eighties. She was quick and soft-spoken and seemed to have all her faculties about her. She was also as plump as a pincushion and she smelled of Joy perfume. "I'm Lettie Bowers," she said, as she shook my hand and invited me in.

Her skin felt delicate and powdery, her palm two or three degrees warmer than my own. I wasn't sure she should be so trusting, inviting a stranger into her house, but it suited my purposes.

Her living room was sparsely furnished, frothy curtains at the windows, faded carpet on the floor, faded paper on the walls. The Victorian-style furniture had a vaguely depressing air about it, which suggested it was authentic. The rocker I sat down in had a horsehair seat, which you couldn't get away with now. To the right of the front door, on the Fredricksons' side of the house, French double doors opened onto a wood balcony crowded with flowerpots. I explained who I was and that I was working as an investigator on behalf of the insurance company Gladys Fredrickson was suing in the wake of her accident. "Would you mind if I ask you a few questions."

"Fine. I'm happy for the company. Would you like tea?"

"No, thanks. I take it you're aware of the claim?"

"Oh yes. She told me she was suing and I said, 'Good for you.' You should see the poor thing hobbling around. What happened was terrible and she's entitled to recompense."

"I don't know about *that.* These days, hitting up an insurance company is like going to Vegas to play the slot machines."

"Exactly. All that money is paid in and very little is paid out. The insurance companies as good as dare you to try to collect. They've got all the power on their side. If you win, they dump you or they double your premiums."

This was discouraging. I'd heard these sentiments expressed before, the belief that insurance companies were fat cats and the mice deserved anything they could get. "In this case, the facts are in dispute, which is why I'm here."

"The facts are obvious. There was an accident. It's as simple as that. Gladys told me it was covered on their home-owner's policy and the company had refused to pay. She said suing was the only way to force their hand."

"Auto."

" 'Auto'?"

"It's not their home-owner's policy. She's suing the company that carries the defendant's car insurance." Personally, I wondered if I was shooting myself in the foot. We were clearly working at cross-purposes, but I got out my tape recorder and went through my drill; identifying myself, Lettie Bowers, blah blah blah. Then I said, "How long have you known the Fredricksons?"

"If you want the truth, I don't know them well and I don't like them much. Am I under oath?"

"No ma'am, but it would be helpful if you could tell me what you know as truthfully as possible."

"I always do that. I was raised that way."

"I take it Gladys Fredrickson's talked to you about the accident."

"She didn't have to. I saw it."

I leaned forward slightly. "*You* were at the intersection?"

She seemed confused. "There wasn't any intersection. I was sitting right here, looking out the window."

"I don't understand how you could have seen what went on."

"I couldn't miss it. I do my pickup work by the window, which gives me good light and offers a nice view of the neighborhood. I used to do needlepoint, but lately I've gone back to knitting and crochet. Less strain on my eyes and easier on my hands. I'd been watching them at work, which is how I happened to see the tumble she took."

"Gladys fell?"

"Oh my, yes. It was entirely her fault, but the way she explained it to me, the insurance company will have to pay anyway if everything goes well."

"Could we back up a few paragraphs and start this again?"

I took a few minutes to go back over the lawsuit, filling in the details while she shook her head.

"You must be talking about someone else. It didn't happen that way."

"Fine. Let's hear your side of it."

"I don't mean to sound judgmental, but she and her husband are penny-pinchers and they hate to hire help. The rain gutters were jammed with leaves. We'd had a number of spring storms and the water had been pouring down in torrents, right over the edge instead of going into the down spouts. First week of nice weather, she got up on a ladder to clean the gutters and the ladder toppled. She landed on the wooden deck and the ladder came down and clunked her in the head. I was surprised she didn't break her back, as much as she weighs. The sound was awful, like a bag of cement. I ran out, but she said she was all right. I could see she was woozy and limping badly, but she wouldn't accept help. Next thing I knew, Millard pulled the van around in front and honked. They had a heated discussion and then she got in."

"Did she tell you this in confidence?"

"Not in so many words. She said it was just between the two of us and then she gave me a wink. And here all this time, I thought the claim was legitimate."

"Would you be willing to testify in the defendant's behalf?"

"Of course. I don't approve of cheaters."

"Nor do I."

Late afternoon, as a special treat, I took myself up to Rosie's and ordered a glass of wine. I'd wait and eat when I got home, but I'd done a good day's work and I deserved a reward. I'd just settled into my favorite booth when Charlotte Snyder appeared. I hadn't seen her for weeks, since she and Henry had quarreled. I thought her presence was coincidental, but she paused in the doorway, looking around, and when she spotted me, she headed straight for my table and sat down across from me. She had a scarf tied over her hair, which she removed and put in her coat pocket while she shook her hair back to its natural shape. Her cheeks were pink from the cold and her eyes were bright. "I took a chance on catching you here when you didn't answer your door. If you tell me Henry's on his way in, I'll disappear."

"He's having dinner with William. It's boys' night out," I said. "What's up?"

"I'm hoping to redeem myself in Henry's eyes. I heard the court appointed a woman named Cristina Tasinato as Gus Vronsky's conservator."

"Don't remind me. I was nearly sick when I heard."

"That's what I wanted to talk about. According to the bank, she's taking out a big construction loan, putting the house up as collateral."

"News to me."

"I gather she wants to remodel and upgrade, add a wheelchair ramp, redo electrical and plumbing, and generally bring the house up to snuff."

"The place could use a face-lift. Even with the cleanup Solana's done, it's still a mess. What's the size of the loan?"

"A quarter of a million bucks."

"Wow. Who told you?"

"Jay Larkin, a friend of mine in the loan department. We used to date years ago and he was a big help when I was getting into real estate. He knew I'd been interested in listing the property and when this came up, he assumed I'd made a deal. It struck me as curious because I told Solana the two parcels together were worth far more than the house. This block is already zoned multiple-family. Any buyer with savvy would purchase both lots and tear the old house down."

"But it makes sense to remodel with Gus so adamant about hanging on."

"That's just what I'm getting at. She put the house on the market. Well, maybe not Solana, but the conservator."

"For sale? How so? I haven't seen a sign out front."

"This is a pocket listing. I'm guessing she'll pay off the construction loan with the proceeds from the sale. I wouldn't have known about it, but an agent in our Santa Teresa office is handling the deal. She remembered I'd done comps when my client came through town so she was calling to ask if I wanted a referral fee. I was sorely tempted, but with Henry so burned at me, I didn't dare."

"What's the asking price?"

"A million two, which is a joke. Even fixed up, it'll never sell for that. I thought it was odd after Solana swore up and down Gus would rather die than part with the place. What I can't understand is why the house was listed with my company. Didn't anybody realize I'd get wind of it?"

"The conservator probably had no idea you were ever involved," I said. "Solana doesn't seem that sophisticated about real estate. If this is her doing, maybe she wasn't aware how closely you work with one another."

"Or maybe she's thumbing her nose at us."

"This is being done through Gus's bank?" I asked.

"Sure. One big happy family, but the whole thing stinks. I thought you should know."

I said, "I wonder if there's any way to gum up the works?"

Charlotte pushed a piece of paper across the table. "This is Jay's number at the bank. You can tell him we talked."

30

I slept poorly that night, my brain abuzz. Lettie Bowers's revelations had been a gift, but instead of feeling good, I was kicking myself for not interviewing her earlier. She and Julian both. If I'd talked to neighbors before my first meeting with the Fredricksons, I would have known what I was dealing with. I felt like I was slipping, distracted by the miscalculations I'd made in my dealings with Solana Rojas. Not to beat myself to death here, but Gus was in big trouble and I was the one who'd put him there. What more could I do? I'd called the county so there was no point in going over that ground again. Nancy Sullivan had doubtless drawn and quartered me in her report. Beyond that, I hadn't witnessed verbal, emotional, or physical abuse that warranted calling the police. Which left me where?

I couldn't persuade my mind to shut up. There was nothing I could do about any of it in the middle of the night, but I couldn't let it go. Finally, I sank into some deep canyon of sleep. It was like slipping into a trough in the ocean's floor, dark and silent, the weight of the water pinning me in place. I wasn't even aware I'd fallen asleep until I heard the noise. My leaden senses registered the sound and invented a few quick stories to account for it. None of them made sense. My eyes popped open. What *was* that?

I checked the clock, as though noting the time would make a difference. 2:15. If I hear the cork pop from a champagne bottle, I automatically check the time in case it turns out to be a gunshot and I'll be asked later to file a police report. Someone was riding a skateboard in front of the house; metal wheels on concrete, repeated clicks as the skateboard rolled across cracks in the sidewalk. Back and forth, the sound surging and receding. I listened, trying to determine how many skateboarders there were—only one as far as I could tell. I could hear the kid try kickflips, the board slamming down when he made it, clattering off when he missed. I thought about Gus railing at the two nine-year-olds on skateboards in December. He was at his crankiest back then, but at least he was on his feet. Despite his complaints and the nuisance calls he made, he was alive and vigorous. Now he was failing and no one else in the neighborhood was irritable enough to protest the racket outside. The board clacked and banged, off the curb, into the street, back up on the curb again, and down the sidewalk. This was getting on my nerves. Maybe I'd be the cranky neighbor from now on.

I pushed the covers aside and made my way across the carpeted loft in the dark. There was sufficient illumination from the Plexiglas skylight above that I could see where I was going. Barefoot, I went down the spiral stairs, my oversized T-shirt leaving my bare knees exposed. It was cold in the studio and I knew I'd need a coat if I went out to shake a fist as Gus would have. I went into the downstairs bathroom and stepped into the fiberglass tub and shower surround, with its window that looked out on the street. I'd left the light off so I could see out without the skateboarder knowing I was there. The sound seemed farther away—muted, but persistent. Then silence.

I waited, but heard nothing. I crossed my arms for warmth and peered out at the dark. The street was empty and remained so. Finally, I climbed the spiral stairs again and crawled back in my bed. It was 2:25 and my body heat had dissipated, leaving me shivering. I pulled the covers over my shoulders and waited to get warm. Next thing I knew, it was 6:00 A.M. and time for my morning run.

I started to feel more optimistic as I put away the miles. The beach, the damp air, the sun painting gauzy layers of color across the sky—everything suggested this would be a better day. When I reached the dolphin fountain at the foot of State, I took a left and headed toward town. Ten blocks later I made the turn and jogged back toward the beach. I didn't wear a watch, but I could time my progress as I reached the *ding-ding-ding*ing signal gates near the train station. The ground began to vibrate and I heard the train approach, its warning howl subdued in deference to the hour. Later in the day, when the passenger train came through, the horn would be loud enough to halt conversations up and down the beach.

As a self-appointed site foreman, I took the opportunity to peek through the wooden barrier surrounding the new Paramount Hotel pool. Much of the construction debris was gone, and it looked as though the plaster coat had been sprayed over the gunite. I could imagine the completed project: deck chairs in place, tables with market umbrellas protecting the hotel patrons from the sun. The image faded, replaced by my worries about Gus. I debated putting a call through to Melanie in New York. The situation was distressing and she'd blame me. For all I knew, Solana had already given her an annotated version of the story, appointing herself the good guy while I was the bad.

Once I reached home, I went through my usual morning routine, and at 8:00 I locked the studio and went out to my car. There was a black-and-white police cruiser parked at the curb directly across the street. A uniformed officer was deep in conversation with Solana Rojas. Both were looking in my direction. What now? My first thought was of Gus, but there was no ambulance and no fire department rescue vehicle on hand. Curious, I crossed the street. "Is there a problem?"

Solana glanced at the officer and then pointedly at me before she turned her back and moved away. I knew without being told that the two had been discussing me, but to what end?

"I'm Officer Pearce," he said.

"Hi, how're you? I'm Kinsey Millhone." Neither of us offered to shake hands. I didn't know what he was doing here, but it wasn't to make friends.

Pearce wasn't a beat officer I knew. He was tall, broad shouldered, maybe fifteen pounds overweight, with that staunch police presence that speaks of a well-trained professional. There was even something intimidating about the way his leather belt creaked when he moved.

"What's going on?"

"Her car was vandalized."

I followed his gaze, which had shifted to Solana's convertible, parked two cars down from mine. Someone had taken a sharp instrument—a screwdriver or a chisel—and scratched the word dead in deep gouges on the driver's-side door. The paint was stripped and the metal had been dented by the force of the tool.

"Oh, wow. When did that happen?"

"Some time between six o'clock last night when she parked the vehicle and six forty-five this morning. She caught a glimpse of someone passing the house and came out to check. Were you aware of any activity out here?"

Over his shoulder, I saw that the neighbor from across the street had come out in her robe to get the paper and she'd engaged Solana in much the same conversation I was having with the officer. I could tell from Solana's gestures she was agitated. I said, "That was probably me she saw this morning. Weekdays, I jog up State, starting at six ten or so and returning thirty minutes later."

"Anyone else out and about?"

"Not that I saw, but I did hear a skateboarder in the middle of the night, which seemed odd. It was two fifteen because I remember looking at the clock. Sounded like he was riding back and forth on the sidewalk, up the curb and down, some in the street. It went on so long I got up to take a look, but I didn't see a soul. One of the other neighbors might have heard him."

"One kid or more."

"I'd say, one."

"That's your place?"

"The studio, yes. I rent from a gentleman named Henry Pitts, who occupies the main house. You can ask, but I don't think he'll be able to contribute much. His bedroom's on the ground floor rear so he's not subjected to the same street noises that I catch upstairs." I was babbling, giving Pearce more information than he needed, but I couldn't help myself.

"When you heard the skateboarder, you came out to the street?"

"Well, no. It was cold out and pitch dark so I stood in my downstairs bathroom and looked out the window. He was gone by then so I went back to bed. It's not like I heard him gouging and bashing away out here." I meant it as a bit of levity, but the look he turned on me was flat.

"You and your neighbor have a good relationship?"

"Solana and me? Uh, not really. I wouldn't go that far."

"You're on the outs?"

"I guess you could put it that way."

"And what's that about?"

I waved the question aside, already at a loss for words. How was I supposed to summarize the weeks of covert cat-and-mouse we'd played. "Long story," I said. "I'd be happy to explain, but it would take a while and it's irrelevant."

"The bad blood between you isn't relevant to what?"

"I wouldn't call it 'bad blood.' We've had our differences." I caught myself and turned to look at him. "She's not suggesting *I* had anything to do with this."

"A dispute between neighbors is serious business. It's not like you can walk away from the conflict when you live right next door."

"Wait a minute. This is crazy. I'm a licensed investigator. Why would I risk a fine and county jail time to settle a personal dispute?"

"Any idea who might?"

"No, but it certainly wasn't me." What else could I say that wouldn't sound defensive? The mere suggestion of wrongdoing is sufficient to generate skepticism in the eyes of others. While we give lip-service to "presumed innocent," most of us are quick to *presume* quite the opposite. Especially an officer of the law who's heard every possible variation on a theme.

"I should get on in to work," I said. "You need anything else from me?"

"You have a number where you can be reached?"

I said, "Sure." I took a business card out of my wallet and passed it to him. I wanted to point and say, *Look, I'm a no-fooling PI and a law-abiding citizen*, but that only put me in mind of the many times I'd crossed the law-abiding line this past week alone. I adjusted my shoulder bag and crossed to my car, acutely aware of the officer's eyes on me. When I dared to glance back, Solana was watching me as well, her expression poisonous. The neighbor standing next to her regarded me uneasily. She smiled and waved, perhaps worried that if she wasn't nice to me, I'd vandalize her car, too.

I started the Mustang and of course when I backed up to pull out of the slot, I tapped the bumper of the car behind. It didn't seem sufficient to warrant getting out to look, but as surely as I didn't, I'd get dinged for thousands in repair work, plus an additional citation for leaving the scene of an accident. I opened the car door and left it ajar while I walked around to the back of my car. There wasn't any sign of damage and when the officer walked over to see for himself, he seemed to agree.

"You might be a little more careful."

"I will. I am. I can leave a note if you think it's necessary." You see that? Fear of authority will reduce a grown woman to this kind of groveling, like I would have licked his belt buckle to a high shine if he'd grace me with a smile. Which he didn't.

I managed to drive away without any further mishap, but I was rattled.

* * *

I let myself into the office and put on a pot of coffee. I didn't need the caffeine; I was already wired. What I needed was a game plan. When the coffee was done I poured myself a mug and took it to my desk. Solana was setting me up. I had no doubt she'd scratched the car herself and then called the police. The move was a wily one in her campaign to establish my enmity. The more vengeful I appeared, the more innocent she looked by comparison. She'd already made a case for my calling the county hotline as a gesture of spite. Now I was a candidate for charges of vandalism. She'd have a hell of a time proving it, but the point was to damage my credibility. I had to find a way to counteract her strategy. If I could stay one step ahead of her I might be able to beat her at her own game.

I opened my bag, found the scrap of paper Charlotte had given me, and phoned the bank. When the call was picked up I asked for Jay Larkin.

"This is Larkin," he said.

"Hi, Jay. My name is Kinsey Millhone. Charlotte Snyder gave me your number . . ."

"Right. Absolutely. I know who you are. What can I do for you?"

"Well, it's a long story, but I'll give you the condensed version." Whereupon I laid out an account of the situation in as succinct a manner as possible.

When I finished, he said, "Not to worry. I appreciate the information. We'll take care of it."

By the time I got back to my coffee it was stone cold, but I was feeling better. I sat back in my swivel chair and put my feet up. I laced my hands on the top of my head and stared at the ceiling. Maybe I could put a stop to this woman yet. I've dealt with some very bad folks in my day—thugs, brute killers, and scamsters, with a number of truly evil people thrown into the mix. Solana Rojas was cunning, but I didn't think she was smarter than I was. I may not have a college degree, but I'm blessed (she said, modestly) with a devious nature and an abundance of native intelligence. I'm willing to match wits with just about anyone. That being true, I could (therefore) match wits with her. I simply couldn't go about it in my usual blunt-force fashion. Going head-to-head with her had landed me where I was. From now on, I'd have to be subtle and every bit as cunning as she. Here's what else I thought: If you can't go through a barrier, find a way around. There had to be a crack in her armor somewhere.

I sat up, put my feet on the floor, and opened the bottom right-hand desk drawer where I kept her file. There wasn't much in it: the contract with Melanie, the original job application, and the written report of what I'd learned about her. As it turned out, all the personal recommendations were horseshit, but I didn't know that then. I'd tucked Lana Sherman's résumé at the back of the file and I studied that now. Her comments about Solana Rojas had been hostile, but her criticisms only reinforced the notion that Solana was hardworking and conscientious. No hint of abusing the elderly for fun and profit.

I placed Solana's application on the desk in front of me. It was clear I'd have to go back and fact-check every line, starting with the address she'd given out in Colgate. The first time I'd seen the street name, I'd had no idea where it was, but I realized I'd seen it since. Franklin ran parallel to Winslow, one block over from the twenty-four-unit building Richard Compton owned. It was the Winslow property where the Guffeys had so enjoyed themselves, ripping out cabinets and demolishing the plumbing fixtures, thus generating their very own rendition of the Flood, minus Noah's Ark. The neighborhood was a hotbed of low-life types, so it made sense that Solana would be comfortable in such a setting. I picked up my jacket and my shoulder bag and headed for my car.

I pulled up across from the apartment building on Franklin, a drab beige three-story structure, free of architectural flourishes—no lintels, no windowsills, no shutters, no porches, and no landscaping, unless you find drought-tolerant dirt aesthetically pleasing. There was a pile of dead bushes near the curb and that was the extent of the vegetation. The apartment number on Solana's application was 9. I locked my car and crossed the street.

A cursory survey of the mailboxes suggested that this was a twenty-unit complex. Judging from the numbered doors, Apartment 9 was on the second floor. I made my way up the stairs, which consisted of iron risers with pebbly rectangular slabs of poured concrete forming the treads. At the top I took a moment to reconsider. As nearly as I could tell, Solana was living at Gus's full-time, but if the Franklin address was still her permanent residence, she might come and go. If I ran into her, she'd know she was under scrutiny, which was not good.

I returned to the ground floor, where I'd seen a white plastic sign on the door to Apartment 1, indicating the manager was living on the premises. I knocked and waited. Eventually a fellow opened the door. He was in his fifties, short and rotund, with pudgy features in a face that age had sucked into the collar of his shirt. The corners of his mouth were turned down and he had a double-chin that made his jaw look as formless and flat as a frog's.

I said, "Hi. Sorry to bother you, but I'm looking for Solana Rojas and wondered if she was still living here."

In the background I heard someone call, "Norman, who's that?"

Over his shoulder he called, "Just a minute, Princess, I'm in a conversation here."

"I know that," she called, "I asked who it was."

To me he said, "Nobody named Rojas in the building unless it's someone subletting, which we don't allow."

"Norman, did you hear me?"

"Come see for yourself. I can't be yelling back and forth like this. It's rude."

A moment later his wife appeared, also short and round, but twenty years younger with a mop of dyed yellow hair.

"She's looking for a woman named Solana Rojas."

"We don't have a Rojas."

"I told her the same thing. I thought it might be someone you knew."

I looked at the application again. "This says Apartment Nine."

Princess made a face. "Oh, her. The lady in Nine moved three weeks ago—her and that lump of a son—but the name's not Rojas. It's Tasinato. She's Turkish or Greek, something of the kind."

"*Cristina* Tasinato?"

"Costanza. And don't get us started. She left us with hundreds of dollars in damages we'll never recoup."

"How long did she live here?"

The two exchanged a look and he said, "Nine years? Maybe ten. She and her son were already tenants when I took over as the manager and that was two years ago. I never had occasion to check her place until she was gone. The kid had kicked a big hole in the wall, which must have created a draft because she was using old newspapers as insulation, stuffed between the studs. The dates on the papers went back to 1978. A family of squirrels had taken up residence and we're still trying to get them out."

Princess said, "The building was sold two months ago and the new owner raised the rent, which is why she moved. We've got tenants flocking off the premises like rats."

"She didn't leave a forwarding address?"

Norman shook his head. "Wish I could help you out, but she disappeared overnight. We went in and the place stunk so bad, we had to have a crew that usually handles crime scenes come in . . ."

Princess chimed in, "Like if a body's been rotting on the floor for a week and the boards are soaked with that bubbly-looking scum?"

"Got it," I said. "Can you describe her?"

Norman was at a loss. "I don't know, average. Kinda middle-aged, dark . . ."

"Glasses?"

"Don't think so. She might have wore them to read."

"Height, weight?"

Princess said, "On the thin side, a little chunky through the middle, but not as big as me." She laughed. "The son you couldn't miss."

"She called him Tiny, sometimes Tonto," Norman said. "Babyfaced—great big hulk of a guy . . ."

"Real big," she said. "And not right in the head. He's mostly deaf so he talked all in grunts. His mom acted like she understood him, but none of the rest of us did. He's an animal. Prowling the neighborhood at night. Scared the crap out of me more than once."

Norman said, "Couple of women were attacked. He

beat the shit out of this one gal. Hurt her so bad, she nearly had a nervous breakdown."

"Charming," I said. I thought about the goon I'd seen while I was cruising through Gus's house. Solana had been charging Gus's estate for the services of an orderly, who might well be her kid. "You wouldn't happen to have the tenant application she filled out when she moved in."

"You'd have to ask the new owner. The building's thirty years old. I know there's a bunch of boxes in storage from back when, but who knows what's in 'em."

"Why don't you give her Mr. Compton's phone number?"

Startled, I said, "Richard Compton?"

"Yeah, him. He also owns that building across the alley."

"I do business with him all the time. I'll call and ask if he objects to my searching the old files. I'm sure he won't mind. In the meantime, if you hear from Ms. Tasinato, would you let me know?" I took out a business card, which Norman read and then passed to his wife.

"You think her and this Rojas woman are the same?" she asked.

"Looks that way to me."

"She's a bad one. Sorry we can't tell you where she went."

"Never mind. I know."

Once the door was closed, I stood for a moment, relishing the information. Score one for me. Things were finally making sense. I'd done a background check on Solana Rojas, but in reality I was dealing with someone else—first name Costanza or Cristina, last name Tasinato. At some point there'd been a switch in ID, but I wasn't sure when. The real Solana Rojas might not even be aware that someone had borrowed her résumé, her credentials, and her good name.

When I returned to my car, there was a white Saab parked behind me and a fellow was standing on the sidewalk, his hands in his pockets, looking at the Mustang with a discerning eye. He wore jeans and a tweed jacket with leather elbow patches: middle-aged, neatly clipped brown beard laced with gray, wide mouth, a mole near his nose and another on his cheek. "This yours?"

"It is. Are you a fan?"

"Yes ma'am. It's a hell of a car. You happy with it?"

"More or less. Are you in the market?"

"I might be." He patted his jacket pocket and I almost expected him to take out a pack of cigarettes or a business card. "Are you Kinsey Millhone, by any chance?"

"Yes. Do I know you?"

"No, but I believe this is yours," he said, offering a long white envelope with my name scrawled across the front.

Puzzled, I took it and he touched my arm, saying, "Baby, you've been served."

I felt my blood pressure drop and my heart skipped a beat. My soul and my body neatly detached from one another, like cars in a freight train when the coupling's been pulled. I felt as if I were standing right next to myself, looking on. My hands were cold but shook only slightly as I opened the envelope and removed the Notice of Hearing and Temporary Restraining Order.

The name of the person asking for protection was Solana Rojas. I was named as the person to be restrained, my sex, height, weight, hair color, home address, and other relevant facts neatly typed in. The information was more or less accurate except for the weight, mine being ten pounds less. The hearing had been scheduled for

February 9—Tuesday of the following week. In the meantime, under Personal Conduct Orders, I was forbidden to harass, attack, strike, threaten, assault, hit, follow, stalk, destroy personal property, keep under surveillance, or block the movements of Solana Rojas. I was also ordered to stay at least one hundred feet away from her, her home, and her vehicle—the low number of feet apparently taking into account the fact that I lived right next door. I was also forbidden to own, possess, have, buy or try to buy, receive or try to receive, or in any other way get a gun or a firearm. At the bottom of the paper in white letters on a block of black, it said **This is a Court Order**. Like I hadn't guessed as much.

The process server watched me with curiosity as I shook my head. He was probably accustomed, as I was, to serving restraining orders on individuals in need of anger-management classes.

"This is so *bogus*. I never did a thing to her. She's invented this shit."

"That's what the hearing's for. You can tell the judge your side of it in court. Maybe he'll agree. In the meantime, I'd get a lawyer if I were you."

"I have one."

"In that case, best of luck. Pleasure doing business. You made it easy for me."

And with that, he got in his car and drove away.

I unlocked the Mustang and got in. I sat, engine off, my hands resting on the steering wheel while I stared out at the street. I glanced down at the restraining order I'd tossed on the passenger's seat beside me. I picked it up and read it for the second time. Under **Court Orders**, in Section 4, the box marked "b" had been checked, specifying that if I didn't obey these orders, I could be arrested and charged with a crime, in which case I might have to (a) go to jail, (b) pay a fine of up to $1,000, or (c) both. None of the choices appealed to me.

The bitch of it was she'd outmaneuvered me again. I'd thought I was so smart and she was already one step ahead of me. Which left me what? My options were now limited, but there had to be a way.

On the way home I stopped at a drugstore and picked up some 400 ASA color film. Then I drove back to my apartment and left my car in a weedy patch in the alleyway behind Henry's house. I slipped through a gap in the back fence and let myself into my studio. I went upstairs and cleared the surface of the footlocker I use as a bed table, setting the reading lamp, alarm clock, and a big stack of books on the floor. I opened the trunk and took out my 35mm single-lens reflex camera. It wasn't cutting-edge equipment, but it was all I had. I loaded the film and went down the spiral staircase. Now all I had to find was a vantage point that would allow me to fire off multiple views of my nemesis next door, making certain, at the same time, she didn't catch sight of me and call the police. Surreptitious picture-taking would certainly qualify as surveillance.

When I told Henry what I was up to, he smiled impishly. "Your timing's good at any rate. I saw Solana driving off as I was coming back from my walk."

It was his clever idea to use a flexible silver sunscreen against the windshield of his station wagon, which he insisted on my borrowing. Solana knew my car too well and she'd be watching for me. He went out to the garage and came back with the screen he used to keep the interior temperatures down when he was parked in the sun. He cut a couple of nice round lens-sized holes in the material and handed me the car keys. I tucked the sunscreen under my arm and tossed it on the passenger's seat before I backed the station wagon out of his garage.

There was still no sign of Solana's car, though there was a handsome length of curb where she'd been parked earlier. I drove around the block and found a spot across the street, being careful to keep the requisite hundred feet between my person and hers, assuming she stayed where she belonged. Of course, if her parking spot was taken and she pulled her car in behind mine, I'd be jail bait for sure.

I popped open the sunscreen and set it against the windshield, then positioned myself, camera in hand, and zeroed in on Gus's front door. I shifted my focus to the empty section of curb and adjusted the lens. I slouched down on my spine to wait, watching the front of the house through a narrow gap between the dashboard and the bottom of the screen. Twenty-six minutes later Solana turned the corner onto Albanil, half a block down the street. I watched her reclaim her parking place, probably feeling pleased with herself as she eased the car nose-first into the space. I sat up and braced my arms on the steering wheel as Solana emerged. The click and whir of the camera were soothing as I shot frame after frame. She stopped in her tracks and her head came up.

Uh-oh.

I watched her survey the street, her body language suggesting her hypervigilance. Her gaze swept the block to the corner and then swung back and fixed on Henry's car. She stood and stared as though she could see me through the sunscreen. I shot six more frames, taking advantage of the moment, and then held my breath, waiting to see if she'd cross the street. I couldn't very well start the car and drive away without first removing the sunscreen, thus exposing myself to view. Even if I managed that, I'd have to pass right by her and the game would be up.

31

SOLANA

Solana sat in the old man's kitchen, smoking one of Tiny's cigarettes, a guilty pleasure she allowed herself on rare occasions when she needed to concentrate. She'd poured herself a tot of vodka to sip while she counted and bundled up the cash she'd amassed. Some was money she'd kept in a savings account, acquired over the years from other jobs. She had $30,000 that had been happily earning interest while she worked in her current position. She'd spent the past week selling off the jewelry she'd collected from Gus as well as her prior clients. Some pieces she'd held for years, worried that the items might have been reported as stolen. She'd run an ad in the classified pages of the local paper, indicating a sale of "estate jewelry," which sounded hoity-toity and refined. She'd had many calls from the bloodhounds who routinely combed that section, looking for a bargain born of someone else's desperation. She'd had the jewelry appraised and she'd carefully calculated selling prices that would be tempting without generating questions about how she came by Edwardian and Art Deco diamond rings and bracelets by Cartier. Not that it was anybody's business, but she'd invented a number of stories: a rich husband who died and left her with nothing but the jewelry he'd given her over the years; a mother who'd smuggled the bracelets and rings out of Germany in 1939; a grandmother who'd fallen on hard times and had no choice but to sell the treasured heirloom necklaces and earrings she'd been given by her own mother years before. People liked sob stories. People paid more for an item with a tragedy attached. These personal accounts of hardship and yearning imbued the rings and bracelets, brooches and pendants, with a value that exceeded the gold content and the stones.

She'd called the gallery owner every day for a week, asking if she'd located a buyer for the paintings. She suspected the woman was just putting her off, but she couldn't be sure. In any event, Solana couldn't afford to alienate her. She wanted the money. Gus's antique furniture she'd sold piece by piece to various high-end dealers around town. He spent his days in the living room or his bedroom and didn't seem to notice that the house was slowly being stripped. From those sales she'd netted a little over $12,000, which was not as much as she'd hoped. Adding that sum to the $26,000 the old man still had tucked away in combined savings, plus the $250,000 she was borrowing from the local bank as a loan against the house, she'd have $288,000, plus the 30 grand in her private account. The $250,000 wasn't in her hands quite yet, but Mr. Larkin at the bank had told her the loan was approved and it was only a matter now of picking up the check. Today she had personal shopping to do, leaving Tiny to babysit Gus.

Tiny and the old man got along well. They liked the same television shows. They shared the same thick pizzas, loaded with junk, and the plastic tubs of cheap cookies she bought at Trader Joe's. She'd taken lately to letting them smoke in the living room though it annoyed her no end. They both were hard of hearing, and when the high volume on the TV started wearing on her nerves she banished them to Tiny's room, where they could watch the old TV set she'd brought from the apartment. Unfortunately, living with the two of them had spoiled the joys of the house, which now felt small and claustrophobic. Mr. Vronsky insisted on keeping the thermostat set at seventy-four degrees, which made her feel as though she were suffocating. It was time to disappear, but she hadn't quite decided what to do with him.

She packed the cash in a duffel that she kept in the back of her closet. Once she was dressed, she checked her reflection in the full-length mirror on the back of the bathroom door. She looked good. She was wearing a business suit, dark blue and plain, with a simple blouse underneath. She was a respectable woman, interested in settling her affairs. She took her purse and paused in the living room on her way to the front door.

"Tiny."

She had to say his name twice because he and the old man were engrossed in a TV show. She picked up the remote and muted the volume on the set. He looked up with surprise, irritated at the interruption. She said, "I'm going out. You stay here. Do you understand me? Don't go anywhere. I'm counting on you to look after Mr. Vronsky. And keep the door locked unless there's a fire."

He said, "Okay."

"Don't answer the door to anyone. I want you here when I get back."

"Okay!"

"And no back talk."

* * *

She took the freeway out to La Cuesta, to the shopping mall she liked. She was especially fond of Robinson's Department Store, where she bought her makeup, her clothing, and occasional household goods. Today she was shopping for suitcases for her upcoming departure. She wanted new luggage, handsome and expensive to mark the new life she was entering. It was almost like a trousseau, which she didn't think young women set much store by these days. Your trousseau was everything fresh, carefully assembled and packed before you left on your honeymoon.

As she entered the store, there was a young woman coming out who held the door politely, allowing Solana to pass through. Solana glanced at her and then looked away, but not quickly enough. The woman's name was Peggy something—maybe Klein, she thought—the granddaughter of a patient Solana had cared for until she died.

The Klein woman said, "Athena?"

Solana ignored her and walked into the store, heading for the escalator. Instead of letting the matter drop, the woman followed her in, calling after her in a strident voice. "Wait just a minute! I know you. You're the woman who looked after my grandmother."

She moved swiftly, hard on Solana's heels, grabbing at her arm. Solana turned on her savagely. "I don't know what you're talking about. My name is Solana Rojas."

"Bullshit! You're Athena Melanagras. You stole thousands of dollars from us and then you—"

"You're mistaken. It must have been somebody else. I never laid eyes on you or anybody else in your family."

"You fucking liar! My grandmother's name was Esther Feldcamp. She died two years ago. You raided her accounts and you did worse, as you well know. My mother filed charges, but you were gone by then."

"Get away from me. You're delusional. I'm a respectable woman. I've never stolen a cent from anyone." Solana got on the escalator and faced forward. The moving stairs carried her upward as the woman hung on to her from one step down.

The Klein woman was saying, "Someone help! Call the police!" She sounded deranged and others had turned to stare.

"Shut up!" Solana said. She turned and shoved her.

The woman stumbled down another step but clung to Solana's arm like an octopus. At the top of the escalator, Solana tried to step away, but she ended up dragging the woman through the sportswear department. A clerk at the cash register watched with mounting concern as Solana took the Klein woman's fingers and prized them off one by one, bending her index finger back until she shrieked.

Solana punched her once in the face, then shook herself free and hurried away. She tried not to run because running would only call greater attention to herself, but she needed to put as much distance as she could between herself and her accuser. She was frantic to locate an exit, but there was no sign of one, which meant it was probably behind her somewhere. Briefly she thought about finding a hiding place—one of the dressing rooms perhaps—but she was worried she'd be trapped. Behind her the Klein woman had persuaded the clerk to call security. She could see the two of them huddled together at the counter while over the intercom a voice intoned a store code that signified god knew what.

Solana scurried around the corner where she spotted the down escalator. She held on to the moving rail and took the steps down two at a time. People opposite her on the up escalator turned to look at her idly, but they didn't seem to grasp the drama taking place.

Solana looked behind her. The Klein woman had trailed her and she was coming down the escalator steps at a pace that had her breathing down Solana's neck. At ground level, as the woman drew close, Solana hauled back with her purse, swinging it hard until it caught the woman on the side of the head. Instead of backing off, the woman grabbed the purse and gave it a yank. The two wrestled with the bag, which was now hanging open. The Klein woman snatched her wallet, and Solana yelled, "Thief!"

A male customer in the men's department moved in their direction, uncertain whether the situation required intervention. Everyone was fearful these days, reluctant to get involved. Suppose one of the struggling parties had a gun and a Good Samaritan was killed while trying to be of help? It was a stupid way to die and no one wanted to take the chance. Solana kicked the Klein woman twice in the shins. She went down, crying out in pain. The last flash Solana had of the woman, there was blood running down her legs.

Solana moved away as swiftly as she could. The woman had her wallet, but she still had everything else she needed: house keys, car keys, compact. The wallet she could do without. Thankfully she carried no cash, but it wouldn't take the woman long to check the address listed on her driver's license. She should have left the Other's address as it was, but it seemed wiser at the time to change it to the apartment where she herself had been living. Once before, she'd applied for a job, retaining the Other's address instead of substituting her own. The patient's daughter had gone to the real address and knocked on the door. It didn't take a minute for her to realize the woman she was talking to was someone other than the woman who was caring for her aged mother. Solana'd been forced to abandon that job, leaving behind additional precious cash she'd hidden in her room. Even the late-night trip back had netted her nothing since the locks had been changed.

She pictured the Klein woman talking to the police, weeping hysterically and babbling the story of her grammy and the larcenous companion hired to care for her. Solana didn't have a record, but Athena Melanagras had been arrested once for drug possession. Just her bad luck. If she'd known, she never would have borrowed the woman's identity. Solana knew complaints had been filed against her under her various aliases. If the Klein woman went to the police, the descriptions would add up. In the past, she'd left fingerprints behind. She knew now that was a terrible mistake, but it hadn't occurred to her until later that she should have wiped down each place thoroughly before she moved on.

She hurried through the parking lot to her car and headed back to the freeway, taking the 101 south now to the Capillo off-ramp. The bank was downtown and despite the upsetting incident at the store, she wanted her money in hand. Luggage she could buy somewhere else. Or maybe she wouldn't bother. Time was running short.

When she reached the intersection of Anaconda and Floresta, she circled the block, making sure no one was following her. She parked and went into the bank. Mr. Larkin, the manager, greeted her warmly and showed her to his desk, where he seated her graciously, treating her like a queen. Life was like this with money, people fawning; bowing and scraping. She held her purse in her lap like a prize. It was an expensive designer bag and she knew it made a good impression.

Mr. Larkin said, "Will you excuse me for just one second? I have a phone call."

"Of course."

She watched him cross the bank lobby and disappear through a door. While she waited she took out her compact and powdered her nose. She looked calm and confident, not like someone who'd just been attacked by a lunatic. Her hands were shaking, but she breathed deeply, working to appear nonchalant and unconcerned. She closed the compact.

"Ms. Tasinato?"

A woman had appeared behind her unannounced. Solana jumped and the compact flew out of her hand. She watched the arc of its descent, time slowing as the plastic casing hit the marble floor and bounced once. The refillable disk popped out and the hard circle of compressed powder broke into several pieces. The mirror in the lid of the compact shattered as well and fragments littered the floor. The one shard of mirror that remained in the case looked like a dagger, pointed and sharp. She pushed the broken compact aside with her foot. Someone else would have to clean up the mess. A broken mirror was bad luck. Breaking anything was bad, but a mirror was the worst.

"I'm so sorry I startled you. I'll have someone take care of that. I don't want you cutting your hand."

"It's nothing. Don't worry about it. I can get another one," she said, but the heaviness had descended. Things had already gone wrong and now this. She'd seen it happen before, calamity piling on calamity.

She turned her attention to the woman, trying to suppress her distaste. This was no one she knew. She appeared to be in her thirties, definitely pregnant and probably in her seventh month, judging by the taut mound under her maternity smock. Solana checked for a wedding ring, which the woman wore. She disapproved nonetheless. She should quit her job and stay home. She had no business working in a bank, flaunting her condition without a hint of embarrassment. In three months' time, Solana would see the ad she placed in the classifieds: *Working mom needs experienced and reliable baby nurse. References required.* Disgusting.

"I'm Rebecca Wilcher. Mr. Larkin was called away and asked me to assist you." She sat down in his place.

Solana didn't like doing business with women. She wanted to protest, but she held her tongue, anxious to get the transaction over with.

"Let me just take a quick look to familiarize myself with your loan papers," she said. She began to flip pages, reading much too carefully. Solana could see her eyes tracing every line of print. She looked up and smiled briefly at Solana. "I see you were appointed Mr. Vronsky's conservator."

"That's correct. His home is in desperate need of attention. The wiring's old, the plumbing's bad, and there's no wheelchair ramp, which keeps him a virtual prisoner. He's eighty-nine years old and unable to care for himself. I'm all he has."

"I understand. I met him when I first started working here, but we haven't seen him for months." She set the file on the desk. "Everything seems to be in order. This will be submitted to the court for approval and once that's done, we'll be funding the loan. It looks like we'll need one more form filled out, if you don't mind. I have a blank one here you can complete and return."

She reached in the drawer, checked through the files, and came up with a paper that she passed across the desk.

Solana looked at it with irritation. "What's this? I filled out all the forms Mr. Larkin asked for."

"It must have been an oversight. I'm sorry for the inconvenience."

"What's the problem with the forms I gave you?"

"There's no problem. This is something new the government requires. It shouldn't take long."

"I don't have time for this. I thought everything was done. Mr. Larkin said all I had to do was stop by and he'd issue a check. That's what he told me."

"Not without the court's approval. That's standard procedure. We need a judge's okay."

"What are you saying, you doubt I'm entitled to the funds? You think the house doesn't need work? You should come and see for yourself."

"It's not that. Your plans for the house sound wonderful."

"The place is a fire hazard. If something isn't done soon, Mr. Vronsky could burn to death in his bed. You can tell Mr. Larkin I said so. It will be on his head if anything happens. And yours, too."

"I apologize for any misunderstanding. Perhaps I can have a quick word with the bank manager and we can straighten this out. If you'll excuse me . . ."

The minute she'd moved away from her desk, Solana stood up, clutching her bag. She reached across the desk and picked up the manila folder containing all the paperwork. She moved toward the entrance, being careful to behave like someone with a legitimate purpose. Nearing the door, she looked down, holding up the file to conceal her features from the surveillance camera she knew was there. What was the matter with the woman? She hadn't done anything to warrant suspicion. She'd been cooperative and agreeable, and this was how she was treated? She'd call later. She'd talk to Mr. Larkin and raise a fuss. If he insisted on her filling out the form, she'd do so, but she wanted him to know how annoyed she was. Maybe she'd take her business elsewhere. She'd mention that to him. Court approval could take a month and there was always the chance the transaction would come under scrutiny.

She retrieved her car from the parking lot and made a beeline for home, too upset to worry about the paintings in the trunk. She noticed other drivers glancing at the word DEAD scratched on her driver's-side door. Maybe that hadn't been such a good idea. The little hooligan she'd hired had done a good job, but now she was stuck with the damage. She might as well have been toting a banner, LOOK AT ME. I'M STRANGE. Her parking place was still available out in front of the house. She pulled in nose-first and then had to maneuver until the car was properly lined up with the curb.

It wasn't until she got out and locked the car door behind her that she realized something was wrong. She stood stock-still and searched the street, her gaze moving from house to house. She tracked the scene to the corner and then her gaze slid back. Henry's station wagon was parked on the far side of the street, three doors down, a silver sunscreen against the windshield, blocking any view of the interior. Why had he taken it out of the garage and left it on the street?

She watched the dappled sunlight reflecting off the glass. She thought she discerned small irregular shadows on the driver's side, but at this remove, she wasn't sure what she was looking at. She turned away, debating whether to cross the street and take a closer look. Kinsey Millhone wouldn't dare defy the court order, but Henry might be watching her. She couldn't think why he would, but it was wiser to behave as though she didn't suspect.

She went into the house. The living room was empty, which meant that Tiny and Mr. Vronsky had gone down for their naps like good little boys. She picked up the telephone and dialed Henry's number next door. After two rings, he picked up, saying, "Hello?"

She lowered the handset to the cradle without saying a word. If it wasn't Henry, then who? The answer was obvious.

She went out the front door and down the steps. She crossed the street at an angle and walked directly to his car. This had to stop. She couldn't have people spying on her. The rage rising in her throat threatened to choke her. She could see the door locks were up. She yanked open the driver's-side door.

No one.

Solana took in a deep breath, her senses as keen as a wolf's. Kinsey's scent hung in the air—a light, but distinct mix of shampoo and soap. Solana put her hand on the seat, which she could have sworn was still warm. She'd missed her by moments and her disappointment was so sharp she nearly wailed aloud. She had to get herself under control. She closed her eyes, thinking, *Calm. Be calm.* No matter what was going on, she was still in charge. So what if Kinsey'd watched her getting out of her car? What difference did that make?

None.

Unless she was armed with a camera taking photographs. Solana put a hand to her throat. Suppose she'd seen the photo of the Other at the nursing home and wanted a recent photo of her to compare? She couldn't take that chance.

Solana went back to the house and locked the front door behind her as though at any minute the authorities would arrive. She went into the kitchen and retrieved a spray bottle of cleanser from under the sink. She wet a sponge, squeezed out the moisture, and then saturated it with the cleaning solution. She began to wipe the place down, erasing all traces of herself, working her way through the house room by room. She'd catch the boys' rooms later. In the meantime, she'd have to pack. She'd have to get Tiny's things together. She'd have to get the car filled with gas. On the way out of town, she'd stop and pick up the paintings and take them to a gallery somewhere else. She'd be thorough this time, making no mistakes.

32

According to the restraining order, within twenty-four hours of my being served, I was required to turn in or sell any guns or firearms in my possession. I'm not a nut about guns, but the two I have I'm quite fond of. One is a 9mm Heckler & Koch P7M13; the other, a little Davis .32 caliber semiautomatic. Often I carry one of them, unloaded, in a briefcase in the backseat of my car. I keep ammunition close by as well; otherwise, what's the point? My favorite gun of all time, the no-brand .32 caliber semiautomatic my aunt Gin had given me, was destroyed in a bomb blast some years before.

Reluctantly, I removed both guns from my office safe. I had two choices in dispossessing myself of my weapons. I could go to the police station and surrender them, watching as they were booked in and I was given a receipt. The problem with this option was that I knew a number of STPD officers and detectives, Cheney Phillips being one. The notion of running into one of them was more than I could bear. I chose instead to hand the guns over to a licensed gun dealer on upper State Street, who completed items 5 and 6 of the form I'd been given, which I then returned to the court clerk for filing. My guns would be returned to me only by judge's orders.

On the way back to town I stopped at the courthouse and filed a response in opposition to Solana's temporary restraining order, on the grounds that her assertions were factually untrue. Then I stopped by Lonnie Kingman's office and had a chat with him. He agreed to go with me for my court date on Tuesday of the following week. "I don't guess I have to remind you that if you violate the terms of the TRO, you can have your license yanked."

"I have no intention of violating the court order. How else can I earn a living? I've done too many shit jobs in life. I'm partial to my current occupation. Anything else?"

"You might want to line up a couple of witnesses who'll back up your version of events."

"I'm sure Henry would be willing. I'll have to think if there's anyone else. She was clever about conducting our exchanges in private."

When I got into the office there was a message from Lowell Effinger's secretary, Geneva, on my answering machine, saying that Melvin Downs's deposition subpoena for personal appearance was ready to be picked up. I was antsy anyway, not inclined to sit around the office waiting for the next blow to fall. Oddly enough, Melvin Downs had begun to feel like a pal, and my relationship with him cozy compared to my dealings with Solana, which had gone from bad to disastrous.

I got in the Mustang, made a quick stop at Effinger's office for the paperwork, and headed for Capillo Hill. I turned left into the alley just shy of Palisade and parked behind the building that housed the Laundromat and the dropoff location for Starting Over. The back door to the place was closed, but when I tried the handle it opened easily.

Melvin was perched on a stool at a counter that served as a work space. He'd filled a ceramic mug with lollipops, and I could see the cellophane wrapper he'd removed from the one he had in his mouth. The back rooms were cold and he'd kept on his brown leather bomber jacket. A damp breeze emanating from the Laundromat in front smelled of powdered soap, bleach, and cotton garments being tumbled in oversized dryers. On the work space in front of him, there was a dismantled toaster. He'd removed the chassis from the frame. The naked appliance looked small and vulnerable, like a chicken denuded of its feathers. He shook his head slightly when he caught sight of me.

I put one hand in my jacket pocket, more from tension than the chill. In the other, I held the subpoena. "I thought you worked Tuesdays and Thursdays."

"Day of the week doesn't matter much to me. I've got nothing else to do." The lollipop must have been cherry, because his tongue was bright pink. He caught my look and held up the mug, offering me a sucker. I shook my head. The only flavor he'd stocked was cherry and while it was my favorite, it seemed inappropriate to accept anything from him.

"What's wrong with the toaster?"

"Heating element and latch assembly. I'm just working on the latch."

"You get a lot of toasters?"

"Those and hair dryers. Nowadays when a toaster goes bad, the first thing you think about is throwing it away. Appliances are cheap and if something breaks down, you buy new. Most of the time, the problem's as simple as people not bothering to empty the crumb tray."

"What, the sliding thing underneath?"

"Yes, ma'am. With this one, pieces of bread had fallen into the base and shorted out the heating element. Crumbs were jamming the assembly as well so I had to blow the latch clean and then lubricate it. Once I put it all back together, it should be right as rain. How'd you find me this time?"

"Oh, I have my little ways."

I watched for a moment, trying to remember when I'd last emptied my crumb tray. Maybe that's why my toast tended to be burned on one side and soft on the other.

He nodded at the paperwork. "That for me?"

I put it on the counter. "Yes. They've scheduled the deposition and this is the subpoena. If you like I can pick you up and bring you back here afterwards. They set it up for a Friday because I told them which days you were busy here."

"Thoughtful."

"That's the best I can do."

"No doubt."

My gaze strayed to his right hand. "Tell me something. Is that a prison tattoo?"

He glanced at his tattoo, then put his thumb and index finger together to form a pair of lips, which seemed to part in anticipation of the next question. The eyes permanently inked on his knuckle really did create the illusion of a little face. "This is Tía."

"I heard about her. She's cute."

He held his hand up close to his face. "Did you hear that?" he said to her. "She thinks you're cute. You want to talk to her?"

He turned his hand and Tía seemed to study me with a certain bright interest. "Okay," she said. The unblinking black eyes settled on mine. To him she said, "How much can I tell her?"

"You decide."

"We were inside twelve years," she said, "which is where we met."

The falsetto voice he projected seemed real enough to me and I found myself addressing my questions to her. "Here in California?"

She turned and looked at him and then looked back at me. Despite her resemblance to a toothless crone, she managed to appear coy. "We'd prefer not to say. I will tell you this. He was such a good boy, he got out on an early release." Tía bobbed over to him and gave him a big buss on the cheek. He smiled in response.

"What was he in for?"

"Oh, this and that. We don't discuss it with people we've just met."

"I figured it was a child molest since his daughter won't let him see his grandsons."

"Well, aren't you quick to condemn," she said, tartly.

"It's just a guess."

"He never laid a hand on those little boys and that's the truth," she said, indignant in his behalf.

"Maybe his daughter feels sex offenders aren't that trustworthy," I remarked.

"He tried talking her into supervised visits, but she wasn't having any of it. He did everything he could to make amends, including a little side deal with some unsavory gents."

"Meaning what?"

Tía tilted her head and gestured me closer, indicating that what she was going to say was highly personal. I leaned down and allowed her to whisper in my ear. I could have sworn I felt her breath stir against my neck. "There's a house up in San Francisco where they take care of guys like him. Very tacky place. N-O-K-D."

"Pardon?"

" 'Not our kind, dear.' "

"I don't understand."

"Castration." Tía's lips pursed at the word. Melvin watched her with interest, his expression blank.

"Like a hospital?"

"No, no. This is a private residence, where certain surgeries are done under the table, as it were. These weren't licensed medical doctors, just men with tools and equipment who enjoyed cutting and sewing, relieving other fellows of their urges."

"Melvin volunteered for that?"

"It was a means to an end. He needed to gain control of his impulses, instead of them controlling him."

"Did it work?"

"In the main. His libido's down to almost nothing and what desires he has left, he manages to subdue. He doesn't drink or do drugs because he can't predict what Demons will emerge. Sly? You have no idea. There's no way to bargain with the Evil Ones. Once they're up, they take charge. Sober, he's a good soul. Not that he'll ever convince his daughter of that."

"She's a hard-hearted girl," he said.

Tía turned on him. "Hush. You know better. She's a mom. Her first job is to protect her little kids."

I spoke to Melvin. "Aren't you required to register? I called the probation department and they never heard of you."

"I registered where I was."

"If you move, you're supposed to reregister."

Tía intervened. "Technically, yes, hon, but I'll tell you

how it goes. People find out what he was convicted of. Once they know, the whispering starts and then the outraged parents march up and down outside his house with picket signs. Then the news trucks and the journalists and he never has another moment's peace."

I said, "It's not about him. It's about the kids he abused. They'll never get out from under that curse."

Melvin cleared his throat. "I'm sorry for the past. I admit I did things and things were done to me . . ."

Tía cut in, "That's right. All he wants to do now is watch over the little ones and keep them safe. What's wrong with that?"

"He's not supposed to have contact. He's not supposed to be within a thousand yards of little kids. No schools, no playgrounds. He knows that."

"All he does is look. He knows it's wrong to touch so he doesn't do that anymore."

I looked at Melvin. "Why put yourself in harm's way? You're like a dry alcoholic working in a bar. The temptation's right there and a day's going to come when it's too much."

Tía clucked her disapproval. "I've told him that a hundred times myself, hon, but he can't keep away."

I couldn't listen to any more of this stuff. "Can we discuss the deposition? You must have questions."

Melvin's attention remained fixed on the toaster. "If I agree, what prevents the opposing attorney from going after me? Isn't that how they do it? You testify to something they don't like and they turn it back on you. Show you're a despicable ex-con and no one should listen to a word you say?"

I thought about Hetty Buckwald. "Probably. I won't lie to you about that. On the other hand, you don't show up and you'll be cited for contempt of court."

Tía bobbed up and down, saying, "Oh please. You think he gives a shit about that?"

"Can't you talk him into it?"

"Give the man a break. He's paid enough already."

I waited, but neither one said another word. I could only push the point so far. I left the subpoena on the counter and went out the front.

Just to make the afternoon perfect, when I reached the office I received a phone call from Melanie Oberlin, who jumped right in. "Kinsey, what the hell is going on? Solana said she had to get a restraining order out on you."

"Thanks, Melanie. I appreciate the support. Would you like to hear my side of it?"

"Not particularly. She told me you called the county on her and they dismissed the complaint."

"Did she also mention that a woman named Cristina Tasinato has been appointed Gus's conservator?"

"His what?"

"I'm assuming you know the term."

"Well, yes, but why would anyone do that?"

"A better question is, who's Cristina Tasinato?"

"Okay. Who is she?"

"She and the woman we know as Solana Rojas are the same person. She's busy working her way through every cent he has. Hold on a second and I'll check my notes so I can give you the exact figures. Here we go. By way of compensation, she's submitted invoices to the court for $8,726.73 for Gus's home care, courtesy of Senior Health Care Management, Inc. That includes paying her half-witted son, who's posing as an orderly while he sleeps all day long. There's also an invoice from her attorney for $6,227.47 for 'professional services' as of January 15, 1988."

There was a wonderful moment of silence. "Can they *do* that?"

"Kiddo, I hate to sound cynical, but the point is to *help* the elderly with big nest eggs. Why have yourself appointed a conservator for someone living on a fixed income? It makes no sense."

"This is making me sick."

"As well it should."

"But what's this about the county?"

"That's the question you started with. I reported Solana to the Tri-Counties Agency for the Prevention of Elder Abuse and they sent out a caseworker to investigate. Solana told the gal she'd begged you repeatedly to come to Gus's aid, but you refused. She said Gus was incompetent to handle his daily needs and she nominated herself—I should say, Cristina Tasinato—to oversee his affairs."

"That's crazy. Since when?"

"A week, maybe ten days ago. Of course everything's been backdated to coincide, fortuitously, with the phony Solana's arrival on the scene."

"I don't believe this!"

"I didn't either, but it's true."

"You know I never refused to help him. That's a goddamn lie."

"As is much of what Solana says about me."

"Why didn't you call me? I don't understand why I'm just now hearing this. You could have *warned* me."

I squinted at the phone, amazed at how accurately I'd predicted her reaction. She'd already shifted all the blame to me.

"Melanie, I've been telling you Solana was up to something, but you refused to believe me. What's the point of another call?"

"You're the one who said she was okay."

"Right, and you were the one who told me to limit my investigation to her degree, the last place she worked, and a couple of references."

"I said that?"

"Yes, dear. I make a habit of writing down the instructions I'm given in a case like this. Now will you get off your high horse and help me out?"

"Doing what?"

"For one thing, you could fly out and testify on my behalf when I make my court appearance."

"For what?"

"The restraining order. I can't get close to Gus because Solana's there full-time, but you're still entitled to see him unless she gets an order out on you. You could also initiate the paperwork challenging her appointment. You're his only living relative and you're entitled to a say. Oh, and while I have you on the line, I might as well alert you. Once I type up my report, I'm sending a copy to the DA. Maybe they can step in and put a stop to her."

"Fine. Do that. I'll be out as soon as I can make arrangements."

"Good."

That matter taken care of, I put a call through to Richard Compton, who said he'd get in touch with Norman and tell him to give me free rein searching records in the basement of the complex. I gave him a rough estimate of when I'd be there and he said he'd clear it. I had two stops to make before I hit Colgate, the first being the drugstore where I'd left the canister of film the day before. Prints in hand, I drove over to the Sunrise House and pushed through the front door, feeling an easy familiarity since I'd been there before. I'd called in advance and spoken to Lana Sherman, the LVN I'd consulted during the background check on Solana Rojas. She said she could spare me a few minutes as long as no emergencies arose.

In the lobby, the white-flocked artificial Christmas tree had been dismantled and stuffed back in its box until the holidays came around again. On the antique table that served as a reception desk, a white-painted branch had been placed in a Chinese ginger jar and hung with pink and red hearts in honor of Valentine's Day, coming up in two weeks.

The receptionist directed me to One West, the post-surgery floor. Passing down the hall, I caught sight of Lana in a four-bed ward distributing meds in white pleated paper cups. I waved and pointed, indicating that I'd wait for her at the nurse's station. I found a molded gray plastic chair in a little visitors alcove and picked up a tattered magazine called *Modern Maturity*.

Lana appeared moments later, rubber-soled shoes squeaking on the vinyl tile. "I've already had my break so I don't have long." She sat down in a matching plastic chair next to mine. "So how's Solana doing with the job?"

"Not well," I said. I'd been debating how candid to be, but I couldn't see an advantage in holding back. I wanted answers and there was no point in beating around the bush. "I'd like you to look at some photographs and tell me who this is."

"Like a lineup?"

"Not quite." I took the bright yellow envelope of photographs from my shoulder bag and passed them over to her. Out of the roll of thirty-six pictures, I'd netted ten clear shots, which she sorted through rapidly before she handed them back. "That's a nurse's aide named Costanza Tasinato. She worked here the same time as Solana."

"Did you ever hear her use the name Cristina?"

"She didn't use it, but I know it was her first name because I saw it on her driver's license. Costanza was her middle name and she went by that. What's this about?"

"She's been passing herself off as Solana Rojas for the past three months."

Lana made a face. "That's illegal, isn't it?"

"You can call yourself anything you like as long as there's no intent to defraud. In this case, she's claiming she's an LVN. She's moved herself into the patient's house, along with her son, who I gather is a lunatic. I'm trying to put a stop to her before she does any more harm. You're sure this is Costanza and not Solana?"

"Take a look at the wall near the nurse's station. You can judge for yourself."

I followed her into the corridor where photographs had been framed and hung, showing the Employee of the Month for the past two years. I found myself staring at a color photograph of the real Solana Rojas, who was both older and heavier than the one I knew. No one acquainted with the real Solana would be fooled by the impersonation, but I had to give Ms. Tasinato credit for the subterfuge. "You think they'd let me borrow this?"

"No, but the woman in the office will make you a copy if you ask nice."

I left Sunrise House and drove to Colgate, parking as I had before across from the apartment complex on Franklin Avenue. When I knocked at Apartment 1, Princess came to the door, holding a finger to her lips. "Norman's napping," she whispered. "Let me get the key and I can take you down."

"Down" turned out to be a basement, a rare phenomenon in California, where so many buildings are constructed on slab. This one was dank, a sprawling warren of cinder block rooms, some subdivided into padlocked wire enclosures the tenants used for storage. Lighting consisted of a series of bare bulbs that hung from a low ceiling overrun with furnace ducts, plumbing, and electrical pipes. It was the kind of place that made you hope earthquake predictions were off the mark instead of imminent. If the building collapsed I'd never find my way out, assuming I was still alive.

Princess showed me into a narrow room entirely lined with shelves. I could almost identify by type the managers who had come and gone in the thirty years the building had been occupied. One was a neatnik, who'd filed all the paperwork in matching banker's boxes. The next guy took a haphazard approach, using a strange mix of liquor cartons, Kotex boxes, and old wooden milk crates. Another had apparently purchased his boxes from a U-Haul company and each was neatly stenciled with the contents in the upper left-hand corner. In the past ten years, I counted six managers altogether. Norman and Princess surprised me by favoring opaque plastic bins. Each had a slot in front where one or the other had neatly printed and date-ordered a list of rental applications and assorted paperwork, including receipts, utilities, bank statements, repair bills, and copies of the owner's tax returns.

Princess left me to my own devices, as eager as I was for sunlight and fresh air. I followed the line of boxes toward the far end of the room where the light wasn't as good and cracks in the outside wall created an illusion of dripping water, though there was none in evidence. Naturally, as an ex-cop and highly trained investigator, I was worried about vermin: millipedes, jumping spiders, and the like. I followed the dates on the boxes, back as far as

1976, which was in excess of the parameters Norman had suggested. I started with the banker's boxes, which seemed friendlier than the boxes that had the word KOTEX stamped all over them. The earliest date I spotted was 1953 and I assumed the building had been completed right about then.

One at a time, I hauled the first three 1976 boxes from the shelf and carried them to the better-lighted end of the room. I took the lid off the first and finger-walked through two inches of files, trying to get a feel for the order. The system was random, consisting of a series of manila folders, grouped according to the month, but with no attempt to alphabetize the names of the tenants. Each banker's box contained three or four years' worth of applications.

I shifted my attention to 1977. I sat on an overturned plastic milk crate, pulled a quarter of the folders out, and placed them on my lap. My back was already hurting, but I proceeded doggedly. The paper smelled like mildew and I could see where the occasional box had sucked up water like a wick. The years 1976 and 1977 were a bust, but in the third pile of folders for 1978, I found her. I recognized the neat block lettering before I saw the name. Tasinato, Cristina Costanza, and her son, Tomasso, who was twenty-five at the time. I got up and crossed the room until I was standing directly beneath a forty-watt bulb. Cristina worked cleaning houses, employed by a company called Mighty Maids, which had since gone out of business. On the assumption that she lied on a regular basis, I ignored most of the data except for one line. Under "Personal References," she'd listed an attorney named Dennis Altinova, with an address and phone number I already knew. In the space marked "Relationship," she'd block-printed the word "BROTHER."

I set the application aside and repacked the boxes, which I returned to the shelf. I was tired and my hands were filthy, but I was feeling jazzed. I'd packed a lot into my day and I was close to nailing Cristina Tasinato.

It wasn't until I'd left the basement and was coming up the stairs that I spotted the woman waiting at the top. I hesitated at the sight of her. She was in her early thirties, wearing a suit with a short skirt, hose, and low heels. She was attractive and well groomed, except for the heavy bruises marking both shins and the right side of her face. The dark red streaks around the orb of her eye would turn black and blue by nightfall. "Kinsey?"

"That's right."

"Princess told me you were down here. I hope I'm not interrupting your work."

"Not at all. What can I do for you?"

"My name is Peggy Klein. I think the two of us are looking for the same woman."

"Cristina Tasinato?"

"When I knew her she was using the name Athena Melanagras, but the address on her driver's license is this one." She held out the license and I found myself looking at Solana Rojas, who now had one more alias to add to her string.

"Where did you get this?"

"We had a knock-down, drag-out fight at Robinson's earlier today. I was going out the side door as she was coming in. She was wearing glasses and her hair was different, but I knew her right away. She worked for my grandmother toward the end of her life when she needed full-time care. After Gram died, my mother discovered she'd forged Gram's signature on thousands of dollars' worth of checks."

"She knew you'd recognized her?"

"Oh sure. She spotted me about the same time I spotted her, and you should have seen her take off. She made it as far as the escalator before I caught up with her."

"You went after her?"

"I did. I know it was dumb, but I couldn't help myself. She dragged me all over the place, but I wouldn't let go. I was doing all right until she punched me. She whacked me with her purse and kicked the shit out of me, but I grabbed her wallet in the process and that's what brought me out here."

"I hope you filed a police report."

"Trust me. There's already a warrant out for her arrest."

"Good for you."

"There's more. Gram's doctor told us she died of congestive heart failure, but the pathologist who did the autopsy said asphyxiation and heart failure share some of the same features—pulmonary edema and congestion and what he called petechial hemorrhages. He said someone put a pillow over her face and smothered her to death. Guess who?"

"Solana killed her?"

"Yes, and the police suspect she'd probably done it before. Old people die every day and nobody thinks a thing about it. The police did what they could, but by then she was gone. Or so we thought. We just assumed she'd left town, but here she is again. How stupid could she be?"

"*Greedy*'s a better word. She's all over the poor old guy who lives next door to me and she's sucking him dry. I've tried to put a stop to her, but I'm operating at a disadvantage. She has a restraining order out against me so if I even look at her cross-eyed, she'll have me in jail."

"Well, you better find a way around it. Killing my Gram was the last thing she did before she disappeared."

33

I had Peggy Klein follow me home in her car, which she parked in the alley behind Henry's garage. I found parking on the street in front, six cars away from Solana's. I went through the gate and around the side of the studio. Peggy was waiting by the gap in the back fence, which I held aside for her as she slipped through. Henry had a real gate, but it was unusable because both his gate and the fence were weighted down with morning glories. While we crossed the back patio, I brought Peggy up to speed on recent events. Jay Larkin had called me back to tell me about Solana's meltdown at the bank. Peggy was quick to suggest the next step in the plan. I said, "Great timing, your showing up at Solana's apartment complex when you did."

"When I showed Norman and Princess the driver's license, they knew exactly what was going on."

Peggy followed me to Henry's back door, and when he came to let me in I did the introductions.

"What's up?" he asked.

"We're going to get Gus out of there. I'll let her fill

you in while I whip over to my place and pick up a few tools."

I left the two of them to sort themselves out. I unlocked my door and went up the spiral stairs. For the second time in two days, I cleared the top of my footlocker and opened the lid. I took out my fanny pack. I found the flashlight and checked the batteries, which were strong, and I tucked it in my pack along with a set of key picks in a nifty leather case given to me by a burglar of my acquaintance some years before. I was also the proud possessor of a battery-operated pick gun, given to me by another dear friend who was currently in jail and therefore had no need for such specialized equipment. In the interest of virtue, I hadn't done any serious breaking and entering for some time, but this was a special occasion, and I hoped my skills weren't too rusty to do the job. I snapped the fanny pack around my waist and returned to Henry's in time to catch the back end of Peggy's tale. Henry and I exchanged a look. We both sensed we'd have one chance to rescue Gus. If we didn't pull it off, then Gus might well end up like Gram.

Henry said, "Oh, boy. You're taking a hell of a risk."

"Any questions?"

"What about Solana?"

"I'm not harassing her," I said.

"You know that's not what I mean."

"Yeah, well, I've got that under control. Peggy's going to make a call. I gave her the rundown on the situation and she suggested a plan just about guaranteed to send Solana scurrying. Mind if we use your phone?"

"Be my guest."

I wrote Gus's number on the scratch pad Henry kept by the phone and I watched Peggy punch in the numbers. Her expression shifted when the line was picked up and I tilted my head close to the handset so I could hear the conversation.

"May I speak to Ms. Tasinato?" she said, smoothly. She had a lovely phone manner, pleasant and authoritative, with a hint of warmth in her voice.

"Yes, this is she."

"This is Denise Amber. I'm Mr. Larkin's assistant at Santa Teresa Savings and Loan. I understand there was a problem about the funding of your loan. He asked me to call and tell you how sorry he is for any distress it might have caused."

"That's right. I was very upset and I'm thinking about changing banks. You can tell him I said so. I'm not used to being treated like that. He told me to come in and pick up the check and then that woman—the pregnant one—"

"Rebecca Wilcher."

"That's her. She handed me another form to fill out when I'd already given Mr. Larkin everything he asked for. And then she had the nerve to tell me the funds wouldn't be available until the judge approved."

"Which is why I'm calling. I'm afraid Mrs. Wilcher and Mr. Larkin got their wires crossed. She wasn't aware he'd already cleared the matter with the court."

"He did?"

"Of course. Mr. Vronsky's been a valued customer for many years. Mr. Larkin made a point of expediting the approval process."

"I'm happy to hear that. I have a contractor coming here on Monday with a proposal all drawn up. I promised him a deposit so he can start the electrical work. Right now, the wiring's so frayed, I can smell the scorches. I plug in an iron and the toaster at the same time and all the lights go out. Mrs. Wilcher didn't even express her concern."

"I'm sure she had no idea what you've been dealing with. The reason I called is that I have your check at my desk. The bank closes at five o'clock, so if you like I can tuck it in the mail and save you the trip through rush-hour traffic."

Solana was silent for half a beat. "That's very kind of you, but I may be going out of town soon. The mail in this neighborhood is slow to arrive and I can't afford a delay. I'd prefer to pick it up in person and deposit the money in an account I set up especially for this purpose. Not your bank. This is the trust company I've been dealing with for years."

"Whatever's most convenient. If tomorrow works better for you, we open at nine."

"Today's fine. I'm tied up with a little something at the moment, but I can set that aside and be there in fifteen minutes."

"Wonderful. I'm leaving for the day, but all you have to do is ask at the teller's window. I'll have the check in an envelope with your name on it. I'm sorry I can't be here to deliver it personally."

"Not a problem. Which window?"

"The first. Just inside the door. I'll walk the envelope over as soon as we finish our conversation."

"I appreciate this. It's a great relief," Solana said.

Peggy hung up, smiling with satisfaction. I was happy to introduce her to the joy of telling fibs. She'd been worried she couldn't pull it off, but I told her anyone who lied to little kids about Santa Claus and the Easter Bunny could surely manage this.

Henry positioned himself at the dining room window and kept an eye on the street. Within minutes, Solana appeared and hurried to her car. As soon as Henry signaled that she'd pulled away, I was out the back door and slipping through the hedge. Peggy pushed through the bushes after me, doing god knows what damage to her panty hose. "Who cares?" she said, when I cautioned her.

"You have your car keys?" I asked.

She patted her pocket. "I locked my purse in the trunk so we're good to go."

"You have a talent for skulduggery, I admire that. What sort of work do you do?" I asked, as we climbed the porch steps.

"I'm a stay-at-home mom. We're a rare breed these days. Half the mothers I know hang on to their jobs because they can't handle being at home with their own kids full-time."

"How many do you have?"

"Two girls—six and eight. They've got a playdate at a friend's, which is why I'm free. You have kids?"

"Nope. I'm not entirely sure I'm the type."

Henry had gone out to the street with his canvas gloves and a few gardening tools, stationing himself close to Gus's front walk, where he'd dig industriously. The grass at the curb was dormant and looked as dead as dirt, so if Solana found him weeding, I wasn't sure how he was going to explain himself. He'd think of some way to bamboozle her. She probably knew as much about gardening as she did about real estate.

My big worry was Solana's son. I'd warned Peggy about him, but I hadn't gone into much detail for fear of scaring her off. I peered through the glass-paneled back door. The kitchen lights had been turned off. The living room lights were out as well, but I could hear the constant blast from a television set, which meant Tiny was probably home. If Solana had taken him to the bank with her, Henry would have said so before we embarked. I tried the knob just in case she'd left the house open. I knew better, but think how silly I'd have felt using a pick gun on an unlocked door.

I hitched the fanny pack around my waist from the back to the front and removed my torque wrench and the pick gun, my best bet for a speedy entry. The five picks in the leather case required more time and patience, but might come in handy as backup. In my younger days, I was more skilled with a rocker pick, but I was out of practice and didn't want to take the chance. By my calculations, Solana's trip to the bank and back would occupy fifteen minutes each way. We were also counting on an additional delay while she argued with the teller about the nonexistent check promised to her by the nonexistent Ms. Amber. If Solana became belligerent, security would step in and have her escorted off the premises. In any event, it wouldn't take her long to figure out she'd been duped. The question was, would she make the connection between the ruse and our assault on the fort? She probably thought she had me under her thumb with the restraining order in place. Peggy Klein, she hadn't counted on. Bad break for her—Peggy, the housewife, was game for anything.

I took out the pick gun and set to work. It was a two-handed operation, employing a torsion wrench in my left and the pick gun in the right. The mechanism was ingenious. Once the pick gun was inserted in the lock, the squeezing of the trigger activated an internal mallet that compressed an adjustable spring. If all went well, the rapid oscillation of the pick would coax the pins up one by one, holding them above the shear line. By applying a steady pressure with the torque wrench, once all the pins had been breached, the plug would be free to turn and I'd be in.

The mechanism made a pleasant little clicking noise as

I maneuvered it. The sound put me in mind of an electric stapler firing staples into paper. Peggy hovered at my shoulder but mercifully asked no questions. I could tell she was nervous because she shifted restlessly, arms folded tightly as though to keep herself in check. "I should have peed while I had the chance," was the only comment she made. Already, I was wishing she hadn't mentioned it. We were in enemy territory and we couldn't afford to pause to take a whiz.

I'd been at it less than a minute when the lock yielded. I tucked my tools away and opened the kitchen door with care. I stuck my head in. The booming from the television originated from one of the three bedrooms that opened off the hall, and the sound of canned laughter was loud enough to make the kitchen curtains vibrate. There was a strong smell of bleach and I could see a bottle of cleanser sitting on the counter with a damp sponge nearby. I moved into the room and Peggy slipped in after me. I peered around the kitchen door into the corridor. The auditory onslaught was coming from Tiny's room at the end of the hall. I signaled to Peggy, pointing to the third bedroom, where the door was slightly ajar. I heard Tiny shout out a sentence in response to something on the TV, but his words were formless. I hoped his limited intelligence wouldn't interfere with his ability to pay attention to the program.

My first job was to slip into the living room and unlock the front door in case we needed Henry's assistance in the house. He'd apparently left his tools at the curb, mere props in the drama that was playing out. I could see him standing on the porch, his attention riveted to the empty street. He was the lookout man and our success depended on his spotting Solana's car and giving us sufficient warning to get the hell out. I turned the thumb lock and secured it in the open position, then returned to the hall where Peggy was waiting, her face pale. I could see she hadn't developed my appetite for danger.

Gus's bedroom was the first on the right. The door was shut. I closed my fingers around the knob and turned it with caution until I felt the latch bolt ease out of the switch plate. I opened the door halfway. Curtains had been drawn and the light coming through the window shades gave the room a sepia cast. The air smelled of unwashed feet, menthol, and urine-damp sheets. A humidifier was hissing away in one corner of the room, giving us another layer of sound cover.

I stepped into the room and Peggy followed. I left the door open a crack. Gus was propped up against the pillows, motionless. His face was turned toward the door and his eyes were closed. I stared at his diaphragm, but there was no comforting rise and fall. I hoped I wasn't looking at a guy in the early phases of rigor mortis. I crossed to the bed and laid two fingers on his hand, which was warm to the touch. His eyes came open. He was having trouble with his focus, his eyes not quite tracking in unison. He seemed disoriented and I wasn't sure he remembered where he was. Whatever meds Solana had him on, he wasn't going to be much help.

Our immediate problem was to get him on his feet. His pajamas were flimsy cotton, his bare feet as long and thin as a saint's. As frail as he was, I didn't want him navigating the outdoors without a wrap of some kind. Peggy got down on her hands and knees and fished a pair of slippers from under the bed. She gave me one slipper and we each took a foot. I had a problem because his toes were curled and I couldn't force the slipper onto his foot. When she saw my plight, she reached over and pressed her thumb against the ball of the foot with all the skill of a mother wrestling a toddler into hard-soled shoes. His toes relaxed and on the slipper went.

I checked the closet, which yielded nothing in the way of an overcoat. Peggy started opening and closing dresser drawers, apparently without success. She finally came up with a woolly sweater, which didn't look all that warm but would have to suffice. She freed Gus from the tangle of covers while I moved him forward and away from the pillows. I was working to get him into his sweater, noting that his arms were hinged wrong. Peggy moved me aside and employed another mommy trick that got the job done. Together we grabbed his legs and swung them over the side. There was an afghan folded at the foot of the bed. I shook it out and wrapped it across his shoulders like a cloak.

From down the hall I heard manic theme music erupt as a game show came on. Tiny was singing along in a loud tuneless moan. He yelled a word and I realized belatedly he was calling Gus's name. Peggy and I exchanged a look of dismay. She swung Gus's legs back and pulled the spread up to conceal his slippered feet. I whisked off the afghan and flung it to the bottom of the bed while she removed the sweater in a single smooth action and shoved it under the blanket. We heard Tiny clump into the bathroom. Seconds later, he was pissing with a force that mimicked a waterfall pouring into a metal bucket. For emphasis, he farted one long musical note.

He flushed the toilet—good boy—and shuffled down the hall in our direction. I pushed Peggy and the two of us took silent giant steps, trying to clear the field. We stood motionless behind the door as he swung it open and leaned in. Big mistake. I could see his face reflected in the mirror hanging above the chest of drawers. I thought my heart would stop. If he glanced to his right, his view of us would be as clear as our view of him. I'd never actually seen him, except for the one encounter where I'd stumbled across him sleeping in what I'd thought was an empty house. He was enormous, with a wide meaty neck and ears set low on his head like a chimp's. He had a ponytail down his back, secured with what looked like a rag. He vocalized what might have been a sentence, complete with an upward tilt at the end to indicate a question. I gathered he was urging Gus to join him for the laugh-fest in the other room. I could see Gus on the bed guilelessly flick a look in our direction. I wagged a finger like a metronome and then put it to my lips.

In a feeble voice, Gus said, "Thank you, Tiny, but I'm tired now. Maybe later." He closed his eyes, as though to nap.

Out came another garbled sentence and Tiny withdrew. I listened to him shuffling down the hall, and as soon as I judged he was settled on his bed, we went into high gear again. I pulled the covers back. Peggy guided Gus's arms into his sweater and then swung his legs over the side of the bed. I draped the afghan across his shoulders. Gus understood our intentions but he was too weak to assist us. Peggy and I each took an arm, mindful of how painful our touch must be when he had so little flesh on his bones. The minute he was on his feet, his knees buckled under him and we had to shore him up before he fell.

We guided him toward the door, which I pushed open to the full. At the last minute, I placed his hand on the frame for balance and whipped into the bathroom, where I snagged his medications and zipped them into my fanny pack. At his side again, I took Gus's weight on my shoulder, anchoring his arm for stability. We struggled out into the hall. The high-decibel sounds from the television masked our halting advance, at the same time making the threat of discovery seem more immediate. If Tiny stuck his head out of the bedroom door, we were screwed.

Gus's pace was slow, progressing by way of baby steps that advanced him inches at a time. Covering the fifteen feet from the bedroom to the end of the hall took the better part of two minutes, which doesn't sound like much time unless Solana Rojas was on her way home. When we reached the kitchen door, I glanced to my right. Henry didn't dare bang on the glass, but he was waving and pointing frantically, making hurry-up motions and sawing an index finger across his throat. Solana had apparently turned the corner from Bay to Albanil. Henry disappeared and I had to trust him to save himself while Peggy and I focused on the task at hand.

Peggy was about my size, and we were both laboring to keep Gus upright and on the move. He was light as a stick, but his balance was off and his legs would give way every couple of steps. The journey across the kitchen floor proceeded as though in slow motion. We eased him out the back door, which I had the presence of mind to close behind us. I wasn't sure what Solana would think when she found the front door unlocked from inside. I was hoping she'd blame Tiny. From the street, I heard the muffled slamming of a car door. I made a little sound in my throat and Peggy shot me a look. We doubled our efforts.

Getting down the back porch steps was a nightmare, but time was too short to worry about what would happen if Gus fell. The afghan trailed behind him and first one of us and then the other would get a foot tangled in the wool. Peggy and I were half a step away from stumbling, and I could picture all three of us going down in a heap. We didn't exchange a word, but I could tell she was feeling the same strain as I was, trying to hurry him to safety before Solana entered the house, checked his room, and discovered he was gone.

Halfway down the back walk, in a wonderful grasp of the obvious, Peggy reached down and put an arm under Gus's legs. I did the same and we lifted him, forming a chair with our arms. Gus had a trembling arm around each of us, holding on for dear life as we sidled the length of the walk as far as Gus's back gate. There was a shriek of rusty metal hinges when we opened it, but by then we were so close to freedom that neither of us hesitated. We staggered the twenty steps down the alley to her car. Peggy unlocked the front door, flung the back door open, and settled him on the backseat. He had the presence of mind to lie down to conceal himself from view. I took his prescription meds from my fanny pack and put them near him on the seat. I was arranging the afghan over him when he grabbed my hand. "Careful."

"I know it hurts, Gus. We're doing the best we can."

"I mean, you. Be careful."

"I will," I said, and to Peggy, "Go."

Peggy closed the car door, shutting it with the tiniest click. She moved to the driver's-side door and slid under the wheel, shutting her door with scarcely any sound. She started the car as I slipped through the fence into Henry's backyard. She pulled away slowly, but then accelerated with a snap of gravel. The plan was for her to take Gus straight to the ER at St. Terry's, where she'd have a doctor examine him and admit him if necessary. I wasn't sure how she'd explain their relationship unless she simply presented herself as a neighbor or friend. No reason to mention the conservatorship that had made him a virtual prisoner. We'd had no discussion on the subject beyond the initial rescue, but I knew that in saving Gus, she was reaching back in time far enough to save her Gram.

Henry appeared around the corner of the studio and racewalked across the patio. There was no sign of his garden tools so he'd apparently abandoned them. When he was in range of me, he took me by the elbow and herded me toward his back door and into the kitchen. We shed our jackets. Henry turned the thumb bolt and then sat down at the kitchen table while I went to the phone. I put a call through to Cheney Phillips at the police department. Cheney worked vice, but I knew he'd be quick to grasp the situation and set the proper machinery in motion. Once I had him on the line, I bypassed the niceties and told him what was going on. According to Peggy, there was already a warrant out for Solana. He listened intently and I could hear him tapping away on his computer, pulling up wants and warrants under her various aliases. I gave him Solana's current whereabouts and he said he'd take care of it. That was that.

I joined Henry at the kitchen table, but both of us were too anxious for idleness. I picked up the newspaper, opened it at random to the op-ed page. People were idiots if the opinions I read were any indication. I tried the front section. There were the usual troubles in the world, but none of them matched the drama we'd launched here at home. Henry's knee was jumping and his foot made little tapping sounds on the floor. He got up and crossed to the kitchen counter, where he plucked an onion from a wire basket and removed the papery outer skin. I watched as he cut the onion in half and again in quarters, reducing it to a dice so small it sent tears running down his cheeks. Chopping was his remedy for most of life's ills. We waited, the silence broken only by the ticking of the clock as the second hand swept the face.

With a rattle of newsprint, I turned to the "Business" section and studied a spiky graph that depicted major market trends from 1978 to the present. I hoped the boring article would settle my nerves, but it didn't seem to help. I kept expecting to hear Solana shriek at the top of her lungs. She'd start by abusing her son, and after berating him at length she'd appear like a banshee pounding on Henry's door, wailing, screaming, and otherwise denouncing us. With luck, the cops would show up and take her away before she managed any further acting out.

Instead of uproar, there was nothing.

Silence and more silence.

The phone rang at 5:15. I reached for the handset myself because Henry was busy assembling a meatloaf, his fingers squishing oatmeal, ketchup, and raw eggs into a pound of ground beef.

"Hello?"

"Hey, this is Peggy. I'm still at St. Terry's, but I thought I better bring you up to date. Gus was admitted. He's a mess. Nothing major, but serious enough to require a couple of days' care. He's malnourished and dehydrated. He has a low-level bladder infection and his heart is acting up. Bruises galore, plus a hairline fracture in the radius of his right arm. From the X-rays, the doctor says it looks like it's been there a while."

"Poor guy."

"He'll be fine. Of course, he didn't have his ID or his Medicare card, but the admissions clerk looked up his records from a previous hospitalization. I explained the security issues and the doctor agreed to admit him under my last name."

"They didn't make a fuss about that?"

"Not at all. My husband's one of the neurologists on staff. His reputation is the stuff of legend, but more to the point, he has a temper like a junkyard dog's. They knew if they made a stink, they'd have to deal with him. Aside from that, in the past ten years, my father's donated enough money to add a wing to this place. They were kissing my ring."

"Oh." I'd have verbalized my surprise, but her husband's occupation and her dad's financial status were two facts out of the many I didn't know about her. "What about the girls? Shouldn't you be home by now?"

"That's the other reason I called. They're having supper at their playmate's. I talked to her mom and she was cool, but I did assure her I'd pick 'em up within the hour. I didn't want to take off without giving you the low-down."

"You're incredible. I can't thank you enough."

"Don't worry about it. I haven't had that much fun since grade school!"

I laughed. "It was a hoot, wasn't it?"

"Totally. I did make it clear to the charge nurse that Gus was to have no visitors except for you, me, and Henry. I told her about Solana . . ."

"Naming names?"

"Of course. Why should we protect her when she's a piece of shit? It was obvious he'd been badly abused so the nurse got right on the phone and put in calls to the police and the Elder Abuse hotline. I gather they're sending someone out. What about you? What's happening on your end?"

"Nothing much. Sitting here waiting for the bomb to go off. Solana must know by now he's been snatched. I can't understand why she's so quiet."

"That's unnerving."

"For sure. In the meantime, I called a friend of mine at the police department. Given the warrant out on Solana, a couple of officers should be arriving shortly to arrest her fat ass. We'll come over after that."

"There's no big rush. Gus is sleeping, but it'd be nice if he saw a familiar face when he wakes up."

"I'll be there as soon as possible."

"Don't forfeit the chance to see Solana handcuffed and thrown in the back of a black-and-white."

"I'm looking forward to it."

After she rang off, I gave Henry the update on Gus's medical status, some of which he'd gathered from listening to my end of the conversation. "Peggy's put everyone on notice about the possibility that Solana might show up and try to see him. She won't get anywhere so that's good news," I said. "I wonder what she's up to? You think the cops have arrived?"

"There hasn't been time enough, but hang on a sec."

He washed his hands in haste and toted the dish towel with him as he left the kitchen and stepped into the dining room. I followed, watching as he pushed the curtain aside and peered out at the street.

"Anything?"

"Her car's still there and I don't see any sign of life so maybe she hasn't figured it out yet."

That was certainly a possibility, but neither of us was convinced.

34

By then it was close to six. Henry packed his meatloaf in a cake pan, covered it, and put it in the fridge. His plan was to bake it for supper the next day. He extended an invitation, which I accepted, assuming we would both be alive. In the meantime, his homely activities had introduced a note of normalcy. Given that it was happy hour, he took out an old fashioned glass and poured his ritual Black Jack over ice. He asked if I wanted wine, which in truth I did, but I decided to decline. I thought I better have my wits about me in case Solana showed up. I was of two minds about the possibility. On one hand, I thought if she were going to blow her stack, she'd have done it by now. On the other hand, she might be out buying guns and ammo in order to give full expression to her ire. Whatever the reality, we deemed it unwise to keep ourselves on prominent display in the brightly lighted kitchen.

We removed ourselves to the living room, where we closed the drapes and turned on the TV set. The evening news was all bad, but restful by comparison. We were beginning to relax when the knock came at the front door. I jumped and Henry's hand jerked, slopping half his drink.

"You stay there," he said. He set his glass on the coffee table and went to the door. He flipped on the porch light and put his eye to the spy hole. It couldn't have been Solana because I watched him remove the burglar chain, prepared to let someone in. I recognized Cheney's voice before I caught sight of him. He stepped into the room, accompanied by a uniformed officer whose name tag read J. ANDERSON. He was in his thirties, blue-eyed and ruddy-complexioned, with features that spoke of Irish ancestry. I flashed on the only line of poetry I retained from my days of making mediocre grades in my high school English class: "*John Anderson, my Jo, John, when we were first acquent* . . ." That was the extent of it. No clue who the poet was, though the name Robert Burns lurked somewhere at the back of my brain. I wondered if William's father was correct in his belief that memorizing poetry served us later in life.

Cheney and I exchanged a look. He was adorable, no lie. Or maybe my perception was colored by the comfort of his being on the scene. Let him deal with Solana and her goon of a son. While Cheney and Henry chatted, I had the opportunity to study him. He wore dress slacks and a shirt with a button-down collar, over which he'd pulled a caramel-colored cashmere coat. Cheney came from money, and while he had no desire to work in his father's bank, he was smart enough to enjoy the perks. I could tell I was weakening in the same way I weaken at the notion of a QP with Cheese. Not that he was good for me, but who cared?

"Did you talk to her?" Henry asked.

Cheney said, "That's why I'm here. We're wondering if the two of you would step next door with us."

Henry said, "Certainly. Is something wrong?"

"You tell us. When we pulled up, we found the front door standing open. All the lights are on, but there doesn't seem to be anyone there."

Henry left with Cheney and Officer Anderson, without bothering to put a coat over his short-sleeved shirt. I paused long enough to retrieve my jacket from the back of the kitchen chair. I grabbed Henry's as well and scooted after him. The night was chilly and the wind was picking up. There was an empty expanse of curb where Solana's car had been. I trotted along the walk, reassured by the notion that Cheney had the situation under control. He was right about Gus's house. Every room was ablaze with light. By the time I crossed his front yard, I could see Anderson on his way around the side of the house with his flashlight, the wand of white zigzagging across windows, the walkway, and surrounding shrubbery.

Cheney had Solana Rojas's arrest warrant in hand and I gathered that gave him a certain leeway to check the premises in search of her. He'd also uncovered two outstanding warrants for the arrest of Tomasso Tasinato, one on charges of aggravated battery, and the other for battery with great bodily harm. He told us Tiny had twice been caught on tape shoplifting items from a Colgate minimart. The owner had identified him but then decided not to file charges, saying he didn't want the hassle over some beef jerky and two packages of M&M's.

Cheney asked us to wait outside while he went in. Henry shrugged himself into his jacket and tucked his hands in the pockets. Neither of us said a word, but he must have worried, as I did, that something awful was in store. Once Cheney assured himself the place was empty, he asked us to walk through with him to see if we noticed anything out of the ordinary.

The premises had been picked clean of personal items. In my earlier unauthorized home invasion, I hadn't noticed how barren the house was. The living room was intact, furniture still in place: lamps, the desk, a footstool, fake roses on the coffee table. The kitchen was untouched as well, nothing out of place. If there'd been dirty dishes in the sink, they'd been washed, dried, and put away. A damp-looking linen dish towel had been folded and hung neatly across the rack. The spray bottle of cleanser was gone, but the smell was still strong. I thought Solana was taking her compulsive tidiness a bit too far.

Gus's room was just as we'd left it. The covers were flung back, sheets and spread rumpled and looking not quite clean. Drawers still stood half-open where Peggy'd hunted up a sweater for him. The humidifier had run dry and no longer hissed with steam. I continued down the hall to the first of the two spare bedrooms.

Compared with the last view I'd had, Solana's room was empty. The carved mahogany bed frame remained, but the other antique pieces were gone: no burled walnut rocking chair, no armoire, no plump-shouldered fruitwood chest of drawers with ornate bronze drawer pulls. She couldn't have loaded furniture in her car in the scant hour she had available after she returned home. For one thing, the items were too cumbersome, and for another, she was in too great a hurry to bother. This meant she'd disposed of the furniture earlier, but who knew what she'd done with it? In the closet, the hangers had been shoved apart and most of her clothes were gone. Some garments had tumbled to the floor and she'd left them in a heap, indicating the haste with which she'd packed.

I moved to Tiny's room. Henry and Cheney stood in the doorway. I kept expecting to find a body—his or hers—shot, stabbed, or hanged. Uneasily, I eased in behind Cheney, hoping he would shield me from anything gross. The air in Tiny's room was dense with "guy" smell: testosterone, hair, sweat glands, and dirty clothes. Overlying the ripe odor was the same smell of bleach I'd noticed throughout. Had she been using the spray cleanser to wipe the surfaces free of prints?

The two heavy blankets that served as blackout curtains were still nailed to the window frames, and the overhead light was tawny and ineffectual. The television set was gone, but all of Tiny's toiletries were still strewn across the counter in the bathroom he shared with his mom. He'd left his toothbrush behind, but he probably didn't use it anyway so no big deal.

Officer Anderson appeared in the hallway behind us. "Anybody know what kind of car she drives?"

Cheney said, "A 1972 Chevrolet convertible with the word 'dead' scratched into the driver's-side door. Pearce made a note of the plate number in his field notes."

"I think we got it. Come take a look at this."

He went out the back door, flipping on the porch light as he passed. We followed him down the steps and across the yard to the single-car garage at the rear of the lot. The old wooden doors were padlocked, but he held his flashlight against the dusty window. I had to stand on tiptoe to see in, but the car inside was Solana's. The convertible top was down and the front and rear seats were empty to all appearances. It was clear Cheney'd need a search warrant before he went further.

"Did Mr. Vronsky own a vehicle?" he asked.

Henry said, "He did, a 1976 Buick Electra, metallic blue with a blue interior. His pride and joy. He hadn't driven it for years and I'm sure the tags on the license plate expired. I don't know the license number, but a car like that shouldn't be hard to spot."

"The DMV will have the information. I'll notify the sheriff's department and the CHP. Any idea which direction she might've headed?"

"No clue," Henry said.

Before he left, Anderson secured both the house and garage with crime scene tape in anticipation of a return with a warrant and a fingerprint technician. Cheney wasn't optimistic about recovering the cash and other valuables Solana'd stolen over the years, but there was always a chance. At the very least, latent fingerprints would tie the cases together.

"Hey, Cheney?" I said, as he was getting in his car.

He looked across the top of his car at me.

"When the techs dust for prints? Tell 'em to try the vodka bottle in the cabinet above the sink. She probably didn't think to wipe that down before she left."

Cheney smiled. "Will do."

Henry and I went back to his house. "I'm heading over to the hospital and after that, I'll hit Rosie's," I said. "Care to join me?"

"I'd love to, but Charlotte said she'd stop by at eight. I'm taking her to dinner."

"Really. Well, that's interesting."

"I don't know how interesting it is. I treated her poorly over the business with Gus. I was a butt and the time has come to make that right."

I left him to get himself gussied up and walked the half block to my car. The drive to St. Terry's took less than fifteen minutes, which gave me time to ponder Solana's vanishing and Cheney's reappearance. I knew it wouldn't be smart to renew that relationship. On the other hand (there's always that other hand, isn't there?), I'd caught a whiff of his aftershave and nearly whimpered aloud. I parked on a side street and headed for the brightly lighted hospital entrance.

My intended visit with Gus was short-lived. When I reached the floor and identified myself, I was told he was still asleep. I chatted briefly with the charge nurse, making sure she was clear about who was allowed to see him and who was not. Peggy had laid all the necessary groundwork, and I was assured his safety was uppermost in everyone's mind. I did peek in at him and spent half a minute watching him sleep. His color had already improved.

There was one bright moment that made the whole excursion worthwhile. I'd rung for the elevator and I was waiting. I heard the whir of cables and the ping announcing its arrival from the floor below. When the doors opened I found myself face-to-face with Nancy Sullivan. She had her good Girl Scout briefcase in one hand and she was wearing her sensible shoes. As proof there's justice in the world, she'd been assigned to Gus's case after having blown me off. She greeted me coolly, using a tone that implied she hoped I'd fall in a hole. I didn't say a word to her, but I did gloat in my heart. I resisted the urge to smirk until after the elevator doors closed, shutting her from sight. Then I mouthed the sweetest four words in the English language: *I told you so.*

I drove home, fantasizing about my dinner at Rosie's. I was going for the fat and cholesterol sweepstakes: bread and butter, red meat, sour cream on everything, and a big gooey dessert. I'd take a paperback novel with me and read while I stuffed my face. I could hardly wait. When I turned onto Albanil, I could see how scarce the parking was. I'd forgotten it was hump night again, and the mid-week revelers had put parking places at a premium. In search of a spot, I cruised the street at half-speed, scanning for two other things as well: the sight of a black-and-white, indicating the police had returned to Gus's house, or the sight of a telltale metallic blue Buick Electra, a sign that Solana was close by. No sign of either.

I turned the corner onto Bay and drove to the end of the block without seeing a car-length of empty curb. I turned right on Cabana and right again on Albanil, checking the block again. Ahead on the sidewalk, I spotted a woman in a trench coat and high heels. My headlights picked up a flash of hair too blond to be real—hooker hair, all tarted up and dyed. This gal was huge and even from the rear I could tell something was off. It wasn't until I passed that I realized it was a guy in drag. I turned my head and squinted. Was that Tiny? I kept an eye on him in my rearview mirror. A spot had opened up and I angled into it.

Before I shut down the engine, I glanced back at the sidewalk. No sign of the "babe," so I rolled down my window an inch to listen for the clopping of her high heels on concrete. The street was quiet. If it was Tiny, he'd either retraced his steps or turned the corner. I didn't like it. I removed the key from the ignition, clutching the ring in my fist, keys through my fingers. I looked over my right shoulder once more, checking the sidewalk before I opened the car door.

The handle was jerked out of my hand and the door was flung open. I was hauled up by the hair and yanked from the car. I hit the pavement on my backside, pain searing my tailbone. I recognized Tiny by smell—corrosive and foul. I flailed, glancing back at him. His platinum wig was askew and I could see the stubble on his face that even a late-afternoon shave hadn't fully eradicated. He'd shucked his trench coat and kicked off his high heels. He wore a woman's blouse and his XXXL-sized skirt now rode up over his hips, allowing him freedom of movement. His hands were still buried in my hair. I grabbed them, lifting myself in an effort to keep him from ripping off my scalp. My keys had fallen on the street half under the car. No time to worry about that now. I was struggling for purchase. I managed to get my feet under me and kicked his right knee. The heel on my boot might have done some damage except for his bulk, which made him almost impervious to pain. He was pumped up on adrenaline, doubtless hyped on his sense of himself. The hair on his calves and the lower part of his thighs was pressed flat by a pair of queen-sized panty hose. Runners snaked down from the crotch where the nylon had been stretched to the limit. He was making guffing sounds deep in his throat, half exertion, half excitement at the notion of the injuries he'd inflict before he was done with me.

We grappled, both of us down on the pavement now. He was on his back and I lay on my back as well, sprawled awkwardly on top of him. He was scissoring his legs in an attempt to encircle me and lock my body between his thighs. I reached back and clawed at his face, hoping to gouge an eye. My nails raked his cheek, which he must have felt because he punched me in the head so hard I swore I could feel my brain bouncing against the inside of my skull. The fucker outweighed me by a good two hundred pounds. He pinned my arms against me. His grip was viselike, and close up against him like that my elbows were of no use. He rocked back, thrusting himself forward, trying to hook one foot around the other for leverage. I managed to turn my body halfway and I used the bony structure of my pelvis as a wedge to keeping his big knees apart. I knew what he'd do—clamp down, force the air out of my lungs with the increased pressure of his thighs, clamp down again. He'd use compression, like a boa constrictor, tightening his legs around me until I ceased to draw breath.

I couldn't make a sound. In the heaving silence I marveled at the sense of solitude. There was no one else on the street, no one even remotely aware that we were out here joined in this strange embrace. He'd begun to mew—joy, sexual arousal—I wasn't sure which. I slipped down, the heavy flesh of his thighs now pressing on each side of my face. He was hot, sweating between his legs as he squeezed. His weight alone was sufficient to crush me. Without exerting any other effort, he could have sat on my chest and it would've taken less than thirty seconds before the dark came down.

I was deaf. His thighs had shut out all sound except for the hush of blood moving through his veins. I squirmed and rotated myself by inches. I turned again until my nose was smashed up against the crotch of his panty hose with its soft, helpless bulge in range. He didn't have a hard-on. That much was obvious. Any clothing other than panty hose would have offered him protection—heavy jeans or sweats serving as a jock strap or a codpiece of sorts—shielding his nuts. But he was turned on by the feel of silkiness against his naked skin. Such is life. We all have our preferences. I opened my jaws and bit down on his scrotum. I closed my eyes and clamped down until I thought my upper and lower teeth would meet in the middle. The wad in my mouth had the consistency of foam rubber with a touch of gristle at the core. I held on, like a terrier, knowing the searing message of pain was streaking like lightning through his frame.

A howl went up and his thighs popped open as though they were spring-loaded, letting the cold air rush in. I rolled over on my side, scrambling on my hands and knees as far as the car. He was thrashing on the ground behind me, gasping and groaning. He clutched his crotch where I hoped I'd inflicted permanent damage. He wept, his cries hoarse with anguish and disbelief. I felt around for my car keys and snatched them up. I was shaking so badly I dropped them and had to scoop them up again. He'd managed to pull himself upright, but he paused to puke before he staggered to his feet. His face was sweaty and pale, and he held himself with one hand while he limped in my direction. His obesity and his lumbering gait slowed him just long enough to allow me to open the car door and slide in. I slammed the door and banged the knob into the locked position as he grabbed the door handle and yanked. I flung myself across the passenger's seat and banged the knob down on that door as well. Then I sat there, lungs heaving while I gathered my strength.

He slammed both his hands down on the roof of the car and pushed, trying to rock it with the force of his weight. If I'd been trapped in my beloved VW, he'd have rolled the car over on its side and then over on its roof. The Mustang he couldn't budge beyond the faintest shudder. He had no tolerance for frustration. He grabbed the windshield wiper and twisted it, bending it until it stuck out like a dislocated finger. I could see him search for something else to destroy.

He circled the car. Mesmerized, I kept him in sight, turning my head as he moved around the rear and reappeared on my left. He was making sounds that might have been English, but the words were flattened and formless, without the dots and dashes of vowels and consonants to make them distinct. He skipped back two steps and ran at the car. He side-kicked the door. I knew he'd put a dent in the metal, but given that he was shoeless and clad in panty hose, he'd hurt himself more than he'd hurt the car. He yanked at the door again. He banged a fist against the glass and then tried to force his big meaty fingers into the crack between the window and the post. I felt like a mouse in a glass case with a snake outside, hissing and striking ineffectually while fear shot through me like zaps from a Taser gun. There was a hypnotic quality to his assault, fierce and relentless. How long would it take him to breach my small fortress? I didn't dare abandon the safety of the car, which was at least keeping him at bay. I leaned on the car horn until the sound filled the night air.

He moved around the car again, prowling, looking for a weakness in my fortifications. He was clearly infuriated to have me in plain sight but inaccessible. He stood on the driver's side staring at me and then abruptly, he turned away. I thought he was leaving, but he walked across the street and at the far side, turned to face me again. There was something in his eyes so crazy that I hummed with fear.

With a jangle of keys I managed to jam the right one in the ignition. I turned it and the engine roared to life. I jerked the wheel to my left and swung away from the curb. I knew it would take two tries before I cleared the bumper of the car in front of me. I backed up and turned the wheel again. I glanced over as Tiny began to run at the car with more speed than I'd have thought possible for a guy his size. He'd pulled his right fist back and when he reached the car, he drove it straight through the window, shattering the glass. I screamed and ducked as jagged shards flew by, some landing in my lap. The glass that remained in the window tore into his flesh. His punching arm was extended as far as his shoulder blade, but when he tried to pull free, glass bit into the fabric of his blouse like the angled teeth of a shark. He groped for me blindly and I felt his fingers close around my throat. The simple fact of physical contact jolted me into action.

I shoved the stick into first, popped the clutch, and floored it. The Mustang shot forward with a squeal of burning tires. Out of the corner of my eye I could still see Tiny's arm and hand, like the branch of a tree driven through a wall by a gale-force wind. I slammed on the brakes, thinking I could shake him off. That's when I realized I was suffering a misperception. Between his own weight and my speed, I'd left him half a block behind. It was only his arm that remained, resting lightly on my shoulder like an old chum's.

35

I won't go into a moment-by-moment account of what followed in the wake of that grisly incident. Much of it I've forgotten, in any event. I do remember Officer Anderson arriving in his patrol car and Cheney arriving later in his slick little red Mercedes convertible. My car was parked where I'd left it and I was, by then, sitting on the curb in front of Henry's house, shaking as though suffering from a neurological disorder. Having battled with Tiny, I sported sufficient contusions and abrasions to lend credibility to my account of his attack. My head was still ringing from the punch. Since there were already warrants out on him for similar offenses, no one suggested that I was to blame.

These were the facts that worked in my favor:

At the time of the accident, I stopped and approached the injured man with every intention of rendering assistance if necessary, which it wasn't because he was dead.

According to the Breathalyzer and later blood analysis, I was not driving under the influence of alcohol or drugs.

When the officer from the traffic division arrived on the scene, I gave him my name, address, registration, and proof of insurance. I had a valid California driver's license in my possession. He ran my name, license number, and plate, and determined that my record was clean. I was worried he'd pick up on the tiny matter of the TRO, but since we hadn't yet appeared in court, the restraining order probably wasn't in the system. Besides which, I hadn't done a thing to *her.*

There was a suggestion to the effect that I might have used excessive force in defending myself, but that opinion was quashed forthwith.

The Mustang was in the shop for repairs for a week. The windshield wiper and the window on the driver's side would have to be replaced. The driver's-side door was dented and the white vinyl bucket seat on the driver's side was a loss. No matter how often or how thoroughly the upholstery was cleaned, there would always be traces of red in the seams. Whether I'd hang on to the Mustang was another matter altogether. Owning the car was like owning a fine Thoroughbred racehorse—beautiful to behold, but expensive to maintain. The car had saved my life, no doubt about that, but I wondered if every time I drove it, I'd see Tiny starting that fatal run with his right fist pulled back.

Gus was discharged after two days in the hospital. Melanie went through a local agency and made arrangements for a new companion for him. The woman did light housekeeping, prepared his meals, ran errands, and went home at night to a family of her own. Of course, Gus fired her at the end of two weeks. The subsequent companion has survived to date, though Henry reports hearing a good deal of bickering from the far side of the hedge. A week after Tiny's death, Gus's Buick Electra was found six blocks from the Mexican border. It had been wiped clean of prints, but there was a stack of oil paintings locked in the trunk that were later valued at close to a million dollars. Solana must have hated abandoning such assets, but she couldn't very well disappear while continuing to hang on to a carload of stolen art.

One happy side effect of her disappearance was that she was a no-show in court the day of the hearing on the restraining order. The matter was dismissed, but I was still going to need a judge's orders to get my guns back. I knew in my heart of hearts, I wasn't done with her, nor she with me. I'd been responsible for the death of her only child and I'd pay for that.

In the meantime, I told myself there was no point in worrying. Solana was gone and if she came back, she'd come back and I'd deal with her then. I put the matter behind me. It was done, done, done. I couldn't change what had happened and I couldn't give in to the emotions that ran like a riptide under the placid surface I presented to the world. Henry knew better. Tactfully, he probed, wondering aloud how I was coping with Tiny's death, suggesting that perhaps I might benefit from "talking to someone."

"I don't want to talk to anyone," I said. "I did what I had to do. He didn't have to attack me. He didn't have to jam his fist through the glass. Those were his choices. I made mine. What's the big deal? It's not like he's the first guy I ever killed."

"Well, that puts it in a fresh light."

"Henry, I appreciate your concern, but it's misplaced."

I was aware that I sounded testy, but aside from that, I felt fine. At least that's what I told him and anyone else who asked. Despite the brave face I wore, I went through my days with a low-level dread I could scarcely acknowledge. I wanted closure. I needed to have all the loose ends tied up. As long as she was out there, I didn't feel safe. I was afraid. "Terrified" was a better word. I realized later I was experiencing a form of post-traumatic stress disorder, but at the time all I knew was how hard I had to work to suppress my anxiety. I had no appetite. I didn't have trouble falling asleep, but I'd wake up at 4:00 A.M. and that would be the end of it. I couldn't concentrate. I was fearful of crowds and unnerved by loud noises. At the end of every day, I was exhausted from having to maintain such a tight grip on myself. Fear, like any other strong emotion, is difficult to hide. Much of my energy was devoted to denying it was there.

My only relief came from my early morning run. I craved movement. I loved the feeling of flying over the ground. I needed to be sweaty and out of breath. If my legs hurt and my lungs burned, all the better. There was something tangible about the calm that came over me when I was done. I started pushing myself, adding a mile to the three I typically put in. When that wasn't quite enough, I ramped up the pace.

The lull was short-lived. Sunday, February 14, was the last day I'd be able to enjoy the quiet—artificial though it may have been. In the coming week, though I didn't know it yet, Solana would make her move. Valentine's Day was Henry's birthday, and Rosie treated us to dinner to celebrate his turning eighty-eight. The restaurant was closed on Sundays, so we had the place to ourselves. Rosie put together a feast and William helped serve. There were just the four of us: Rosie, William, Henry, and me. We had to do without Lewis, Charlie, and Nell because the Midwest was socked in with snow and the sibs were stranded until the airport opened again. Henry and Charlotte had mended their fences. I thought for sure he'd invite her, but he was reluctant to stir up any suggestion of romance between them. She would always be too driven and single-minded for his laid-back lifestyle. He said he wanted only his nearest and dearest with him while he blew out his candles, beaming at our lusty rendition of "Happy Birthday to Yooouuu!" Rosie, William, and I pooled our money and bought him three copper-bottom saucepans that he adored.

Monday morning, I got to work at eight—early for me, but I hadn't slept well and I'd ended up going out for my run at five thirty instead of six, which put me at the office half an hour ahead of my usual time. One virtue of my office—perhaps the only virtue—was that there was always parking available in front. I parked, locked my car, and let myself in. There was the usual hillock of mail piled on the floor under the slot. Most of it was junk that would go straight into the trash, but topmost was a padded envelope that I assumed was another set of documents from Lowell Effinger's office. Melvin Downs had failed to appear for his deposition, and I'd promised Geneva that I'd go after him again and have another heart-to-heart. Clearly, he'd been unimpressed by the threat of contempt of court.

I dropped my shoulder bag on my desk. I slid out of my jacket and draped it over the back of my chair. I tackled the manila envelope, which was stapled shut and took a bit of doing before I opened it. I separated the flaps and looked in. At the first glance, I shrieked and flung the envelope across the room. The action was involuntary, a reflex triggered by revulsion. What I'd glimpsed was the hairy appendages of a live tarantula. I literally shuddered, but I didn't have time to calm myself or gather my wits.

Horrified, I watched the tarantula feel its way out of the padded mailer, one hairy leg at a time, tentatively testing the characteristics of my beige carpeting. The spider looked huge, but, in fact, the squat body was no more than an inch and a half wide, suspended from a set of eight bright red legs that seemed to move independently of one another. The front and rear parts of its body were round and its legs appeared to have joints, like little bent elbows or knees, which terminated in small flat paws. Body and legs together, the spider could have filled a circle four inches across. With mincing steps, the tarantula crawled across the floor, looking like an ambulatory wad of black and red hair.

If I didn't find a way to stop it, it would scuttle into one of the spaces between my file cabinets and reside there for life. What was I supposed to do? Stepping on a spider that size was out of the question. I didn't want to get that close to it and I didn't want to see stuff squirt out when I crushed it to death. I certainly wasn't going to whack it with a magazine. My distaste aside, the spider represented no danger. Tarantulas aren't poisonous, but they're ugly as sin—mossy with hair, eight glittering round eyes, and (I kid you not) fangs that were visible from half a room away.

Oblivious to my concerns, the tarantula tiptoed out of my office with a certain daintiness and proceeded to cross the reception area. I was afraid it might stretch and elongate, insinuating itself under the baseboard like a cat slipping under a fence.

I kept a wary eye on it, rapidly backing down the hall to my kitchenette. On Friday I'd washed the clear glass coffee carafe and set it upside down on a towel to dry. I grabbed it and sped back, amazed at the distance the tarantula had covered in just those few seconds. I didn't dare pause to consider how repellant it was at close range.

I made my mind a blank, turned the carafe upside down, and set it over him. Then I shuddered again, a groan emanating from some primitive part of me.

I backed away from the carafe, patting myself on the chest. I'd never use that carafe again. I couldn't bear to drink from a coffeepot that spider feet had touched. I hadn't solved my problem; I'd only delayed the inevitable issue of how to dispose of it. What were my choices? Animal Control? A local Tarantula Rescue group? I didn't dare set it free in the wild (that being the patch of ivy outside my door) because I'd always be searching the ground for it, wondering when it was going to pop out again. It's times like these when you need a guy around, though I'd have been willing to bet most men would have been as disgusted as I was and just about as squeamish at the idea of spider guts.

I went back to my desk, sidestepping the empty manila envelope, which I'd have to burn. I took out the telephone book and looked up the number for the Museum of Natural History. The woman who answered the phone didn't behave as though my situation was unusual. She checked her Rolodex and recited the number of a fellow in town who actually bred tarantulas. Then she informed me, with a certain giddiness, that his lecture, complete with a live demonstration, was a favorite among elementary-school kids, who liked having the spiders crawl up and down their arms. I put the image out of my mind as I dialed the number she'd given me.

I wasn't sure what to expect of someone who made a living consorting with tarantulas. The young man who arrived at my office door half an hour later was in his early twenties, big and soft, with a beard that was probably meant to lend him an air of maturity. "Are you Kinsey? Byron Coe. Thanks for the call."

I shook his hand, trying not to bubble over with gratitude. His grip was light and his palm was warm. I looked at him with the same devotion I accorded my plumber the day the hose on the washing machine came loose and spewed water everywhere. "I appreciate your being so prompt."

"I'm happy to be of help." His smile was sweet and his thicket of blond hair was as big as a burning bush. He wore denim overalls, a short-sleeved T-shirt, and hiking boots. He'd brought with him two lightweight plastic carriers that he set on the floor, one medium and one large. The coffee carafe had attracted his attention the minute he arrived, but he'd been polite about it. "Let's see what you got here."

He eased himself down to the floor on one bent knee and then stretched out on his tummy and put his face near the carafe. He gave the glass a tap, but the spider was too busy to care. He was feeling his way around the perimeter, hoping for a little doorway to freedom. Byron said, "He's a beauty."

"Oh, thanks."

"This fellow's a Mexican red-legged tarantula, *Brachypelma emilia*, maybe five or six years old. A male judging by his color. See how dark he is? The females are closer to a soft brown. Where'd you find him?"

"Actually, he found me. Someone left him for me in a padded envelope."

He looked up with interest. "What's the occasion?"

"No occasion, just a very sick practical joke."

"Some joke. You can't buy a red-legged spiderling for less than a hundred and twenty-five dollars."

"Yeah, well, nothing but the best for me. When you

say Mexican red-legged, does that mean they're only found in Mexico?"

"Not exclusively. In states like Arizona, New Mexico, and Texas, they're not uncommon. I breed Chaco golden knees and cobalt blues. Neither cost as much as this guy. I have a pair of Brazilian salmon pinks I picked up for ten bucks each. You know you can actually train tarantulas as pets?"

"Really," I said. "I had no idea."

"Heck, yes. They're quiet and they don't shed. They do molt and you have to be a little bit careful about bites. The venom's harmless to humans, but you'll have swelling at the site and sometimes numbness or itching. Goes away pretty quick. It's nice you didn't kill him."

"I'm a conservationist at heart," I said. "Listen, if you're going to pick him up, please warn me. I'm leaving the room."

"Nah, this guy's had enough trauma for one day. I don't want him thinking I'm the enemy."

While I watched, he removed the ventilated lid from the medium-size clear plastic box. He took a pencil from my desk, picked up the carafe, and used it to coax the spider into the carrier. (The pencil was going, too.) He snapped the lid in place and used the pop-up handle to lift him up to face level again.

"If you want him, he's yours," I said.

"Really?" He smiled, his face flushing with delight. I hadn't given a fellow that much pleasure since Cheney and I broke up.

"I'll also be happy to pay for your time. You really saved my life."

"Oh man, this is payment enough. If you change your mind, I'll be happy to bring him back."

I said, "Go and god bless."

* * *

Once the door closed behind him, I sat at my desk and had a nice long chat with myself. A Mexican red-legged. Bite my ass. This was Solana's doing. If her purpose was to scare the shit out of me, she'd done well. I wasn't sure what the tarantula represented to her, but from my perspective it spoke of a twisted mind at work. She was putting me on notice and I got the point. Any relief my morning run had generated went straight out the window. That first glimpse of the spider would be with me for life. I still had the willies. I put together the files I'd need, picked up my portable Smith-Corona, locked the office door behind me, and loaded the car. The office felt contaminated. I'd work from home.

I made it through the day. Though easily distracted, I was determined to be productive. I needed comfort, and for lunch I allowed myself a sandwich made with half an inch of olive pimento cheese spread on whole grain bread. I cut it in quarters the way I had as a child and I savored every tangy bite. I wasn't all that strict about dinner either, I must confess. I needed to sedate myself with food and drink. I know it's very naughty to use alcohol to relieve tension, but wine is cheap, it's legal, and it does the job. Up to a point.

When I went to bed that night I didn't have to worry about lying awake. I was ever so slightly inebriated and I slept like a stone.

It was the faintest whiff of cold air that woke me. I was sleeping in sweats, in anticipation of my early morning run, but even suited up, I was cold. I glanced at the digital clock, but the face was black, and I realized the usual soft purring of appliances had ceased. The power had gone out, an irksome business for someone as time-oriented as I was. I stared up through the Plexiglas skylight but couldn't estimate the hour. If I'd known it was early, 2:00 or 3:00 A.M., I'd have pulled the covers over my head and slept until my inner alarm clock woke me at 6:00. Idly I wondered if the outage included the whole neighborhood. In Santa Teresa, if the wind blows wrong, there are tiny breaks in the service and the flow of electricity cuts out. Seconds later the clocks might flash on again, but the numbers continue to blink merrily, announcing the upset. In this instance there was none of that. I could have groped across the bed table for my watch. By squinting and angling the face, I might have been able to see the hands, but it didn't seem to matter much.

I was puzzled by the cold air and I wondered if I'd left a window open somewhere. It didn't seem likely. In winter, I keep the studio snug, often closing the interior shutters to eliminate drafts. I looked down to the foot of my bed.

There was someone, a woman, standing there. Motionless. The nighttime darkness is never absolute. Given the city's light pollution, I can always distinguish gradients of light, starting with the paler shades of gray and deepening to charcoal. If I wake during the night, this is what allows me to wander the studio without bothering to turn on lights.

It was Solana. In my house. In my loft, staring down at me while I slept. Fear spread through me slowly like ice. The cold moved out from my core all the way to the tips of my fingers and toes in the same way water gradually turns solid when a lake freezes over. How had she gotten in? I waited, wondering if the specter would resolve into an ordinary object—a jacket thrown over the railing, a garment bag hanging from the hinge on my closet door.

At first, my mind was blank with disbelief. There was no way—no *way*—she could have gained entry. Then I remembered Henry's house key attached to a white cardboard tag with PITTS neatly printed on it by means of identification. Gus kept the key in his desk drawer, where I'd come upon it the first time I searched for Melanie's phone number. Henry had told me there was a time when Gus had brought in the mail and watered the plants when Henry was out of town. Henry's locks and mine were keyed the same, and when I thought about it, I couldn't remember securing the burglar chain, which meant once she unlocked the door, there was nothing preventing her from coming in. What could be easier? I might just as well have left my front door ajar.

She must have sensed I was awake and looking at her. We stared at each other. There was no need for conversation. If she was armed with a weapon, this was the moment she'd strike, knowing I was aware of her, but powerless to fight. Instead, she moved away. I saw her turn toward the spiral stairs and disappear. I sat straight up in bed, my heart banging. I pushed the covers aside and reached for my running shoes, shoving my bare feet into them. The lighted clock face shone bright again, numbers flashing. It was 3:05. Solana must have found the breaker box. Now the power was on and I skittered down the stairs. My front door stood open and I could hear her unhurried footsteps receding along the walk. There was an insolence in the leisurely way she left. She had all the time in the world.

I closed the door, turned the thumb lock, slid on the chain, and hurried into the downstairs bathroom.

Through the window I could see a squared-off view of the street. I pressed my forehead against the glass, checking in both directions. There was no sign of her. I expected to hear a car start, but the quiet was unbroken. I sank down on the rim of the tub and rubbed my face with my hands.

Now that she was gone, I was more afraid than I'd been when she was there.

In the dark of the bathroom, I closed my eyes and projected myself into her head, seeing the situation as she must view it. First the tarantula, now this. What was she up to? If she wanted me dead—which she did without doubt—why hadn't she acted while she had the chance?

Because she wanted to demonstrate her power over me. She was telling me she could walk through walls, that it would never be safe for me to close my eyes. Wherever I went and whatever I did, I'd be vulnerable. At work, at home, I was at her mercy, alive purely at her whim, but possibly not for long. What were the other messages embedded in the first?

Starting with the obvious, she wasn't in Mexico. She'd left the car near the border so we'd assume she'd fled. Instead, she'd doubled back. By what means? I hadn't heard a car start, but she could have parked two blocks away and made the rest of the trip to and from my bedside on foot. The problem from her perspective was that buying or renting a car required personal identification. Peggy Klein had snatched her driver's license and without that she was screwed. She couldn't be certain her face, her name, and her various aliases hadn't been burning up the wires. For all she knew, the minute she tried to use her phony credit cards, she'd announce her location and law enforcement would close in.

In the weeks she'd been gone, she probably hadn't

applied for work, which meant she was living on cash. Even if she found a way to bypass the issue of ID, buying or renting a car would eat up valuable resources. Once she killed me, she'd have to lie low, which meant she'd have to save her cash reserves to support herself until she found someone new to prey on. Those matters took patience and careful planning. She hadn't had time enough to set up a new life. So how had she managed to get here?

By bus or by train. Traveling by bus was cheap and largely anonymous. Traveling by train would allow her to disembark a scant three blocks from where I lived.

First thing the next morning, I told Henry about my night visitor and my theory of how she'd gotten in. After that, I called a locksmith and had my locks changed. Henry and Gus had their locks changed as well. I also called Cheney and told him what had happened so he could put the word out on his end. I'd given him photographs of Solana so the officers on every shift would be familiar with her face.

Once again, my nerves were on edge. I pressed Lonnie about getting the judge's order signed so I could have my guns back in my possession. I don't know how he did it, but I had the order in hand and retrieved them from the gun shop that afternoon. I didn't picture myself walking around like a gunslinger, armed to the teeth, but I had to do something to make myself feel safe.

Wednesday morning when I returned from my run, there was a photograph taped to my front door. Solana again. What now? Frowning, I pulled it free. I let myself in, locked the door behind me, and turned on the desk lamp. I studied the image, knowing what it was. She'd snapped a picture of me the day before somewhere along my jogging route. I recognized the dark blue sweats I'd worn. It had been nippy out and I'd wrapped a lime green scarf around my neck, the first and only time. It must have been late in the run because my face was flushed and I was breathing through my mouth. In the background, I could see part of a building with a streetlamp in front. The angle was odd, but I couldn't think what that meant. The message was clear enough. Even the run, which had been my salvation, was under siege. I sat down on the couch and put a hand over my mouth. My fingers were cold and I found myself shaking my head. I couldn't live this way. I couldn't spend the rest of my life on red alert. I stared at the photo and another thought occurred to me. She wanted me to find her. She was showing me where she was, but she wouldn't make it easy. Being sly was her way of maintaining the upper hand. Wherever she was, all she had to do was wait while I was forced to do the legwork. The challenge was to see if I was smart enough to track her down. If not, she'd send me another clue. What I couldn't "get" was her game plan. She had something in mind, but I couldn't read her well enough to figure out what it was. It was an interesting display of power. I had more at stake than she did, but she had nothing to lose.

I showered and dressed in sweats and running shoes. For breakfast, I ate cold cereal. I washed the bowl and spoon and set them in the rack to dry. I went upstairs and took out my fanny pack. I left the key picks in their compact leather folder but removed the pick gun to make room for the H&K, which I loaded and tucked in its place. I left the house with Solana's photo of me in hand. The other snapshots I carried were of her. I walked my route—down Cabana, left on State. I kept an eye on the passing landscape, trying to identify the point from which the photo had been taken. It looked like the eye of the camera was angled downward, but not by much. If she'd been out in the open, I would have seen her. During a run, I keep my focus on the run itself, but not to the exclusion of all else. I was usually out before the sun came up, and as empty as the streets appeared to be, there were always other people about and not all of them good. I was interested in being fit, but not at the cost of being foolish.

I was torn between a natural desire to be thorough and a need to get to the point. I compromised by walking half the route. My hunch was that her location was on the beach side of the freeway. The buildings along the upper part of State had a very different look to them than the one in the photograph. I'd taken this route for weeks and it surprised me how different the streets looked when I traveled at a walking pace. Retail stores were still closed, but the popular sidewalk cafés were filled. People were heading off to the gym or returning to their cars, damp from their workouts.

At the intersection of Neil and State, I turned and retraced my steps. It helped that there weren't that many lampposts—two to every block. I scanned the buildings as high as the second floor, checking fire escapes and balconies where she might have hidden. I looked for windows located at a level that would reproduce the angle from which the snapshot had been taken. I'd almost reached the railroad tracks by then and I was running short of geography. It was the section of building she'd caught in the frame that finally tipped me off. It was the T-shirt shop across the street. The skirting beneath the plate-glass window was quite distinct now that I looked at it. Slowly I walked on until the slice of background matched the picture. Then I turned and looked behind me. The Paramount Hotel.

I checked the window visible just above the marquee. It was a corner room, probably large because I could see a deep balcony that wrapped around both sides of the building at that point. Maybe the original hotel had had a restaurant up there, with French doors that opened onto the balcony so patrons could enjoy the morning air at breakfast and, later, the setting sun at the cocktail hour.

I went into the lobby through the front doors. The remodel had been done with an impeccable eye for detail. The architect had managed to capture the old glamour without sacrificing current standards of elegance. It looked like all the old brass fixtures were still in place, burnished to a high shine. I knew this to be untrue as the originals had been looted in the days just after the hotel closed. Murals in muted tones covered the walls, with scenes depicting the fashionable set in residence at the Paramount Hotel in the 1940s. The doorman was on hand, as well as numerous bellhops toting luggage for the patrons checking in. A party of rail-thin women in jaunty hats played a hand of bridge in one corner of the lobby. Two of the four had foxtail furs tossed over their suit jackets with the big shoulder pads. There was no hint that a war was going on except for the scarcity of men. The patio and pool area had been brushed in, the images lifted from old photographs. I could see six cabanas on the far side of the pool, which was flanked with ponytail palms and the larger, more graceful queen palms. What I hadn't realized, peering at the construction through the barrier, was that the pool extended under a glass wall into the lobby itself. The lobby portion was largely decorative, but the overall effect was nice. In the mural there were vintage automobiles parked at the street and no hint of the various tourist-oriented businesses that now stretched along State. Just to the right, there was a wide carpeted stair in trompe l'oeil curving up to the mezzanine. I turned and saw the same stairway in reality.

I went up and at the top turned to my right so that I was facing the street. What I'd imagined was a restaurant or lounge was actually a lavish corner suite. The brass number on the door was an ornate 2. I could hear a television set blaring inside. I went to the window at the end of the hall and looked out. Solana must have snapped the picture from a window in the suite because the perspective was slightly off from the place where I stood.

I went down the wide stairs to the lobby. The desk clerk was in his thirties with a thin, bony face and hair slicked back with pomade in a style I'd seen only in photographs taken during the '40s. His suit had a retro look to it as well. "Good morning. May I help you?" he said. His nails had the shine of a recent manicure.

"Yes. I'm interested in the suite on the mezzanine," I said, and gestured toward the stairs.

"That's the Ava Gardner Suite. It's occupied at the moment. How soon would you need the reservation?"

"Actually, I don't. I think a friend of mine checked in and I thought I'd pop in and surprise her."

"She asked not to be disturbed."

I frowned slightly. "That doesn't sound like her. Usually she has a steady stream of visitors. Of course, she's in the process of divorcing and maybe she's worried her ex will try tracking her down. Can you tell me what name she used. Her married name was Brody."

"I'm afraid I couldn't give you that information. It's against hotel policy. The privacy of our guests is our first priority."

"What if I showed you a photograph? You could at least confirm that it's my friend? I'd hate to bang on the door if I'm making a mistake."

"Why don't you give me your name and I'll ring her?"

"But that would spoil the surprise." I brought my fanny pack around from the back to the front and unzipped the smaller of the two compartments. I took out the photo of Solana and put it on the counter.

"I'm afraid I can't help," he said. He was careful to maintain eye contact, but I knew he couldn't resist a peek. His eyes flicked down.

I said nothing, but I gazed at him steadily.

"Anyway, she has company at the moment. A gentleman just went up."

So much for his respect for her privacy. "A gentleman?"

"A handsome white-haired fellow, tall, very trim. I'd say he was in his eighties."

"Did he give you his name?"

"He didn't have to. She called down and said she was expecting a Mr. Pitts and when he arrived I should send him right up, which is what I did."

I could feel the color leave my face. "I want you to call the police and I want you to do it right now."

He looked at me, a quizzical smile playing across his lips, as though this were a hoax being filmed by hidden cameras to test his response. "Call the police? That's what the gentleman said. Are you two serious?"

"Shit! Just do it. Ask for a detective named Cheney Phillips. Can you remember that?"

"Of course," he said, primly. "I'm not stupid."

I stood there. He hesitated and then reached for the phone.

I moved away from the desk and took the stairs two at a time. Why would she have called Henry? And what could she have said that would get him over here? When I approached the Ava Gardner Suite for the second time, the volume on the blaring television had been turned down. The modernization and restoration of the hotel, happily from my perspective, hadn't included the installation of card-operated locks. I didn't recognize the lock brand, but how different could it be? I unzipped my fanny pack and took out the leather folder with its five picks. I'd have preferred the cover of loud music and talk, but I couldn't take the chance. I was just about to set to work when the door opened and I saw Solana standing there.

She said, "I can save you the effort. Why don't you come in? The desk clerk phoned to tell me you were on your way."

The fuck-head, I thought. I stepped into the room. She closed the door behind me and secured the burglar chain.

This was the sitting room. Doors on the left stood open revealing two separate bedrooms and a bathroom done in an old-fashioned white marble streaked with gray. Henry was out cold, lying on the plump upholstered sofa with an IV line in his arm, the needle taped in place. His color was still good and I could see the steady rise and fall of his chest. What worried me was the loaded syringe lying on the coffee table beside a crystal bowl filled with roses.

The French doors stood open, sheers lifted by a breeze. I could see the newly planted palms near the flagstone patio surrounding the pool. The terracing was still under construction, but it looked like work had been completed on the pool, which was now in the process of being filled. Solana allowed me time to get my bearings, enjoying the fear that must have been written in my face.

"What have you done to him?"

"Sedated him. He was upset when he realized you weren't here."

"Why would he think I was here?"

"Because I called him and told him so. I said you'd come to the hotel and attacked me. I said I'd hurt you very badly and now you were close to death and begging me to let you see him. He didn't believe me at first, but I insisted and he was afraid of being wrong. I told him I'd put a tap on his phone line and if he called the police, you'd be dead before he hung up. He was very quick, knocking on my door in less than fifteen minutes."

"What did you inject him with?"

"I'm sure the name of the drug would be meaningless to you. It's used to render a patient immobile before surgery. I hit him with something else first, an injection in his thigh. Very fast-acting. He went down like a tree toppling in a high wind. He doesn't seem to be conscious, but I can assure you he is. He can hear everything. He just can't move."

"What do you want from me?"

"Just the pleasure of watching your face as he dies," she said. "You took away the love of my life and now I'll take yours. Ah. But first let me have your fanny pack. Gus told me you own a gun. It wouldn't surprise me if you had it with you."

"I don't, but you're welcome to look." I unbuckled the pack and held it out to her. When she reached for it, I grabbed her by the arm and jerked her toward me. She lost her balance and toppled forward as I brought my right knee up to meet her face. There was a lovely popping sound that I hoped was her nose. Sure enough, blood poured down her face. Her eyelids fluttered briefly and she sprawled to her knees, her hands thrown out in front of her as she tried catching herself. I kicked her in the side and stomped on one of her outstretched hands. I snatched the syringe from the coffee table and crushed it with my heel. I stood beside Henry and pulled the tape from his arm. I wanted that IV line out of him.

Solana saw what I was doing and came after me in a flying tackle. I stumbled backward onto the coffee table and dragged her with me. The coffee table tipped over. The bowl of roses bounced on the carpet and settled upright, the roses still perfectly arranged. I grabbed the crystal bowl by the rim and hit her on her upper arm, which loosened her grip. I flipped over to my hands and knees and she launched herself at me again. She hung on, while I rammed her in the side repeatedly with my elbow. I kicked back at her, catching her on the thigh, inflicting as much damage as I could with the heel of my running shoe.

The woman was relentless. She came after me again and this time grabbed me around the arms, pinning my elbows to my sides. We were in such close contact I couldn't shake her off. I laced my hands together and brought them straight up, which broke her hold. I torqued myself to one side, grabbed her by the wrist, and pivoted. Her body arced across my hip and she went down. I hooked an elbow around her neck and dug my fingers into one eye socket. She shrieked in pain and covered her face with her hands. I pushed her away from me, breathing heavily. I could hear sirens in the street and I prayed they were heading toward us. With one eye bloody, she turned, her expression wild with pain. She found Henry in her visual field and in two strides was on him with her hands around his throat. I leaped at her. I boxed her ears, caught her by the hair, and hauled her off him. She staggered two steps back and I shoved her hard in the chest. She banged backward through the French doors onto the balcony.

I was gasping for breath and so was she. I watched her

use the railing to pull herself up. I knew I'd hurt her. She'd hurt me, too, but I wouldn't find out to what extent until the adrenaline receded. For the moment, I was tired, and not altogether certain I could take her on again. She glanced toward the street where I could hear police cars, sirens wailing, come screeching to a stop. We were only one floor above and it wouldn't take them long to come pounding up the steps.

I made my way to the door and removed the burglar chain. I turned the thumb lock and opened the door and then leaned against the frame. When I turned to look at her, the balcony was empty. I heard a scream from below. I crossed to the French doors and went out on the balcony. I looked over the rail. The water in the pool showed a spreading cloud of pink. She struggled briefly and then went still. It made no difference whether she'd fallen or jumped. She'd landed facedown, hitting her head on the edge of the pool before she slid into the water. At the shallow end, the water was only two feet deep, but that was sufficient. She drowned before anyone could get to her.

EPILOGUE

Henry was taken to St. Terry's by ambulance. He recovered from his ordeal without incident. I think he felt foolish that Solana had deceived him, but I'd have done the same thing in his place. We're each of us more protective of the other than we are of ourselves.

The Fredricksons' suit against Lisa Ray was dropped. I came close to feeling sorry for Hetty Buckwald, who'd been convinced their claim was legitimate. By the time I was able to swing by the Laundromat to tell Melvin he was off the hook, the milk truck had disappeared and so had he. I completed an Affidavit of Inability to Serve Process and filed it with the court clerk, which ended my official connection to the man. I wasn't surprised to find him gone, but it was hard to believe he'd give up his vigil over his youngest grandson. I kept wishing there were some way to make contact, but I'd never heard his daughter's name, first or last. I had no idea where she lived or where her youngest boy was enrolled. It might have been the preschool near City College or another day care center I'd spotted six blocks away.

Even now, I find myself driving around the neighborhood where Melvin worked, checking nursery schools, scanning children on the playground. I coast by parks in the area, thinking I might catch sight of a white-haired gentleman in a brown leather bomber jacket. Every time I see a kid with a lollipop, I study the grownups nearby, wondering if one of them offered the child a piece of candy in that first tentative overture. At the kiddie pool, I stand near the fence and watch the little kids at play, splashing water on each other, gliding on their tummies in the wading pool while they walk their hands along the bottom and pretend to swim. They are so beautiful, so sweet. I can't imagine anyone willfully harming a child. Yet some people do. There are thousands of convicted sex offenders in the state of California alone. Of those, a small but unsettling number are unaccounted for on any given day.

I don't want to think about predators. I know they exist, but I prefer to focus on the best in human nature: compassion, generosity, a willingness to come to the aid of those in need. The sentiment may seem absurd, given our daily ration of news stories detailing thievery, assault, rape, murder, and other treacheries. To the cynics among us, I must sound like an idiot, but I do hold to the good, working wherever possible to separate the wicked from that which profits them. There will always be someone poised to take advantage of the vulnerable: the very young, the very old, and the innocent of any age. Though I know this from long experience, I refuse to feel discouraged. In my own unassuming way, I know I can make a difference. You can as well.

Respectfully submitted,
Kinsey Millhone

TURN THE PAGE FOR AN EXCERPT

It's April 1988, and Kinsey Millhone is alone in her office doing paperwork when Michael Sutton arrives unannounced. He wants Kinsey's help in locating a four-year-old girl's remains and finding the men who kidnapped and killed her twenty-one years earlier. As her investigation unfolds, Millhone discovers Sutton has an uneasy relationship with the truth. Is his current story true or simply one more in a long line of fabrications?

PUTNAM
Penguin Random House

1

Wednesday afternoon, April 6, 1988

What fascinates me about life is that now and then the past rises up and declares itself. Afterward, the sequence of events seems inevitable, but only because cause and effect have been aligned in advance. It's like a pattern of dominoes arranged upright on a tabletop. With the flick of your finger, the first tile topples into the second, which in turn tips into the third, setting in motion a tumbling that goes on and on, each tile knocking over its neighbor until all of them fall down. Sometimes the impetus is pure chance, though I discount the notion of accidents. Fate stitches together elements that seem unrelated on the surface. It's only when the truth emerges you see how the bones are joined and everything connects.

Here's the odd part. In my ten years as a private eye, this was the first case I ever managed to resolve without crossing paths with the bad guys. Except at the end, of course.

My name is Kinsey Millhone. I'm a private detective, female, age thirty-seven, with my thirty-eighth birthday coming up in a month. Having been married and divorced twice, I'm now happily single and expect to remain so for life. I have no children thus far and I don't anticipate bearing any. Not only are my eggs getting old, but my biological clock wound down a long time ago. I suppose there's always room for one of life's little surprises, but that's not the way to bet.

I work solo out of a rented bungalow in Santa Teresa, California, a town of roughly 85,000 souls who generate sufficient crime to occupy the Santa Teresa Police Department, the County Sheriff's Department, the California Highway Patrol, and the twenty-five or so local private investigators like me. Movies and television shows would have you believe a PI's job is dangerous, but nothing could be further from the truth . . . except, of course, on the rare occasions when someone tries to kill me. Then I'm ever so happy my health insurance premiums are paid up. Threat of death aside, the job is largely research, requiring intuition, tenacity, and ingenuity. Most of my clients reach me by referral and their business ranges from background checks to process serving, with countless other matters in between. My office is off the beaten path and I seldom have a client appear unannounced, so when I heard a tapping at the door to my outer office, I got up and peered around the corner to see who it was.

Through the glass I saw a young man pointing at the knob. I'd apparently turned the dead bolt to the locked position when I'd come back from lunch. I let him in, saying, "Sorry about that. I must have locked up after myself without being aware of it."

"You're Ms. Millhone?"

"Yes."

"Michael Sutton," he said, extending his hand. "Do you have time to talk?"

We shook hands. "Sure. Can I offer you a cup of coffee?"

"No, thanks. I'm fine."

I ushered him into my office while I registered his appearance in a series of quick takes. Slim. Lank brown hair with a sheen to it, worn long on top and cut short over his ears. Solemn brown eyes, complexion as clear as a baby's. There was a prep school air about him: deck shoes without socks, sharply creased chinos, and a short-sleeve white dress shirt he wore with a tie. He had the body of a boy: narrow shoulders, narrow hips, and long, smooth arms. He looked young enough to be carded if he tried to buy booze. I couldn't imagine what sort of problem he'd have that would require my services.

I returned to my swivel chair and he settled in the chair on the other side of the desk. I glanced at my calendar, wondering if I'd set up an appointment and promptly forgotten it.

He noticed the visual reference and said, "Detective Phillips at the police department gave me your name and address. I should have called first, but your office was close by. I hope this isn't an inconvenience."

"Not at all," I said. "My first name's Kinsey, which you're welcome to use. You prefer Michael or Mike?"

"Most people call me Sutton. In my kindergarten class, there were two other Michaels so the teacher used our last names to distinguish us. Boorman, Sutton, and Trautwein—like a law firm. We're still friends."

"Where was this?"

"Climp."

I said, "Ah." I should have guessed as much. Climping Academy is the private school in Horton Ravine, K through 12. Tuition starts at twelve grand for the little tykes and rises incrementally through the upper grades.

I don't know where it tops out, but you could probably pick up a respectable college education for the same price. All the students enrolled there referred to it as "Climp," as though the proper appellation was just, like, *sooo* beside the point. Watching him, I wondered if my blue-collar roots were as obvious to him as his upper-class status was to me.

We exchanged pleasantries while I waited for him to unload. The advantage of a prearranged appointment is that I begin the first meeting with at least *some* idea what a prospective client has in mind. People skittish about revealing their personal problems to a stranger often find it easier to do by phone. With this kid, I figured we'd have to dance around some before he got down to his business, whatever it was.

He asked how long I'd been a private investigator. This is a question I'm sometimes asked at cocktail parties (on the rare occasion when I'm invited to one). It's the sort of blah-blah-blah conversational gambit I don't much care for. I gave him a rundown of my employment history. I skipped over the two lackluster semesters at the local junior college and started with my graduation from the police academy. I then covered the two years I'd worked for the Santa Teresa PD before I realized how ill suited I was to a life in uniform. I proceeded with a brief account of my subsequent apprenticeship with a local agency, run by Ben Byrd and Morley Shine, two private investigators, who'd trained me in preparation for licensing. I'd had my ups and downs over the years, but I spared him the details since he'd only inquired as a stalling technique. "What about you? Are you a California native?"

"Yes, ma'am. I grew up in Horton Ravine. My family lived on Via Ynez until I went off to college. I lived a couple of other places, but now I'm back."

"You still have family here?"

His hesitation was one of those nearly imperceptible blips that indicates internal editing. "My parents are gone. I have two older brothers, both married with two kids each, and an older sister who's divorced. We're not on good terms. We haven't been for years."

I let that pass without comment, being better acquainted with family estrangement than I cared to admit. "How do you know Cheney Phillips?"

"I don't. I went into the police department, asking to speak to a detective, and he happened to be free. When I told him my situation, he said you might be able to help."

"Well, let's hope so," I said. "Cheney's a good guy. I've known him for years." I shut my mouth then and let a silence descend, a stratagem with remarkable powers to make the other guy talk.

Sutton touched the knot in his tie. "I know you're busy, so I'll get to the point. I hope you'll bear with me. The story might sound weird."

"Weird stories are the best kind, so fire away," I said.

He looked at the floor as he spoke, making eye contact now and then to see if I was following. "I don't know if you saw this, but a couple of weeks ago, there was an article in the newspaper about famous kidnappings: Marion Parker, the twelve-year-old girl who was abducted in 1927; the Lindbergh baby in 'thirty-two; another kid, named Etan Patz. Ordinarily, I don't read things like that, but what caught my attention was the case here in town . . ."

"You're talking about Mary Claire Fitzhugh—1967."

"You remember her?"

"Sure. I'd just graduated from high school. Little four-year-old girl taken from her parents' home in Horton Ravine. The Fitzhughs agreed to pay the ransom, but the money was never picked up and the child was never seen again."

"Exactly. The thing is, when I saw the name Mary Claire Fitzhugh, I had this flash—something I hadn't thought about for years." He clasped his hands together and squeezed them between his knees. "When I was a little kid, I was playing in the woods and I came across these two guys digging a hole. I remember seeing a bundle on the ground a few feet away. At the time, I didn't understand what I was looking at, but now I believe it was Mary Claire's body and they were burying her."

I said, "You actually saw the child?"

He shook his head. "She was wrapped in a blanket, so I couldn't see her face or anything else."

I studied him with interest. "What makes you think it was Mary Claire? That's a big leap."

"Because I went back and checked the old newspaper accounts and the dates line up."

"What dates?"

"Oh, sorry. I should have mentioned this before. She was kidnapped on July 19, which was a Wednesday. I saw the guys on Friday, July 21, 1967 . . . my birthday, the year I turned six. That's how I made the association. I think she was already dead by then and they were getting rid of the body."

"And this was where?"

"Horton Ravine. I don't know the exact location. My mother had errands to run that day so she dropped me off at some kid's house. I don't remember his name. I guess his mom had agreed to look after me while she was gone. Turns out the other kid woke up with a fever and sore throat. Chicken pox was going around and his mom didn't want me exposed in case that's what it was, so she made him stay in his room while I hung around downstairs. I got bored and asked if I could go outside. She said I could as long as I didn't leave the property. I remember finding this tree with branches that hung down to make a little room, so I played there for a while, pretending I was a bandit in a cool hideout. I heard voices and when I peeped through the leaves, I saw the two guys walk by with shovels and stuff and I followed them."

"What time of day?"

"Must have been late morning because after I came in again, the kid's mother fed me lunch—a plain lettuce and tomato sandwich, no bacon, and it was made with Miracle Whip. Our family didn't eat Miracle Whip. My mother wouldn't have it in the house. She said it was disgusting compared to real homemade mayonnaise."

"Your mother made *mayonnaise?*"

"The cook did."

"Ah."

"Anyway, Mom always said it was rude to complain, so I ate what I could and left the rest on my plate. The kid's mom hadn't even cut the crusts off the bread."

"There's a shock," I said. "I'm impressed your memory's so clear."

"Not clear enough or I wouldn't be here. I'm pretty sure the two guys I saw were the ones who abducted Mary Claire, but I have no idea where I was. I know I'd never been to the house before and I never went there again."

"Any chance one of your siblings would remember who the kid was?"

"I guess it's possible. Unfortunately, we don't get along. We haven't spoken in years."

"So you said."

"Sorry. I don't mean to repeat myself. The point is, I can't call them up out of a clear blue sky. Even if I did, I doubt they'd talk to me."

"But *I* could ask, couldn't I? That would be the obvious first move if you're serious about this."

He shook his head. "I don't want them involved, especially my sister, Dee. She's difficult. You don't want to mess with her."

"All right. We'll scratch that for now. Maybe the kid's mother was being paid to babysit."

"That wasn't my impression. More like she was doing Mom a favor."

"What about your classmates? Maybe she left you with one of the other moms, like a playdate."

Sutton blinked twice. "That's a possibility I hadn't thought of. I've kept in touch with the other two Michaels, Boorman and Trautwein, but that's the extent of it. I didn't like anybody else in my kindergarten class and they didn't like me."

"It doesn't matter if you *liked* them or not. We're trying to identify the boy."

"I don't remember anyone else."

"It should be easy enough to come up with a list. You must have had class photos. You could go back to the school library and check the 'sixty-seven yearbook."

"I don't want to go back to Climp. I hate the idea."

"It's just a suggestion. So far, we're brainstorming," I said. "Tell me about the two guys. How old would you say?"

"I'm not sure. Older than my brothers, who were ten and twelve at the time, but not as old as my dad."

"Did they see you?"

"Not then. I decided to spy on them, but where they ended up was too far away and I couldn't see what they were doing. I sneaked up on them, crawling through the bushes and crouching behind a big oak. It was hot and they were sweating so they'd taken off their shirts. I guess I wasn't as quiet as I thought because one of them spotted me and they both jumped. They stopped what they were doing and asked what I wanted."

"You actually talked to them?"

"Oh, sure. Absolutely. We had this whole conversation. I thought they were pirates and I was all excited about meeting them."

"Pirates?"

"My mother was reading me *Peter Pan* at bedtime, and I loved the illustrations. The pirates wore bandanas tied around their heads, which is what the two guys had done."

"Beards? Earrings? Eye patches?"

That netted me a smile, but not much of one. He shook his head. "It was the bandanas that reminded me of pirates. I told them I knew that because of *Peter Pan*."

"What'd you talk about?"

"First, I asked 'em if they were pirates for real and they told me they were. The one guy talked more than the other and when I asked what they were doing, he said they were digging for buried treasure . . ."

As Sutton spoke, I could see him regressing to the little boy he'd been, earnest and easily impressed. He leaned forward in his chair. "I asked if the treasure was gold doubloons, but they said they didn't know because they hadn't found it yet. I asked to see the treasure map and they said they couldn't show me because they were sworn to secrecy. I'd seen the bundle on the ground, over by this tree, and when I asked about it, the first guy said it was a bedroll in case they got tired. I offered to help dig, but he told me the job was only for grown-ups and little kids weren't allowed. And then the other one spoke up and asked where I lived. I told them I lived in a white house, but not on this street, that I was visiting.

The first guy asked what my name was. I told him and the other one spoke up again and said he thought he heard someone calling me so I better go, which is what I did. The whole exchange couldn't have taken more than three minutes."

"I don't suppose either of them mentioned their names?"

"No. I probably should have asked, but it didn't occur to me."

"Your recall impresses me. Much of my life at that age is a total blank."

"I hadn't thought about the incident for years, but once the memory was triggered, I was right there again. Just like, *boom*."

I reran the story in my mind, trying to digest the whole of it. "Tell me again why you think there's a connection to Mary Claire. That still seems like a stretch."

"I don't know what else to say. Intuition, I guess."

"What about the kidnapping. How did that go down? I remember the broad strokes, but not the particulars."

"The whole thing was horrible. Those poor people. The ransom note said not to contact the police or the FBI, but Mr. Fitzhugh did it anyway. He thought it was the only way to save her, but he was wrong."

"The first contact was the note?"

Sutton nodded. "Later they phoned and said he had one day to get the money together or else. Mr. Fitzhugh had already called the police and they were the ones who contacted the FBI. The special agent in charge convinced him they'd have a better chance of nabbing the guys if he and his wife appeared to cooperate, so they advised him to do as he was told . . ."

"Twenty-five thousand dollars, wasn't it? Somehow the number sticks in my head."

"Exactly. The kidnappers wanted it in small bills, packed in a gym bag. They called again and told him where he was supposed to leave the money. He stalled. They must have thought there was a tap on the line because they cut the call short."

"So he dropped off the ransom money and the kidnappers didn't show."

"Right. After a day passed, it was clear the FBI had bungled it. They still thought they had a chance, but Mr. Fitzhugh said to hell with them and took matters into his own hands. He notified the newspapers and the radio and TV stations. After the story broke, Mary Claire was all anybody talked about—my parents and everyone else."

"What day was it by then?"

"Sunday. Like I said before, she was kidnapped on Wednesday and I saw them on Friday. The paper didn't carry the story until Sunday."

"Why didn't you speak up?"

"I did. I'd already done that. When my mother came to get me, I told her about the pirates. I felt *guilty*. Like I'd done something wrong."

"How so?"

"I don't know how to pin it down. I believed what they said about digging for treasure. When you're six, things like that make perfect sense, but on some level I was anxious and I wanted reassurance. Instead, Mom got mad. She said I wasn't supposed to talk to strangers and she made me promise I'd never do it again. When we got home, she sent me straight to my room. On Sunday we heard the news about Mary Claire."

"And your mother didn't see the relevance?"

"I guess not. She never mentioned it and I was too scared to bring it up again. She'd already punished me once. I kept my mouth shut so she wouldn't punish me again."

"But it worried you."

"For a while, sure. After that, I put the incident out of my mind. Then I saw Mary Claire's name and it all came back."

"Did you ever see either guy again?"

"I don't think so. Maybe one of them. I'm not sure."

"And where would that have been?"

"I don't remember. I might have made a mistake."

I picked up a pencil and made a mark on the yellow pad lying on my desk. "When you explained this to Cheney, what was his response?"

His shoulder went up in a half-shrug. "He said he'd check the old case notes, but he couldn't do much more because the information I'd given him was too vague. That's when he mentioned you."

"Sounds like he was passing the buck."

"Actually, what he said was you were like a little terrier when it came to flushing out rats."

"Sucking up," I said. Mentally, I was rolling my eyes because Cheney wasn't far off the mark. I liked picking at problems and this was a doozy. "What about the house itself? Think you'd recognize it if you saw it again?"

"I doubt it. Right after I read the article, I drove around the old neighborhood, and even the areas I knew well had changed. Trees were gone, shrubs were overgrown, new houses had gone up. Of course, I didn't cover the whole of Horton Ravine, but I'm not sure it would have made any difference since I don't have a clear image. I think I'd recognize the place in the woods. The house is a blur."

"So twenty-one years later, you're clueless and hoping I can figure out where you were."

"Yes, ma'am."

"You want me to find an unmarked grave, basically a hole."

"Can you do it?"

"I don't know. I've never tried before."

I studied him, chasing the idea around to see where it might go. "It's an interesting proposition. I'll give you that."

I rocked in my swivel chair, listening to the squeak, while I sifted through the story, wondering what I'd missed. There was something more going on, but I couldn't imagine what. Finally, I said, "What's your stake in the situation? I know it bothers you, but why to this extent?"

"I don't know. I mean, the article talked about how the kidnapping ruined Mrs. Fitzhugh's life. She and her husband divorced and he ended up leaving town. She still has no idea what happened to her little girl. She doesn't even know for sure she's dead. If I can help, it seems like the right thing to do."

"It's going to cost you," I said.

"I figured as much."

"What sort of work do you do?"

"Nothing right now. I lost my job so I'm on unemployment."

"What was the job?"

"I sold advertising for KSPL."

KSPL was the local AM station I sometimes tuned in on my car radio when I was tooling around town. "How long were you there?"

"About a year, maybe a little less."

"What's it mean when you say you 'lost' your job? Were you laid off, downsized, fired, what?"

He hesitated. "The last one."

"Fired."

He nodded.

I waited and when it was clear he had no intention of continuing, I gave him a nudge. "Uh, Sutton, I'd consider it a courtesy if you'd be a bit more forthcoming. Would you care to fill me in?"

He rubbed his palms on his pants. "I said I had a BA from Stanford, but it wasn't really true. I was enrolled and attended classes for a couple of years, but I didn't graduate."

"So you lied on the application?"

"Look, I know I made a mistake . . ."

"That would cover it," I said.

"But I can't do anything about it now. What's done is done and I just have to move on."

I'd heard a host of criminals make the same remark, like boosting cars, robbing banks, and killing folks could be brushed aside, a minor stumble on the path of life. "Have you given any thought to how you're going to pay me out of your unemployment benefits? We're talking about five hundred bucks a day, plus expenses. Assuming I agree to help, which I haven't."

"I have some money set aside. I thought I'd write a check for one day's work and we'd see how it goes from there."

"A *check*?"

A flush tinted his cheeks. "I guess that's not such a hot idea."

"You got that right. What's plan B?"

"If you're going to be here for a while, I could make a quick run to the bank and bring you cash."

I considered the notion. The prime item on my Thursday To Do list was to make a bank deposit and pay bills. I had two reports to write and a few calls to make, but I could shift those to Friday. The job itself might end in folly, but at least when he mentioned "the right thing to do," he didn't turn around and ask me to work for free. I wasn't convinced he was right about what he'd seen, but Cheney must have considered the story credible or he wouldn't have sent him over to me.

"Okay. One day, but that's it. And only if you pay me cash in advance. I'll be here until five o'clock. That should give you plenty of time."

"Great. That's great."

"I don't know how great it is, but it's the best I can do. When you get back, if I happen to be out, you can stick the money through the mail slot. In the meantime, give me a contact number so I'll know how to reach you."

I handed him my yellow pad and watched while he scribbled down his address and telephone number. In return I handed him my business card with my office number and address.

He said, "I really appreciate this. I don't know what I'd have done if you hadn't agreed."

"I'll probably regret it, but what the hell? It's only one day," I said. If I'd been listening closely, I'd have caught the sound of the gods having a great big old tee-hee at my expense.

I said, "You're sure you don't want to make the trip up to Climp? It would save you a few bucks."

"I don't want to. They probably wouldn't talk to me in any event."

"I see." I studied him. "You want to tell me what's going on here? You can't talk to your siblings and now you can't talk to your prep school pals?"

"I already told you I didn't have pals. It has more to do with the administration."

"How come?"

"There were some difficulties. I had a problem."

"Like what, you were expelled?" I love stories about flunking and expulsions. With my history of screwups, those are like fairy tales.

"It's not something I want to get into. It has nothing to do with this." A stubborn note had crept into his voice. "You go up there. They'll let you see yearbooks as easily as me."

"I doubt it. Educational institutions hate handing over information about their students. Especially with the words 'private investigator' thrown into the mix."

"Don't tell 'em you're a PI. Think of something else."

"I didn't even attend Climping Academy so why would I want to see a yearbook? It makes no sense."

He shook his head. "I won't do it. I have my reasons."

"Which you're not about to share."

"Right."

"Okay, fine. It's no skin off my nose. If that's how you want to spend your five hundred bucks, I can live with it. I love driving through Horton Ravine."

I got up, and as we shook hands again, I realized what was bothering me. "One more question."

"What's that?"

"The article came out two weeks ago. Why'd you wait so long before you went to the police?"

He hesitated. "I was nervous. All I have is a hunch. I didn't want the police to write me off as a crank."

"Nuh-uh. That's not all of it. What else?"

He was silent for a moment, color rising in his cheeks again. "What if the guys find out I remembered them? I might have been the only witness and I told them my name. If they're the ones who killed Mary Claire, why wouldn't they kill me?"

2

While Sutton and I were chatting, the mail had been delivered. Walking him to the door, I paused to collect the scattering of envelopes the postman had pushed through the slot. Once he'd gone off to the bank, I moved into my office, sorting and separating the stack as I sat down at my desk. Junk, bill, another bill, junk, junk, bill. I came to a square vellum envelope with my name and address written in calligraphy: *Ms. Kinsey Millhone,* with lots of down strokes and flourishes, very lah-di-dah. The postmark was Lompoc, California, and the return address was printed in the center of the back flap. Even without the sender's name in evidence, I knew it was a Kinsey family member, one of numerous kin whose existence I'd first learned about four years before. Until that strange turn of events, I'd prided myself on my loner status. There was a benefit to my being an orphan in the world, explaining as it did (at least to my way of thinking) my difficulties in forming close bonds with others of my species.

Looking at the envelope, I could guess what was coming up—a christening, a wedding, or a cocktail party—

some formal affair heralded by expensive embossing on heavy card stock. Whatever the occasion, I was either being informed of, or invited to, an event I didn't give a rat's ass about. At times, I'm a sentimental little thing, but this wasn't one. I tossed the envelope on my desk, then thought better of it, and threw it in the wastebasket, which was already brimming with trash.

I picked up the phone and punched in the number for Cheney Phillips at the STPD. When he picked up, I said, "Guess who?"

"Hey, Kinsey. What's up?"

"I just had a chat with Michael Sutton and thought I better touch base with you before I did anything else. What's the deal with him?"

"Beats me. That story sounded just screwy enough to be true. What was your impression?"

"I'm not sure. I'm willing to believe he saw two guys digging a hole. What I'm skeptical about is the relevance to Mary Claire Fitzhugh. He says the dates line up because he went back and checked his recollections against the articles in the paper, but that doesn't prove anything. Even if the two events happened at the same time, that doesn't mean they're related."

"Agreed, but his recollections were so specific he pretty much talked me into it."

"Me, too. At least in part," I said. "Did you have a chance to look at the old files?"

"Can't be done. I talked to the chief and he says the case notes are sealed. Once the FBI stepped in, they put everything under lock and key."

"Even after all this time? It's been twenty years."

"Twenty-one to be precise, and the answer is, definitely. You know how it goes. The case is federal and the file's still active. If the details are leaked then any clown off his meds can walk into the department and claim responsibility."

I caught a familiar racket out on the street. "Hang on a sec."

I put my hand over the mouthpiece and listened, picking up the hydraulic grinding, wheeze, and hiss of a garbage truck approaching from down the block. Shit! Garbage day. The week before, I'd forgotten to take out my trash and my wastebaskets were maxed out.

"I gotta go. I'll call you later."

"Vaya con Dios."

I hung up in haste and headed down the hall to the kitchenette, where I grabbed a plastic bag from a carton under the sink. I did a quick round of the wastebaskets—kitchen, bathroom, and office—shaking trash into the plastic bag until it sagged from the weight. I scurried out the back door, tossed the bag in my trash bin, and rolled it down the walkway on one side of the bungalow. By the time I reached the street, the garbage truck was idling at the curb and I just managed to catch the guy before he hopped back on. He paused long enough to add my contribution to the day's haul. As the truck pulled away, I blew him a kiss and was rewarded with a wave.

I returned to my desk, congratulating myself on a job well done. Nothing makes a room look messier than a wastebasket full of trash. As I settled in my swivel chair, I glanced down and spotted the vellum envelope, which had apparently missed the plastic bag and now lay on the floor. I leaned over, picked it up, and stared at it. What was going on? Instead of happily winging its way to the county dump, the damn thing was back. I'm not superstitious by nature, but the envelope, coupled with Michael Sutton's reference to his family estrangement, had set an old train of thought in motion.

I knew how treacherous and frail family bonds could be. My mother had been the eldest of five daughters born to my grandparents Burton Kinsey and Cornelia Straith LaGrand, known since as Grand. My parents had been jettisoned from the bosom of the family when my mother met my father and eloped with him four months later. She was eighteen at the time and came from money, albeit of the small-town sort. My father, Randy Millhone, was thirty-three years old and a mail carrier. In retrospect, it's difficult to say which was worse in Grand's eyes, his advanced age or his occupation. Apparently, she viewed civil servants right up there with career criminals as undesirable mates for her precious firstborn girl. Rita Cynthia Kinsey first clapped eyes on my father at her coming-out party, where my father was filling in as a waiter for a friend who owned the catering company. Their marriage created a rift in the family that had never healed. My Aunt Gin was the only one of her four sisters who sided with her, and she ended up raising me after my parents were killed in a car wreck when I was five.

You'd think I'd have been pleased to discover the existence of close kin. Instead, I was pissed off, convinced they'd known about me for years and hadn't cared enough to seek me out. I was thirty-four when the first family overtures were made, and I counted their twenty-nine years' silence as evidence of crass indifference for which I blamed Grand. I really didn't have a quarrel with my aunts and cousins. I'd tossed them into the pit with Grand because it was simpler that way. I'll admit it wasn't fair, but I took a certain righteous satisfaction in my wholesale condemnation. For the past two or three years, I'd made a halfhearted attempt to modify my attitude, but it hadn't really worked. I'm a Taurus. I'm stubborn by nature and I had my heels dug in. I shoved the invitation in my shoulder bag. I'd deal with it later.

Sutton returned after twenty minutes with five crisp one-hundred-dollar bills, for which I wrote him a receipt. Once he was gone again, I locked the cash in my office safe. Since I'd be devoting Thursday to Sutton's business, I sat down and did a rough draft of one of the client reports on my To Do list, figuring I might as well get one chore out of the way. By the time I'd finished, it was close to 4:00 and I decided to shut down for the day. One reason I'm self-employed is so I can do as I please without consulting anyone else.

I rescued my car from the semilegal parking spot I'd found earlier. My office is on a narrow side street barely one block long. For the most part, the surrounding blocks are posted No Parking, which means I have to be inventive in finding ways to squeeze my Mustang into any available space. I was due for a parking ticket, but I hadn't gotten one yet.

I drove home along the beach, and within minutes my spirits lifted. Spring in Santa Teresa is marked by early-morning sunshine, which is eradicated almost immediately by dense cloud cover. The marine layer, known as the June Gloom, usually stretches from late May until early August, but that's been changing of late. Here we'd scarcely made it into April and low clouds had already erased the offshore islands. Seabirds wheeled through the fog while sailboats, tacking out of the harbor, disappeared in the mist. In the absence of sunlight, the surf was the color of burnished pewter. Long strands of kelp had washed up on shore. I inhaled the salty essence of damp sand and sea grass. Cars rumbled along the wooden wharf with a sound like distant thunder. It was not quite tourist season, so traffic was light and many of the beach hotels still sported vacancy signs.

I turned left from Cabana onto Bay and left again onto Albanil. I found a length of empty curb across from my apartment and paralleled my way into it. I shut the engine down, locked my car, and crossed the street, passing through the squeaking gate that serves the duel purpose of doorbell and burglar alarm.

Henry Pitts, my landlord, was in the backyard in a T-shirt, shorts, and bare feet. He'd set up a ladder near the house and he was hosing out the rain gutters where a thick, nasty mat of wet leaves had collected over the winter. During the last big rain, small gushers had poured down on the porch outside the kitchen door, drenching anyone who dared to enter or leave.

I crossed the patio and stood there for a while, watching him work. The day was getting chilly and I marveled at his determination to cavort about in so few clothes. "Aren't you going to catch your death of cold?"

Henry had turned eighty-eight on Valentine's Day, and while he's sturdy as a fence post, the fact remains he's getting on in years. "Nope. Cold preserves most things, so why not me?"

"I suppose."

The spray from the hose was creating an area of artificial rain so I stepped back out of range. He turned his hose in the opposite direction, inadvertently watering his neighbor's shrubs. "You're home early," he remarked.

"I gave myself the afternoon off, or what's left of it."

"Hard day?"

I waggled my hand, indicating so-so. "I had a guy walk in and hire me for a day's work. As soon as I said yes, I knew it was dumb."

"Tough job?"

"More pointless than tough. He gave me five hundred dollars in cash and what can I say? I was seduced."

"What's the assignment?"

"It's complicated."

"Oh, good. I like it when you're challenged. I'm just about done with this. Why don't you stop by for a glass of wine and you can bring me up to speed?"

"I'd like that. There's another issue up for grabs and we can talk about that, too."

"Maybe you should stay for supper so we won't feel rushed. I made corn bread and a pot of beef stew. If you come at five-thirty, I'll have time enough to shower and change clothes."

"Perfect. See you shortly."

Henry is the only person alive I'd talk to about a client, with the possible addition of his sister, Nell, who'd be turning ninety-nine in December. His brothers, Charlie, Lewis, and William, were ninety-six, ninety-one, and ninety respectively, and all were going strong. Any talk about the frailties of the elderly has no bearing on them.

I let myself into the studio and dropped my shoulder bag on a kitchen stool. I moved to the sitting area, turning on a couple of lamps to brighten the room. I went up the spiral staircase to the sleeping loft, where I perched on the edge of the platform bed and pulled off my boots. Most days, my work attire is casual—jeans, a turtleneck, and boots or tennis shoes. I can add a tweed blazer if I feel the need to dress up. Though I'm capable of skirts and panty hose, they're not my first choice. I do own one dress that I'm happy to say is suitable for most occasions. It's black, made of a fabric so wrinkle-resistant, if I rolled it up and stored it in my shoulder bag, you'd never know the difference.

At the end of the day, my clothes hurt and I'm eager to be shed of the restraints. I stripped off my jeans and hung them on a peg. I pulled off my shirt and tossed it over the rail. Once I was downstairs again, I'd retrieve it and add it to the garments waiting in the washing machine. In the meantime, I found a set of clean sweats and my slippers, rejoicing, as I always do, that Henry and I are beyond the need to impress each other. As far as I'm concerned, he's perfect and I suspect he'd say much the same thing about me.

I've been his tenant for the past eight years. At one time, my studio was Henry's single-car garage. He decided he needed a larger one to accommodate his station wagon and his pristine 1932 five-window coupe, so he converted the original garage to a rental unit, which I'd moved into. An unfortunate explosion had flattened my apartment six years before, so Henry had redesigned the floor plan, adding a half-story above the kitchen. On the ground floor I have a living room with a desk and a sofa bed that can accommodate overnight guests. The kitchen is small, a galley-style bump-out off the living room. There's also a bathroom and a combination washer-dryer tucked under the spiral stairs. The whole of it resembles the interior of a small boat, lots of highly polished teak and oak, with a porthole in the front door and nautical blue captain's chairs. The new loft, in addition to a double bed, boasts built-in cubbyholes, as well as a second bathroom with a view that includes a small slice of the Pacific Ocean visible through the trees. Henry had installed a Plexiglas skylight above my bed, so I wake to whatever weather's drifted in during the night.

Between the studio and Henry's house there's a glassed-in passageway where he proofs batches of bread, using a Shaker cradle like an enormous buttered bowl. In his working days, he made his living as a commercial baker, and he still can't resist the satiny feel of newly kneaded dough.

At 5:29 I grabbed my shoulder bag, crossed the flagstone patio, and tapped on the glass pane in Henry's back door. Most of the time he leaves it unlocked, but our unspoken agreement is to respect each other's privacy. Unless my apartment was in flames, he'd never dream of entering without permission. I peered through the glass and saw Henry standing at the sink, filling it with hot water into which he was squeezing a long shot of liquid detergent. He took three steps to the side to open the door and then returned to his task. I could see numerous place settings of tarnished silverware on the counter with a roll of aluminum foil and a clean towel laid out. He'd set an eight-quart pan on the stove and the water had just reached a rolling boil. On the bottom of the pan there was a crumpled section of foil. I watched him add a quarter cup of baking soda, after which he placed the silverware in the bubbling water with the foil.

"Oh yum. A pot of flatware soup."

He smiled. "When I pulled the silver from the canteen, most of it was tarnished. Watch this."

I peered into the boiling water and watched as the foil turned dark and the tarnish disappeared from all the forks, knives, and spoons. "That doesn't do any harm?"

"Some people think so, but anytime you polish silver, you're removing a thin layer of oxidation. That's a Towle pattern, by the way. Cascade. I inherited service for eighteen from a maiden aunt who died in 1933. The pattern's discontinued, but if I haunt garage sales, I can sometimes find a piece."

"What's the occasion?"

"Silver's meant to be used. I don't know why I hadn't thought of it before. It lends a meal an air of elegance, even when we're eating in here." He poked the silverware with a set of tongs, making sure all the pieces were totally submerged. "I put an open bottle of Chardonnay in the refrigerator for you."

"Thanks. Will you be having some with dinner?"

"As soon as I finish this."

He paused to take a swallow of the Black Jack over ice that constitutes his usual late-afternoon pick-me-up. I retrieved the Chardonnay, took two wineglasses from the cupboard, and filled mine halfway. Henry, meantime, was using the tongs to move the silver from the kettle to the sink of soapy water. After a quick rinse, he laid the freshly polished silver on the waiting towel. I took a second towel from the linen drawer and dried the pieces; I set places for two at the kitchen table, where Henry had laid out freshly ironed cloth napkins and mats.

We postponed our conversation about the job until we'd each eaten two servings of beef stew. Henry crumbled corn bread in his, but I preferred mine on the side with butter and homemade strawberry jam. Am I in love with this man or what? When we finished our meal, Henry put the dishes and silverware in the sink and returned to the table.

Once he was settled, I gave him the *Reader's Digest* condensed version of the story Michael Sutton had related to me. I said, "Where have I heard the name Michael Sutton? Does it mean anything to you?"

"Not offhand. You know what his father does for a living?"

"Not much. He's deceased. Sutton told me both his parents were gone. He's got two brothers and a sister, but they're not on speaking terms. He didn't explain himself and I didn't ask."

"I wonder if his father was the Sutton who served on the city council. This was maybe ten years ago."

"That I don't know. I suspect the reference will come to me, if there is one."

"In the meantime, you have a game plan?"

"I've got some ideas percolating at the back of my brain. I want to see what the papers have to say about the Fitzhugh girl. Sutton might have forgotten something relevant or embellished where he should have left well enough alone."

"You don't trust him?"

"It's not that. I'm worried he's conflating two separate events. I believe he saw two fellows digging a hole. What I question is the connection to Mary Claire's disappearance. He says the dates line up, but that doesn't count for much."

"I guess time will tell. So what's the other one?"

"The other what?"

"You said there was another issue up for grabs."

"Oh, that."

I leaned toward the empty chair where I'd placed my shoulder bag. I retrieved the still-sealed envelope and passed it across the table. "I don't have the nerve to open it. I thought you could peek and tell me what it is."

He put on his reading glasses and studied the front and back of the envelope in the same way I had. He slid a finger under the flap and lifted it, then removed a card with an overleaf of tissue. Inside, there was a smaller card with a matching envelope, so the recipient could RSVP. "Says, 'The Parsonage. Groundbreaking and Dedication Ceremony, celebrating the removal of the Kinsey Family Homestead to its new location at . . .' blah, blah, blah.

May 28, 1988. I believe that's the Saturday of Memorial Day weekend. Four P.M. Cocktails and dinner to follow at the country club. Very nice."

He turned the invitation so it faced me and I could read it for myself. "Big family do," he said. "Doesn't say black tie optional, so that's good news." He picked up the smaller card with its stamped envelope. "They'd appreciate a reply by May 1. Couldn't be easier. The envelope's already stamped so that will save you return postage. Well, now, what do you think of that?"

"This is just not going to go away, is it?" I said. "Why do they keep harassing me? It's like being nibbled to death by ducklings."

He pulled his reading glasses down low on his nose and looked at me over the rims. "Two contacts a year isn't 'harassment.' This is an invitation to a party. It's not like someone put dog turds on the front seat of your car."

"I barely know these people."

"And you won't if you keep avoiding them."

Reluctantly, I said, "I've dealt with Tasha and she's not so bad. And I'm fond of Aunt Susanna. She's the one who gave me the photograph of my mother and then sent me the family album. I'll admit I was touched by that. So here's what worries me. Am I just being stubborn for the sake of it? What do they call that, 'cutting off your nose to spite your face'? I mean, most families want to be close. I don't. Does that make me wrong?"

"Not at all. You're independent. You prefer being alone."

"True, and I'm pretty sure that's considered the opposite of mental health."

"Why don't you sleep on it and see how it looks in the morning."